A WILL, A WISH, A WEDDING

KATE HARDY

A WINNING SEASON

ROCHELLE ALERS

MILLS & BOON

First Published in Great Britain 2020
by Mills & Boon, an imprint of HarperCollinsPublishers,
1 London Bridge Street, London, SE1 9GF

A Will, a Wish, a Wedding © 2020 Pamela Brooks
A Winning Season © 2020 Rochelle Alers

ISBN: 978-0-263-27897-2

0920

MIX
Paper from
responsible sources
FSC™ C007454

This book is produced from independently certified FSC™
paper to ensure responsible forest management.

For more information visit: www.harpercollins.co.uk/green

Printed and bound in Spain
by CPI, Barcelona

A WILL, A WISH,
A WEDDING

KATE HARDY

To Gerard, Chris and Chloe,
who've supported me all the way
through 90 books, with all my love.

CHAPTER ONE

YOU DON'T BELONG HERE, oik, a posh voice sneered in Alice's head.

Barney and his cronies would've laughed themselves sick if they could've seen her standing at the foot of a set of white marble steps. What business did the girl from the council estate have here, in the poshest bit of Chelsea?

She lifted her chin to tell the voice she wasn't listening. Ten years ago, she'd been so naive that she hadn't realised that Barney—the most gorgeous man at the Oxford college where they were both studying—was only dating her for a bet. She'd found out the truth at the college ball where she'd thought he was going to propose, while he'd been planning to collect his winnings after proving he'd turned the oik into a posh girl. He hadn't loved her for herself or even wanted her; instead, it had been a warped kind of Eliza Doolittle thing. He and his friends had been laughing at her all along, and she'd been so hurt and ashamed.

Now Dr Alice Walters was a respected lepidopterist. She was comfortable with who she was professionally and was happy to give keynote speeches at high-powered conferences; but socially she always had to silence the voice in her head telling her that she wasn't good enough—especially if her surroundings were posh.

Why *had* Rosemary Grey's solicitor asked to see her?

Maybe Rosemary had left some specimens to the university. Or maybe this was about the project they'd worked on together: editing the journals and writing the biography of the butterfly collector Viola Ferrers, Rosemary's great-grandmother. Alice had visited her elderly friend in hospital several times after her stroke and, although Rosemary's sentences had been jumbled, her anxiety had been clear. Alice had promised Rosemary that she'd see the project through. Hopefully, whoever had inherited the journals would give her access to them, but she needed to be in full professional mode in case there were any doubts. Now really wasn't the time for imposter syndrome to resurface and point out that she looked a bit awkward in the business suit and heels she hardly ever wore, there was a bit of hair she hadn't straightened properly, and her make-up wasn't sophisticated enough.

The one thing Barney's callousness had taught her all those years ago was that image *mattered*—even though she thought people should judge her by what was in her head and her heart, not by what she looked like. For now she'd go with the superficial and let them judge the butterfly by its chrysalis.

'This is for you and Viola, Rosemary,' Alice said softly. She walked up the steps to the intimidatingly wide front door with its highly polished brass fittings and pushed it open.

'May I help you?' the receptionist asked.

Alice gave her a very professional smile. 'Thank you. I'm Dr Alice Walters. I have an appointment with Mr Hemingford at two-thirty.'

The receptionist checked the screen and nodded. 'I'll let him know you're here, Dr Walters. The waiting area's just through there. Can I offer you a cup of coffee while you're waiting?'

Alice would have loved some coffee, but she didn't want

to risk spilling it all over her suit—and right now she was feeling nervous enough to be clumsy. 'Thank you for the offer, but I'm fine,' she said politely, and headed for the waiting area.

There were a couple of others sitting there: a middle-aged woman who kept glancing at her watch and frowning, as if her appointment was running a bit late, and a man with floppy dark hair and the most amazing cobalt-blue eyes who was staring out of the window, looking completely lost.

For one crazy moment, she thought about going over to him and asking if he was all right. She knew from working with her students that if someone was having a rough day, human contact and a bit of kindness could make all the difference.

But the man was a stranger, this was a solicitor's office, and whatever was wrong was none of her business. Besides, she needed to make sure she was prepared for anything, given the infuriating vagueness of the solicitor's letter. So she sat down in a quiet corner, took her phone from her bag, and re-read the notes she'd made about the butterfly project.

Hugo Grey still couldn't quite believe that his eccentric great-aunt was dead. He'd thought that Rosemary would live for ever. She'd been the only one of his family he could bear to be around when his life had imploded nearly three years ago. Unlike just about everyone else in his life, she hadn't insisted over and over that he shouldn't blame himself for Emma's death, or tried to make him talk about his feelings; she'd simply asked him to come and help her with an errand that almost always didn't materialise, made him endless cups of tea and given him space to breathe. And there, in that little corner of Notting Hill, he'd started to heal and learn to face the world again.

He'd spent the first three months of this year in Scotland, so he hadn't been able to visit Rosemary as much as he would've liked, but he'd still called her twice a week and organised a cleaner and a weekly grocery delivery for her. Once he was back in London, he'd popped in on Monday and Thursday evenings, and she'd been fine—until the stroke. He'd visited her in hospital every other day, but it had been clear she wouldn't recover.

And now he was to be her executor.

Just as he'd been for Emma. Hugo knew exactly how to register a death, organise a funeral, plan a wake, write a good eulogy and execute a will, because he'd already done it all for his wife.

He clenched his fists. He'd let Emma down—attending an architectural conference thousands of miles away in America instead of being at her side when she'd had that fatal asthma attack. If he'd been home, in London, he could've got medical help to her in time to save her. He couldn't change the past, but he could learn from it; he wasn't going to let his great-aunt down. She'd trusted him to be her executor, so he'd do it—and he'd do it *properly*.

He glanced round the waiting room. There were two others sitting on the leather chairs: a middle-aged woman who was clearly impatient at being kept waiting, and a woman of around his own age who looked terrifyingly polished.

It was nearly half-past two. Thankfully Philip Hemingford was usually punctual. Hugo could hand over the death certificate, and then start working through whatever Rosemary wanted him to do. He knew from the copy of the will she'd given him that she'd left nearly everything to his father and there were some smaller bequests; he'd make sure everything was carried out properly, because he'd loved his eccentric great-aunt dearly.

A door opened and Hugo's family solicitor appeared. 'Mr Grey, Dr Walters?'

Dr Walters?

Hugo had been pretty sure this appointment was for him alone; he was representing his father, who wasn't well. Who on earth was Dr Walters?

The terrifyingly polished woman stood up, surprising him. She didn't look like the sort of person who'd pop in to see Rosemary for a cup of tea and a chat. Hugo knew all Rosemary's neighbours, and his great-aunt hadn't mentioned anyone moving into the street recently. This didn't feel quite right.

'Please, have a seat,' Philip Hemingford said, gesturing to the two chairs in front of his desk as he closed the door behind them. 'Now, can I assume you already know each other?'

'No,' Hugo said. And she looked as mystified as he felt.

'Then I'll introduce you. Dr Walters, this is Hugo Grey, Rosemary's great-nephew. Mr Grey, this is Alice Walters, Rosemary's business associate.'

Since when had his great-aunt had business arrangements? As far as Hugo knew, she'd been living on the income from family investments, most of which ended with her death. 'What business associate?'

The solicitor neatly sidestepped the question by saying, 'My condolences on your loss. Now, Mr Grey—before we begin, we need to follow procedure. I believe you have Miss Grey's death certificate?'

'Yes.' Hugo handed over the brown manila envelope.

'Thank you.' The solicitor extracted the document and read through it swiftly. Clearly satisfied that all was in order, he said, 'We're here today to read the last will and testament of Miss Rosemary Grey.'

Hugo didn't understand why this woman was here. Her name wasn't on the list of people who'd been left bequests.

Hugo had assumed that today's appointment was mainly to start the ball rolling with his duties as Rosemary's executor, so he could sort out the funeral.

Philip Hemingford handed them both a document. 'I witnessed the will myself, three months ago,' he said.

The will Hugo knew about dated from five years ago, when his great-aunt had first asked him to be her executor. Why had she changed it—and why hadn't she told anyone in the family?

'Dr Walters, Miss Grey has left you the house.'

What? Rosemary had left her house to a *stranger*?

Wondering if he'd misheard, Hugo scanned the document in front of him.

It was clearly printed.

Last will and testament...
...of sound mind...
To Dr Alice Walters, I leave my house...

A house in Notting Hill was worth quite a lot of money, even if it needed work—work that Hugo had tried to persuade his great-aunt to have done so that she'd keep safe and warm, but she'd always brushed his concerns aside. And Hugo had a really nasty feeling about this. He'd been here before, with something valuable belonging to his aunt and a stranger persuading her to hand it over.

'Just to clarify, Mr Hemingford,' Hugo said, giving Alice a steely look. 'My great-aunt left her house to someone that nobody else in my family has ever heard of before, and she changed her will three months ago?'

At least the woman had the grace to blush. As well she should, because he'd just stated the facts and they all very clearly added up to the conclusion that this woman had taken advantage of Rosemary's kindness. It wasn't the first time someone had taken advantage of his great-aunt. The last time had been Chantelle, the potter who'd befriended Rosemary and told her all kinds of sob stories. Rosemary had given Chantelle her William Moorcroft tea service; Chantelle had sold it to a dealer for a very large sum of money and—worse, in Hugo's eyes—stopped visiting Rosemary. Hugo had quietly bought the tea service back with his own money, returned it to his aunt, and kept a closer eye on people who visited his aunt since then.

Except for the mysterious Dr Walters, who'd slid very quietly under his radar.

Unless… Was this the woman his aunt had mentioned visiting, the one she'd said she wanted him to meet? Hugo, fearing this was yet another attempt by his family to get him to move on after Emma's death, had made excuses not to meet the woman. Fortunately this friend had never been available on Mondays or Thursdays, when Hugo visited, so he hadn't had to deal with the awkwardness of explaining to his aunt that he really didn't want to meet any 'suitable' young women.

Now, he wished he hadn't been so selfish. He should've been polite and met her. He should've thought about his aunt and her vulnerability instead of being wrapped up in his own grief and his determination not to get involved with anyone again.

'Miss Grey changed her will three months ago,' the solicitor confirmed, 'and she was of sound mind when she made her will.'

You could still be inveigled into doing something when you were of sound mind, Hugo thought. And Rosemary liked to make people happy. What kind of sob story had this woman spun to make his great-aunt give her the house?

'There are conditions to the bequest,' the solicitor continued. 'Dr Walters, you must undertake to finish the butterfly project, turn the house into an education centre—of which she would like you to assume the position of director, should you choose—and re-wild the garden.'

The garden re-wilding, Hugo could understand, because he knew how important his great-aunt's garden had been to her. And maybe the education centre; he'd always thought that Rosemary would've made a brilliant teacher. But, if Rosemary had left the house to his father, as her previous will had instructed, surely she knew that her family would've made absolutely sure her wishes were carried out? Why had his great-aunt left everything to a stranger instead? And he didn't understand the first condition. 'What project?'

'I'm editing the journals and co-writing the biography of Viola Ferrers,' Dr Walters said.

It was the first time he'd heard her speak. Her voice was quiet, and there was a bit of an accent that he couldn't quite place, except it was definitely Northern; and there was a lot of a challenge in her grey eyes.

Did she really think he didn't know who Viola Ferrers was?

'My great-great-great-grandmother,' he said crisply.

Her eyes widened, so he knew the barb had gone home. This was *his* family and *his* heritage. What right did this stranger have to muscle in on it?

'Miss Grey also specified that a butterfly house should be built,' the solicitor continued.

Rosemary had talked about that, three years ago; but Hugo had assumed that it was her way of distracting him, giving him something to think about other than the gaping hole Emma's death had left in his life. They'd never taken it further than an idea and a sketch or two.

'And said butterfly house,' the solicitor said, 'must be designed and built by you, Mr Grey.'

Rosemary had left him a loophole, then. As an architect, Hugo knew what happened if there was a breach of building and planning regulations, or a breach of conditions in a contract. 'So the bequest is conditional. What happens if the conditions of my great-aunt's will are breached?' he asked, trying to sound more casual than he felt.

'Then the house must be sold and the money given to a dementia charity,' the solicitor explained.

Meaning that any scheming done by this Dr Walters would fall flat, and something good would happen with the money. Which was fine by Hugo. It wasn't the money he was bothered about, even though he knew the house would raise a lot of money at auction; it was the fact that this woman appeared to have taken advantage of his great-aunt's kindness, and in his view that was very far from being OK. 'I see,' Hugo said. It looked as if this was going to be easy, after all. 'Then I'm afraid I won't be designing or building a butterfly house.'

'But you have to,' Dr Walters said. 'It's what she wanted.'

Or what Rosemary had been *persuaded* that she wanted, which was a very different thing. Hugo shrugged. 'We don't always get what we want.'

'Rosemary wanted the book finished and the house turned into a proper memorial to Viola,' Dr Walters said, folding her arms and narrowing her gaze at him.

Was that meant to intimidate him? He'd already survived the very worst life could throw at him. He had nothing left to lose, and he wasn't playing her game.

Philip Hemingford looked uncomfortable. 'This is meant to be a simple reading of Miss Grey's will, not a discussion.'

'That's fine by me,' Hugo said. 'I have nothing to add.' He wasn't letting this woman get away with scamming his great-aunt. And it was going to be very easy to defeat her; all he had to do was refuse to build the butterfly house.

'You can't let Rosemary down,' Dr Walters said, glaring at him.

Oh, was she trying to pretend that she cared? 'Perhaps you'd like to explain, Dr Walters, what your business association was with my great-aunt?'

'As I said earlier, I was working with her on Viola's journals,' she said. 'I'm a lepidopterist.'

The only people Hugo knew who were interested in butterflies were his great-aunt and some of her friends who were from the same generation, all of whom had been slightly eccentric and who hadn't cared about whether their clothes matched or even if they'd brushed their hair that morning. This smart, sleek woman didn't look anything like that kind of person. She looked brittle and fake and completely untrustworthy—much like he remembered Chantelle the potter. 'Indeed,' he drawled, putting as much sarcasm into his voice as he could.

'I lecture on lepidoptera at Roxburgh College at the University of London,' she said. 'Your great-aunt contacted my department and asked if I could help with her project. We've been working on it together part-time for the last six months.'

'She never mentioned the project to me,' he said.

She raised an eyebrow. 'Maybe you didn't talk to her enough.'

Playing that game, was she? His eyes narrowed. 'I was working in Scotland for six months from last October, so I admit I phoned rather than visiting—but I've seen her twice a week since I've been back in London.' Not that it was any of her business.

'Maybe she thought you wouldn't approve of her plans, so she didn't discuss them with you.'

If he'd known of Rosemary's plan to leave her house to a stranger, he would definitely have asked questions. Why hadn't his aunt trusted him? Had this woman coerced her?

'I really don't think this is a helpful discussion,' Philip Hemingford said, looking awkward.

For pity's sake. Why were lawyers so mealy-mouthed? If Hemingford wasn't going to stand up for his great-aunt, then Hugo would. 'Oh, I think it is,' Hugo said. 'I'm sure that professionally you'd want to make quite sure that your client hadn't been cozened into making a bequest. There are laws to prevent such things, I'm sure.'

'As you're such an expert in the law, Mr Grey,' Dr Walters said crisply, before the solicitor could reply, 'I'm sure you'll also be aware of the laws of defamation. I had no idea your great-aunt was going to leave me the house and I certainly didn't ask her to do so.'

'As I wasn't privy to the discussions, I wouldn't know,' he pointed out.

'Exactly,' she said. 'You weren't there.'

Hugo stared at her, outraged. Was she trying to claim that he'd neglected Rosemary? The gloves were coming off, now. 'So if the project goes ahead,' he asked, 'what exactly do you get out of it? Let me see.' He ticked them off on his fingers. '*You'll* be the one to bring any of Viola Ferrers's discoveries to light. *Your* name will appear on any papers written. *Your* name will appear on the cover of the journals as the editor, *your* name will be on the cover of the biography, and *your* name will appear as the director of the education centre. You appear to be doing rather well out of my great-aunt, Dr Walters.' The way he saw it, this woman was using Rosemary to further her career—to further it rather a lot.

'I can assure you, Mr Grey, that Rosemary's name will be on the biography and the journals as co-editor,' Dr Walters corrected, 'and I'll give her full credit on any papers. And, if the education centre goes ahead—which I very much hope it does, because it's clearly what she wanted—then *her* name will be prominent because it was her bequest.' She stared at him. 'And it'll be *your* name on record as the designer and builder of the butterfly house.'

'Ah, but it won't,' he said, 'because I'm not building it. Which means the conditions of the will are breached, so the house will have to be sold and the money given to charity.'

Smug, self-satisfied, *odious* man.

And to think that she'd felt sorry for him in the waiting room—that she'd actually considered going over to ask if he was all right. This man wasn't the sweet nephew Rosemary had mentioned to Alice a couple of times—a man who'd been very busy and struggled to see her. Instead, he was just like Barney and his cronies: posh, entitled and living on a different planet from the rest of the population. This was all just some kind of game to him, and he clearly thought he'd won.

Well, he could think again.

The barely veiled accusation that she was a gold-digger had made Alice angry enough to absorb the shock of the bequest and decide that yes, she'd do this and carry out her friend's dream. Hugo Grey wasn't going to get his own way. At all. He might be able to sell the house, under the terms of Rosemary's will, but he certainly couldn't dictate who bought it.

Alice didn't have the money to buy the property, let alone turn it into Rosemary's vision. But she could apply to the university for a grant to buy the house, and apply to plenty of other places for grants to do the work to convert it into an education centre and build a butterfly house. If she couldn't get enough money through grants, then she'd crowdfund it. *Help save Rosemary's butterflies.*

This man wouldn't know a butterfly if it came flapping past and settled on his arm. Rosemary did, and Alice wasn't going to let her friend down. The solicitor might have referred to her as a 'business associate', but the elderly lady was more than that; Rosemary had become a good friend over the last six months, and she deserved better than this arrogant, self-centred great-nephew slinging his weight around. A man Rosemary had obviously seen through rose-tinted glasses.

'As you wish,' she said.

He looked surprised.

Did he *really* think she was some kind of gold-digger?

She wasn't sure whether anger or pity came uppermost: anger at the insult, or pity for a man who clearly lived in a world full of suspicion and unkindness. It was a confused mixture of both, but anger had the upper hand. Hugo Grey might be gorgeous to look at, with that floppy dark hair and those cobalt-blue eyes, but he was as much of a snake as Barney.

Let him think that the world would go his way. Too late, he'd find out that it didn't. Not in this case.

'Do you have a key to the house?' he asked.

And, damn, her face was obviously very easy to read, because he nodded in satisfaction. 'I thought so. You need to hand it over to Philip Hemingford.'

No way. Not until she'd managed to rescue the last few journals so she could finish her work. 'As Rosemary left the house to me, I think not.'

'The conditions of your bequest have been breached, so technically the house belongs to the dementia charity she named in the will,' he pointed out coolly.

'I'm not the one who breached the conditions.'

'Really, really,' the solicitor interjected, squirming and looking awkward. 'This isn't…'

'What Rosemary wanted. I agree, Mr Hemingford,' Alice finished. 'And I don't have the key with me.' That wasn't actually true, but she was working on moral rights. Rosemary would've approved of the white lie, she was sure.

'Then I suggest,' Hugo Grey said, with that irritating drawl, 'that you bring the key here to Philip Hemingford by ten o'clock tomorrow morning.'

'Provided,' she said, 'that you do the same. Because the house doesn't belong to you, either.'

He looked shocked at that. 'It's my great-aunt's house and I'm her executor. I'm responsible for it.'

And *she* was responsible for the butterfly project. 'I'll hand my key over when you hand yours over,' she said.

'That,' the solicitor said hastily, 'sounds like a good solution for now. Perhaps you could both bring your sets of keys to me—say, tomorrow at ten?'

'I'm in a lecture at ten, but I can make it at twelve if that works for you.'

'Twelve's fine.'

'Thank you for your time, Mr Hemingford,' she said, giving him a brief nod of acknowledgement. Then she gave the younger man a glance of pure disdain. '*Mr* Grey.' And she hoped he interpreted 'Mr' as 'Entitled piece of pond-life', because that was exactly what she meant by the word.

And she walked out, leaving both men open-mouthed.

Normally, Alice didn't take taxis, but she needed to get to Rosemary's house before Hugo Grey did, to make sure she could still access the journals. So she whistled the first black cab that passed her—to her shock, it actually stopped for her—and took a taxi to the house in Notting Hill.

It felt weird, letting herself into the empty house. Right now the only moving things here were herself and the dust motes dancing in the sunlight.

It was weirder still, not seeing her elderly friend pottering around in the garden, or sitting at the kitchen table with her cup of tea and a welcoming smile.

Tears prickled against Alice's eyelids. Rosemary Grey was special. Kind, eccentric and with a lively mind. In a lot of ways, Rosemary reminded Alice of her grandfather, and she was sure they would've enjoyed each other's company—despite the fact that socially they were worlds apart.

'I'm not going to let him win,' she said fiercely. 'You deserve better than that entitled, spoiled buffoon. I'm going to finish our book. And your name is going on the cover before mine. I'm not going to let you down, Rosemary, I promise. And I keep my promises.'

She went into the study and found the last volumes of the journals. No doubt Hugo would figure out very quickly that she'd taken them and demand them back, so today she'd need to photograph every page and make sure she backed up the images in three places for safety's sake. Hugo Grey and his pomposity were absolutely not going to get in the way of Rosemary's plans.

'We're going to win,' she whispered to the empty house, and locked up behind her again.

Hugo had half-expected Alice Walters to be there, stripping out whatever she could, when he got to his great-aunt's house; but it was empty. Nothing but dust-motes and echoes. His great-aunt's vitality had gone from the place.

He let himself into the garden and wandered through it. The shrubs were overgrown and needed cutting back, but he could smell the sweet scent of the roses and the honeyed tones of the buddleia, and for a moment it made him feel as if his great-aunt were walking right beside him.

The butterfly house.

He could see exactly where Rosemary wanted it. They'd talked about it three years ago, when he'd been so broken after Emma's death and desperately needed distracting. Rosemary had suggested using the rickety old wall at the back of the garden for one wall of it; they'd talked about a house of glass, filled with plants that were the perfect habitat for butterflies.

Rosemary had loved glasshouses. So had he. She'd

taken him to see stately homes with amazing conservatories and domes when he was small, as well as the glasshouses at Kew and the Chelsea Physic Garden. They'd had a road trip to the Eden Project, too, when he was in his teens. They'd both been fascinated by the biomes—Rosemary for their contents, and himself for the structure. And Rosemary had been the one who'd championed him when he'd decided to become an architect, specialising in glass.

Had he been so cocooned in his grief that he'd not paid enough attention? He hadn't thought that she'd really meant it about the butterfly house; he'd assumed it was her way of distracting him. Particularly when she'd talked about using the wall of Viola's old conservatory; he'd checked it out and it would've needed completely rebuilding before it could be used to support a structure. He'd assumed that she'd realised the idea was impractical. Had he been wrong?

Standing with his hands in his pockets, he stared at the space in front of him. A lawn that had been cut but not cared for, so it was straggly and patchy, with weeds taking over completely in places. Overgrown flower beds with shrubs drooping, their dead flower heads unpruned. Right at that moment, it was a mess. But, with careful planning and a bit of hard work, he could just imagine the garden transformed and showcasing a butterfly house. A modern twist on a Victorian palm house, perhaps, marrying the past and the present. Something that looked like the past but had modern technology underpinning it; something that would last for the future.

Back in the kitchen, he made himself a black coffee in one of Rosemary's butterfly-painted mugs and sat at the kitchen table.

'What did you really want, Rosemary?' he asked the empty air. 'If the butterfly house was your dream, then I'll back it all the way and I'll build it for you. But if it's this woman trying to use your name and tread on you so she can get to the top, then it's no deal.'

How did he find out which one it was? He knew nothing about Dr Alice Walters. Rosemary had mentioned her friend but Hugo hadn't really paid attention. He'd been caught up in work and brooding—because, without Emma's warmth in his life, he'd been going through the motions. Existing, not living. It had been hard enough to get from the beginning of the day to the end.

Something about this just didn't sit right. It felt as if Alice Walters had taken advantage of Rosemary in the same way as Chantelle had, using a shared interest as a way to befriend her and then cheat her.

He flicked into his phone and looked up the website for Roxburgh College.

And there she was, listed in the staff of the biology department.

Dr Alice Walters.

He clicked on the link. Her photograph made her look much softer than she had in the solicitor's office. Her light brown hair had a natural curl rather than being ironed into the sophisticated smoothness he'd seen. She wasn't wearing make-up, either; her natural beauty shone through and her grey eyes were huge and stunning.

He pushed the thought away. This wasn't about being attracted to a woman who might or might not be a gold-digger. This was about making sure the woman hadn't taken advantage of his great-aunt.

According to her biography on the university's website, Alice had taken her first degree in biology at Oxford, and studied for her Masters and her PhD at London. She was a Fellow of the Royal Entomological Society. Her research interests were in biodiversity, conservation ecology and the impact of land use—all of which fitted with what Rosemary had asked her to do. She'd written an impressive list of papers, including some on re-wilding; she'd been a keynote speaker at several conferences; and she was supervising half a dozen doctoral students.

The academic side of it stacked up.

But were the ideas in the will Rosemary's, or had Alice influenced her? Was Alice Walters involved in this project because she'd liked Rosemary and wanted to help her make a difference, or because she wanted to make a name for herself and had no scruples about taking advantage of others to get there? Had she lied when she'd claimed to have no idea that Rosemary intended to leave her the house?

Until Hugo knew the truth, he wasn't budging.

CHAPTER TWO

TWO WEEKS LATER, Alice slid into a pew at the back of the church. She didn't want any animosity with Rosemary's family, but she did want to pay her respects to her friend at the funeral. It mattered to her. She'd leave quietly after the service, so the Greys wouldn't even know she was here.

There were lots of people in the congregation; she recognised some as Rosemary's neighbours, and a few of them smiled at her or lifted a hand in acknowledgement. And she definitely recognised Hugo Grey; he was sitting in a pew at the very front of the church, comforting an older couple she guessed were his parents.

The service itself was lovely, with the organist playing Chopin's Nocturne in E flat major as the pallbearers brought in the coffin. 'Morning Has Broken' was the first hymn—if Rosemary hadn't suggested it herself, whoever had chosen it had clearly known Rosemary's spirit well.

When it was time for the eulogy, Hugo stood up and went into the pulpit.

For a moment, Alice caught his eye and it felt like an electric shock.

No, absolutely *no*. It was totally inappropriate to feel that tug of attraction towards someone at a funeral, and it was even more inappropriate because she and Hugo were on opposite sides. During the last couple of weeks, he'd continued to refuse to change his position about building the butterfly house, so Rosemary's house was going up for sale. Alice had responded by putting together a business plan for the university, asking them for a grant towards buying the house and building the butterfly house; she'd also set up a crowdfunding page and a campaign to save the house. Finally, she'd applied for outline planning permission for changing the use of the house and building the butterfly house in the garden.

Everything was going at a speed she wasn't entirely comfortable with, but she had no other choice; she needed to be ready in case Hugo decided to put the house up for immediate auction rather than selling it through an estate agency. Without the money—or at least the promise of it—behind her, she couldn't buy the house and she couldn't fulfil Rosemary's dreams.

She looked away, and Hugo began speaking. Unlike the other day, his voice wasn't full of coldness and sneering; it was full of warmth and affection and sadness. And Alice was utterly captivated.

'I feel as if I should be reading Ophelia's speech up here about flowers, suggesting rosemary for remembrance, because we'll always remember Great-Aunt Rosemary. When I was a child, I spent a lot of time in her garden, and she'd tell me all about the butterflies and the birds and the flowers. So I'm choosing to read something by her favourite poet, Thomas Hardy; Rosemary noticed things, and I remember her reading this to me when I was a child and telling me that the first verse was about butterflies.'

This was personal, Alice thought. Heartfelt.

And the way he delivered it was full of love and meaning. His voice was clear and beautifully modulated; although it didn't wobble in the slightest, because he was clearly determined to do well by his great-aunt, she could see the glitter in his eyes to show that tears weren't far away.

"'When the Present has latched its postern behind my tremulous stay, And the May month flaps its glad green leaves like wings, Delicate-filmed as new-spun silk, will the neighbours say, 'He was a man who used to notice such things'?'"

It was the perfect poem to choose. Just as Hugo had suggested, it was full of butterflies, and it reminded her of Rosemary. Rosemary Grey had definitely noticed things—not just the environment, but also people. Alice had found herself able to open up to the older woman.

A woman who used to notice things.

A woman who was kind and passionate and inspirational.

And Alice was really going to miss her.

Hugo could see Alice Walters sitting at the back of the church. Today, she wasn't the polished, sophisticated woman who'd sat in the solicitor's office and argued with him. She was wearing plain black trousers and a silky black top, and her hair had the slight natural curl he'd noticed in her official university photograph.

Was she here to pay her respects to Rosemary, or to keep an eye on her own interests?

Hugo knew about her crowdfunding bid to buy the house, and Alice Walters exasperated him thoroughly; yet, at the same time, there was something about her that intrigued him.

How ironic that the first woman he'd really noticed since his wife's death was on the opposite side to him. And this was his great-aunt's funeral. He needed to finish his eulogy and give Rosemary the send-off she deserved, not start mooning about a woman he didn't really know and whom he strongly suspected of being an ambitious gold-digger.

So he shared his memories, making sure that every

single person in the congregation—except possibly the woman sitting in the last pew—had something to share, too. Rosemary would want to be remembered with love and with smiles, and he was going to make that happen.

Though he had to hold his mother's hand through 'Abide With Me' and clasp his father's shoulder; the verse about death's sting and the grave's victory caused both of them to stop singing, choked by emotion.

He followed his parents behind the coffin as they left the church; again, he couldn't help glancing at Alice. Her face coloured faintly as she caught his gaze, and he was horrified to feel awareness pulse through him again. Not here, not now, and—actually, no, he didn't want this *at all*. He was done with feeling. It had broken him nearly three years ago, and he never wanted to repeat it.

He'd expected her to be gone by the time the committal had finished, but instead she was talking to some of Rosemary's neighbours in the churchyard. From the way they were chatting so easily to her, he was pretty sure they knew her. Liked her, too, because they were smiling rather than giving her suspicious looks, the way half of them had looked at Chantelle.

Had he judged Alice unfairly?

In which case, he'd really let his aunt down. Then again, if Alice was as ambitious as he suspected, he didn't want her to get away with using Rosemary. He needed to get to the bottom of this.

Guilt had the upper hand at that moment, so he walked over to her and gave her a nod of acknowledgement. 'Dr Walters.'

'Mr Grey,' she replied, her tone equally formal.

'Perhaps you'd like to join us for the wake?'

Her eyes widened. 'Seriously? I didn't think I'd be welcome.'

Today, her manners were as blunt as the hint of her

accent. He rather liked that. It suggested that she was straightforward. Or was that a double bluff from an accomplished and ambitious woman?

'I don't want to cause any upset to your family,' she continued. 'Today's about Rosemary and your memories of her, and I don't want to do anything that takes away from that.'

A gold-digger would've said yes to the invitation without hesitating and would've been charming rather than blunt. Maybe he really had misjudged her. Even though she'd set up that crowdfunding site to buy the house.

This wasn't about Rosemary's house. It was about Rosemary. About saying goodbye. And he needed to do the right thing. The kind thing, as Rosemary would've wanted.

'You'll be welcome,' he said. 'It's in the hotel across the road, if you'd like to join us. I'll leave it to you to decide.' He gave her a nod of acknowledgement, then went to join his parents.

Hugo Grey had actually asked her to the wake. Alice couldn't quite get her head round this. They were on opposite sides. He didn't have to be nice to her. Yet today he'd chosen to be kind.

So she followed the straggle of mourners across the road, accepted an offer to sit with Rosemary's neighbours, drank tea from a pretty floral china cup and ate a scone with jam and cream. Rosemary, she thought, would've enjoyed this.

But all the while she was very aware of Hugo Grey.

The way he read poetry.

The sensual curve of his mouth.

And this had to stop. Even if they weren't on opposing sides, she was absolutely hopeless when it came to relationships. After Barney, she hadn't dated for a couple of years, not trusting her judgement in men, but then she'd met Robin, who'd seemed so nice at first—and the opposite of Barney. Down-to-earth. Except Robin had wanted her to change, too; she hadn't been girly enough for him. After Robin, there had been Ed, who hadn't minded how she dressed—but he'd wanted her to be less of a nerdy scientist, so she'd fit in with his artsy crowd. Then there had been Henry, who'd broken up with her because he'd wanted someone whose career would be less stellar than his.

Everyone she'd dated seemed to want to change her. It didn't matter whether they'd met through work, through a friend of a friend, or a dating app that should've screened them so they were the perfect match.

Maybe she was the one at fault, for picking men who couldn't compromise. And every break-up had knocked her confidence a little bit more.

Not that it mattered, because nothing was going to happen between herself and Hugo. He might already be involved with someone else. All she really knew about him was that he was Rosemary's great-nephew and he was an architect. One who'd won a couple of awards, according to the Internet, and was a rising star in the industry; but she hadn't looked up his private life because it was none of her business.

Even as she thought it, he walked over to her, carrying a cup of tea. 'Dr Walters. May I join you?'

Short of being rude, there was only one thing she could say. 'Of course, Mr Grey.'

'Can I get you some more tea, or something to eat?'

'I'm fine, thanks,' Alice said, suddenly feeling gauche and tongue-tied.

And he clearly wasn't going to make it easy for her, with small talk. He simply sat down beside her and waited.

Given that he reminded her so much of Barney and his entitled friends with their over-elaborate code of manners, was he waiting for her to make a mistake? Not hold her cup properly, or use the wrong bit of cutlery, or…

No. She was being unfair to him, especially as he'd been kind earlier. They were strangers, and this was his great-aunt's funeral. She'd try to meet him on common ground. 'Your eulogy was very good.'

He inclined his head. 'Thank you.'

Wasn't it his turn to make a comment, now, to keep the conversation going?

When he didn't, she added, 'I liked the poem.'

'My great-aunt loved poetry,' he said. 'Hardy was her favourite poet, but she loved Keats as well. And Christina Rossetti—whenever I hear leaves rustling in the trees, I think of Rosemary reading me that poem, or when I see the moon in a cloudy sky.'

Hugo Grey liked poetry? Now that she hadn't expected. But she knew the poems he'd mentioned. '"The moon was a ghostly galleon tossed upon cloudy seas."'

He looked surprised. 'You know that one, too?'

She nodded. 'My grandmother loved that one. She read it to me a lot when I was a child.' And she could hear it in her head, in her grandmother's broad Yorkshire accent.

Just for a moment, the crowded room was forgotten: it felt as if it were just the two of them, the poem echoing down the years to them and joining them together.

'"Watch for me by moonlight. I'll come to thee by moonlight,"' he whispered.

And she could imagine Hugo as the highwayman of the poem, with his breeches and his velvet claret coat, lace at his chin and a French tricorn hat on his hair.

Her mouth went dry as she thought of Bess loosening her black hair in the window, and her highwayman lover kissing the dark waves. What would it be like if Hugo kissed her hair, her cheek, the corner of her mouth?

It made her feel hot all over—and ashamed, because

this really wasn't the time or place to be thinking like that. Though, given the sharp slash of colour across his cheeks, she had a feeling that he was thinking something very similar indeed.

And she couldn't make a single word leave her mouth. They were all stuck in her throat.

This was terrifying. She hadn't been this aware of anyone since Barney. But she knew her judgement in men was hopeless and she'd given up trying to find Mr Right. Burying herself in her work had been much safer. Looking at butterfly pheromones and ignoring human ones.

Quoting poetry. How stupid Hugo had been to think that was safe: Hardy, Keats, Rossetti and their images of nature.

But of all things he'd chosen to quote 'The Highwayman'. And it wasn't about the moon as a galleon, the road over the purple moors. It was about Bess the landlord's daughter and the highwayman, the woman plaiting her hair and the man kissing it, promising to be back for her. The jealous ostler with his hair like mouldy hay, betraying the highwayman to the redcoats. Bess saving him temporarily with her own death. Love and passion and death.

Alice Walters's eyes were grey, not dark. Her hair was light brown, almost a nondescript colour, rather than the exotic long, black curls of Bess. She didn't have a red ribbon tied through her hair in a love knot.

And yet remembering the line of the poem made Hugo want to bury his face in Alice's hair.

Would she smell of roses, vanilla or honey?

Oh, for pity's sake.

He hadn't so much as noticed another woman in the last three years. He hadn't wanted to. Emma was the love of his life, and after her death he hadn't wanted anyone else.

So what was it about Dr Alice Walters that drew him, made him actually notice her and react to her like this?

Rosemary would no doubt have said this was a good thing. That Hugo would never forget Emma but it was past time that he started thinking about moving on, finding someone to share his life with rather than spending decades and decades alone. He'd half-suspected that was why she'd tried to get him to meet her friend Ally, and it was why he'd made himself unavailable. He didn't want anyone else.

Maybe he did need to move on. But his first choice definitely wouldn't be an ambitious lepidopterist, a woman whose motives he hadn't yet worked out. He didn't even *like* Alice Walters.

Though he had to acknowledge that he was attracted to her. Not to the glossy, brittle woman from the solicitor's office, but to *this* woman, a woman whose lips had parted ever so slightly and he was incredibly aware of the shape of her mouth. It made him want to lay the palm of his hand against her cheek and rub the pad of his thumb against her lower lip.

And he was at his great-aunt's funeral.

This really wasn't the time or place to be thinking about touching someone, kissing them.

Time seemed to have slowed to treacle. It felt as if he were hearing things from underneath an ocean, slow and haunting like a whale song rather than the trill of birds.

Say something.

He needed to say something.

But moving his lips made him think about *her* lips. How soft they might be against his own. Pliant and warm and—

'Hugo? I'm so sorry about your aunt.'

He looked up. Saved by Millie Kennedy, Rosemary's neighbour.

'Thank you, Millie.' He accepted the elderly woman's hug. 'Have you met Dr Walters?'

'Our Ally? Of course I have. Lots of times. She's been

working on Rosemary's book.' Millie hugged Alice, too. 'Good to see you again, love. I'm glad you could make it. Our Rosemary deserved the best send-off.'

Millie was nice to everyone, Hugo knew. But she seemed to know Alice quite well, accepting her as one of her own. And surely a gold-digger wouldn't want to get too close to anyone other than her target, in case she was caught out? So maybe Alice wasn't one of the bad guys. Maybe he'd just become a miserable cynic since Emma's death, seeing the worst in the world.

'I really ought to get back to my students,' Alice said. 'But I wanted to pay my respects to Rosemary.' She stood up, and Hugo realised that without her high heels Alice was a good six inches shorter than he was. Petite. *Cute*.

And it set alarm bells ringing in his head. This woman could be very dangerous to his peace of mind.

'Thank you for inviting me to the wake, Mr Grey,' she said politely, and held out her hand to shake his.

It would be churlish not to shake her hand, he thought. But he regretted the impulse when the touch of her fingers against his made him feel as if an electric shock had zapped through him.

'Thank you for coming to Rosemary's funeral,' he said, equally politely. There were other things he wanted to say, but absolutely not in front of Millie. 'I'm sure we'll be in touch.'

Touch. What a stupid word. His libido seized on it and threw up all kinds of images of her touching him, and he could feel the heat rising in his face.

What was it about this woman that made him feel like a gauche teenager?

And what was he going to do about it?

Alice surreptitiously checked her hand when she left the hotel. Shouldn't there be scorch marks on her skin from where Hugo Grey had touched her? Because it had felt as if lightning had coursed through her when he'd shaken her hand.

This was crazy.

She didn't react to men like this.

Maybe she was going down with some peculiar virus.

She was very glad to get back to the safety of her office and a tutorial with her students. And she was not going to spend her time mooning over Hugo Grey. She had things to do. Students to teach, Viola's journals to finish editing, a crowdfunding campaign to run...

But it was hard to concentrate. She kept drifting off and thinking about him. Which really wasn't her; she never let anything get in the way of her professionalism. Why was she letting Hugo Grey affect her like this?

'Alice Walters, get a grip,' she told herself out loud. 'He was just being polite when he said he'd be in touch. You're probably never going to see him again. He's going to sell the house, you're going to buy it, and that's that.'

Though she revised her views, the following Monday, when she had the letter from the planning officials rejecting outline permission for the butterfly house.

She'd given them solid reasons for the change of use to the building and the construction of the butterfly house. The fact the planning office had turned her down made her think that someone had pulled strings—someone who clearly had contacts within the department.

And she had a pretty fair idea of who that someone had to be.

Hugo Grey.

Anger simmered in her heart all morning, through all her tutorials, to the point where she had to ask her students to repeat their answers. Her afternoon was scheduled for working on a paper, but she decided to catch up with that later. Right now she had something much more important to do: pin Hugo Grey down and make him fix the mess he'd made.

A quick phone call to his office in Docklands established that yes, he was in, but he was in a meeting until one o'clock.

So far, so good; if she left the university now, she'd reach his office at just about the same time that his meeting finished and she could tackle him face to face.

His office was in part of an old wharf that had been converted; the yellow bricks had been cleaned until they sparkled and the arched windows were huge. Inside, the lobby was light and airy, and the reception area for Hugo's architectural practice was gorgeous, filled with plants and overlooking the river.

'Can I help you?' the receptionist asked.

'I'd like to see Hugo Grey,' Alice said.

'I'm afraid he's in a meeting,' the receptionist said. 'Can anyone else help?'

'Thank you, but I'm afraid it needs to be Hugo himself,' Alice said. 'I'm aware that his meeting's scheduled to finish at one. That's why I'm here now.'

The receptionist looked surprised that the scruffy woman in front of her appeared to possess organisational skills. Alice wished she'd worn her favourite T-shirt, the one with the slogan 'Don't judge a butterfly by its chrysalis'.

'If his meeting overruns, I'll wait,' she said.

'He might not be av—'

'Oh, he'll be available to see me,' Alice cut in, very quietly. 'Unless he'd prefer me to stand in the middle of this waiting area and explain to everyone within earshot why Hugo Grey is completely untrustworthy and they might be better off taking their business to a different practice of architects.'

The receptionist looked alarmed. 'Please don't do that.

I'll talk to his PA and see when he'll be available. Would you mind waiting in the reception area?'

'Thank you. I'm Dr Alice Walters and it's about the butterfly house. And,' she added, 'it's quite urgent.'

Three minutes after the receptionist had made the phone call, Hugo came downstairs, frowning.

'Dr Walters? Why are you here?'

'I think you know why.' She folded her arms and glared at him.

'I'm afraid I have no idea what you're talking about,' he drawled.

'So you're a liar as well as a snake?' She gave a humourless laugh. 'I'm sure your clients will be interested to hear this.'

He narrowed his eyes at her. 'We're not going to discuss this here. Come up to my office.' He looked over to the receptionist. 'Thank you, Anjula. I'm sorry you've got tangled up in this.'

Guilt prickled its way across Alice's skin. It wasn't the receptionist's fault that Hugo had behaved this way; and Alice hadn't exactly been very nice to her. 'I'm sorry, too,' she said.

She followed Hugo up the stairs to his office, allowed him to usher her inside and close the door, and took the chair he offered her.

He sat down opposite her and folded his arms. 'So what is all this about, Dr Walters?'

'It's about you pulling strings with your mates at the planning office, Mr Grey.'

'I have no idea what you're talking about.'

She took the letter from her bag and slapped it down on his desk. 'Just what you wanted to happen, I believe. I'm sure you'll be delighted to learn that the council turned down the outline planning permission for the butterfly house—if you don't know that already.'

'That has nothing to do with me.'

She scoffed. 'You seriously expect me to believe that?'

'If a new building or a change of use doesn't fall within the local planning authority's development plan, then a project will be rejected,' he informed her. 'It has nothing to do with any objections that people might raise about the building or the change of use.'

Alice shook her head. 'Rosemary would be so disappointed in you. She really wanted the butterfly house built and the house turned into an education centre, and you're doing your very best to block it. And, just so you know, I'm not a gold-digger. I don't care about money—what I care about is butterflies.'

The woman sitting in front of him wasn't the sophisticated, brittle woman he'd met at the solicitor's office, nor even the quiet, slightly shy woman from the funeral, Hugo thought. This woman glowed. Right from the top of her very messy hair down to her well-worn hiking boots.

For the first time since he'd known her, Alice Walters actually looked like a lepidopterist—like one of Rosemary's hippy friends he remembered from his childhood. Mixed with a bit of Roman goddess. A pocket-sized one, with freckles on her snub nose.

She was still speaking. 'Did you know that three-quarters of British butterflies are in decline, and the number of moths has gone down by a third in the last forty years?'

He didn't.

'They're not just silly little flappy things that we don't need to worry our pretty little heads about. Butterflies are important as pollinators—they don't have the fur of a bee for the pollen to stick to, but they cover more ground than bees and that means greater diversity in the gene pool. They're important in the food chain, both as prey and predator, and they're important indicators of the health of the ecosystem. Butterflies and moths are fragile, so they react quickly to change, and if they vanish it's an early indicator of problems in an area.'

This was way outside his area of expertise. But she was clearly both knowledgeable and passionate about her subject, and that passion drew him like a magnet. No way was he going to stop her speaking—even if she did have a few of her facts wrong about the planning application.

'They're important in teaching children about the natural world,' she continued, 'and the transformation during their life-cycle from egg to caterpillar to pupa to butterfly.' She ticked the points off on her fingers. 'And if nothing else they're beautiful. Just look at the delight on a child's face when they see butterflies in the garden or the park or the forest. We need all the beauty we can get in this world.'

He remembered being delighted by the butterflies in Rosemary's garden, as a child. And, now he thought about it, there didn't seem to be as many of them around as there had been when he was young.

But this woman was also accusing him of something he hadn't done, and that wasn't acceptable. 'So you think it's OK to march into my office and be rude to my team, without having a shred of evidence of what you're accusing me of?'

'In the solicitor's office, you said you refused to build the butterfly house, meaning that the conditions of the will aren't met and Rosemary's house will have to be sold,' she said. 'And you're an award-winning architect, so it's obvious that any planner will take notice of what you have to say. If you put in an objection, it'll carry more weight than a normal person's.'

'That isn't how planning works,' he said. 'Did you take advice before you submitted the outline application?'

She folded her arms. 'I might have an accent, but that doesn't mean I'm stupid.'

Interesting. She was chippy about her background? Then again, she'd been to Oxford. Having the wrong accent might've made things harder for her there.

'So you took advice.' He tried to make it sound like a statement rather than a question.

'Yes.'

'May I?' He gestured to the envelope she'd slapped down on his desk.

'Help yourself.'

The angry colour on her cheeks was subsiding, now. But she was still slightly pink and flustered, and Hugo had to stop himself wondering what she'd look like if she'd just been kissed. Would she be equally pink and flustered? Would her eyes glow with that same passion?

He forced himself to concentrate on reading the letter. Then he looked at her. 'Judging by their objections, whoever you went to for advice on your application obviously didn't explain what you wanted clearly enough. Did you submit plans? Sketches? Anything to scale?'

'It was an *outline* planning application. I was told it didn't need anything like that.'

'Sketches and plans would have helped. And a proper explanation.' He looked at her. 'You could talk to someone at the planning department and ask them if modifying your application would change their decision.'

She narrowed her eyes at him. 'Are you offering to help me, now?'

'I...' He raked a hand through his hair. Yes and no. He *could* help her; he just wasn't sure if he wanted to. 'My great-aunt was lovely. She was kind, she was generous, and people took advantage of her.'

Her mouth opened in seeming outrage. 'I wasn't taking advantage of Rosemary. I'd never do that. Apart from the fact that I'm not the gold-digger you seem to think I am, she was my *friend*.'

'Philip Hemingford introduced you to me as her business associate.'

'I was her friend, too. I liked her. She was straightforward. She judged people on who they were.'

That chimed with him. But Alice also flustered him—and she made him angry when she added, 'Rosemary mentioned her high-powered nephew. But you never seemed to be around.'

'I had a six-month project in the wilds of Scotland. It's not exactly easy to pop in to Notting Hill from several hundred miles away.'

'What about after your project ended?'

'I visited twice a week—obviously on days you weren't there. But you're welcome to check with her neighbours, if you want proof. Mondays and Thursdays, to be precise.' He stared at her, challenging her to call his bluff. He'd enjoy seeing her back down and apologise, confronted with the proof.

She met his gaze head on, to make the point that he didn't intimidate her.

It felt as if there should be a military drummer in the room, rat-tat-tatting a challenge.

Just when the tension reached screaming point, she inclined her head. 'Your eulogy convinced me that you loved her.'

The quiet words took all the combat out of it. She was acknowledging that, even though she knew nothing about him, she could tell he'd loved his great-aunt.

Maybe it was his turn to make a concession. 'And her neighbours knew you. Millie liked you; she didn't have any time for Chantelle.'

She frowned. 'Who was Chantelle?'

'Someone who befriended Rosemary a few years ago, told her massive sob stories, and as a potter she fell in love with Rosemary's William Moorcroft tea service—so my great-aunt gave it to her.'

'What's William Moorcroft?' Alice looked mystified.

'It's Art Deco china. Pretty—and also worth a great deal of money.' He took his phone from his pocket, did a quick search and then showed her a photograph.

She bit her lip. 'Oh, no. I broke the handle off one of those cups, a couple of months ago. I glued it back on, but...' Her eyes widened as she obviously noticed the auction price guide. 'Oh, my God. I thought it was just a pretty cup and it was one of Rosemary's favourites, so I mended it. I had no idea it was worth that sort of money. It should've been done by a proper specialist. I'm so sorry.' She blew out a breath. 'I'll pay for a proper repair.'

And right at that moment Hugo knew that Alice Walters was absolutely genuine and he'd misjudged her. This wasn't a woman who'd tried to inveigle his aunt into leaving the house to her so she could make lots of money. This was a woman who shared Rosemary's love of butterflies and wanted to help her reach her dream. A woman who'd mended a cup she'd thought was worth only a couple of pounds rather than throwing it away, because it was his great-aunt's favourite; and now she knew it was valuable she was offering to pay for a specialist repair.

'Don't worry about it,' he said. 'But Chantelle wasn't the only one who took advantage of my great-aunt over the years, simply the last of them. There were a few others.'

'I'm sorry. That's a horrible thing to do. Betraying someone's trust is just vile.'

There was something heartfelt about her words, and he wondered who'd betrayed her.

'I had absolutely no idea about her will,' Alice said. 'When I got the solicitor's letter, I thought maybe she might have left me some of Viola's specimens for the university collection. I didn't know she'd planned this. And, even though I love the idea of setting up a proper education centre and a butterfly house in Rosemary's name, I do understand that you wouldn't want all her estate going to a stranger.'

'Technically, it goes to charity,' he pointed out.

'Whatever.' She spread her hands. 'What *does* matter, though, are Viola's journals.'

'The ones you took from the house,' he said. He'd discovered that when he'd looked in the office.

'I returned them to the solicitor, the next day, along with my key. And he gave me a receipt for them, if you'd like to see it.' She paused. 'You obviously know that Rosemary was having trouble with her hip.'

No, he hadn't. His great-aunt was of the generation that just got on with things and didn't make a fuss. She hadn't mentioned a word about a problem with her hip.

'That's why she gave me a key—so she wouldn't have to get up and limp to the front door to let me in every time I visited.'

And now he felt bad. Why hadn't he known? Why hadn't he *noticed* that Rosemary actually let him do things for her instead of being her usual fiercely independent self? He'd been so busy trying to keep himself looking like a functioning human being that he'd had tunnel vision, and it made him feel ashamed. Had the trouble with Rosemary's hip had anything to do with her having a stroke?

'I loved working on the journals with her,' Alice continued softly. 'You've no idea how amazing it is, seeing words that are nearly a couple of centuries old, and hardly anyone else has seen since they were written. Sketches and watercolours that are still as fresh as the day they were painted. And, best of all, to hear about the person who created those journals from someone who actually knew her when she was still alive.'

'Actually, I do,' he said.

She blinked. 'You've seen the journals?'

'When I was younger. I just liked the pictures of butterflies. I was too little at the time to try and work out what the handwriting said. But when I was a student I saw the original plans for the Kew Gardens palm houses and it made all the hairs stand up on my arms—so I'm guessing that's how you felt about the journals.'

'It is,' she confirmed. 'Viola Ferrers deserves her place in lepidopterist history. And Rosemary, too. She was a custodian. She kept Viola's work safe, and the butterfly collection intact. Something that I think is worth sharing with the nation, the way Rosemary wanted it—starting with having Viola's study restored to how it was, because it's important for social history as well as scientific history.'

This wasn't a gold-digger talking. At all.

Hugo saw this with clarity, now. Alice didn't want the house for herself. She wanted it for the butterflies. She wanted it to make a *difference*.

'I have a site meeting this afternoon,' he said, 'and I think this is a discussion that needs a bit longer than a lunch break.'

Hope bloomed on her face. 'Are you saying you're going to work with me instead of against me?'

He wasn't promising anything. Not until he'd looked at everything properly. 'I'm saying,' he said, 'that we should talk further. Are you available this evening?'

'Yes.'

He liked the fact that she hadn't tried to make him feel as if she was doing him a favour, claiming she'd have to shuffle things round to accommodate him. Clearly this project was important to her, and as far as she was concerned anything else could be moved. That was a good sign.

'We should meet on neutral territory,' he said.

'The obvious place,' she said, 'would be Rosemary's house. Except neither of us has a key any more.'

Because he'd backed them both into a corner at the solicitor's office, and he knew it. 'OK. I'll get one of the keys back. For today,' he said. 'Until we've talked. What time can you meet me there?'

'Any time. I'm working on a paper this afternoon, so I can be flexible.'

'Five-thirty, then?' he suggested.

'That works for me.'

He held out his hand to shake hers.

Big mistake.

Just like the last time he'd shaken her hand, every nerve-end in his skin felt electrified.

Given that she suddenly looked pink and flustered, did it affect her the same way? Though he couldn't allow himself to think about that. This was about his great-aunt and the butterflies. Nothing else.

'I'll see you out,' he said, and ushered her down to the reception area.

And why was it that he found himself watching her walk away? Why was it that he was starting to feel things he'd thought were damped down for ever?

This was a potential complication that neither of them needed. By the time he met her at his great-aunt's house, he'd better have his head and his emotions completely back under control.

CHAPTER THREE

As Hugo had agreed to meet her at Rosemary's house, Alice hoped there might be a chance he was going to listen to her and have a proper discussion about the butterfly house instead of being the bull-headed, irritating man who'd judged her without examining the evidence properly. Which in turn meant that he might actually help her to fulfil her promise to Rosemary. If he agreed, then the money she'd raised so far in crowdfunding could be used for renovations, repairs and building the butterfly house, rather than the whole lot having to be used to buy the house itself.

Hugo Grey was a businessman first, so she needed to show him the plans she'd made for grant applications. Plans that showed potential footfall and revenue, so he could see that the project would be self-supporting. And then she'd show him the things that really made a difference: Viola's journals, her butterfly collection and the garden itself. She knew he'd probably seen them all before—but she was also willing to bet that he'd never seen them from her particular point of view.

Armed with her laptop, Alice took the Tube to Notting Hill and walked to Rosemary's house. Hugo was already there waiting for her, leaning against the gate. She'd expected him to let himself inside to stake his claim to the house; the fact that instead he'd waited for her outside made her feel a lot more relaxed about the situation. Though, at the same time, her heart skipped a beat as she drew nearer to him. His cobalt-blue eyes really were stunning. He'd changed into jeans instead of the sharp business suit he'd worn in the office and taken off his tie; it was odd how such tiny differences could make him look so much more approachable.

'Thanks for meeting me here,' she said.

'You're welcome.'

Was she? Was that mere politeness, or did he actually mean it? She'd never been able to tell with Barney's set. She'd taken them at face value—and then she'd learned that they'd been laughing at her all along, mocking the working-class girl who'd been stupid enough to think that the privileged classes would ever accept her for who she was.

'Shall we?' He gestured to the front door; once he'd unlocked it, he stood aside for her to enter.

She caught her breath as she walked into the kitchen. 'It doesn't feel right, being here without Rosemary.'

'That's how I feel, too,' he admitted.

'I'd always put the kettle on and make us some tea before we started work on the journals.'

'Proper loose-leaf tea, and make sure you warm the pot first,' he added.

She could almost hear Rosemary saying that; clearly it had been the same for him when he'd visited. She looked at the teapot on the dresser. 'Given what I know now about the tea service, I don't think I'd dare use that teapot ever again. I'd be too scared of dropping it. I can't believe she let me think it was just ordinary.'

'I can,' he said wryly. 'She once told me not to save things for best. She said you need to use things *now* and enjoy them, rather than save them for a special occasion that might never come.'

'She was full of wise words.' Alice felt her voice thicken in her throat. 'I miss her.' But getting emotional wasn't going to help anything. She needed to keep this business-like. Professional. She looked at him. 'But that's not why we're here.' She set her laptop on the kitchen table. 'What do you want to start with, the journals or the butterfly house?'

'The journals,' he said. 'I assume you had copies made when you borrowed them.'

'Yes. I photographed them myself.' She looked him straight in the eye. 'And, before you ask, the reason I took them was in case you refused me access. I promised Rosemary I'd finish writing Viola's biography and editing her journals, and I think it's important to keep promises.' Especially as she knew how it felt when someone broke a promise to you. 'Just so I don't waste time running through stuff you already know, what do you know about Viola Ferrers?'

'She was born in 1858 into a fairly wealthy family, and she followed the fashion of Victorian women collecting butterflies,' he said promptly. 'Her husband bought this house when they married, and it's stayed in the family since then.'

'OK. First off, Viola was a proper entomologist, so please don't dismiss her as an amateur collector with a "little hobby",' Alice said, making quote marks with her fingers and giving him a hard stare. 'She was much more than that. She studied butterflies scientifically. She wrote papers, though because she was a woman she never got to hear her papers read at the Linnean Society—just like Beatrix Potter.'

He blinked. 'That was a reason for them not to read her papers? Because she was a woman?'

'Oh, they *read* the papers, all right,' Alice said. 'But Viola wasn't allowed to hear them being read. At the time, women weren't allowed to be members of the society. She couldn't even go along to meetings as a guest. But she didn't let any of that nonsense stop her studying butterflies. Let me show you.'

Again, Hugo noticed how vital and animated Alice was when she talked about the project; he really, really liked that. He followed her into Rosemary's study, and she took one of the narrow leather-bound books from the shelf.

'I know you've already seen them, but I want to put them in an academic context for you. Viola kept these journals from the age of sixteen,' she said. 'She used them as a sketchbook as well. She travelled around the country to see botanical gardens; she wrote down the details of the butterflies she saw there and sketched them, too.' She opened the book, flicked through a couple of pages and held the book out to him. 'See?'

Viola's handwriting was very neat and regular, and Hugo noticed that all the diagrams were labelled. 'She's called the butterflies by their Latin names,' he said, surprised; that hadn't registered when he'd been young. There was a water colour of a copper and black butterfly on the page Alice showed him. *'Boloria euphrosyne.'*

'The Pearl-bordered Fritillary. It used to be widespread throughout the country, and now it's mainly found in parts of Scotland, Cumbria, Devon and Cornwall,' Alice said, looking sad. 'They're one of the early spring butterflies; their caterpillars feed on violets.'

'I'm not sure I remember ever seeing any of these in real life,' he said thoughtfully.

'There are some specimens in Viola's collection.' Alice went over to the large display cabinet, opened one of the drawers and slid out one of the frames. 'Here.'

It was a long, long time since Hugo had seen the frames of butterflies. And it still amazed him that these specimens were more than a hundred and fifty years old, yet the colours were still fresh. 'That's beautiful. And also really sad, because—well, shouldn't butterflies be flying, not pinned to a board?'

'I'm glad you said that,' Alice said. 'I agree. Though at the same time we do need to curate the collectors' frames we still have. So many of these haven't been kept properly and the butterflies have just crumbled into dust over the years.'

'I remember Rosemary showing me the big blue butterflies when I was very young,' he said. 'They fascinated me.'

'Those would've been tropical ones from South America,' she said. 'I'm guessing that was *Morpho didius*. That's one of my favourites, too.' She put the frame back carefully and fished out another. 'Here.'

'That's what I remember,' he agreed. 'The colour. Though obviously I've never seen a live one.'

'You wouldn't, in England, unless you've been to a butterfly house. Though there are some blue British butterflies,' she said. She tipped her head very slightly to one side, as if thinking about something, and then said, 'I could show you.'

'In London?'

She nodded. 'Or a bit further afield.'

She was asking him to go on a butterfly expedition with her?

Right then, she looked exactly like what she was: a butterfly specialist. Scruffy, not caring about fashion in the slightest, and totally in love with her subject.

'All right,' he said. Because going further afield with her wasn't the same as going on a date, was it? Alice was proposing a scientific expedition to back up her argument on the butterfly house project, and as he was on the opposite side it made sense for him to accompany her so they were both in full possession of all the facts.

But what if it was a date?

He checked himself. Of course it wasn't. Though, if he was honest with himself, Alice Walters intrigued him. And he was definitely attracted to the scientist, the woman who glowed with passion when she spoke about her subject. That snub nose. The freckles. The light in her grey eyes.

Reining in his thoughts, he brought the subject back to the butterflies. 'The specimens in these frames: are they butterflies that Viola collected herself?'

Alice nodded. 'She went on expeditions abroad. In Victorian times, you didn't actually need a passport to travel, so we don't have exact dates of when she went. But she wrote up her expeditions in her journal. Some of her specimens are in the British Museum.'

Hugo hadn't known that, either. 'And that's important?'

'It means the specimens are of really, really high quality. Lots of collectors in those times offered specimens to the British Museum and were rejected.'

'And hers were accepted? That's pretty special,' Hugo said.

'Exactly. You should be proud of her,' Alice said. 'And she didn't get the specimens solely from expeditions; she used to breed butterflies here in this garden, working out what food plants and habitats helped to produce the best specimens.'

Now he was beginning to understand why Alice thought the journal project was so important. 'And that was rare for a woman in her time?'

'Probably not,' Alice said. 'A lot of women did academic work that their husbands took the credit for—which isn't me having a feminist rant at you, it's just stating how things were back then. Women couldn't even study at university until a decade after Viola was born. Even when they were allowed to attend university, at first they couldn't graduate; they were given a certificate of completion for their exams rather than a proper degree.'

'I had no idea,' he said.

'The University of London was the first one to allow women students and the first one to confer degrees on women. Viola studied there—at my college, which is why Rosemary contacted me in the first place—and she fell in love with one of her fellow students. Luckily for her, he was pretty enlightened and he encouraged her to keep up her scientific work, even after they got married. She bred her butterflies, did her experiments and wrote papers for entomology magazines.' Alice folded her arms and gave him a level stare. 'And I think her name should be a lot better known.'

'Did my great-aunt do something similar?' he asked. What Rosemary actually did had always been a bit of a mystery to him.

'Yes. But she took photographs of butterflies, rather than going out with a net and a killing jar. That's how I do things, too. I want to conserve butterflies, not preserve them.' Alice put the frame back in the cabinet. 'Which leads me to the butterfly house. Shall we go into the garden?'

'Sure.' He went to the back door; after he'd unlocked it, he stood aside so she could lead him into the garden.

He noticed there were several butterflies resting on the buddleia, soaking up the sunshine.

'Peacocks,' she said, seeing his gaze. 'The blue eye-spots make it obvious why they get their common name—but I bet you didn't know they hiss.'

He stared at her. 'Really? Butterflies *hiss*?'

'Well—it's not *actual* hissing,' she amended. 'It's their third line of defence against predators. The first one is the underside of their wings looking like a leaf; if a bird works out that it's potential food and not a leaf, then the butterfly will open its wings to flash those eye-spots—it's called a startle display. If that doesn't make the bird back off, then the butterfly rubs its wings together and it sounds like hissing.'

'That's amazing.' Hugo could see now why Rosemary had wanted Alice to set up the educational centre. This was the sort of fact that would hold a child spellbound. The way Alice talked held *him* spellbound, too.

'Butterflies are amazing,' she said. 'That buddleia needs a bit of work so it'll have better growth next year. But you already know from Rosemary's will that she wanted the garden properly re-wilded and filled with plants that attract butterflies and bees.'

'And a winding path through it, so you don't see the butterfly house itself until the very last minute.'

She stared at him. 'That wasn't stated in her will, but it's something she said to me a couple of times. So did she discuss it with you?'

'Years ago, but...' He didn't want to tell Alice why he'd needed distracting. He didn't want her to start pitying him. 'There was a lot going on in my life at the time. I guess I didn't pay enough attention to what she was telling me. She hadn't said anything to me about it for quite a while, so I thought she'd shelved the idea.'

'And now?'

'I don't know.' He looked at her. 'You're not like you were at the solicitor's.'

'Not wearing a suit and make-up and high heels, you mean?' She rolled her eyes. 'I'm a scientist, not a fashion plate.'

'So that's what you normally wear for work?' He gestured to her faded jeans and ancient khaki T-shirt.

'Yes.' She shrugged. 'If you're doing fieldwork, wearing strappy sandals is the quickest way to give yourself a sprained ankle, wearing a dress with bare legs instead of trousers tucked into boots will make you vulnerable to ticks, and little strappy tops are no protection at all against sunburn. So I dress sensibly.'

'I don't think I've ever met anyone who wears hiking boots,' he said.

She frowned. 'Surely you have to wear boots and a hard hat on building sites?'

'If it's a working site, like the one I went to this afternoon, yes. Otherwise, ordinary shoes will do.'

She looked at his feet and raised an eyebrow. 'Handmade Italian shoes are *ordinary*?'

Why did that make him feel so defensive? 'They're comfortable.'

'They're the male equivalent of Louboutins.'

Although her tone was slightly acidic, there was a little glint of amusement in her eye. She was teasing him—and, now he thought about it, he was enjoying being teased.

He hadn't felt like this in a long, long time. It was the sort of comment Emma would've made to him.

Emma.

Loneliness washed over him. Would he ever stop missing his wife? Would he ever stop wishing he could turn back time and turn down the invitation to that conference, so he would've been there when Emma had that fatal asthma attack and he could've saved her?

He didn't want to dwell on his feelings, so he switched the topic back to something safe. 'So how do you see the butterfly house working?'

'Rosemary had photographs of the orangery that used to be here—the one Viola used when she bred her caterpillars. There might even still be traces of it on the wall.'

'And you think it should be recreated?' he asked.

'No, because we'll be using the building for a different purpose. We'll need a mix of butterflies, and that includes tropical ones,' she said. 'And I need the kind of tech that means we get the right intensity of light and humidity, as well as the right temperature; the plants can't do all the work. And we need a good design.' She paused. 'Which is where you come in.'

Two choices: he could design the butterfly house, or he could block everything.

He thought about it again. A butterfly house. A confection of glass. A house of dreams.

He loved working with glass, and he was so tempted to build it. 'What sort of thing are you thinking about? A biome, like the ones at the Eden Project?'

'It could be anything you like. The butterfly house at London Zoo is shaped like a caterpillar, and the one in Vienna is a gorgeous Art Nouveau building. The way I see it, you're the glass and architecture specialist. Your imagination is the limit. Well, and the site itself,' she amended. 'Obviously the shape of the garden and the way the sunlight falls will affect what you build.'

He liked the fact that she'd realised that.

A glass building. Complete freedom with the design. Fulfilling his great-aunt's dream. This was the perfect commission. 'The Palm House at Kew,' he said. 'That was the first glass building I fell in love with. And glass domes. Like the one at the Reichstag in Berlin with its double staircase.'

'A dome filled with butterflies free to fly wherever they like. Kind of like a snow globe, except summery,' she said thoughtfully.

Alice Walters actually got it, Hugo thought. She understood the kind of stuff that filled his head. Knowing that made his skin prickle with excitement.

'There isn't really room to build a dome in the garden here. And I'm not making any promises,' he said, 'but maybe we could look at the possibilities.'

'That would be good.' She smiled at him—the first

genuine smile she'd ever given him—and it made him catch his breath. It felt as if the world had just flashed into technicolour for a moment before fading back to its usual monochrome.

For pity's sake. He had to get a grip. This wasn't about him. Or her. It was about his great-aunt's dreams and whether they could make it work.

Her stomach rumbled audibly, and she winced. 'Sorry. I kind of forgot about lunch today.'

She'd turned up at his office at lunchtime, he remembered, and thrown that hissy fit on him. 'Because you were too angry with me to eat?'

'Something like that,' she admitted, wrinkling her nose. 'And then I was busy.'

He forced himself not to think about how cute she looked. 'We could get a pizza delivered.' Just to make sure she didn't think he was coming on to her, he added, 'Seeing as we still have a lot to discuss about Rosemary's project, we might as well refuel while we work.'

'Pizza's fine by me,' she said. 'We'll go halves.'

He liked that, too. She hadn't assumed that he was going to pay, just because it had been his suggestion.

Sharing.

Could they share? Was this their chance to start compromising? 'There could be a topping issue,' he said. 'Pineapple or no pineapple?'

'I don't object hugely to pineapple,' she said. Then she tipped her head on one side. 'But olives are essential.'

It sounded as if she was thinking the same thing: they needed to find common ground so they could start negotiating properly. Negotiation by pizza... He'd started it, and she seemed to be running with it. He might as well see where it took them. 'OK. Ham?'

She gave a deep, dramatic sigh. 'Oh, *please*. Prosciutto cotto at the very least.'

He couldn't help grinning. 'You're a pizza snob—and you were lying about the pineapple, weren't you?'

'Yes. I was trying to be conciliatory. I'm prepared to agree to your demands for pineapple,' she said. 'But if you want deep pan or stuffed crust, the deal's off. Proper pizza comes in thin crust only.'

He wasn't quite sure whether she was teasing him or whether she was serious. She was a bit more difficult to read than he'd expected. 'Did you ever eat pizza with Rosemary?'

'Generally I use fresh basil on pizza,' she said, her expression deadpan and her voice dry.

That was a definite tease. Nobody in his life teased him any more.

And then it hit him.

Obviously Alice didn't know about Emma, because she wasn't treading on eggshells round him the way everyone else in his life did; she was reacting to him as if he was a normal human being. And he really, really liked that feeling. It was refreshing enough for him to want to spend more time in her company. 'All right. Thin crust, olives, pineapple, prosciutto cotto. Anything else?'

'No. That all works for me.'

'It's a deal.' Once he'd called the local pizzeria and arranged delivery, they headed back to the kitchen. 'So how would the education centre work?' he asked.

'We might need to remodel the inside of the house. For a start, we need an exhibition room,' she said. 'And a space where children can learn how to help butterflies and wildlife by doing practical things—planning their own butterfly gardens with food plants for both caterpillars and for butterflies, how to build a bug hotel, that sort of thing. I'd like a screen where they can see things like a time-lapse film of a butterfly going through its life stages.' She tapped into her laptop. 'Like this. It's only a couple

of minutes long, but it always wows my first-years and I
think you might enjoy it.'

He watched the film in silence, marvelling at the pho-
tographer's skills. 'That's amazing. I had no idea it was
that complicated.'

'And that's only on my laptop. Imagine seeing that on
a really big screen, then following the trail through the
garden, seeing those exact plants growing, seeing butterfly eggs on leaves and caterpillars munching their way
through plants, seeing pupa suspended from canes or even
hatching, and then seeing butterflies flying round in the
butterfly house. How cool is that?'

Very. But he needed to be businesslike about it. This
couldn't be a decision based on emotions. 'Rosemary's investment income died with her. There isn't any money to
fund the running costs of an education centre.'

'Which is why we need grants,' she said. 'We can do
some crowdfunding, to cover the set-up costs, and then the
grants will help keep us going. We'll also charge admission
fees—reasonable prices, though, because we want schools
to visit in term time and families to visit out of term time.
And we also want to attract anyone who's vaguely interested in butterflies or conservation or re-wilding, or just
wants a nice morning out with friends. So we'd have a
pop-up café on the patio, serving drinks and healthy food.
Probably a shop, for books and postcards and butterfly-
related goods. I've put together a business plan with some
projected footfalls, for my grant applications.' She opened
another file and let him look at it. 'I can email this across
to you, to give you time for a proper read.'

'That would be helpful,' he said, and gave her his business card with all his contact details so she could send the
file across to him.

'Do you think you could pause the house going on the

market, just until you've seen what the possibilities are and had time to make an informed decision?' she asked.

She wasn't asking him to stop the sale completely, he noticed. She was giving him the choice of continuing their discussions, but without making assumptions that he'd fall in with her plans.

'And what I've put together so far isn't set in stone,' she said. 'It's simply a start. A working document for discussion, if you like.'

'So my family could have input.'

She inclined her head. 'Including the butterfly house design, which Rosemary wanted to be yours. Though maybe I should take you to visit a few, so you can see what sort of things are possible.'

He remembered what she'd said earlier about site visits to see blue butterflies. 'So you're suggesting we should visit butterfly houses and botanical gardens.'

'Butterfly houses,' she said, 'and sites of scientific interest. I suppose we could include formal botanical gardens, but as we're looking at re-wilding the garden I think it would make more sense to look at nature reserves, so you can see the kind of habitat we can try to create.'

This was treading a very fine line indeed between a date and a business proposition.

He wasn't sure if the fluttering in his stomach was terror or excitement. Probably both.

'I appreciate,' she said, 'that you have demands on your time from work—as do I. But maybe we can look at our diaries and find a few windows for field trips: some local, some a bit further afield.'

Now Hugo could see that Alice Walters wasn't the ambitious gold-digger he'd first thought she was, he was more inclined to listen to her.

'All right,' he said. 'I'll tell Philip Hemingford to put the sale of the house on hold for a couple of weeks and we'll do some field trips.'

'Thank you.'

He looked at her. 'What about your crowdfunding?'

'That stays,' she said. 'If you decide to put the house on the market after all, the trust will need all the money we can get. If you don't sell the house, then the money will pay for remodelling and building the butterfly house.'

'Trust?' He narrowed his eyes at her. 'What trust?'

'I was thinking, it should be called the Ferrers-Grey Butterfly Education Trust,' she said. 'Honouring both Viola and Rosemary. Oh, and that reminds me: we should have a garden centre section of the shop with butterfly-friendly plants and seeds, obviously including violas and rosemary.'

Acknowledging his great-great-great-grandmother and his great-aunt with plants as well as with the name of the building? He liked that. But that still left him with questions. 'What about you?'

She frowned. 'What do you mean?'

'Don't you want your name on the project?'

'I told you before,' she said quietly, 'it isn't about me. It's about the butterflies. And I'm disappointed that you still think I'm doing this because I'm some power-crazed, ambitious bitch. Clearly you mix with the wrong sort of women.'

He felt the flush of embarrassment and awkwardness creep under his skin. 'I'm sorry. I didn't mean it quite like that.'

'No?' Her eyes narrowed a fraction.

The pizza arrived, at that moment; when he came back from answering the door, he gave her a wry smile. 'Can we agree to a truce over dinner?'

'I guess. How much do I owe you?'

'This one's on me,' he said, cutting the pizza into slices. 'Next meeting, you buy the pizza or whatever.'

Without further comment, Alice fetched plates from the cupboard and cutlery from the drawer and found two glasses. 'Water?'

'Thank you.'

It was weird, sharing a pizza with a near-stranger, one who'd been pretty much hostile up until now. And Alice found herself feeling unexpectedly shy with him.

Oh, for pity's sake. Just because he was posh, it didn't mean that he was superior—or even that he had a superiority complex. She really had to stop letting what had happened with Barney get in the way of how she handled things. She was older, wiser and much more able to hold her own.

And she needed to be practical about this. 'I could do a field trip on Saturday,' she said. 'Would that fit in with you, or do you need to check with your partner?'

For a second, it was as if someone had closed a shutter over his expression. And his voice was very cool when he said, 'No partner.'

Uh-oh. Did he think she was coming on to him? Maybe she ought to invent a boyfriend. Then again, her love life was a complete disaster zone. Better, perhaps, to suggest something else. 'If you want anyone else from your family to come along, that's fine. Where I have in mind can be rough ground, though, and it's also prime tick season, so I'd recommend whoever joins us wears strong shoes and trousers that can be tucked into socks.'

'That's fine,' he said. 'It'll be just me.' He looked at her. 'Is your partner going to be OK with it?'

'I,' she said, 'am married to my butterflies.' Just so it would be clear to him that she saw this purely as work.

Her fingers accidentally brushed his as they reached for

a slice of pizza at the same time, and again she felt that weird flicker of electricity along her skin.

Even if she admitted to being attracted to Hugo Grey, she wasn't going to act on it. Her relationships never worked out, and she wouldn't let anything jeopardise the butterfly project. 'OK,' she said, cross with herself when her voice went slightly breathless. She made an effort to sound professional. 'Do you mind an early start? It'll take us about three hours to get to the first site, maybe more if we get stuck in traffic.'

'How early?' he asked.

'Given that the butterflies I have in mind are usually more active in the morning, six o'clock?'

He looked wary; maybe he wasn't a morning person. 'OK. I'll pick you up.'

'I'll pick *you* up,' she corrected. 'Let me know your address.'

For a moment, she thought he was going to argue, but then he nodded and gave her his address. 'Do you need anything from Rosemary's study, while we're here?' he asked when they'd finished eating.

'No. I've already got copies of the photographs she had of Viola.'

'OK. I'll clear up here, then, and I'll see you on Saturday.'

'All right. I'll email over the files I promised you.' She paused. 'Thank you. I appreciate you listening to what I had to say.'

He inclined his head. 'And I apologise for my earlier prejudice.'

She appreciated that apology; and it was her turn to compromise, now. 'I can understand it, now you've told me about the people who took advantage of her. In your shoes, I think I would've felt the same. Maybe we both started off on the wrong foot.'

'Maybe,' he agreed.

'Can I help with the washing up?' she asked, glancing at the crockery on the table.

'No, it's fine. See you Saturday.'

'Saturday, six a.m. sharp,' she echoed, closed her laptop and left the house.

This field trip absolutely wasn't a date: it was part of a business proposition. So why were all her senses humming?

Probably, she thought, because Hugo Grey was the first man who'd attracted her like this in several years.

But nothing was going to happen between them. She needed to be sensible about this. Her relationships always ended in disaster; and she and Hugo were pretty much complete opposites. Well-worn hiking boots versus handmade, highly polished Italian shoes. It simply wouldn't work, so it was pointless letting anything start.

Even if he did have the most gorgeous eyes...

CHAPTER FOUR

DURING THE REST of the week, Hugo found himself thinking about the butterfly project whenever he had a spare moment. The doodles on his desk blotter were all of potential butterfly house designs—except for the sketches that started to creep in on Friday morning. Little line-drawings of a woman with untamed hair, a snub nose and freckles.

Sketches of Alice Walters.

Not good.

He didn't want to start thinking about Alice, or about anyone else. Emma's death had broken him; although on the surface it looked as if he'd managed to put himself back together, deep down he wasn't so sure he had. Without her, there was a huge hollow in the middle of his life and he didn't know how to fill it. His family and friends had encouraged him to date again, saying he needed someone in his life to stop him being lonely. But Emma wasn't replaceable. And anyway he didn't want to risk loving and losing again. It was easier just to avoid social situations and use work as an excuse. The only person he really saw much of nowadays was his best friend, and—since an incident where Kit and his wife had tried to set him up with a suitable woman, and Hugo had backed off for a couple of weeks—Hugo's non-existent love life was a topic firmly off limits.

Saturday's butterfly expedition with Alice was a field

trip, not a date. Hadn't she told him herself that she wasn't interested? You didn't tell someone that you were married to your job if you were even vaguely interested in dating them. This was business.

He dragged himself out of bed on Saturday morning at what he considered an unearthly hour, showered and dressed, ate a banana for breakfast, and was considering whether he had enough time to make himself a coffee to wake himself up properly when his doorbell rang.

Six o'clock precisely.

At least Alice was punctual. He would've been seriously annoyed if he'd dragged himself out of bed and then she'd made him wait around for ages.

She was wearing bright red canvas shoes instead of hiking boots today, he noticed when he opened the door to her. Her faded jeans emphasised her curves, and the slogan on her equally faded T-shirt was very pointed: 'Don't judge a butterfly by its chrysalis.'

She wore absolutely no make-up, and her light brown hair was tied back with a brightly coloured silk scarf, though little tendrils had already escaped at the front. Next to the women he was used to at the office in their sharp business suits, she should've looked a scruffy mess: but actually she looked incredibly cute, completely natural and guileless. When she smiled at him, his pulse actually leapt.

Oh, help.

He didn't want to be attracted to anyone. Particularly to someone whose life had almost nothing in common with his.

He needed to get a grip.

He also needed more sleep.

Why on earth had he agreed to this ridiculous field trip at this even more ridiculous time of day?

'Good morning. Ready to go?' she asked.

How could she possibly be this chirpy at six o'clock? 'You're a morning person, then,' he muttered.

Her smile broadened. 'Of course. It's the best part of the day. You've already missed the sunrise.' She raised an eyebrow. 'Owl, are we?' And then, just to make it worse, she gave a soft, mocking 'Tu-whit, tu-whoo.'

He glared at her, his synapses not firing quite quickly enough to let him make a suitably sarcastic retort.

She just laughed. 'You can always nap in the car, because it's going to take us about three hours to get there, if we're lucky with traffic. Or, if you need coffee, I've a flask and a spare reusable cup in my backpack.'

Of *course* she'd have reusable cups. 'Thanks.' Though he was aware of how ungracious and grumpy he sounded, and winced inwardly.

She glanced at his feet. 'I'm glad you're not wearing your posh shoes. I forgot to warn you that it can be a bit boggy underfoot in the wetlands.'

'Wetlands? I thought we were looking at butterflies?'

'We are. But one of the sites we're visiting is in the Norfolk Broads.' She spread her hands. 'By definition, it can be a bit wet.'

'Oh.' He looked at her feet again. 'No hiking boots for you, today?'

'They're in the car. I don't drive in them,' she said.

'I'm a bit surprised someone with your green credentials has a car,' he said.

She smiled. 'I don't. But if I can't get somewhere any other way, I hire one.'

'Oh.' And then he felt stupid.

'Feel free to change the temperature or the music,' she said when he'd climbed into the passenger seat.

She was being nice, and he was being impolite and grouchy. 'This is fine,' he said. 'And sorry. I don't mean to sound grumpy.'

She patted his forearm, and his skin tingled where her fingertips touched him. 'Poor little owl. I promise what we're going to see will be worth the early start. Well, as long as the weather holds.'

'Butterflies don't like rain?'

'Or wind. They like calm, bright weather,' she said. 'Or just calm will do. Overcast is all right, if there isn't a wind. I have something with me in case I need to cheat a bit, though.'

'Cheat?' He was mystified.

'Later.' She started the car. 'Go back to sleep, if you want to.'

Hugo had no intention of doing that, though he was glad that she didn't want to chatter inanely. However, lulled by the warmth of the sunlight through the windows and the soft piano music she was playing in the car, he did actually doze off; when he opened his eyes again, they were in the middle of nowhere. The road before them wasn't even a proper road; it appeared to be a dirt track.

'Where are we?' he asked.

'Milk Parsley Fen—named after one of the plants that grows here.' She drove through a gap in the hedge into what seemed to be a field, though there were a couple of other cars parked underneath the trees. 'Do you want some coffee before we go for a walk?'

He wasn't going to cut off his nose to spite his face. 'Yes, please.'

'It's black, no sugar,' she warned. 'I never quite got out of my student habits.'

'That's fine. Coffee's coffee,' he said.

She took a backpack from the back seat, removed a metal flask and two cups, and poured them both a coffee.

'Thanks. Butterflies on your cups?' he asked as she fitted a silicone lid to a cup and handed it to him.

'Of course.' She changed into her hiking boots, put the

backpack on her shoulder and slung a camera round her neck. 'Ready?'

'Ready.' The coffee was already making him feel more human. He followed her down a narrow path; the ground felt a bit spongy to walk on, and there were fronded grasses everywhere he looked. But what he'd expected to see was absent.

'There aren't any butterflies,' he said, knowing he sounded accusatory and a bit like a spoiled child denied a promised treat, but not being able to stop himself.

'They're probably skulking around in the reeds,' she said. 'Wait until we get further in. The reserve managers have cut some paths through the fen so we'll get a decent view of the milk parsley, but at the same time the really vulnerable plants aren't in danger of being trampled on.'

He could follow that line of thinking. 'So paths need to be cut in a re-wilded garden?'

'Absolutely. These are wetlands, so they're not quite what Rosemary had in mind—but there's a specific butterfly I want you to see here,' she said.

There was a stream running alongside them, he noticed, and a small bridge; as they drew closer, a large swan waddled out of the reeds and sat in the middle of the bridge, staring at them.

'Looks as if we're going to have to wait for a bit,' she said.

'We can't just walk past the swan?'

She shook her head. 'My guess is his mate and his cygnets are somewhere nearby. He's likely to be a bit protective. Let's give him some space,' she said. 'Look—there's a Painted Lady and a Peacock.' She gestured to the purple flowers lining the route, and he could see butterflies resting on the plant with their wings outstretched.

And then, all of a sudden, he could hear a kind of peeping noise.

'Cue the cygnets,' she said with a smile.

The swan stood up and started to walk over the bridge, his movements slow and deliberate.

'Let's follow him,' she suggested.

The peeping noise grew stronger; the swan veered off to the side, shaking his tail as he stepped towards a large pool. And then he glided majestically across the water towards another swan and a bevy of cygnets, whose peeping noises grew even louder.

'I love this.' Alice took Hugo's free hand and squeezed it. 'You can just hear them yelling, "Hurry up, Dad, we're going exploring!", can't you?'

He would never have thought of that if he'd been on his own; but now she'd said it he could almost hear it. 'Yes. And I don't think I've ever seen anything like this before.' And now she was holding his hand it felt as if she was leading him into an enchanted landscape. Part of him was skittish—he hadn't expected to hold hands with anyone again—but part of him felt as if he was being drawn back to life. Step by step. Noticing tiny details he'd blanked out before.

He stared at the swans and their cygnets, entranced as they glided to the other side of the pool and then filed out of the water again, the adults walking at each end of the line with the cygnets protected between them. 'That's *such* a privilege.'

'Isn't it just?' Then her eyes widened as she clearly realised that she was still holding his hand. 'Sorry. I tend to get a bit carried away when I see things like this.'

'It's fine.' But how crazy was it that he actually missed her holding his hand when she took her fingers away from his?

They carried on through the marshes, with Alice pointing out various butterflies. It was a long time since Hugo had seen that many butterflies in a single place, and it amazed him. The birds were singing; the sun was bright and warm; and, even though there had been other cars in the field where she'd parked, they hadn't seen another human since they'd arrived. It felt a bit as if they were wandering through some kind of magical oasis.

'I think I'm going to have to cheat a tiny bit,' she said, 'because there's one particular butterfly I really, really want you to see. We're right at the start of first brood, and the weather's almost perfect, but I'm not taking any chances. I don't want you to miss this.' She took the backpack from her shoulder and removed a bunch of sweet williams, which she placed carefully on the ground.

He looked at her, surprised. 'Are butterflies super-attracted to these flowers, then?'

'Yup,' she said, coming over to stand next to him. 'The caterpillars only eat milk parsley—which is why the fenland in this part of the country is the main habitat for them—but the butterflies just love them. It's a combination of the scent and the nectar.' She smiled. 'And now, we wait. I probably should've warned you that there's a bit of waiting around on field trips.'

Hugo, who absolutely loathed wasting time, was a little surprised to discover that he didn't actually mind waiting around with Alice. Time didn't seem to be important when he was with her. It felt as if he was in a different place, somewhere much more carefree than his usual regimented life.

And then he saw it flying gracefully over the reeds before it landed on the bunch of flowers: a butterfly the size of his palm, creamy yellow and black, with a dark blue line and two red spots on the lower pair of wings, which curved down like a swallow's tail.

'That's incredible,' he whispered.

'An English Swallowtail,' she whispered back. '*Papilio*

machaon. You only find them here in England in the Norfolk Broads.'

She'd brought him here to see a rare butterfly. The biggest butterfly he'd ever seen flying. And all of a sudden he got why she loved the creatures so much. He was spellbound by it.

Spellbound by her.

Not that he was going to let himself think too much about that. He didn't feel ready for this.

She'd taken the camera out of its case and was taking photographs of the butterfly; Hugo's attention was caught between them both, the concentration and the joy on Alice's face and the sheer beauty of the butterfly.

Once the butterfly had taken its fill of the nectar from the sweet williams, it flew off again.

'That,' he said, 'was stunning. I know you said you only find them around here, but is it possible to get them to breed in London?'

'Not native ones. They'd have to be imported,' she said, 'and they'd need to live in a butterfly house.'

She didn't say anything more. Hugo realised she was letting the butterflies make the case for her.

'And look there,' she said.

He followed where she was pointing, to the gorgeous turquoise insects darting about. 'Dragonflies?'

'Damselflies,' she said with a smile. 'If we're lucky, we'll get to see some rare dragonflies as well.'

He was entranced by the whole thing. She was right: it was definitely worth the early start. And, best of all, on the way back to the car they saw some more Swallowtails flying across the fen and landing on a patch of yellow flag irises.

'That,' he said, 'was amazing.'

'I'm glad you enjoyed it. The first time you see a Swallowtail is a bit special.' She smiled at him. 'And now we're going north. Not wetlands, this time—I want you to see the kind of wildflower meadow that I think would work with Rosemary's plans.'

'Bring it on,' he said.

That smile gave Alice hope that the butterflies were convincing Hugo to give the project a chance.

Yet, at the same time, his smile worried her because it made her heart feel as if it had done a backflip. Nearly all the men she'd fallen for in the past had hurt her—letting her think they wanted her for who she was, yet then they'd wanted to change her. She wasn't posh enough, wasn't girly enough, was too nerdy...

What you looked like shouldn't matter. But, in Hugo's world, it did. And Hugo himself was a fashion plate, with his designer shoes and sharp suits; it was so obvious that she'd be setting herself up for yet another crack in her heart, if she let herself fall for him. She didn't want to take that risk. It would be much more sensible to keep things strictly business between them and avoid the heartache in the first place. As for the way he made her stomach feel as if it swooped, the way her skin prickled with awareness whenever he accidentally brushed against her—she'd just have to ignore it.

It was an hour's drive to their next site and she kept the conversation light on the way. As she drove into the nearest village, Hugo's stomach rumbled audibly.

'Is that a hint you want to stop for lunch?' she asked.

He winced. 'Sorry. We had an early start. I only had time for a banana for breakfast.'

'If you'd said,' she told him, 'we could've stopped on the way for a bacon sandwich.'

'Your butterflies distracted me.'

'They'll do that,' she agreed with a smile. 'Look, there's a pub just up here. Let's stop and grab some lunch.'

She insisted on paying for their paninis and coffee, on the grounds that he'd bought the pizza earlier in the week, then drove them out of the village.

'So this is somewhere else in the middle of nowhere?' he asked wryly.

'That's why it's called a field trip.' Though then Alice made the mistake of looking at him, and the expression in his eyes caused her pulse to jolt again. Worse still, she noticed the curve of his mouth. How easy it would be to reach out and run a fingertip along his lower lip...

She pulled herself together with an effort, parked the car on the verge of a narrow country road, then led him down a track between two high hedges.

'It's as if that little brown butterfly's leading us,' he said.

'It's a Ringlet—*Aphantopus hyperantus*,' she said.

'Named after the little circles on its wings?'

She smiled. 'Absolutely.'

At the end of the track, they reached a stile with an information board next to it.

'This place is an Iron Age fort?' he asked, sounding surprised.

'It's the best-preserved Iron Age fort in East Anglia,' she said, 'and it's home to a lot of butterflies. This place always blows my students' minds, so I hoped you'd like it.'

'Are we actually allowed to walk among this?'

'We are indeed.' She indicated the people walking along the top of the massive circular earthwork; others were half-way down the steep slopes with cameras, bending down and clearly taking photographs of butterflies. 'Come and take a look.'

They made their way to the top of the outer circle. 'The wind's got up a bit, so the butterflies will be looking for sheltered spots,' she said. 'We might see more on the slopes than we do up here.'

'So all the flowers on the slopes and down in the middle of the rings are wildflowers?' he asked.

'And grasses,' she said. 'There are some rare orchids here, but you'll find the common flowers here as well—red clover, oxeye daisies, that sort of thing. And this is pretty much how I'd see Rosemary's re-wilded garden looking.'

'All different colours,' he said, 'like a kind of kaleidoscope. I can see that working.' He frowned. 'What's the shimmery stuff?'

'Butterflies,' she said. 'Stand still for a moment and watch.' Though she found herself looking at Hugo rather than at the butterflies; she enjoyed seeing the expression on his face change as he realised that there were lots of butterflies on the wing, just above ground level. She loved the way he'd clearly just realised how magical their surroundings were, the way his eyes lit up with pleasure as he worked out exactly what he was seeing.

'Blue butterflies,' he said. 'Just what you promised me.'

'Not quite as spectacular as the Morphos in Viola's collection,' she said, 'but I adore the Chalk Hill Blues. The females are actually more brown than blue, but they both have all these pretty circles on their underwings.'

'To make them look more like leaves if a bird happens to be passing?' he asked.

So he'd actually been paying attention to what she'd told him, and remembered it? Funny how that made her feel warm inside. 'Yes.'

To stop herself doing anything stupid—like holding his hand again—she took her camera out of its case and snapped a few pictures of the butterflies. They wandered round the hill fort, walking on the slopes as well as the top, and every so often Hugo stopped to watch the butterflies, looking entranced.

'I can't remember the last time I saw a blue butterfly,'

he said. 'Or quite as many butterflies in one place. They're beautiful. Thank you for bringing me here.'

'My pleasure,' she said, meaning it. 'I can take you to some reserves nearer London, next time. I just wanted to show you these two places today.'

'I'm glad you did. It's been a while since...' He stopped.

She said nothing, giving him the space to talk, and eventually he said, 'Since I've been anywhere that made me feel this light of heart.'

The butterflies, the landscape—or sharing it with her? Though she didn't quite dare ask him, because she didn't want him to turn back into the grouchy, suspicious man she'd first met.

'So what made you choose to study butterflies?' he asked.

'My grandad used to take me to the park on a Sunday afternoon and show me all the butterflies on the plants there, whether they were the cultivated lavender in the posh bit or the wildflowers by the hedges,' she said. 'He died when I was ten. I was torn between studying botany and lepidoptery, but I think he would've been pleased about my career choice.' She glanced at him. 'What about you? Why architecture?'

'I guess, like a lot of kids, I liked building things with toy bricks. I spent hours and hours creating things. And then I noticed the way things were built, whenever I went out. I loved the Natural History Museum—but it wasn't just because of the dinosaurs or the big blue whale. I liked the shape of the building and the windows, and the colours of the bricks.' He smiled. 'Rosemary took me to Kew when I was about ten, and I fell in love with the Palm House. It's all the light. That's why I like working with glass.'

Alice really didn't understand what made Hugo Grey tick. But maybe this was her chance to get to know him better. 'What's your favourite thing you've designed?' she asked.

'The project I've been working on in Scotland for the last year,' he said. 'It's a country house on the buildings at risk register.'

'So you like restoring old buildings rather than designing new ones?'

'A mixture of the two,' he said. 'But this one was a bit special. There's a glass dome in the centre of the main hall—sadly, there were only a few fragments of the original glass left, but at least we had some photographs to work with. And there's an amazing spiral staircase beneath the dome.'

The tone of his voice made Alice feel sure that Hugo felt the same way about staircases and glass domes as she did about butterflies. So maybe they weren't quite as far apart as she'd thought.

'So that's what you specialise in? Domes and staircases?'

'Glass and staircases,' he said. 'Some historic, some modern.'

He was surprisingly easy to talk to, now she'd got him onto his favourite subject. She really enjoyed the drive home, to the point where she didn't want the day to end. When she finally parked in his road, it shocked her that she actually felt a lurch of sheer disappointment that their trip was over.

Maybe he felt the same, because he said, 'Would you like to come in for a coffee?'

She did—and, at the same time, she didn't. Getting close to him made her feel twitchy. She opened her mouth to make a polite excuse, and was surprised to find herself saying, 'That'd be nice.'

From the outside, his house was a Victorian redbrick terrace, with large windows and a front door with a very fancy arch of glass above it. Inside, the house was startlingly modern and minimalist, with the walls painted a soft dove-grey and the flooring pale wood. The hallway had a flight of stairs leading off it; and a door to the left led to an enormous living room with an old-fashioned fireplace, a sofa and a desk with a drawing table. Though there was no artwork of any description on the walls, she noticed, just a very workmanlike clock. No bookshelves, either; or maybe all his shelves were hidden in a clever architectural way.

He shepherded her into a kitchen with white marble worktops, dark grey wooden cupboards and rectangular white tiles on the walls; the lighting was very modern, almost industrial. At the far end of the room there was a dining table and chairs; but what caught her eye was the entire wall of glass looking out onto the garden.

'That's spectacular,' she said. 'Was it like this when you bought it?'

'No. I opened it up,' he said. 'The glass doors fold inwards, so in summer you can open up the whole wall and step straight from the house to the garden.'

She loved the idea of it; though the garden was as minimal as the house, with a stone patio containing a bistro table and a couple of chairs, a square lawn mown very short indeed, and that was it. No shrubs. No herbaceous border. Not even a pot containing a plant of some kind. There wasn't a flower in sight.

'It's lovely,' she said, meaning that it *could* be lovely if he put a bit of effort in. Though maybe, as an architect, he saw the building rather than its surroundings. Given how minimalist the house was, the garden matched it. Though in her view that garden was all wrong. If it were hers, she'd fill it with roses. There would be herbs and shrubs to attract butterflies and bees. And there would most definitely be a wild patch at the end, with cornflowers and poppies and clover and vetch. Maybe a tiny pond. It would be glorious.

'Espresso?' he asked, breaking into her thoughts.

'Thanks. That'd be nice,' she said politely.

'Feel free to grab a seat.' He indicated the dining table by the glass wall.

And of course he had a posh coffee machine—a proper bean-to-cup machine that ground the beans and made coffee with the perfect *crema* on top, which he brought over to her in a double-walled glass cup.

Posh.

So very different from her world.

Hugo belonged in Barney's world—and she never had. Even though she knew Hugo was trying to make her welcome, she couldn't help remembering the way Barney's set had reacted to her, scoffing that the girl from the council estate really thought she could step into a world of privilege.

You don't belong here, the voice said in her head.

But Hugo had asked her here without a hidden agenda. Feeling wary was ridiculous and stupid, and she needed to stop it. Right now.

To shut the voice up, she asked, 'So do you have any photographs of the house you were working on?'

'Yes.' He took his laptop from a drawer, tapped a few keys, then slid it across the table to her. 'All the photographs are in the same album. Help yourself.'

'Thanks.' She scrolled through them. 'Wow. I can see why you fell in love with it. That's an incredible staircase. And that glass dome...'

'It's pretty special,' he said. 'It's as near a reproduction to the original as I could get. And we managed to save all the original glass that was left in the external windows.'

'That's impressive,' she said, handing the laptop back to him.

* * *

Again, when her fingers brushed against his, it made Hugo's skin tingle.

What was it about this woman that drew him?

He was seriously tempted to ask her to stay for dinner, but he knew it would probably be wise to put a little distance between them, so he could get his head back in the right place.

So he kept the conversation light until she'd finished her coffee. 'Thank you for today,' he said. 'The butterflies were amazing.' And then his mouth ran away with him and spoiled his good intentions. 'Are you busy tomorrow?'

'Do you want to do another field trip?' she asked.

'I was thinking we could take a look at some glass,' he said. 'The British Museum, perhaps, and then Kew.'

'All right,' she said. 'I'll meet you at the British Museum. It opens at ten—is that too early for you?'

'It's a lot later than today,' he said wryly, 'so it's fine.'

'Ten o'clock on the steps,' she said.

He nearly—nearly—kissed her cheek, but managed to hold himself back.

And he intended to spend the rest of the evening working with figures and formulae, until he'd got himself back under his usual control. He was absolutely not going to kiss Alice Walters.

'See you tomorrow,' he said, shepherding her out to the door.

And when he closed the door behind her, he realised that he was regretting not kissing her.

Utterly ridiculous. He'd get a grip before tomorrow. For both their sakes.

CHAPTER FIVE

HUGO FELT LIKE a teenager about to go on his first date with a new girlfriend. Given that he was meeting a lepidopterist, how ironic it was that he had butterflies in his stomach.

Today was supposed to be about his great-aunt's legacy. But his heart still felt as if it had done a somersault when he walked through Bloomsbury and peered through the railings around the British Museum to see Alice standing on the steps beneath the famous pediment, waiting for him. As she'd done the previous day, she was wearing faded skinny jeans; when he drew nearer, he saw that today's T-shirt bore the slogan 'Butterflies do it with pheromones'.

'Nice T-shirt,' he said.

She grinned. 'Here's your fun fact for the day: a male butterfly can sense female butterfly pheromones from ten miles away.'

'Ten miles?' Was she teasing him?

His confusion must've shown on his face, because she smiled. 'Really. I'm full of facts like that.'

'They must have amazing noses.'

'Butterflies don't actually have noses, the way we do,' she said. 'They smell with their antennae and taste with their feet. If you'd said you wanted an anatomy lesson, Mr Grey, I would've brought one of my presentations with me.'

Anatomy lesson. Why did that suddenly make him feel hot all over? For pity's sake. The last woman Hugo had dated was his late wife. He'd closed down his emotions and his libido since Emma's death—at least, he'd thought he had. But, since he'd met Alice, that part of him seemed to have woken up again. She'd shown him things on their field trip that had enchanted him, and now the woman herself was enchanting him. Everything from that sassy slogan on her T-shirt, to the sparkle in her grey eyes and the way she smiled when she'd spotted something that interested her.

'I don't need an anatomy lesson, Dr Walters,' he said—a little more brusquely than he'd intended, because she really flustered him. 'Besides, today is about glass.'

'Indeed. Time to strut your stuff, Mr Glass Expert.'

But there was no mockery in her eyes. She actually looked interested.

Interested in glass, or—his heart skipped another beat—interested in him? He wasn't sure whether the idea scared him or thrilled him more.

Keep it professional, he reminded himself, and ushered her into the Great Court. 'This,' he said, 'is one of my favourite buildings in London.' That was it. Talk about his passion for architecture. Don't think about emotions. Keep it focused on the abstract. Something *safe*. 'I love the way the shadows of the steel beams change as you walk round.'

Hugo's gorgeous blue eyes were suddenly all lit up as he talked about the roof, and he'd lost that slight grouchiness. Clearly he felt the same way about glass as she did about butterflies, Alice thought. And seeing him in love with his subject made him so much easier to deal with.

Though, at the same time, it made him dangerous. Mesmerising.

She needed to get a grip; she'd been burned too often by men she'd been attracted to and then it had all gone wrong. That wasn't going to happen again. 'Tell me about the glass,' she said.

'There are three thousand, two hundred and twelve panes in that roof,' he said. 'And no two are identical.'

'Seriously?' She couldn't understand how you'd build a roof from what seemed to be a jigsaw puzzle. Besides, to her most of the panes looked identical.

'Seriously. It's because the roof undulates,' he said. He took his phone from his pocket, flicked into the Internet and brought up a photograph. 'This is it from above.'

It was nothing like she'd expected. 'It looks like a turquoise cushion, with an ancient brooch in the centre—but, from down here, the glass seems clear. And what's that in the centre?'

'It's the dome of the old Reading Room,' he said. 'And, actually, it's not very much smaller than the dome of the Pantheon in Rome.'

She stared at him, as amazed by the statistic as he'd seemed when she'd explained about butterfly pheromones. 'Seriously? But it looks tiny! I've been to Rome, with my best friend, and the Pantheon's enormous.'

'Which shows you just how huge this courtyard is—it's the biggest covered square in Europe,' he said. 'I would've loved to work on something like this, merging the old and the new.'

Just as he had with the Scottish country house and its dome, she thought. Could he be tempted to build something new—the butterfly house—that would fit into the garden of Rosemary's old house?

Together, they walked around the Great Court; just as Hugo had said, the light and the pattern of shadows changed as they moved round the area.

'This is pretty stunning,' she said. 'Though I'm not sure we could make a design like this work for a butterfly house.'

'It wouldn't.' He smiled. 'You wanted to show me an amazing butterfly yesterday, before you showed me the wildflower site. I wanted to show you my favourite bit of new architectural glass before we go and see the other stuff.'

'It's spectacular,' she said. 'Obviously I've been here before, but I never really noticed it. You've shown it to me in a very different way.'

'Like your Iron Age hill fort yesterday,' he said. 'I know this is going to make me sound a complete heathen, given the treasures within these walls, but I'd really like to skip the rest of the building now and go to the second bit of our field trip.'

Field trip. Of course that was what it was. They were going to Kew together because of the butterfly house project, not because he wanted to spend time with her, she reminded herself. Part of her wanted it to be a date; but at the same time part of her was scared she'd be sucked into trusting someone again and end up being let down. Pushing away the mingled disappointment and wariness, she said brightly, 'Sure.'

At Kew, they grabbed a quick coffee and a sandwich, then wandered through some of the formal gardens; Alice laid her palm against Hugo's upper arm to direct his attention to some butterflies, and instantly regretted the impulse when her fingertips started tingling where she touched him.

'Butterfly,' she said, knowing how stupid she sounded. For pity's sake, she should be speaking to him in full sentences, not mumbling single words at him. What was wrong with her? Why was she being so inarticulate?

'What is it?'

Focus on the science, she told herself. Take your hand off his arm. Stop being flustered. *Focus.* 'It's a *Polygonia c-album*—more commonly known as a Comma.'

'Because of the shape of its wing-edges?' he asked.

She liked the fact he'd tried to be logical. 'No, because of the white mark on its underwing.'

'I love the colour. Especially the contrast with the purple flowers.'

'It's not necessarily purple to a butterfly,' she said.

His eyes widened. 'It's not?'

'They don't see colour and resolution in the way that humans do—even though they have eyes in the back of their head and near three-hundred-and-sixty-degree vision, they can't see the fine detail,' she explained. 'And they can see the ultraviolet patterns on flower petals that we can't.'

'What ultraviolet patterns?' he asked.

'The nectar guides.' She gestured to one of the plants in the lawn. 'To a butterfly, this yellow dandelion looks white at the edges, but red at the centre where the nectar is. And a horse-chestnut flower is yellow to them when it's producing nectar, and red when it's not.'

'That's amazing,' he said, smiling. And that smile made her heart feel as if it had done a backflip. He actually listened to what she said. So far, he hadn't tried to change her.

Could she take a risk?

Or should she be sensible, and find a way of putting some distance between them?

Yet she couldn't. As they walked through the gardens together, their hands brushed against each other. Once. Twice. And then their fingers interlocked, just one at first, and then another, and another, until they were actually holding hands.

She could barely breathe.

This wasn't supposed to be happening.

They were absolutely *not* a couple.

Yet here they were, holding hands, as if they were on a proper date. It was thrilling and terrifying, all at the same time.

'This is what I wanted to show you. The Palm House,' he said. 'Victorian glass and iron.'

Was it her imagination, or did his voice sound a bit funny? As if he was just as flustered by this thing happening between them as she was, and he was trying really hard to keep it businesslike...and failing, the same way she was.

'It's like an upside-down ship,' she said.

'Well spotted. It was the first glasshouse built on this scale,' he said, 'so they used techniques from shipbuilding. And here you see sixteen thousand panes of glass.'

He let her hand go when he opened the door for her—but within moments they were back to holding hands. Neither of them said a word about it or even looked at their hands to draw attention to what was happening. But it was there. A fact. They liked each other enough to hold hands. And Alice wondered if Hugo, too, was feeling the little fizzy bubbles of pleasure that seemed to be filling her own veins.

The fact that Hugo really seemed to be considering building the butterfly house made her heart feel light with hope.

She had no idea how long they spent wandering through Kew, exploring the glasshouses and the gardens, with Hugo pointing out his favourite bits of various buildings and herself pointing out the butterflies flitting over the plants. All she could really concentrate on was the warmth of his fingers curled round hers, and how good it made her feel.

Time blurred, seeming to go in the blink of an eye and yet stretch for a week at the same time. But finally the gardens were closing and all the tourists appeared to be heading for the exits.

'Time to leave, I guess,' Hugo said, sounding regretful.

'I guess,' she said.

They walked back to the Tube station together. Alice knew they'd be taking completely different trains—Hugo to Battersea and herself to Shadwell. He'd sounded wistful earlier; would he want to prolong the time with her and maybe suggest dinner? Should she suggest it, maybe? Or were they back in the real world again, now they'd left the glasshouse behind? Would he want to put some distance between them?

'Thank you for a nice day,' Hugo said, which pretty much sealed it for her.

Distance it was.

Separate trains and separate lives.

She could ask him if he'd like to have dinner with her; but perhaps it would be better to spare them both the embarrassment of him refusing. Instead, she smiled. 'I enjoyed it, too. Thank you for showing me the glass.'

He looked awkward, as if debating something in his head; and then he bent forward and kissed her swiftly on the cheek.

Warmth spread through her, along with some courage. 'Maybe we can go to see a butterfly house, next.' She took a deep breath. 'Wednesday afternoons are usually free for me.'

He took his phone from his pocket and checked something. 'I can do Wednesday, this week.'

They were talking as if this was a business appointment, but it felt like a date. And she was shocked to realise how much she wanted it to be a date.

Forcing herself to sound calm, she said, 'We could meet at Canary Wharf station at, say, one o'clock?'

'I'll put it in my diary,' he said. 'See you then.'

'See you then.' She held her breath, just in case he decided to lean forward and kiss her other cheek—or, even, her mouth.

But he didn't.

He just smiled at her and walked away.

Was she about to make a colossal fool of herself? Should she back off?

But all the same Alice found herself touching her cheek when she sat down on the train, remembering how his lips had felt against her skin.

Would he kiss her again, the next time they met?

Would it be a proper kiss?

And, if so, what was she going to do about it?

Butterfly fact of the day: a butterfly's body temperature needs to be thirty degrees C before it can fly.

Alice regretted the impulse, the second she'd sent the email.

Supposing Hugo thought she was trying to flirt with him?

Well, she *was* trying to flirt with him. Even though her head knew it was dangerous and reckless and a very bad idea, that flare of attraction was strong enough to make her ignore her common sense. She couldn't stop thinking about the way he'd held her hand all afternoon, and that kiss on the cheek, and wondering just how his mouth would feel against hers.

He didn't reply. Which served her right, and she forced herself to concentrate on her students and stop mooning over him. But, at the end of the day, there was an email waiting in her inbox.

Glass fact of the day: when glass breaks, the cracks move at three thousand miles an hour.

Flirting by nerdiness?

It was delicious. And addictive. She sent him a nerdy fact by text on Tuesday morning; he replied in kind, later in the day. By Wednesday lunchtime, Alice was practi-

cally effervescent with excitement. She couldn't wait to
see him.

Just as they'd arranged, Hugo was waiting for her at
Canary Wharf station. He was wearing his sharp suit and
posh shoes, and she wished she'd thought to dress up a
bit, too, instead of being her usual scruffy scientist self.

'Hi,' she said, suddenly shy now she was with him.

'Hi.' And now he looked equally ill-at-ease.

What now? They weren't *officially* dating, so she could
hardly greet him with a kiss. But this wasn't just business
any more, either. There was definitely something personal.

'Shall we, um…?' She gestured to the platform, where
the train was waiting.

He didn't hold her hand on the train. He didn't hold
her hand on the way to the butterfly house, either. And he
didn't look that impressed as they walked up to the very
ordinary glasshouse. Well, he was an architect who spe-
cialised in glass. Of course a square building with a gable
roof would be dull and functional, in his view.

Then again, this was the man who'd built a removable
glass wall between his house and his garden, and yet his
garden was the dullest and most minimalist in the universe.
So, the way she saw it, he really didn't have the right to be
picky about this place.

'Don't judge it from the outside,' she said.

'Uh-huh.' His expression and the tone of his voice were
both firmly neutral.

She'd just have to hope that the inside of the building
would work the same magic on him as it did on her. Without comment, she opened the first set of doors and ushered
him inside, before closing the doors behind them. And then
she opened the inner doors.

She'd timed it deliberately: this was the afternoon lull,
when the younger children had gone home for a nap and
the older children were still at school, so she and Hugo

had the whole building to themselves. The glasshouse was filled with large ferns and tropical plants; dozens of butterflies flitted through the air, a mix of sizes and shapes and glorious colours.

She stopped by one of the feeding stations, primed with slices of banana and pineapple and melon; huge owl butterflies had settled on the fruit and were feeding on the sugar.

'That's impressive,' he said.

Yes, but it wasn't the bit she hoped would really attract him. 'Come this way,' she said, taking his hand.

They passed several Zebra Longwing butterflies that were settled on the greenery, idly flapping their long, black-and-white-striped wings.

'I didn't realise that butterflies could be that shape,' he said. 'They're more like a dragonfly than a butterfly.'

'They're the *Heliconius* type,' she said. 'You'll see other butterflies in here that are the same shape, but with splashes of red on their wings; they're the Postman.'

'Postman because they're red, like a post box?' he guessed.

'No, because they do a daily "round" of their flowers—like a postman delivering letters.'

His eyes lit up. 'That's brilliant. And that one over there's really vivid. I had no idea that butterflies could be lime green.'

'That's a Malachite,' she said. *'Siproeta stelenes.'*

She knew she was babbling, just naming things for him, but it was the only way she could cope. Hugo Grey made her head feel all mixed up.

She took a video on her phone of one of the butterflies hovering above a flower, switching the recording to slow motion mode so she could show him something later that she hoped would amaze him, then continued to walk through the butterfly house with him.

His fingers suddenly tightened round hers. 'The big blue

butterflies I remember Rosemary showing me: there's one flying over there in the corner.'

'A Morpho.' The thing she thought—*hoped*—might make the difference. 'Stand still,' she said, 'because they're really curious and they'll come over to have a closer look at you.'

'Seriously?'

'Seriously.'

He did as she suggested, and she watched his expression as one of the butterflies flapped lazily over to them, its wings bright iridescent blue, then landed on his arm. His eyes were full of wonder; all the cynicism had gone from his face. At that moment, it felt as if he lit up the whole butterfly house for her. It was the sweetest, sweetest feeling. As if they were sharing something special. Something private. Their own little world.

'You can breathe, you know,' she said softly. 'You won't hurt it.'

'That's just…' He shook his head, clearly lost for words.

She couldn't resist standing on tiptoe and brushing her mouth against his.

He froze for a moment; and then, as the Morpho flew away again, he wrapped his arms around her waist, returning the kiss. She slid her arms round his shoulders, drawing him closer. And then he really kissed her, teasing her lips with his until she leaned against him and opened her mouth, letting him deepen the kiss. All around them, butterflies flapped their iridescent wings, and she closed her eyes, letting all her senses focus on the feel of Hugo's mouth against hers.

When he finally broke the kiss, she opened her eyes, startled.

'Sorry,' he said. 'I shouldn't have done that.'

'Sorry,' she said. 'Blame it on the butterflies—the excitement of seeing the blue Morpho.'

'Absolutely,' he said.

She was lying; and she was pretty sure he knew it. She was pretty sure he was lying, too. But she had no idea what they were going to do about this. She hadn't felt this attracted to someone for years; but at the same time she didn't want to put the butterfly house project in jeopardy. How did she deal with this, without making a huge mess of things?

'Come and see the pupae,' she said, and slid her hand through the crook of his elbow—just to steer him towards the right place in the butterfly house. It had absolutely nothing to do with wanting to touch him. Though, when he drew her a tiny bit closer, it made tingles run down her spine.

'They're in a box?' He stared at the wooden box with its lines of horizontal canes.

'It's a puparium—the safest place for them to hatch.'

'And they're stuck to the canes?'

She nodded. 'So, once they've wiggled out of the chrysalis, they can hang freely to let their wings dry and fill with blood, ready for flying. In a set-up like this, they might hatch overnight and they'll be let out in the mornings when they're ready to fly. Then they look for a mate and start the courtship ritual...'

Just as she and Hugo were doing. Of sorts. Holding hands. Kissing. Making eye contact, and shying away again, because both of them were so unsure about this whole thing. She felt the colour seep through her cheeks and she couldn't quite look him in the eye. 'The females lay the eggs, and the cycle starts all over again: egg, caterpillar, pupa, butterfly.'

He looked thoughtful. 'It's hotter than I expected in here.'

Did he mean literally or figuratively? It felt hot in here for her, too. Especially when he kissed her. She pulled herself together. Literally, she reminded herself. 'It's the right temperature and humidity for the plants and the butterflies.'

'And it's noisier than I expected, too.'

'That's the air heating,' she explained.

'Maybe we could look at different ways of heating,' he suggested.

Which sounded as if he was thinking seriously about the possibilities of building the butterfly house. Maybe she hadn't ruined everything with that kiss, after all.

'This place is magical. It's a bit like walking through a summery snow globe crossed with a rain forest,' he said.

Did he have a picture of that in his head? Something perhaps that he could do with her project? 'I know a dome wouldn't work, but have you any other thoughts?'

He shook his head. 'Maybe we could have a domed roof. A cylindrical building, with arched windows.'

'Like the ones in the Palm House?'

'That could work.'

If she put the butterfly house first, maybe afterwards she and Hugo could explore what was happening between them.

What was it about this place? Hugo wondered. He'd mused earlier that it was like walking through a summery snow globe. But it wasn't just the brightly coloured butterflies that made it feel so magical; it was Alice, too. There was something special about her. The way she made him feel—with her, for the first time in so very long, it felt as if there was a point to life. As if he was doing more than just existing and trudging from minute to minute. As if her warmth and sweetness had melted the permafrost where he'd buried his heart.

He'd been the one to break the kiss and call a halt. She'd backed off too, blaming it on the butterflies. But it wasn't the real butterflies that had caused that kiss: it was the metaphorical ones in his stomach. The way she made him feel, that swooping excitement of attraction and desire.

What would happen if he kissed her again? Would she back away, skittish as one of her butterflies?

Then he realised that she was speaking.

'Sorry. Wool-gathering,' he said. 'You were saying?'

She was all pink and flustered, and he wanted to draw her into his arms.

'If you're not busy, I could cook dinner tonight. Show you some more butterfly things.'

Was this Alice's way of acknowledging this thing between them and admitting that she'd like to get closer, but was wary at the same time?

That was exactly how he was feeling, too. Wanting to get closer, but scared.

Baby steps.

Starting with dinner.

'I'd like that,' he said.

The pink-and-flusteredness went up a notch. Good. Because she made him feel that way, too.

The Tube was too crowded for them to talk on the way back to her place. Then she went quiet on him during the walk from the station to her flat in Shadwell, which turned out to be in a modern development overlooking a quayside.

'It's a fair bit smaller than your place,' she said, 'but it's home.' She gave him a wry smile. 'Though I do envy you your garden. The nearest I have is a window box of herbs.'

'But you get a view of the water,' he pointed out.

'I guess.'

He realised that her assessment was right when she opened the front door and ushered him inside; her flat really *was* compact. 'The bathroom's there if you need it,' she said, indicating a door off the hallway, then led him into the living room.

There was a bay window with space for her desk and a small filing cabinet; the rest of the room was taken up by a small sofa, a bistro-style table and two chairs, and a floor-to-ceiling bookcase stuffed with books. The walls were all painted cream, but there were strategically placed framed artworks; some were old-fashioned botanical prints of butterflies, and others were small jewel-like modern pieces. And how very different it was from his own stark and monochromatic home; her flat was full of colour and beauty.

'Is that Van Gogh?' he asked, gesturing to a framed poster.

She nodded. 'It's his *Butterflies and Poppies.* They're Clouded Yellows. I saw the original with my best friend—she's an art historian, and she wanted to go to the Van Gogh museum in Amsterdam to see their collection because he's her favourite painter.' She smiled. 'Ruth also took me to the gardens at Giverny, because she's a huge Monet fan. She was waxing lyrical over the bridge and the lily pond, and there I was on the hunt for butterflies. I guess we're as nerdy as each other.'

'My best friend's nerdy, too. He's got this passion for Regency doors, and whenever we go anywhere he's always darting off to take a photograph. His Instagram's full of shots of fanlights and door knockers.' Kit was one of the few people Hugo saw regularly—but a couple of months back Kit and Jenny had invited one of her single friends over to dinner to make up a foursome, and it had annoyed Hugo to the point where he'd pleaded a headache and left early. Things had been a bit strained between them since then; he knew Kit meant well, but he really didn't want to be set up with a suitable woman.

Yes, he was lonely and miserable. Stuck. Things weren't

getting better; the more time passed, the lonelier he felt, and the more aware he was of things he and Emma hadn't had the time to do together. All that stuff about time being a great healer was utter rubbish. He was just *stuck*.

Emma would be furious with him.

He was furious with himself.

But he didn't know how to get unstuck again.

Alice was the first person in a long time who'd made him feel connected with someone. He'd probably spent as much time in her company during the last week or so as he'd spent with anyone else outside the office in the previous six months, apart from his parents and Rosemary. But he couldn't expect her to help push him out of his rut. That was too much to ask from someone who'd known him for less than a month—especially as he'd been at odds with her for more than half that time.

'Can I help with dinner?' he asked instead.

'No, you're fine,' she said with a smile. 'My kitchen's a bit on the small side.'

He could see that for himself from the doorway. It was practically a galley kitchen, with just enough room for a cooker, fridge, and washing machine. He noticed that there was a large cork board on the wall with photographs and postcards pinned to it; it was perfectly neat and tidy, but the personal touches made her flat feel like a home rather than just a place to live, as his own house was.

'Let me grab you a glass of wine,' she said. 'Red or white?'

'I ought to provide the wine, as you're making dinner,' he said. And then he was cross with himself. Why hadn't he thought of that earlier?

She flapped a dismissive hand. 'It's fine. Red or white?'

'What goes better with dinner?'

She tipped her head on one side as she considered it; yet again, he was struck by how cute she was. 'White,' she said. 'Though, before I start cooking, do you have any food allergies or are there any particular things you hate?'

'No allergies and I eat most things,' he confirmed.

The kitchen was definitely too small for two people to work in, because she accidentally brushed against him when she took the wine out of the fridge. He almost wrapped his arms round her and kissed her again, but he held himself back. Just.

'Can I do anything? Lay the table?' he asked instead.

She took cutlery from a drawer. 'You can lay the table and then come back for the salad, if you like. Then feel free to amuse yourself with the TV or whatever.'

He laid the bistro table; when he came back to collect the bowl of salad and his glass of wine, she was busy chopping mushrooms and boiling water in a pan. He could smell something delicious; funny, it had been so long since he'd noticed food. He'd seen it as nothing more than fuel ever since Emma had died.

Rather than bothering with the television, he glanced through the books on Alice's shelves; there were some very academic tomes on ecology and butterflies, and a few glossy coffee-table-type books with gorgeous shots of butterflies, mixed in with a smattering of crime novels. There were also photographs on the shelves; the young child was recognisable as her, with an elderly couple he assumed were her grandparents. The graduation photos of Alice were at Oxford and London, with a couple who were obviously her parents. There was another picture of her wearing a bridesmaid's dress, with her arm wrapped around the bride: obviously a close friend, maybe the one she'd mentioned going with to Rome and Amsterdam and France.

And how very different this was from his own house; he didn't have any photographs on display at all. They were tucked away for safekeeping, along with his memories. Where they didn't hurt.

A few minutes later, Alice came in carrying two bowls of pasta. 'Fettuccine Alfredo,' she said. 'I hope that's OK with you.'

He joined her at the table. 'This is lovely,' he said after his first taste.

She inclined her head in acknowledgement of the compliment. 'Thank you, but it's just a very simple pasta dish, not something I've slaved over for hours and hours.'

'It's still lovely,' he said.

Strangely, given that they were in her flat, her space, she'd gone all quiet and shy on him. Hugo had the feeling that, even though Alice had fought like a tigress for Rosemary's butterfly house and she teased him, there was also something about her that was as fragile as the butterflies she studied. A vulnerability that she kept hidden.

'Who are the people in the photographs?' he asked, hoping to draw her out a bit more.

'The one of me when I'm small is with my grandparents, the graduation photos are with my parents, and the wedding is when my best friend Ruth got married last year,' she said, confirming his guesses.

'Nice pictures,' he said.

'Thank you.' She looked at him. 'You didn't have any art or photos in your house. Have you only just finished the renovations?'

'No. I've been there for just over two years,' he admitted. 'I finished the renovations last summer.' He just couldn't face putting up photographs which underscored the hole in his life, or the pictures Emma had chosen, because just looking at them made him miss her.

To his relief, she didn't push him to explain; she merely topped up his glass of wine and then turned the conversation to something much lighter.

And how good it was to spend time with someone else. It made him realise he should've made more of an effort with the people around him instead of trying to hide away from the world and lick his wounds in silence.

After dinner, she let him help with the washing up, then offered him a coffee. 'Though I don't have a fancy machine or fancy glass cups like yours,' she said. 'The best I can do is a cafetière and a mug.'

'A mug with butterflies on it, I presume,' he said, trying for lightness.

'Of course,' she said, and proceeded to make a cafetière of coffee. 'Oh, and I meant to show you the film I took earlier.' She put the mugs on the table, found the film on her phone, and handed it to him.

A black and red butterfly was flapping its wings frantically; and then suddenly it went into slow motion. The two upper wings flapped completely separately from the bottom pair of wings, he realised. 'It looks like a swimmer.'

'Doing the butterfly stroke,' she said. 'Isn't it incredible?'

'When it's at normal speed, you just see the mad flapping. But this—it's really amazing.'

She looked pleased. 'I thought you'd enjoy it.'

And there it was: the warmth and sweetness that had been missing from his life for so long. He wanted more of this in his life, but he was so out of practice at dating. He wasn't sure how to reach out to her. Then again, even if he did reach out to her, and even if Alice responded— could he take the risk of falling in love again, and losing her? Intellectually, he knew that the chances of losing her in the same way he'd lost Emma were tiny; but emotionally the fear of going through all the pain and loss again thudded through him, making him want to back away and keep what was left of his heart safe.

He drained his coffee and said, 'I'd better let you get on with your evening.'

'Of course,' she said, all calm and professional; but Hugo had seen the hurt in her eyes before she'd masked it, and felt guilty.

He didn't mean to make her feel bad. But he couldn't explain, either, not without things getting a whole lot more awkward.

'Thank you for dinner,' he said. 'I'll, um, catch you later.'

'Sure,' she said. 'Thanks for coming to the butterfly house.'

And all the way home Hugo kicked himself. Why hadn't he just opened up to her, admitted that he liked her and wanted to see her but he was scared about things going wrong? Why hadn't he been honest about Emma? Alice had made him feel amazing, that afternoon. And the moment when he'd kissed her and she'd kissed him back...

He was an idiot for not kissing her again. For not asking her out properly. For not taking the risk. Life was too short to spend all your time hiding.

He'd call her tomorrow, he decided. Apologise for being rude. Explain.

And he'd just have to hope that she'd listen.

Alice scrubbed the coffee pot clean. And then she scrubbed it again, because it gave her something to do.

What a fool she was. Why on earth had she thought it was a good idea to cook dinner for Hugo? Just because he'd kissed her in the butterfly house and made her feel amazing?

Then again, maybe it was better that he'd realised this early on that she didn't fit into his world. He'd seen her for who she was: and she simply didn't measure up. Further proof that Barney and his cronies had been right all along and it was what you looked like, what you sounded like, that was most important.

She'd just have to hope that she hadn't jeopardised the butterfly house project with her stupidity.

CHAPTER SIX

ALICE SENT HUGO a text with a butterfly fact on Thursday morning, hoping that she could find some way back to the working relationship they'd established, but there was no reply.

Until her phone pinged almost at the end of the day.

Sorry. Tied up in meetings all day. Fact for you: glass isn't a solid.

It wasn't a liquid or a gas, either. And that statement was definitely an opening. She could ignore it; or she could give in to temptation and reply.

So what is it?

Amorphous solid—molecules can still move inside it, but too slowly for us to see.

He was still playing the nerdy facts game with her, then; but it didn't feel quite as reassuring as she would've liked. Especially as he'd left her house so abruptly, the previous day.

OK, so he'd made it clear that he didn't want to take their relationship further. But that didn't necessarily mean he was giving up on the butterfly house project. She just needed to try and keep things light and easy between them.

Friday was Emma's birthday and Hugo woke with a ball of misery in his stomach. He headed for his office early, but keeping busy didn't help. If he was honest with himself, he wasn't keeping busy, either; he was just staring out of the window at the river. Stuck. Miserable as hell.

Life moved on, so why couldn't he?

Then his phone chimed to signal an incoming text. He knew before he looked at the screen who it would be from: Alice.

Your butterfly fun fact of the day: butterfly wings are transparent because they're made of chitin, the same protein as an insect's exoskeleton.

Funny, she was the one person he felt he could handle communicating with today. Probably because she didn't know what had happened, so she wasn't going to tread carefully round him and make things worse. And her text was a really welcome distraction.

She was telling him that butterflies were transparent, but the ones she'd shown him were all different colours. He called her on it.

So how come they look different colours?

Scales. As they get older, the scales fall off and leave transparent spots on their wings. Except for a Glasswing, which is transparent to start with.

He could just hear her saying that. And then she'd find a picture on the Internet to illustrate her point, and maybe she'd test him to see if he knew what the butterfly was and whether this was a male or female of the species. He really liked her nerdy streak; it intrigued him and delighted him in equal measure, and it made him feel as if the world was opening up around him again, as if he was stepping away from the oppression of his heartbreak. Just being with her made him want to smile.

Right at that moment he really, really wanted to see her. The only time he felt vaguely normal nowadays was when he was with her. How crazy was that? Before he could overanalyse things and talk himself out of it, he sent her a text.

Are you busy at lunchtime or do you want to come and see a staircase?

To his relief, she didn't make him wait for a reply. Alice wasn't a game-player. What you saw was what you got.

Staircase at lunchtime is doable. I need to be back for a seminar at three.

Meet at St Paul's? When's a good time?

Half-twelve?

OK. See you by the main entrance at half-twelve.

And how weird it was that, for the first time that day, Hugo felt as if he could actually breathe—that there wasn't a huge weight on his chest, making every breath a shallow effort.

At half-past twelve, he was standing on the cathedral steps, looking out for Alice; it was easy to spot her in the crowd. He lifted a hand in acknowledgement, and his heart gave a little skip when she waved back.

'Thanks for coming,' he said when she reached him.

'I'm looking forward to seeing this staircase,' she said. 'And I know it's not glass, but I assume you're going to tell me about that, too.' She gestured up to Wren's enormous dome.

What he really wanted to do was wrap his arms round her, feel her warmth melting the permafrost around his heart. But that would involve explanations he didn't want to give right now, so he duly smiled and escorted her into the cathedral. 'We've actually got a slightly different tour. Maybe we'll come back another day and I'll show you the dome. Today we're focusing on a staircase.'

'I owe you for my ticket,' she said.

He shook his head. 'My idea, my bill.'

'Then I'm buying coffees and sandwiches after,' she said firmly. 'No arguments.'

They were just in time to join the tour, and when they got to the end of it—the bit he'd really been waiting for—Hugo watched Alice's face, pleased to see how amazed she was by the Dean's Stair.

'It's a spiral staircase, but it doesn't have a column in the middle,' she marvelled. 'I don't get how it just floats in the air like that, without falling over.'

'It's cantilevered,' he said. 'Each step is shaped so it can bear the weight of the next. And it's not going to fall over—it's been there for more than three hundred years.'

He held her hand all the way to the top, pleased that she seemed to enjoy the elegant stonework and wrought-iron railings as much as he did.

'What a view,' she said at the top, looking down at the elegant spiral with the eight-pointed star at its centre. 'I need to take a picture of this for Ruth.'

'The art historian,' he remembered.

She nodded, and snapped the picture on her phone.

And then he heard the cathedral organist start to play.

Something he knew well. Bach. A piece Emma had loved and had used to play on the piano he'd given back to her parents, knowing they'd find it comforting. The piece the organist had played at her funeral. And suddenly the weight was right back in the centre of his chest, along with sapping misery.

Something was wrong. Alice didn't know what, but Hugo looked terrible. There were lines of pain etched round his mouth and smudges beneath his eyes. Once the guide had led them back out into the main part of the cathedral, she said gently, 'I think we need coffee and a sandwich. And somewhere nice to eat it.'

'Sure.'

His voice was flat, worrying her further. She quickly bought coffee, muffins and sandwiches at a shop nearby, then shepherded him to a quiet garden not far from St Paul's.

'I had no idea this place even existed,' he said as they sat down. 'Where are we?'

'Christchurch Greyfriars garden,' she said. 'The church was pretty much lost to the Blitz, apart from the tower, but the authorities have kept the land as a garden. The pergolas are full of bird boxes for sparrows and finches. I love this place because it's full of the most gorgeous blue, purple and white flowers.'

'And butterflies.'

Even now, one was skimming past them. She inclined her head. 'Indeed, because a lot of the plants here are nectar-rich.'

'I'm guessing you know a lot of hidden gardens in London?'

She smiled. 'It kind of goes with my job. I need to know where I can take my students on a field trip semi-locally at different times of the year. Here. Have your lunch.' She handed him a cup of coffee and a sandwich.

'Thank you.'

They ate in silence; it wasn't completely awkward, but Alice could see that he was wrestling with something in his head. She had a feeling that talking about whatever was wrong didn't come easily to him. So, when they'd both finished their sandwich and he was staring into his coffee, she reached out to take his free hand. 'I'm probably speaking out of turn here,' she said softly, 'but you look like you did the very first day I met you—lost.'

'It's how I feel,' he admitted. He looked at her and his eyes were full of misery. 'It's selfish of me, but I wanted to see you today because you don't tread on eggshells round me. You stomp about and you tease me and you teach me things and you...' He shook his head. 'You make me see things in a different way.'

Which was an incredible compliment, but it wasn't what had snagged her attention. 'Why do people tread on egg-shells round you?'

He took a deep breath. 'Emma—my wife. It's her birth-day today.'

He was married?

But, before she had a chance to absorb that, he contin-ued, 'She died nearly three years ago.'

Widowed, then. And she was pretty sure he wasn't that much older than she was. Her heart broke for him. 'That's rough, losing her so young.'

He nodded. 'She had asthma. After she died, I found out there's something called Peak Week—it's a week in September when allergies and asthma just spike be-cause there's a big rise in pollen and mould, plus the kids have just gone back to school so there are loads of germs and what have you that compromise people's breathing. Emma was a middle school teacher. I was in America giving a paper at a conference when she had a severe asthma attack.'

Obviously in that week in September, Alice realised.

'She called the ambulance and they came straight away, but she collapsed before she even had a chance to unlock the front door. She had a cardiac arrest and she never regained consciousness.' His expression grew bleaker. 'I never got a chance to say goodbye to her.'

No wonder he'd looked so lost, that day at the solicitor's. The meeting had been about his great-aunt's estate, and it must have brought back all the memories of his wife's death. She put her arms round him and just held him. 'That,' she said softly, 'is so sad. I've never lost anyone near my own age—the only person I've lost is Grandad, and although he went a bit before his time it still felt in the natural order of things. Your wife was so young. It must've felt like the end of the world.'

'It did. And then in the cathedral just now...the organ music. It was something she played on the piano at home. A piece—' his breath caught '—played at her funeral.'

Music that had brought back everything he'd lost. 'I didn't know Emma,' she said, 'but she mattered to you, so she must've been special.'

'Very.'

'Do you have a photo of her?'

For a moment, Alice thought she'd gone too far; but eventually Hugo nodded and took out his phone. He skimmed through the photos, then handed the phone to her.

It was clearly their wedding photograph, with Hugo in a tailcoat and Emma in a frothy dress with her veil thrown back; they were both laughing, radiant with happiness, while confetti fluttered down around them. Emma was utterly beautiful.

'She looks lovely, really warm and kind,' Alice said.

* * *

'She was,' Hugo said. And, although Alice was a very different woman, she had that same warmth and kindness about her. The thing that had been missing from the centre of his life. The thing he'd tried so hard to live without. But he'd just been existing, not living. Putting one foot in front of the other, taking it step by step. It was all he could do, without Emma. On his own, nothing made sense.

'Remember the love, not the loss,' Alice said gently. 'I know it's hard when you're missing someone and want them beside you, when you want to share things with them and you can't—but you can still share things in spirit. When I see the first butterfly of spring, I think of Grandad and I kind of send him a mental phone call. I sit down wherever I am and I talk to him about it, remember times we'd seen that same species together, and it makes things not hurt quite so much. Maybe you need to give Emma a mental phone call. Talk to her. Tell her about your staircases and your glass.'

Hugo's throat felt as if it were full of sand. He couldn't speak, so he just nodded.

'And you can still celebrate her birthday with cake, because that's how birthdays should be celebrated.' She produced two muffins from a bag. 'It's white chocolate and raspberry. I hope that's OK. I'm sorry I don't have a candle to put in it and light, but we can pretend we have candles and wish Emma happy birthday.'

Hugo's eyes stung. He and Alice had kissed. They'd started to get close, taken the first tentative steps towards a relationship. Yet she still had a big enough heart to make room for his late wife and celebrate Emma's birthday instead of putting herself first.

'I'll spare you the singing,' she said. 'But happy birthday, Emma.' She raised her muffin in a toast.

'Happy birthday, Emma,' he said, his voice thick with unshed tears.

And how odd that eating cake and wishing his late wife happy birthday made him feel so much better, taking the weight of the misery off his heart. He really hadn't expected this to work.

'Emma used to make amazing cakes,' he said. It was why he rarely ate cake nowadays; the memories were too much for him.

'Then,' she said, 'if the butterfly house project goes ahead, maybe we can call the cafe after her. Emma's Kitchen. And then she'll be part of it, too, along with Viola and Rosemary.'

How on earth had he ever thought Alice was an ambitious gold-digger who didn't care who she trampled on her path to the top? She was nothing of the sort. She was inclusive. Kind. Thoughtful. This was so much more than he deserved, given the way he'd misunderstood her.

And she still wasn't taking for granted that the butterfly house would go ahead. She wasn't seeing his feelings as a weakness and using them to pressure him into getting her own way. She was being *kind*.

It made him feel too emotional to speak again. He just took her hand and raised it to his mouth, pressing a kiss into her palm and folding her fingers over it. He hoped she understood what he was trying to say. How much he appreciated her being there. How he wanted things to be different.

She rested her palm against his cheek. 'I have half a dozen students expecting me this afternoon, but I can call them now and reschedule our seminar.'

He shook his head. 'That's not fair.'

'It's not fair of me to leave you right now,' she said.

'I have meetings, in any case.' Meetings that he'd force himself to get through, and he'd do his job well, the way he always did. He had his professional pride. He took a deep breath. 'You've made me feel so much better today. Thank you.'

Her grey eyes were unsure. 'Do you want me to walk you back to your office?'

'No. But I'll walk you back to the Tube.'

'All right.'

She didn't push him to speak on the way back to the station; she just let him be. No wrapping him in platitudes and pity, and he was grateful for that. How often did you find someone who'd just let you be you, with no pressure?

'I'll call you later,' he said.

'OK.' She stood on tiptoe and kissed his cheek. Just once. 'Give that mental phone call a try. It always makes me feel better.'

And then the train pulled up at the station and she'd gone.

Hugo was thoughtful all afternoon, between meetings.

A mental phone call.

Better than that, he'd visit. Just as he always did on Emma's birthday, his own birthday, their wedding anniversary and the anniversary of her death.

He took stocks, her favourite flowers, to the churchyard, and rinsed out the vase on her grave, filling it with fresh water before adding the new flowers.

'Happy birthday, my love,' he said, sitting down next to the grave. 'I can't believe it's nearly three years, now. I miss you so much, still.' He swallowed hard. 'And I know you'd be furious with me for moping. I know I need to move on—to live life to its fullest, the way you used to do. But it's just so hard without you, Em.'

He wrapped his arms round his knees. 'I miss you. And this is incredibly crass of me to say this on your birthday—it's wrong on so many, many levels—but I've been so lost and lonely without you. And I've met some-one. She would've liked you, and I think you would've liked her.'

He sighed. 'I'd like to ask her out. I think we could make each other happy. And she's not replacing you—I'll always love you, and I'll always keep your memory alive. She doesn't want to push you out of my life, either; she thinks we ought to call the cafe at the butterfly house after you. This whole thing makes me feel so mixed up. I want to move on, but I feel as if I'm letting you down all over again. If I hadn't gone to that conference...' Would Emma still have been here? Would he have managed to get help to her in time? Or would she still have collapsed and had that heart attack, and the medics still wouldn't have been able to save her and he would still have felt guilty? He blew out a breath. 'Is it selfish of me to want to find happiness again?'

A moment later, a white butterfly landed on the stocks and basked in the sunlight as it fed on the flowers.

Hugo stared at the butterfly. This felt like a sign. As if Emma was giving him her blessing to ask Alice out—and telling him to build the butterfly house.

Emma's Kitchen it was, then.

'I love you, Em,' he said as the butterfly flittered away again.

And now he knew what to do.

'You really do make the best Buddha bowl in the universe,' Alice said, smiling at her best friend as she laid her fork down on the empty bowl. 'Spicy chicken, wild rice and extra avocado. It doesn't get better than that.'

Ruth laughed. 'Indeed.'

And then Alice's phone pinged. Normally she would've ignored a text during dinner, but she noticed Hugo's name on the notification.

'From the look on your face,' Ruth said, 'I'm guessing that's something you need to deal with.'

'I've come to have dinner with you, not be glued to my phone,' Alice said.

'I know, but I'm going to get the ice cream. I think you can be forgiven for reading a text while I've left the table.'

'Thanks.' Alice opened the message, and frowned.

Can I take you to dinner tomorrow night?

Did this mean that Hugo wanted to talk about the butterfly house?

Then her phone pinged again.

That's a social invitation, not a butterfly/glass discussion. Keeping things separate.

Alice stared at the phone, not sure whether she was more thrilled or terrified.

Unless she was being very dense, Hugo Grey had just asked her on a date.

'Everything OK?' Ruth said, coming back with two dishes, a bowl of raspberries and a tub of caramel ice cream.

'Yes. No.' Alice dragged a hand through her hair. 'I don't know.'

'Spill,' Ruth said.

'It's Hugo.'

'Rosemary's great-nephew, the man you wanted to throttle?' Ruth asked.

'We've moved on a bit, since then,' Alice said. 'We've been talking about the project and having field trips.'

'Field trips,' Ruth said, with a knowing look.

'Not dates,' Alice corrected.

'But?'

Alice squirmed. Trust her best friend to notice the invisible 'but'. 'There appears to have been some hand-holding.' When Ruth didn't say anything, just looked levelly at her, Alice caved further. 'And some kissing.'

'That, honey, doesn't sound remotely like what a field trip should be. It sounds as if you're dating.'

Which was what Hugo was proposing now. Something Alice wanted to say yes to—but she was scared that it would all go wrong.

'It's complicated,' Alice said. 'I send him nerdy facts about butterflies. He sends me nerdy facts about glass.'

'Flirting by nerdiness. That sounds good,' Ruth said. 'It means he gets you. So do I take it that he's just asked you out officially?'

Alice nodded.

'Then say yes.'

'You know how rubbish I am at relationships. I always pick someone who wants to change me. Robin, Ed, Henry —and Barney.' She grimaced. 'Hugo's from the same kind of background as Barney, one where I don't fit in.'

'Maybe it'll be different, this time,' Ruth suggested.

'Maybe it won't.' Alice sighed. 'He's a widower.'

Ruth raised her eyebrows. 'He's a lot older than you, then?'

'No. His wife died tragically young—an asthma episode caused a heart attack.' She swallowed hard. 'I think I'm the first woman he's asked out since she died. Nearly three years ago.'

'And you haven't dated in a year. It sounds to me as if you might be good for each other,' Ruth said.

'What if I get it wrong?'

'Then you get it wrong. But if he's as nerdy as you, in his own way, that's a good thing. You'll understand each other.'

'I just don't want to get it wrong,' Alice repeated.

'What if you get it right?' Ruth asked. 'Then, if you say no, you'll miss out. I know Barney really hurt you, but you're an amazing woman and I'm proud to call you my friend. If you back off from the chance of a relationship, you're letting Barney win—and you're worth more than that.' Ruth squeezed her hand. 'The only way you'll find out is to date him. What have you got to lose?'

Alice bit her lip. 'The whole of the butterfly house project. I can't risk that.'

'What did he say?'

Alice handed her phone over.

Ruth read the texts swiftly. 'He's pretty clear about wanting to keep things separate. He's asking you out for dinner. As a date. Nothing to do with the butterfly house. I think you should say yes.'

Alice looked at her in an agony of indecision.

Ruth tapped in a reply. 'OK. Done.'

'What? Ruth! No! What did you say?' Alice asked, horrified.

Ruth handed the phone back.

'"I'd love to. Let me know where and when,"' Alice read aloud, and groaned. 'Oh, no.'

'Ally, you've admitted that you've kissed him and you've held hands and you've been flirting by text. This is the next step, that's all.' Ruth leaned across the table and hugged her. 'I just want you to be as happy as I am with Andy. I know you don't need a partner to be a valid person, but I worry that you're lonely.'

'I've got good family and good friends—the best, when they don't commandeer my phone and send texts under my name,' Alice said pointedly, 'and good colleagues.'

'Which is not the same as sharing your life with someone.'

Alice's phone pinged with another text.

Pick you up at seven tomorrow.

So it was a definite date. 'Oh, help. What do I do now?'

Ruth had known her for long enough to be able to guess what the issue was. 'Ask him where you're going,' Ruth said, 'and I'll tell you what to wear.'

Alice duly texted Hugo.

Surprise was the answer.

'That doesn't help at all.' Alice bit her lip. 'What if I wear completely the wrong thing?' Just as she had in Oxford, and Barney's set had all mocked her for it. 'We're talking about a man who wears handmade Italian shoes.'

Ruth smiled. 'It sounds to me like a good excuse to go and buy a new dress.'

'I hardly ever wear dresses.'

'I wish,' Ruth said, 'you'd get over how Barney made you feel. What you wear isn't as important as feeling comfortable in it.'

'And I don't feel comfortable in a dress.'

'Because you can't hide behind a T-shirt slogan, hiking boots and a camera?' Ruth asked, raising one eyebrow.

'The first time I met Hugo, I was wearing a business suit, and I...didn't come across well.'

'Neither did he, from what you told me. It's got nothing to do with what you look like.' Ruth frowned. 'Ask him if a little black dress is appropriate or if he can suggest a dress code.'

'I don't have a little black dress.'

'I do,' Ruth said, 'and you're the same size as me, so there are no excuses. Text him.'

Alice knew if she didn't, Ruth would simply steal her phone and do it for her, so she gave in and texted him. When her phone pinged, she read the text. 'He says wear whatever I like, but a little black dress would be just fine.'

'It's you he's dating, not your clothes,' Ruth said. 'I like the sound of that. It's a good thing. Make that leap of faith, Ally. He's not Barney.'

'But I already told you, he's from the same kind of background as Barney,' Alice pointed out. 'The kind of people who judge me and find me wanting.'

'You're a woman who has three degrees and a heart as big as the world: in what *possible* way can you be found wanting?' Ruth asked.

The answer to that was burned into Alice's heart. She'd learned that from Barney and his friends and their mocking laughter. 'The wrong background. The wrong clothes. The wrong manners.'

'Anyone who's that shallow isn't worth your time,' Ruth said. 'And not everyone from that background is like Barney. You've just always chosen Mr Wrong.'

'So what makes Hugo any different?'

'That,' Ruth said, 'is for you to answer. And the only way you're going to find the answer is to date him.'

Alice couldn't really reply to that.

'Now stop fussing and eat your ice cream,' Ruth said, 'because we have a dress to sort out.'

Working on Viola's journals, her current favourite part of her job, didn't manage to calm Alice's nerves, the next day.

Would dating Hugo Grey turn out to be a huge mistake?

Even if he didn't hold her background against her or want to change her, there was the fact that he'd lost his wife in such tragic circumstances. How could she ever measure up to the love of his life?

With her borrowed dress, the shoes she'd worn the first time she'd met Hugo, and the butterfly necklace her parents had given her for her thirtieth birthday, she felt polished enough to cope with wherever he was taking her. Though, when the doorbell rang, she had butterflies in her stomach. Stampeding ones. A whole forestful of Monarchs in the middle of a long-distance migration.

'Hi. You look lovely,' he said.

'Thank you. So do you.' And her voice *would* have to go all squeaky, wouldn't it?

Hugo looked gorgeous in a dark suit that she would just bet was custom-made, teamed with a crisp white shirt and an understated silk tie…and yet another pair of handmade Italian shoes. The man was a walking fashion-plate. And, although it would normally have made her worry that she wasn't stylish enough, the way he looked at her—the heat in his eyes, the way he was smiling just for her—made her feel special. The fact that a man as gorgeous and talented as Hugo had called her 'lovely' made her feel as if she were walking on air.

'For you,' he said, handing her a bouquet of delicate flowers in shades of blue and cream—cornflowers, cream-and-pink-swirled Californian poppies, honeysuckle and columbines.

'Thank you. They're beautiful,' she said.

'I asked the florist for something different, because I didn't think you'd enjoy hothouse blooms. And you said you liked blue flowers.'

'I do.' And she loved the fact he'd made such an effort, instead of grabbing the first bouquet he saw. There was real thought behind this. Substance, not just style. She breathed in the scent of the honeysuckle. 'These are so lovely. I ought to put them in water before we go. Have we got time?'

'Sure.'

'Come in.'

The cornflowers were almost the same shade of blue as his eyes, and it made her smile. She put the flowers in water and stood the vase on the kitchen windowsill. 'They're perfect. Thank you.'

'Pleasure.' He smiled at her. 'Are you OK to walk in those shoes?'

'I didn't think my hiking boots would quite go with this dress,' she said, aiming for lightness.

'Perhaps not. I thought we'd get the Tube to the restaurant, then maybe have a walk along the river and get a taxi back, if that's OK with you?'

'That'd be nice,' she said, wondering just how flashy the restaurant was going to be and how out of her depth she was going to feel.

But, when they arrived at the restaurant, it was nothing like she was expecting. The waitress led them to the rooftop where there were several glass pods, all containing pots of enormous ferns decked with fairy lights as well as tables and chairs. Most of the pods were already full but there was one clearly waiting for them.

'We're eating in one of these glass pods?' she checked.

'I thought it might be nice to have a view of the sunset over the river,' he said. 'Is this OK with you?'

'It's more than OK,' she said. A glass dome—his favourite thing—plus beautiful plants and a view of the sunset. It was the perfect first date.

Once they'd ordered and the waitress had brought them a bottle of wine, he said, 'When I asked you to dinner, last night, I wasn't sure if you'd say yes.'

'I wasn't sure, either,' she admitted. 'You're still grieving for Emma.'

'But I need to move on. And you're the first woman I've really noticed since she died.' He took a deep breath. 'I took your advice.'

'The mental phone call?'

He nodded. 'I went to her grave. I talked to her about you, and about how I'd like to ask you to dinner. And I'd just finished talking when this white butterfly settled on the flowers I'd taken with me. It felt like a sign. So I texted you when I got home.'

'I was at my best friend's,' Alice said. 'Actually, this is her dress. I, um, don't often wear dresses.'

'Because of the ticks?'

So he remembered what she'd said. That made her feel a lot more confident. 'Something like that. So what does an architect do in his spare time?'

'Work,' he said. 'Make calculations.'

Which sounded very lonely, to her.

'What does a lepidopterist do in her spare time?' he asked.

'Have dinner with friends, go to the cinema, and visit art exhibitions with my best friend—on condition she visits an SSSI with me.'

'A Site of Special Scientific Interest?' he asked.

She nodded. 'When I'm planning a field trip for my students, I scope it out first. So Ruth and I have a girly road trip.'

'Like our field trips?'

'Something like.' She looked at him. 'This is odd. Being here together, not talking about the butterfly house project.' The thing that scared her. 'Actually on a date.'

'On a date.' He met her gaze head-on. 'You know why I haven't dated since Emma died. You told me you're married to your job. Why don't you date?'

Oh, help.

She didn't want to tell Hugo about Barney. About how pathetic and worthless she'd felt when she'd learned the truth about why Barney was really dating her. How pathetic and worthless she still felt, thanks to the men she'd dated since. 'Let's just say I'm not great at picking Mr Right.'

But he didn't let her weasel out of answering his question.

'What normally makes them Mr Wrong?' he asked.

She'd soon find out if he was another of them, so she

might as well be honest. 'They want to change me,' she said simply.

He frowned. 'You're supposed to date someone because you like them and you want to get to know them better, not because you want to make them into someone else.'

That was reassuring. 'How do you get to know someone better?' she asked.

'Search me. I'm out of practice,' he said. 'Emma and I met at university, in our last year. Friend of a friend at a party sort of thing. We just clicked, and I never looked at anyone else after that.'

She blinked. 'Are you telling me this is your first "first date" since you were twenty-one?' She wasn't sure whether that made her feel special—or scared that she wouldn't live up to his expectations.

'Yes. So I'm a bit out of practice.' He grimaced. 'I apologise if I'm making a mess of it.'

So was he feeling as nervous as she was? Wanting to reassure him, she said, 'You're not. Whereas I have a PhD in making a mess of first dates. The wrong clothes, the wrong conversation...' She shrugged. 'The wrong everything.'

'Maybe,' he said, 'we shouldn't call this our first date.'

Because he'd already seen enough of her to change his mind? Because she'd crashed and burned yet again?

Her thoughts must've shown in her expression, because he added quietly, 'To take the pressure off both of us. This is dinner between people who might become friends—and who might become something else.'

'So it's a getting-to-know-you sort of thing.' Which was a lot less scary. At his nod, she said, 'As a scientist, I get to know things by asking questions.'

'Go for it,' he said.

She'd start with an easy one. Something that didn't have any real emotional investment. 'What's your favourite food?'

'Cheese. Really salty, crumbly, strong Cheddar, with oatcakes and a glass of good red wine. You?'

'Parkin, like my gran makes,' she said promptly, 'with a cup of proper Yorkshire tea. Strong.'

'So *that's* your accent,' he said. 'I wasn't sure.'

She tried not to flinch. 'Just so you know, I'm proud of being from South Yorkshire.' Even though Barney's crowd had sneered at her heritage. *The lass from t'pit. The oik.*

'And so you should be. Yorkshire's given us Yorkshire pudding, the Brontës and Wensleydale cheese. Kit—my best friend—is from York,' he said.

'My best friend's a Cockney,' she said. 'We have fights about whether London or Yorkshire is better. Our last fight was traditional dishes—jellied eels versus parkin.' She spread her hands. 'I won that one. No contest.'

'Jellied eels are definitely not my thing. Though I couldn't judge fairly, because I've never eaten parkin,' he said.

'Even though your best friend is from Yorkshire?' At his nod, she said, 'Then I'm taking that as a challenge.'

'Good,' he said, 'because tonight might not be our first date—but as far as I'm concerned I don't want it to be our last.'

She was glad of their food arriving, because she didn't have a clue what to say next. The possibilities of where they went from here had completely flustered her.

'OK. So you like the sweet stuff and I'm more savoury,' he said. 'Music?'

'Whatever's on the radio. Though at Christmas I like proper carols, like they sing at home.'

'Kit made me go to a folk festival with him in Yorkshire, when we were students.' He grinned. 'Beforehand, I was planning to tease him about brass bands and Morris dancers—except I absolutely loved the music. And the beer was really good.'

'So you like live music?'

'Pretty much anything,' he said. 'Not super-heavy classical, though I've been to a few proms with Em.'

'Ruth and Andy had an amazing group at their wedding. Quartus. A string quartet which played a mix of popular classical music and pop—it was really romantic,' she said.

'You like dancing?'

She had—until the ball where she'd learned the truth about Barney. That had put her off. Though telling Hugo the whole truth made her feel too ashamed. 'I'm not very good at it,' she said instead. 'You?'

'I have two left feet. I can't do much more than sway, and even then I might not do it to the right beat,' he admitted.

So far, they seemed compatible. 'What kind of thing do you read?' she asked.

'Background reports on architectural projects,' he said. 'Strictly non-fiction.'

'Which explains why you don't have any bookshelves.'

He shrugged. 'Em was the reader, not me,' he said.

And books reminded him of her, so he didn't keep them in his house? she wondered. Before she could find the right words to ask him, he said, 'I already know you read scientific stuff about Lepidoptera, have gorgeous photographic books of butterflies, and you read crime novels.'

'Not gory ones,' she said. 'I like the clever ones where you solve a puzzle.'

'So from a scientist's point of view,' he said.

'I guess.' She smiled. 'I don't like gory films, either. The ones I see with Ruth tend to be arthouse movies or costume dramas.'

'Em loved costume dramas. Anything Jane Austen.' He looked at Alice. 'Do you mind me talking about her?'

'Of course not. She was a big part of your life and you loved her. Not talking about her would be weird.'

'You're so easy to talk to,' he said. 'Yet, the first day I met you, you were terrifyingly polished and unapproachable.'

'That was the idea,' she said. 'To look professional, in case the meeting was about Viola's journals and you were on the side that could cancel the project.'

'But that wasn't who you are,' he said.

She went very still. 'Meaning?'

'You're not a suit. You're a scientist. You're about seeing the world in a different way,' he said.

She felt the colour flood into her face. 'That might be the nicest compliment anyone's ever given me.' She could tell he meant it. He saw her for who she was and, although she found it hard to believe this was real, he actually seemed to like her for who she was. 'Thank you.'

'It wasn't meant to be schmoozy—more trying to say that the real you is a lot more approachable,' he said. 'When I found out who you were... I didn't think you looked like a butterfly expert. Not in that suit. That's why I didn't think you were genuine.'

'Remember what my favourite T-shirt says: "Don't judge a butterfly by its chrysalis".'

'I like that.' He paused. 'I'm glad I'm getting to know you.'

'Me, too.' Even though part of her still worried. Hugo's world was like Barney's. When he got to know her better, would he realise that she wouldn't fit in? Would he change his mind about dating her? Or, worse—despite what he'd said about not wanting to turn someone into something else—once he got to know her better, would he want her to change, the way almost all her past boyfriends had?

The waitress arrived with the food, which was excellent. And thankfully Hugo turned the conversation to food and all the dangerous moments were averted. They watched the sun set over the Thames, the sky looking almost airbrushed and reflecting on the river; after coffee, they walked along the river, holding hands.

'If I was any good at dancing,' he said as they passed a group of people dancing in a fairy-lit square on the South Bank, 'I'd suggest we stop here and join them.'

'Better not. Your posh shoes would be in severe danger,' she said with a smile.

He stopped and drew her close to him. 'But, on the plus side, if I was dancing with you I'd have an excuse to do this.' He brushed his mouth very lightly against hers.

Heat bloomed through her, and she slid one hand round the nape of his neck. 'There are fairy lights. That's all the excuse you need.'

'I'll remember that,' he said, and kissed her again.

Alice had no idea how far they walked, after that; all she was aware of was the floaty feeling being with him gave her, and the warmth of his fingers twined with hers.

He hailed a taxi to take them back to her flat, and walked her to the front door.

'Would you like to come in?' she asked.

'Not tonight,' he said, and kissed her again on her doorstep. 'But if you're not busy tomorrow, maybe we can have a field trip.'

The heat in his eyes made her ask, 'A field trip or a date?'

'A bit of both,' he said.

'What's the dress code?' she asked.

'Whatever you're comfortable in,' he said, and frowned. 'Why do you worry so much about what to wear?'

Explaining that would open up a can of worms she'd rather leave closed. 'Thinking about ticks,' she said lightly. 'Urban or countryside?'

'Both,' he said. 'Your hiking boots are fine. And maybe I can cook us dinner tomorrow night.'

So he wanted to spend the whole day with her? 'That would be lovely,' she said. 'Where do you want to meet, and what time?'

'Chelsea Physic Garden at half-past eleven,' he said.

She grinned. 'I notice you've gone for an owl-type hour.'

'It means we can have brunch,' he said. 'See you tomorrow.' He kissed her lightly.

'Thank you for tonight,' she said. 'It was amazing.'

'Good. And tomorrow's mainly a date, by the way,' he said.

She kissed the corner of his mouth. 'I'll look forward to it.'

CHAPTER SEVEN

THE NEXT DAY, Alice was already waiting by the entrance to the gardens when Hugo got there, and his heart skipped a beat when he saw her.

'Hi.' He'd said goodbye to her with a kiss, yesterday. Could he say hello with a kiss, too? He was so out of touch with dating, and he didn't want to get this wrong. It was ridiculous to feel this nervous and awkward; he was thirty-two, not fifteen. But he had a feeling that Alice could really matter to him, and he didn't want to make a mistake that could take all the possibilities away.

She blushed. 'Hi.'

Her voice was slightly breathy and shy, and that decided him. He kissed her cheek. 'Thank you for coming.'

'I really thought we'd be heading to see a dome or a staircase,' she said, and he loved the slightly cheeky, teasing look in her eyes.

He smiled and took her hand. 'The staircase I want to show you next isn't open at weekends. Maybe Wednesday lunchtime?'

'That works for me,' she said. 'So why did you pick here?'

'I used to come here with Rosemary when I was small. I haven't been for a few years,' he said, 'but I wanted to take a look at the glasshouses.'

'Is that what you meant by *mainly* a date?' she asked.

'Are you in the running to restore the glasshouses or something and you wanted to check them out?'

'Possibly, but that's not what I had in mind,' he said. 'Let's go for a wander.'

She handed him a ticket, pre-empting any arguments over who was going to pay for their admission. 'Seeing as I got here before you,' she said, 'and you took me to dinner last night, our admission's on me.'

'It's my idea, so it's my bill,' he protested.

'No. We're sharing,' she said firmly.

He sighed. 'Alice, I've apologised for ever thinking you were a gold-digger. I know you're not like that.'

'Good. But let's not fight,' she said, and tucked her arm into the crook of his.

Strolling round the gardens with her was a delight. She pointed out her favourite flowers, and several different species of butterflies; but, more than that, Hugo just liked being with her. He didn't have to pretend, with her; he could just be himself. She knew about Emma, and she hadn't judged him or told him what he should be doing. Not having to fake being a normal, functioning human being was so refreshing; and, in a weird way, taking that pressure off meant that he could actually function normally and focus on things he usually didn't have the energy to notice because he was too busy trying to get through the day.

When they stopped at the cafe for brunch of coffee and a bacon sandwich, he said, 'I want to run something by you.'

'Is this the non-date part?' she asked.

'Yes.' He paused. 'I've been looking at your figures for the butterfly house.'

She went very still. 'Uh-huh.'

'Tomorrow I'll instruct Philip Hemingford to fulfil my great-aunt's will.' He smiled. 'Though you've probably already guessed that.'

'I hoped you would,' she said. 'But you hadn't actually said you'd build the butterfly house—just that you'd think about it. I'm so glad.'

'Good. We need to revise our planning application,' he said. 'And I can't guarantee they'll say yes.'

'But it's more likely they'll say yes if you've had a hand in it.'

'Not because of who I am,' he reminded her. 'Just that I'd word it in a different way—I know the guidelines of most planning departments and the words that work for them.'

Her eyes filled with tears. 'I'm so glad you're going to do it. But, just to be clear, that isn't why I agreed to date you.'

'Good. I was hoping it was because you wanted to see me for *me*.'

She nodded. 'It is. But what you've just told me—I think you've scrambled my brain, because now I'm...' she spread her hands '...speechless.'

He reached across the table, took her hand, pressed a kiss into her palm and folded her fingers over where he'd kissed her. 'That's one of the things I value about you. What you see is what you get.'

She didn't reply, but her eyes sparkled again with unshed tears.

'I thought maybe I could show you some rough ideas for the butterfly house, later this afternoon.'

'I'd love that,' she said.

And he was looking forward to seeing her reaction. He'd spent half the night sketching, and it was the first time he'd felt really inspired since Emma's death—the first time his designs had flowed instead of feeling mechanical and as if he was simply ticking boxes. It was all because of Alice: without her, he wouldn't have remembered how much it made his heart sing to work with glass, or discovered how amazing a butterfly house was. It felt like coming back into the spring after a very long, dark winter. New shoots everywhere, green starting to soften the bare branches, birds singing madly in the morning. He was starting to get the joy back in his life, and he wanted more.

After lunch, Alice wanted to visit the shop. She emerged with a recyclable shopping bag slung over her shoulder; she didn't say what she'd bought, and Hugo didn't want to be pushy and ask.

'Do you want me to carry that for you?' he asked instead.

She smiled. 'Thank you, but I can manage.'

So instead he held her hand while they crossed the river and walked back through Battersea park, past the rose garden and under the pergola.

'I know it's pretty much past its best now, but the wisteria's still so pretty,' she said. 'I love walking through Kensington in wisteria season.'

He'd never really been bothered about wisteria before, but he couldn't resist kissing her under the pergola, with the lilac blooms hanging down. 'Works for me,' he said with a grin.

Back at his house, he opened the glass wall to the garden.

'Is it OK for me to potter round your garden?' she asked.

'Sure. Have a seat on the patio. I'll make coffee,' he said.

'I brought something to go with it.'

When he'd finished making the coffee, she was sitting down, looking at something on her phone. It took him another ten minutes to notice that the bag she'd had slung over her shoulder was missing—and there was something in his garden that definitely hadn't been there before.

'There's a pot of flowers in my garden.'

'A *small* pot,' she said.

'Flowers.' That must've been what she'd bought from the shop at the Chelsea Physic Gardens. 'I don't do flowers.'

'They're Leucanthemums—Shasta daisies,' she said.

Big white ones. Flowers he didn't have a clue what to do with.

'They're beginner flowers. You can neglect them and they'll still be fine,' she reassured him, clearly guessing at his concerns. 'They don't mind full sun or partial shade, they're hardy, and they're not fussy about soil type. The main thing is that they're great for pollinators.'

He still couldn't get his head round this. 'You bought me a plant.'

'Call it a garden-warming present.'

'I moved here two years ago.'

'Late garden-warming, then. Because I didn't know you two years ago.'

She'd just put flowers into his very plain outdoor area, showing him he didn't have to be surrounded by plain boxes. Although she'd only moved him a tiny fraction out of his rut, it was enough to make him slightly unnerved. He'd wanted to move on, but now it was happening he wasn't entirely sure he was quite ready for this.

As if he'd spoken aloud, she put her arms round him and kissed him. 'I'm sorry. I'll take it back with me if you really hate it.'

How could she take it with her, when she didn't have a garden? And he was being ungrateful. The gift had been motivated by kindness. 'It's not that I hate it. I'm just not a gardener.' He knew about buildings, about glass and staircases. Even though Rosemary had talked to him a lot about plants when he was young, and his mother was very fond of her outdoor space, Hugo didn't have a clue about how to maintain a garden. Alice had pushed him out of his comfort zone.

'Was Emma the gardener? Because I didn't mean to trample on a sore spot. I'm sorry.'

'We didn't have a garden at our flat,' he admitted. 'And, no, she wasn't really a gardener.'

She looked thoughtful. 'So technically you're a garden virgin.'

Just when he thought he'd worked her out, she said something that threw him. 'Did you just call me...?'

She kissed him again. 'I apologise. But just watch. I promise this will be worth it.'

Ten minutes later, there was a bee buzzing round the pot of daisies. And, ten minutes after that, there was a butterfly.

'See?' she asked softly. 'The difference one little pot can make. When was the last time you saw a bee or a butterfly out here?'

'Hmm,' he said, refusing to be drawn.

'So now can I see your sketches?' she asked.

'They're indoors.'

She followed him into the kitchen, and he brought out his files and spread the sketches on the table. He'd sketched a cylinder with a domed top, more or less what he'd suggested at Kew. 'The panels on the sides remind me of the Victorian glasshouses we saw at Kew. The ones from Viola's era. This is perfect,' she said. 'There's plenty of space for the plants and the butterflies, as well as the heating system and the puparium.' She looked at him. 'But what *I* think isn't important. What really matters is the planning committee's view.'

'I tweaked your application—*our* application,' he corrected. 'Hopefully we can get outline permission now, then work on the detail later. Have a look at what I've done. If it sounds right to you, I'll submit it tomorrow.'

'OK.' She took a small box from her handbag. 'By the

way—parkin. I made some this morning. It'll go nicely with coffee.'

'From your gran's recipe?' he asked.

She nodded. 'Which isn't me trying to fill Emma's shoes by baking stuff. Just that you said you'd never tried it, and it's my turn to bring in departmental goodies tomorrow, so I saved you a bit from the batch I made.'

'Good plan,' he said. He opened the box and tasted the gingerbread. 'Now I know why Kit raves about this. Thank you. It's lovely.' He pulled up a file on his laptop and passed it across to her. 'Here's the revised application. Does this work for you or do you want me to change anything?'

She read through it. 'You've said everything I did, except it sounds slightly different.'

'Little tweaks in the wording, that's all.' He raised his mug of coffee. 'Here's to the butterfly house. And may the planners love it.'

'May the planners love it,' she echoed.

After dinner, Hugo drove Alice home. He kissed her lingeringly on her doorstep, enjoying the warmth of her mouth against his and the feel of her arms wrapped round him, holding him close. He'd been at such a low ebb; and Alice made him feel as if he were slowly coming towards the light at the end of a very long and lonely tunnel.

'I'll see you later in the week,' he said when he finally broke the kiss.

'Staircase or butterflies?' she asked.

'Both, if you've got time,' he said.

'Call me. Wednesdays are always good for me,' she said.

'I'll check my diary and move things around, if need be,' he promised, and kissed her again. 'Wednesday it is.'

He waited until she was safely indoors before going back to his car and driving home. Funny how she'd made such a difference to his life. Her butterflies and the way she encouraged him to talk about glass and staircases made him feel so much lighter of heart. He actually found himself looking forward to the day when he woke up, now, because he knew he'd talk to Alice at some point—even if it was only a brief text exchange of nerdy facts. And how much better that was than the last three years, when he'd been dragging himself from one dismal minute to the next and the struggle had exhausted him.

Back at his house, Hugo sat at the kitchen table with a mug of tea, looking out at the garden. That one bright pot of white daisies made the whole space feel different—as if the garden had a focus. Just the way that Alice herself had brought brightness and focus into his life again.

Could it be that his life was finally changing for the better?

On Wednesday, Hugo took Alice to see the helical staircase at City Hall. 'This is something I wish I'd built. And just imagine this as a butterfly house,' he said.

She looked thoughtful. 'Or the Sky Garden. Thousands and thousands of butterflies. It'd be amazing, like seeing a migration of Monarchs—did you know they sound like a waterfall when they fly on migration because there are so many of them?'

'No, but I can imagine it. I still haven't got over that Blue Morpho landing on me. Or seeing the Swallowtail in the fens.'

'I'd like a mix of butterflies in our house, based on Viola's journals,' she said. 'And I definitely want her drawings of those species on the website. Ruth's husband is a website designer, so I was hoping he might be able to help us out.'

'That'd be great,' he said. 'I was going to check with my father, in case he has any more family papers or photos that would be useful.'

'That would be brilliant,' she said. 'And maybe tonight I can show you where I've got to.'

'I'd like that,' he said. 'We could get a takeaway for dinner.'

'There's a really good Chinese near me,' she said. 'They do the best dim sum ever.'

'Sounds perfect,' Hugo said.'

He kissed her goodbye at the Tube station. 'See you tonight. I've got a late meeting, so would seven be OK?'

'It's fine.' She stole a last kiss. 'See you then.'

Over the next couple of weeks, Alice and Hugo were busy at work—Alice with marking and exams, and Hugo with a project—but they managed to see each other a couple of evenings a week and spent the weekends at Rosemary's house. Hugo made lists of what needed to be done in the house and which contractors to ask for quotes, while Alice worked out what needed to be done in the garden—which plants would go where, how the re-wilding would work, and which plants and species they needed for the butterfly house. In between, Alice continued to work on the journals and Viola's biography, and Hugo made more detailed plans for the butterfly house, checking sizes and volumes with Alice to make sure it was the right space for the number of butterflies she wanted to keep in the house.

'Some of this we can do ourselves,' Hugo said at the end of the second week. 'Maybe we can talk friends into coming here to wield a paintbrush or do some weeding and planting.'

'Not until we've got the outline planning permission,' Alice said. 'I don't want to jinx anything by starting things too early.'

'Superstitious?' He stole a kiss. 'OK. But maybe we can make a start on tidying the garden. Whatever happens with the planning, that needs to be done.'

'Says the man who doesn't garden,' she reminded him with a smile.

'Just tell me what's a weed and what isn't.'

'I don't necessarily want to get rid of the weeds. They're good host plants for caterpillars.'

'I can follow directions,' he said.

She frowned. 'You'd take directions from me?'

'Where you have more knowledge and experience than I do, of course.' He looked surprised. 'It would be very stupid not to.'

She really, *really* had to stop assuming he would behave like Barney and want to be in charge all the time. 'All right,' she said. 'Maybe I can ask Ruth and her husband to come and help us at the weekend.'

'And I could ask Kit and his wife,' he said.

Meaning they'd be meeting each other's best friends.

It was another step forward in their relationship, letting each other that tiny bit closer.

Would Kit like her? Would Ruth approve of him? What if they didn't like each other? If their closest friends didn't think they were right for each other, there was a good chance that their families wouldn't, either. And Alice didn't intend to repeat her mistake of not being accepted by her partner's friends.

In the end, Hugo arranged for them all to meet at Rosemary's house to spend the day working on the garden, following up with a barbecue at Hugo's house in the evening.

Alice was already busy working in the garden when Kit and Jenny arrived.

'Nice to meet you, my fellow countrywoman,' Kit said, greeting her with a hug. He reminded Alice of her uncles, with his broad Yorkshire accent and his ready smile, and she warmed to him immediately.

She was just making coffee when Ruth and Andy arrived. Once the introductions were done, Alice asked, 'So do you all want a tour of the house and the garden before we start work?'

At everyone's nod, she led them through into the house. 'We're moving Rosemary's study upstairs, and arranging it so it looks like it would've done in Viola's day,' she said. 'The other rooms on the upper floor will be teaching areas and a library. Downstairs, we'll keep the kitchen for making refreshments, though we'll need to tweak it a bit, and the dining room will be the cafe. Rosemary's study will be the shop, and the living room will be an exhibition area.'

'Is that a William Moorcroft tea set on the dresser?' Ruth asked when they were back down in the kitchen.

'It is,' Hugo confirmed. 'And I'll make you a cup of tea in it later.'

'Seriously? You do know it qualifies as artwork in its own right and it's—'

'—worth quite a lot of money,' Hugo finished with a smile. 'Yes. But my great-aunt believed in using things rather than saving them for best.'

Ruth picked up a cup. 'This is stunning. I love the colours. I've never actually touched any of his work before. This is such a privilege.' She smiled at Hugo. 'Thank you.'

In the garden, Alice showed them the areas they were going to tidy up and the bits they were planning to re-wild; Hugo explained where the butterfly house was going to be and showed them the plans.

'This is going to be amazing,' Andy said.

'*If* we get planning permission,' Alice said. 'If we don't...'

Hugo rested a hand on her shoulder. 'Then we'll keep submitting plans until we make it work. And we'll get public opinion on our side—like your crowdfunding thing. Emma's best friend is in PR, so maybe we can talk her into helping.'

Over the course of the day, Alice thoroughly enjoyed working with Kit and Jenny, chatting to them about what she was trying to achieve with the garden. 'I want it to help children to connect with nature, and maybe take some of the ideas back to their school or even their home. Although not everyone has access to the garden—I only have plants on the windowsill of my flat—even a plant in the window can help.'

'I'd like to see more butterflies and bees in our garden,' Jenny said. 'Maybe you and Hugo could come for dinner one night and you can give me some advice?'

'I'd love that,' Alice said.

'I'd love that, too. It might distract her from the guerrilla gardening at my house,' Hugo said.

'Guerrilla gardening?' Ruth asked.

'My neat, square garden seems to sprout a new plant every time Alice visits,' Hugo explained. 'She started with these big white daisies, and then...' He shook his head sorrowfully. 'They just seem to pop up from nowhere. Triffids, the lot of them.'

'He means lavender, salvia and white cosmos. But they're easy to look after,' Alice said. 'Think how many bees and butterflies you've seen in your garden since I sneaked the flowers in, Hugo.' She gave him a hopeful look. 'It would be even better if you had a tiny wild corner.'

'Which translates as unrestrained nettles,' Hugo grumbled.

'And thistles,' Alice added cheerfully. 'Which is why we've got them here in Rosemary's garden. The emerging caterpillars can't travel far so they need good host plants.'

'You're actually making that horrible square of his into a proper garden?' Jenny asked. At Alice's nod, she beamed. 'Good.'

'You're all ganging up on me,' Hugo mock complained.

'I'm going to make tea. Even though none of you deserve any.'

'I'll help,' Ruth offered.

'Thank you, Alice,' Kit said when Hugo left the garden. 'It's good to have my best friend back. He's been struggling for a while and the only place he seemed to function was at the office, and even there he wasn't happy. Jen and I tried to support him, but nothing we've done seemed to help. We tried to fix him up with one of her friends, to stop him being quite so lonely, but that made things worse, and...' He shook his head sadly. 'We were idiots. Thank you. You've made a huge difference to him.' He paused. 'I assume you know about Emma?'

'I do, and we're going to call the cafe after her—Emma's Kitchen,' Alice confirmed.

Kit looked pleased. 'That's so nice.'

'It must've been so hard for him, losing her like that,' Alice said.

'It broke him,' Kit agreed. 'But I think you're showing him how to put the pieces back together.'

Just as Hugo was doing for her, Alice thought. He was giving her the confidence in herself that Barney and his cronies had taken away.

At the end of the afternoon, they all headed back to Hugo's house for the barbecue.

'That's another pot for my garden, isn't it?' Hugo accused on the train to Battersea, staring at Alice's recyclable bag.

'I can't hear you. It's too loud on the Tube,' Alice said with a grin.

'I can't see a pot,' Jenny said, looking around at everything except Alice's bag.

'Me, neither,' Kit said, putting his hands over his eyes.

'What pot would that be?' Ruth asked.

Andy looked out of the window. 'No pots here, my friend.'

'Oh, for pity's sake. I give in,' Hugo said, rolling his eyes.

Kit and Alice did a fist bump, and everyone laughed.

Back at Hugo's place, Alice added the pot of lavender to the collection she'd started at the sunny edge of the patio.

'That looks amazing—so much better than that boring square of lawn,' Jenny said. 'And look! There are butterflies.'

'Plus the lavender's from Rosemary's garden. It belongs with Hugo—a family legacy sort of thing,' Alice said.

'Agreed,' Kit said. 'Now let's get this barbecue started.'

Kit and Jenny had organised the wine, Ruth and Andy had brought bread and salads, Alice had sorted out puddings and Hugo had bought meat, fish and veggie options. And it was one of the nicest evenings Alice had spent in a while, getting to know Hugo's best friends while he got to know hers.

'I like him a lot,' Ruth said in the kitchen as they were clearing away and making coffee. 'He's one of the good guys. And I like the way he treats you.' She looked Alice straight in the eye. 'I never met Barney, but I know his type. Hugo isn't like that.'

'I know,' Alice said.

'Barney?' Jenny asked.

'Ally's ex from her undergraduate days. Posh, conceited, selfish, and he treated her badly,' Ruth explained.

Jenny rolled her eyes. 'I know the type, too. Hugo's posh, but not the rest of it. He's a sweetheart. He's had a rough time—but you've made a real difference to him, Alice.'

'It's very early days,' Alice said. 'There are no guarantees.' But she was really starting to hope that this would work out. She liked the man Hugo really was—not the uptight, closed-off man she'd met at the solicitor's, but the architect who loved light and glass and space. The man who understood exactly how she felt about butterflies and listened to her ideas.

They spent the rest of the evening sitting on the patio, drinking coffee and chatting. When the others had left, Hugo walked Alice to the Tube station. 'I liked Ruth and Andy,' he said.

'Good. They liked you, too—and I liked Kit and Jenny.'

He kissed her. 'I'm glad. You made a hit with them, too.'

She stroked his face. 'That's good. I mean, I know dating someone doesn't mean you're dating their friends, but it helps if you all get on.'

'It does indeed.' He kissed her as the train came in to the station. 'See you tomorrow.'

The following weekend, Alice was starting to get antsy. 'It's been three weeks now, and we still haven't heard a thing from the planning people.'

'It doesn't necessarily mean bad news,' Hugo reassured her. 'Holiday season can slow things down.'

'What if they don't give approval?' Alice asked.

'Then we look at the reasons why they rejected the plans and tweak our application to take them into account.' He stole a kiss. 'You can wait for hours to see a butterfly, right? This is the same sort of thing. Be patient.'

She sighed. 'Sorry. I'm behaving like a spoiled brat.'

'No, you just want to get on with things. And we've got everything lined up ready for when we finally get a yes. We've got local businesses whose apprentices need a project to work on, my friend James will do the survey, and Emma's best friend Pavani is a PR specialist and she's getting together a list of possible sponsors to add to the crowdfunding you've already done.' He smiled. 'Why don't we do something tomorrow instead of working on the house or the garden?'

'Such as?'

'Go to the sea,' he said. 'I thought maybe we could go and see a rare butterfly on the South Downs on the way to the beach—the Duke of Burgundy.'

She raised her eyebrows. 'Been researching on the Internet, have we?'

He looked pleased with himself. 'Apparently it's a real conservation success.'

'It is,' she agreed. 'But unfortunately you've just missed the season where the adults fly.'

'How? It's only the middle of July.'

'It's still too late.' She smiled. 'But there are other butterflies we could go and see in Sussex. Marbled Whites, Gatekeepers, maybe a Purple Emperor.'

'You're on. I'll drive,' he said. 'We can see the butterflies in the morning, paddle in the sea and eat chips for lunch, and have afternoon tea on the way back to London.'

'That sounds like the perfect day,' she said. 'I'd really like that.'

He stole a kiss. 'I'll pick you up at seven-thirty.'

'Are you sure you want to drive? Wouldn't you rather nap in the car?' Just to hammer the point home, she hooted softly at him.

'Sussex isn't as far as Norfolk so we don't have to leave quite so early. I can cope.'

'You're on,' she said. 'Remember sensible shoes and big socks.'

'Yeah, yeah.' His eyes crinkled at the corners. 'Are you this bossy with your students?'

'Absolutely,' she said. 'One of my colleagues was bitten by a tick, some years back. Because she didn't notice the rash, she didn't go to the doctor early enough. Even a

month of antibiotics didn't cure Lyme's disease, and she
was really ill for a couple of years. It's as debilitating as
chronic fatigue syndrome. She still can't work full time,
and it's so frustrating for her.'

'Point taken,' he said. 'Sensible shoes, big socks, and
I'll see you at seven-thirty.'

CHAPTER EIGHT

HUGO PICKED ALICE up at seven-thirty, as arranged, and they drove to the South Downs. Alice thoroughly enjoyed wandering hand in hand across the footpaths with him, spotting butterflies, and the highlight of her morning was photographing a cluster of Purple Emperors.

'I thought you were teasing about them being purple,' Hugo said. 'They're stunning.'

'Aren't they just?'

From the Downs, they headed to the sea and strolled across the pebbly beach, eating hot, crispy chips.

'I hardly ever go to the sea,' Alice said. 'It's a long way for a day trip. Though when I was small we used to go and stay in Whitby every summer. I'd spend hours beach-combing with Grandad, finding fossils and bits of jet and amber, and we'd eat fish and chips on the cliffs, trying to avoid the seagulls.'

'Living in London, the quickest beach for us to go to was Brighton,' Hugh said. 'I was fascinated by the Pavilion and the pier, but I was always a bit disappointed that the beach was stony. My mother's parents lived in Suffolk, and I loved going to visit them because they lived near this enormous sandy beach and I could spend hours and hours searching for shells and building sandcastles.'

'So what kind of sandcastle does an architect build?' she asked.

'Traditional. Moat, four towers with a flag made of twigs and seaweed, a drawbridge lined with shells, and windows of sea-glass.'

She could just imagine Hugo as a small, intense child, searching for shells and sea-glass to fill his bucket, then making his sandcastle; it made her heart feel as if it had done a backflip.

'So what kind of sandcastle does a butterfly expert build?' he asked.

'Rather less elaborate than yours,' she said with a grin. 'But my gran always went to the beach with flags in her handbag, made from cocktail sticks and pictures she'd cut out of magazines. There were butterflies for me, ponies for my cousin who loved horses, and kittens for my cousin who loved cats.'

'It sounds brilliant,' he said. 'Are you all still close?'

She nodded. 'Grandad's no longer with us, but everyone else is. They all think I'm a bit weird, because I'm the only one in the family who went to uni. My Uncle Jack makes the same terrible joke every single time he sees me about Dr Alice diagnosing someone with butterflies in their tummies, but he doesn't mean any harm by it.'

'It must be nice having a big family,' Hugo said.

'It is. I had a "blink and you'll miss it" spot on a Sunday evening TV programme, last spring. Mum told everyone, and I guess it was a good excuse for a family gathering because she made me come home for the weekend, and everyone came over to ours to watch it and eat cake and drink bubbly.' And Alice had been moved to tears by the pride on their faces as they'd nudged each other and cheered when her face had flashed up on the TV screen.

'That's so nice,' he said.

'I love my family. And I need to make more effort to go up to Yorkshire, because my flat's too small for more than a couple of people to stay at a time.' And maybe, just maybe she could ask Hugo to join her.

Maybe.

Because it was still early days, and she didn't want to get her family all excited at the idea of her finally settling down, when she still didn't know exactly where this thing between herself and Hugo was going.

'So—afternoon tea,' he said when they were back at the car. 'My mother makes the best scones ever, and my father's got some photos and documents he thought you might be interested in.'

When it registered with her, Alice went cold. 'We're going to see your parents?'

'For afternoon tea.' He frowned. 'That's OK, isn't it?

Oh, help. They'd met each other's best friends and it had been fine, but she wasn't sure she was quite ready to meet his parents.

'Alice? What's wrong?'

'I, um…just wasn't expecting this.'

'They're not going to give you a hard time about Rosemary's house,' he said, taking her hand and squeezing it. 'I was always the one in guard dog mode, and I'm on your side. Pa's thrilled about Viola's biography and the journals, and I know he and Ma would love to hear about your plans for the garden.'

What would they think of the scruffy scientist with the messy hair and faded jeans? Hugo came from a posh family. Would they expect cashmere and pearls, the way Barney's family had? Alice remembered the whispers she hadn't been supposed to hear, the disapproval.

Really, Barney, couldn't you have found someone better?

And, although Alice didn't think that Hugo's parents would mock her behind her back, the way Barney's social set had, she was worried that they'd be disappointed in her.

'Uh-huh,' she said, but she was quiet all the way to the

village where the Greys lived. And she was quieter still when she realised that they lived in an old rectory—an enormous place at the end of a really, really long driveway.

You don't belong here, oik.

The words echoed in her head, spinning round and round.

'Alice?' Hugo asked.

Belatedly, she realised he'd parked the car. She had no idea what he'd said to her or how long he'd been waiting for an answer.

'Sorry. Bit of a headache,' she fibbed. And then she had to support the lie by hunting in her handbag for paracetamol.

With every step across the gravel, she felt worse. An impostor. The girl from t'pit; the oik from the council estate. The Northern version of Eliza Doolittle.

The front door opened and Hugo's parents came out to greet them, a small black and white cocker spaniel with a madly waving tail following at their heels.

'Ma, Pa, this is Dr Alice Walters,' Hugo said.

Right now he sounded even posher than he did in London, and it worried Alice. Was this who Hugo really was?

'So nice to meet you, Dr Walters—or may we call you Alice?' Hugo's mother asked, holding out her hand in welcome to shake Alice's.

'Alice, please,' Alice said.

'I'm Serena, and this is Charles.'

'Pleased to meet you,' Alice said, shaking his hand too.

'And this is Soo.' Serena gestured to the little dog. 'Do you mind dogs, Alice?'

'No, I like them,' Alice said. At least that was one thing they had in common. She bent down to make a fuss of the dog, who immediately threw herself onto her back and waved an imperious paw to indicate that she wanted a tummy-rub.

'I've put the kettle on,' Serena said.

Just as Alice's own mother would have done; that forced the voice in Alice's head, which was yammering that she didn't belong here, to drop down a notch in volume.

'Hello, darling.' Serena wrapped her arms round Hugo, who hugged her back and greeted his father just as warmly.

'I'm so thrilled you're writing Viola's biography, Alice. I always loved those trays of butterflies in Rosemary's study,' Charles said. 'I've been digging through the family archives and I've found some things that might be useful for you.'

Alice noticed that Charles' breathing was a little ragged. Was this what Hugo had meant when he'd said his father was unwell?

'Come and sit down, Alice,' Serena urged. 'It's lovely in the garden right now. Would you prefer tea or coffee?'

'I like both, but please don't feel you have to wait on me. Let me help,' Alice said.

Serena patted her arm. 'Charles is dying to show you what he found. But I'll say yes to some help later.'

This wasn't a rejection, Alice reminded herself. 'OK. Thank you.'

Charles had a box sitting on the table on the patio. 'Viola's letters—that is, letters people wrote to her,' he said. 'I've sorted them into bundles from the writers in date order. I thought they might be useful for the biography, so you can borrow them for as long as you need.'

'Thank you—that's wonderful,' Alice said.

'And there are photographs, some of which might be duplicates of Rosemary's,' Charles added. 'Feel free to use anything that works for the book.'

'That's really kind,' Alice said. 'I didn't realise we were dropping in to see you today, or I would've brought my file of photographs for you to look through, too. But I'll be happy to bring them down at any time over the sum-

mer.' She glanced quickly through the contents of the box.
'These are wonderful. Thank you so much. I'll credit you
with anything I use.'

Charles looked pleased.

Soo was clearly Serena's shadow, and her reappear-
ance heralded Hugo's mother arriving with a tray of tea.

'I'm sorry we didn't meet before, Alice,' Serena said.
'Rosemary clearly thought a lot of you, as she entrusted
Viola's biography and journals to you.'

'I thought a lot of her,' Alice said. 'My condolences on
your loss.'

'I saw you at the funeral,' Charles said. 'In the background.'

Alice nodded. 'I wanted to pay my respects—but, given
what was happening at the time, I didn't want to make
things awkward for your family.'

'That's very thoughtful,' Serena said. 'But Hugo's reassured us about what you're both planning to do with the
house—turning it into an education centre and a museum.'

'Named after both Viola and Rosemary,' Alice said.
'Though we're still waiting to hear from the planning people.'

'This is what the butterfly house will look like, if the
plans go through,' Hugo said, taking out his phone and
showing his parents photographs of his sketches.

'The doors remind me of the Palm House at Kew,'
Charles said. 'You fell in love with the place when Rosemary took you there. So did I, when I was a boy.'

'So will you have butterflies there all year round?' Serena asked.

'Yes—we'll have tropical butterflies, and we'll buy the
pupae from sustainable farmers,' Alice explained. 'The
English ones will be in the re-wilded garden during the
spring and summer.'

Serena and Charles were interested in everything she

had to say about the re-wilding; finally, Serena asked, 'So can you recommend things we can do here to attract more butterflies?'

Hugo groaned. 'Ma, I know where this is going. Don't let Alice talk you into giving her pots of stuff for my garden.'

'If you mean that abomination of a square outside your patio, I'd be more than happy to donate pots of stuff,' Serena retorted.

Alice grinned. 'You're out-womanned here, Hugo.'

'Indeed. Come and see the garden, Alice. We'll leave the men to their tea and we can talk about plants.' Serena stood up, tucked her arm through Alice's, and led her further into the garden.

'At least Charles will sit down and rest with Hugo there to talk to him. He has COPD,' Serena said, when they were out of earshot. 'When he overdoes things he struggles to breathe. And then he gets cross. But will he sit down and rest?'

'That's hard,' Alice said sympathetically. 'My grandfather—the one who was a miner—had emphysema, so I know what it's like.'

'Men never listen.' Serena rolled her eyes. 'I also wanted to thank you, without embarrassing Hugo. It's the happiest I've seen him look in nearly three years, and when he's talked to me about the butterfly house he's been designing for Rosemary's garden it's the first time he's sounded enthusiastic about a project since—' She stopped and bit her lip. 'I assume he's told you?'

'About Emma? Yes, he has,' Alice reassured her. 'It must've been so hard for all of you.'

'It was,' Serena confirmed, looking sad. 'And I've worried about Hugo every day ever since. He shuts himself away, and it's so hard to reach him. There's nothing I can do or say that will help. But you—since he's met you, he's sounded so much better. The light's back in his eyes. He doesn't look defeated all the time.' She grimaced. 'I apologise for being an interfering mother and making him bring you here. I just wanted to meet the woman who's brought my son back into the world again, so I could say thank you.'

'Hugo and I are very different,' Alice warned.

'That's a good thing. It means you'll broaden each other's horizons instead of living in an echo chamber.'

No censure. No discreetly rolled eyes about Alice having the wrong accent and the wrong background. Here, she was accepted for who she was. Whatever barriers she and Hugo might face in the future, his family wouldn't be one of them. She wouldn't have to pretend she was somebody she wasn't. And it felt as if a huge weight had been rolled off her chest, letting her breathe normally again.

Alice thoroughly enjoyed wandering round the garden with Serena and Soo, making suggestions of dog-friendly plants for particular corners and tiny tweaks that would encourage butterflies and bees.

'I have to confess, I do have a gardener,' Serena said.

Hugo's parents were posh enough to have a gardener?

Maybe Alice's uneasiness showed in her expression, because Serena grimaced and waggled her fingers. 'Arthritis stops me doing as much as I'd like to do, and Charles has brown fingers, not green. And I couldn't bear to be without a garden. So this was the compromise. Jacob lives in the village. He does all the stuff that makes my hands hurt, but he's all about the vegetable patch and he's terribly sniffy about my flowers.' She smiled. 'I had to bully him into letting me have a herb garden. But even he admits that home-made pesto is the best.'

It sounded, Alice thought, as if Serena and her gardener were good friends and bantered together a lot. So it wasn't the same sort of thing as the way Barney's family had looked down on their domestic staff.

'How would Jacob feel about you having a wild corner in the garden?' she asked.

'He'll stomp about, muttering about slugs,' Serena said. 'And we'll have a huge fight about the damage caterpillars would do to the cabbages.'

Alice smiled. 'I'll send you all the figures so you can guilt him into it.'

'Done,' Serena said. 'Now, if you wouldn't mind doing the cuttings yourself, you can have whatever you like for Hugo's garden.'

'Some of your honeysuckle,' Alice said promptly. 'I'd like some for Rosemary's garden as well, please.'

'Of course. Come to the potting shed.' Serena grinned. 'I know where Jacob keeps the spare key. Third stone from the left.'

Alice retrieved the key, and between them they sorted out some pots and some cuttings.

'So Hugo's actually letting you redo his garden?' Serena asked.

'I'm not giving him any choice,' Alice said. 'I brought lavender from Rosemary's garden, and Kit and Jenny are giving me some plants from their garden next week. That horrible minimalist square is going to be a riot of colour by the time I've finished with it. Kit's going to keep him distracted while Jenny and I sneak in and plant some spring bulbs. He'll complain about it, but secretly he loves it. You can see it in his eyes.'

Serena's eyes filled with tears. 'Emma would have liked you so, so much.' She hugged Alice. 'I'm not going to say any more now. We'll go and make afternoon tea.'

But Alice felt *accepted*. And that made all the difference in the world. Instead of worrying that she was going to say or do the wrong thing, she could relax and just be herself. And it made her hope that she and Hugo really had the chance of a future together.

Serena insisted on both of them taking scones and cake back to London, and the goodbye hug that Hugo's parents gave Alice was very warm indeed.

'Sorry I sprang that visit on you,' Hugo said, once they were out of the village.

'That's the biggest "sorry, not sorry" I've ever heard,' she retorted.

'What, like the one you're about to say about being sorry you raided my mother's garden to put more pots into mine?' he asked archly.

'I'm not sorry about *that* in the slightest,' she said. 'Honeysuckle is one of life's pleasures. If I had a balcony, I'd have a pot of it for there, too.'

He laughed. 'At least you're honest about it.' He paused. 'My parents liked you very much.'

'I liked them, too,' Alice said. And she intended to suggest a field trip to Yorkshire later in the summer so Hugo could meet her family, too. Because now she was confident they'd like each other.

CHAPTER NINE

ON MONDAY, ALICE came home from the university to discover an official-looking envelope in the post. The last time she'd opened an envelope with that particular return address, it had been bad news. Would it be different, this time?

This was so ridiculous. She was far from being a coward, and she'd never been afraid of getting exam results. Then again, she'd always had a good idea how she'd performed in exams. This was all completely out of her control—and of Hugo's. She had absolutely no clue whether the planners were going to say yes or whether the letter would contain another rejection.

She rang Hugo. 'Are you super-busy?'

'Just wrestling with some figures,' he said. 'What's up?'

'I think I've got a letter from the planning people.'

'What does it say?'

'I haven't opened it, yet,' she admitted.

'Why?'

'Because I'm terrified they're going to turn us down.'

'Hang up and I'll video-call you,' he said, 'so then we can open it together. Sort of.'

She ended the call, and he video-called her back.

'Shall I hold the phone so you can see the letter?' she asked.

'For you to show me the whole letter on a phone screen

I'd need a magnifying glass to read it this end,' he said. 'Just open it and read it out loud.'

She undid the flap and took out the contents.

'OK. "Dear Dr Walters, Thank you for your revised planning application—"' She stopped, because she couldn't quite take in the next line.

'Alice? Is everything all right?'

'Yes.' Dazedly, she looked at him on the screen.

'Did they say yes or no?'

'They said—' and she still couldn't quite believe it '—yes.'

He whooped. 'Brilliant! We are so going out to celebrate tonight. If you call Ruth, I'll call Kit, and dinner's my shout. I'll call you in ten minutes.'

But when he called back, they both had bad news. 'Jenny's got a work thing tonight.'

'And Ruth's doing a lecture as part of the university's community project,' she said. 'Our celebratory dinner will have to be another night.'

'We'll have two celebrations, then—because I think this sort of news deserves champagne right now. You, me, a takeaway and my back garden tonight?' he suggested.

'OK. You organise the takeaway and I'll bring the champagne,' she said.

'Perfect. What sort of takeaway?'

'Anything. But just remember pizza only comes as thin crust.'

'Pizza and champagne works for me. See you at seven?'

'I'll be there.'

Although she didn't bother dressing up, Alice changed into clean jeans and a T-shirt. At seven precisely, she arrived at Hugo's house with a bottle of champagne she'd bought from the supermarket chiller cabinet and a pot. 'Celebratory scabious,' she informed him, handing him the pot of pink wildflowers.

'You made that up,' he accused.

'Your point is...?' She spread her hands, laughing.

He laughed back, and kissed her. 'It could've been worse, I suppose. Celebratory nettles.'

'Now that's an excellent idea.'

'We've had this conversation. You are *not* filling my garden with nettles.'

'A tiny pond?' she suggested.

'No.' But she noticed he was smiling when he added the pot to his growing collection. And she also noticed that he had a watering can. A posh metal one, painted green, with a gold-coloured watering rose. She coughed. 'Well, look at that. Been shopping, have we?'

'No. Ma had it delivered to the office this morning, with instructions about how to water the pots,' he said.

'Good, because virgin gardeners should absolutely not choose a watering can without help. Your mum knows what she's doing, so the rose will work.'

'You're putting roses in my garden now?'

'A rose is the thing on the end of the can that does the watering, as I'm sure you know perfectly well. Given that your mum loves her garden and so did Rosemary, I'm calling you on pretending to know a lot less than you really do.'

'Maybe,' he said. 'I like watching you be bossy.'

She had no answer to that, so she kissed him.

There were two glasses and a wine cooler waiting on the patio table; Hugo opened the champagne.

'I want to make a toast,' he said. 'To Viola, who studied butterflies; to Rosemary, who kept all her papers and loved butterflies enough to give us her garden; and to us, because we're going to make the butterfly house happen.'

'To Viola, Rosemary and us,' Alice echoed. 'And to the butterflies.'

After the pizza was delivered and they'd eaten it, followed by the posh salted caramel ice cream and raspberries Hugo supplied for pudding, they continued to sit in the garden, holding hands and talking while the light faded. Finally, Alice started yawning. 'Sorry. My lark tendencies are kicking in. I'd better head for the Tube.'

He met her gaze. 'Or you could stay here tonight.'

Her heart skipped a beat. 'In your spare room?' she checked.

His cobalt-blue eyes were intense. 'Or in my room. With me.'

Stay the night.

Take their relationship to the next level.

Alice wanted to; yet, at the same time, it scared her. This was a big step. They'd gone from hand-holding to dating, to meeting each other's best friends and in her case meeting his family; so far, they'd negotiated all the tricky moments. But this... This was something that could bring them closer together—or it could show just how big the gap was between them.

She didn't think Hugo would deliberately hurt her, the way her exes had, but was he really ready for this? Were they rushing things? Worry made her mouth feel as dry as if they'd been drinking vinegar instead of champagne. She knew she had to be brave and ask the difficult question. 'What about Emma?'

'Emma didn't live here. She never even saw this house,' he said. 'None of the furniture is stuff we chose together. Everything in this house was a fresh start for me.' His fingers tightened briefly round hers. 'You're the only woman I've dated since she died, and the only woman who's been here apart from my mother and a couple of close friends and colleagues.'

She stroked his face, knowing she'd put pressure on a soul-deep bruise. 'Thank you. I just didn't want you to think I'm trying to...' She paused, wanting to find a kind way to say it, except there wasn't one. 'Trying to take her place,' she said in the end.

'I know you're not.' He kissed her lightly. 'And there are no strings. I don't have any condoms, and I don't expect you to have sex with me. But, if you'd like to, tonight I want to go to sleep with you in my arms and wake up with you tomorrow.'

No pressure. No demands. No expectations.

An intimacy that, in some ways, was deeper than just the mechanics of sex.

He'd told her what he wanted. Now she could be brave enough to admit the same. 'I don't have any condoms, either, but I'd like to go to sleep in your arms and wake up with you.'

His kiss was so slow and so sweet that it brought tears to her eyes.

'I'll sort out the laundry overnight,' he said. 'There's a spare new toothbrush in the bathroom. Leave whatever you want washed outside the door, and I'll leave you a T-shirt to sleep in.'

'Thank you.' She loved the fact that he was so organised and so matter-of-fact about things. He'd made it easy.

When she peeked outside the bathroom door, clad only in a towel, there was a plain black T-shirt folded neatly on the floor, large enough to work as a makeshift nightshirt.

Shyness threatened to engulf her, but she put it on and walked into his bedroom.

It was very plain and minimalist, as she'd expected. The bed had a black wrought-iron headboard; the bedding was in tones of blue and grey, matching the curtains. The floor was of sanded boards with a rug next to the bed in the same tones of blue and grey. There was no artwork on the walls, and nothing on top of the chest of drawers except a phone charger.

He was sitting on the end of the bed, looking at something on his phone.

'Thank you for sorting everything out,' she said.

'You're very welcome.' He looked up at her with a smile. 'If you'll excuse me, I'll use the bathroom. Choose whichever side of the bed works best for you. Oh, and just in case you need a phone charger.' He gestured to the dressing table. 'There's a socket either side of the bed.'

She waited until he'd left the room before choosing the right side of the bed and plugging in her phone. Maybe this hadn't been a great idea. Maybe she should've gone home. This was a new level of intimacy, and she wasn't completely sure either of them was ready for it.

Her worries must've shown on her face, because when he came back into the room he sat on his side of the bed, drew her hand to his mouth, kissed her palm and folded her fingers over the kiss. 'No pressure,' he said softly. 'You can use the spare room if you're more comfortable. Or I can.'

'No, I want to. But it's been a while since either of us has done this,' she said.

'It feels weird,' he agreed. 'But I'm glad you're here.'

And that conviction melted some of her worries. 'Me, too.'

He climbed properly into the bed, switched off the light and drew her into his arms. 'No pressure,' he said again.

'No pressure,' she whispered. She brushed her mouth against his, and her lips tingled to the point where she couldn't resist doing it again. And again.

'Alice.' He drew her closer and kissed her back.

Kissing led to touching. Exploring. Discovering where a touch could elicit a sigh of pleasure or a murmur of desire. Her shyness melted away in the dark, and she matched him kiss for kiss, touch for touch.

'I can't do quite everything I want to do,' he whispered, 'but if you'll let me...'

'Yes,' she whispered back, and allowed him to strip the borrowed T-shirt from her, just as she allowed her to remove his pyjamas.

She discovered that Hugo was a generous lover, arousing her with his hands and his mouth until she was breathless, and then pushing her further until she climaxed and shattered in his arms.

Afterwards, he drew her close, so her head was resting on his shoulder and her arm was wrapped round him.

When she was finally able to collect her thoughts, she said, 'Thank you. But this isn't fair. You're...' Left on the edge, unfulfilled, while she was languorous and sated.

He kissed her lightly. 'It's fine. Next time. And in the meantime I'm going to do complicated equations in my head. Go to sleep, my lark.'

'This feels horribly selfish.'

'Tomorrow,' he said, 'you can make it up to me. Any way you please.'

Which put all sorts of pictures in her head. 'Tomorrow,' she promised.

The warmth of his skin against hers and the darkness of the room pushed her swiftly into sleep.

Hugo lay awake when Alice had turned onto her side, spooned against her. Part of him felt guilty; even though he'd made his peace with Emma, this was the first time he'd made love with someone since she'd gone. And it was weird to be sharing his space again instead of lying there, thinking how big and empty the bed felt. Weird, but comforting as well.

Even though he hadn't reached his own release, he was glad Alice had agreed to stay. He'd enjoyed touching her, the way she'd responded to him.

He liked Alice, full stop. More than liked her. If he was honest with himself, he was halfway to falling in love with her. Since she'd burst into his life, as brightly as one of her butterflies, he'd felt lighter of spirit than he had for years. Instead of just existing, he was connecting with the world again. And it felt really, really good.

He had a feeling that someone had hurt her badly in the past; she'd said her exes had wanted to change her. But maybe he could help her past that, the way she was helping him to move forward again. Maybe she'd trust him and open up enough to tell him what was holding her back, and he could help her feel differently about the situation—make her see just what an amazing woman she was.

The next morning, Alice woke, slightly disorientated; then she remembered the previous night.

She was in Hugo's bed.

And he was spooned against her, his arm wrapped round her waist.

She started to twist round and was about to wake him with a kiss, when he murmured, 'Go back to sleep, Emma.'

Emma.

He thought she was Emma.

She swallowed hard. Whatever Hugo had said about wanting to move on, subconsciously he clearly wasn't ready. He was still in love with his late wife; and Alice was making a huge mistake, letting herself fall for an unavailable man. Not one who wanted to change her, this time, but one who wished she were someone else.

And it hurt so much. She'd tried to resist him but over the last few days she'd let herself fall for him. She'd let herself believe that this time love would work out for her; but she'd been so very, very wrong. This wasn't like Barney and his callousness—Hugo wasn't the sort to ride roughshod over other people—but if anything it hurt more because she knew she could never be what Hugo really wanted. She wasn't the woman he'd loved for most of his adult life. She wasn't *enough*.

How was she going to deal with this?

The first thing she needed to do was to collect her clothes, get dressed, and leave Hugo's house before he woke. Give herself some space to think and work out what to say, so she didn't hurt him: but she knew she couldn't be with him until he was *really* ready to move on.

Given that he wasn't a morning person, she hoped that also meant he was a heavy sleeper.

Tentatively, she wriggled out of his arms, then climbed out of the bed. His discarded T-shirt—the one he'd peeled off her, the night before—was on the floor. She slipped it on, took her phone off charge, and managed to tiptoe downstairs without waking him. Once she'd retrieved her clothes from his washer-dryer, she dressed swiftly and wrote him a note, which she propped against his coffee machine.

Had an early meeting.
Will return your T-shirt later.
A

And then she quietly let herself out of his house.

Hugo woke when his alarm shrilled; and then he realised something was wrong.

Alice wasn't beside him.

Had he dreamed last night?

No, because the pillow was rumpled.

Tentatively, he slid his arm across her side of the bed. The sheet was cold, so clearly she'd been gone for a while.

Maybe she was downstairs and had just let him sleep in? After all, she was a lark.

But, when he went downstairs, he discovered that the house was empty.

There was a note propped against his coffee machine. He read it and frowned. It was very businesslike and left him feeling that something had gone very wrong between himself and Alice, but he had no idea what or why.

He tried calling her, but her phone went to voicemail. Maybe she really was in a meeting and it hadn't been a polite excuse. But, when she didn't reply to his message by lunchtime he texted her.

Busy tonight? Think Kit and Jenny are free for our celebratory dinner, if Ruth and Andy are?

The reply came within five minutes.

Sorry, can't. Have a departmental thing tonight.

That definitely felt like an excuse. She hadn't mentioned anything to him about a departmental thing yesterday, when they'd talked about celebrating the planning decision.

He decided to ask her outright.

Is everything OK? Have I done something to upset you?

Instead of texting back, she called him. 'Hi.'

'Are you OK?' he asked.

'Yes. Are you?'

But she sounded distant. Polite. 'What's wrong?' he asked.

She sighed. 'You and me—I think we need to move things back a step.'

What? Last night—he'd felt a real connection with her. He was so sure she'd felt the same. 'Why?'

'Because I don't think you're ready to move on with anyone else, right now,' she said.

But he was. He'd *told* her he was. 'Why?' he asked, confused.

'Because you called me Emma,' she said.

'What?' For a moment, shock paralysed his vocal cords. He swallowed hard. 'I'm sorry. I really didn't mean to do that.' But he didn't remember doing it. 'When?'

'This morning.'

He frowned. 'I didn't speak to you this morning. You were gone before I woke.'

'First thing. When I woke. You were still pretty much asleep.'

'Then how did I…?'

'You told me to go back to sleep. And you called me Emma.'

Her voice was very calm, very even, and he didn't have a clue what was going through her head—though he was pretty sure he'd hurt her. 'I'm sorry,' he said again. 'I didn't mean to do that.'

'I know you didn't. But you called me by her name. That tells me you still haven't fully come to terms with losing her. So I think for now it's better that we stick to being colleagues.'

'Alice, I… This…' She wasn't being fair. She'd said herself that he'd been half asleep. But getting angry about it wasn't going to solve the problem. He needed to prove to her that she'd got this wrong. That he did want her. Yet, right now, she was wary and skittish, and it was important that he didn't push her even further away. He raked a hand through his hair. 'That's not what I want.'

'You're still in love with Emma, which is completely understandable, but it's also not fair to either of us. So it's better for us to be just colleagues.'

No, it wasn't. At all. But she'd really got the wrong end

of the stick and he needed time to regroup and work out just how he could convince her of the truth. 'Are we still celebrating the planning decision with Kit and Ruth?'

'Of course.'

And he'd just bet that she'd make sure she was sitting as far away from him as possible at dinner and would make an excuse to leave before everyone else.

'Let me know dates and times,' he said, 'and I'll arrange something.' And work out how to persuade her to give him another chance.

It was Friday night when he finally got to see her again. Just as he'd predicted, she sat as far away from him as possible. And she was really, really quiet. So quiet that Ruth followed him when he went to the bar to order another bottle of wine.

'What's happened between you and Alice? If you've hurt—'

'Yes, I have hurt her,' he cut in, 'and I've apologised. It wasn't intentional. And, actually, it's hurt both of us.'

Ruth frowned. 'What happened?'

'She stayed with me on Monday night. I'm rubbish in the mornings. You don't get any sense out of me until after my second cup of coffee. I called her Emma's name when I was still half asleep and I didn't even realise I'd done it. She told me, later in the day, and called it off between us.' He blew out a breath. 'She says I'm not ready to move on. I *am*. But she doesn't believe me, and I don't know how to fix it.'

Ruth's eyes widened. 'I had no idea.'

'Is that something that's happened to her before? She said something about her exes wanting to change her. Was it someone who wanted to make her into a carbon copy of his ex or something?' He shook his head in frustration. 'Because I don't want to do that. I know she's not Emma. She's herself, and that's just the way I want her. I want my nerdy scientist with her mad hair and her amazing facts and the way she sees the world.'

'Then find a way to tell her,' Ruth said.

'That's the problem,' Hugo pointed out. 'She's avoiding me. She doesn't answer my calls—she just texts me to say she's busy with a departmental thing, and I know it's not true. What do I have to do to get her to talk to me? Dress up as a butterfly?'

Ruth's mouth twitched at the corners. 'That might be fun.'

'But it wouldn't get her to see that I lo—' He stopped mid-word as it hit him.

He loved Alice.

And it felt as if he'd just fallen off a cliff, because he didn't know how she felt about him. Only that she'd backed away, which made him think that maybe she didn't feel the same way as him.

'That you...?' Ruth prompted.

He shook his head. 'Sorry to be rude, but it's something I want to talk to her about before I talk to anyone else.' And that was the problem. Getting her to talk to him. 'But I need to find a way to persuade her to talk to me.'

'For what it's worth,' Ruth said, 'I think you're good for each other. She's blossomed since she's been with you.'

'Thank you. I think. But I need more practical help, Ruth. I need to find out what really worries her, so I can talk it through with her and find a solution that works.' He looked at her. 'I won't ask you to break her confidence, and to be honest I think she needs to tell me herself. Can you get her to talk to me?'

'I don't know,' Ruth admitted. 'You need the equivalent of nectar guides.'

Nectar guides. The thing that attracted butterflies.

Alice wasn't a butterfly, but there was something to do with butterflies that he knew—at least, *hoped*—would attract her and get her to talk to him. 'Of course. You're a genius.' He hugged her. 'Thank you.'

'What are you going to do?' Ruth asked.

'Arrange nectar guides,' he said. At her mystified expression, he added, 'I'll explain later.'

Alice was quietly polite for the rest of the evening, and Hugo excused himself early. As soon as he was out of earshot, he rang his mother.

'Ma, where can I buy nettle seeds?'

'Nettle seeds?' Serena sounded surprised. 'I have no idea. Who would want to buy nettle seeds?'

He did. Desperately. 'If I can't get seeds, where can I get the plants?'

'Why?'

He explained the situation and what he planned to do.

'That's *incredibly* romantic,' she said. 'Leave it with me and I'll talk to Jacob. Come down tomorrow for lunch and I'll have it sorted.'

'Thanks, Ma.' He paused. 'She's important to me.'

'I know. For what it's worth, I think this is your best shot. If your father did something like that for me…'

'Too much info, Ma,' he said, smiling. 'I love you. See you tomorrow.'

The next morning, he headed for Sussex. Last time he'd driven this way, he'd spent the day walking hand in hand with Alice on the Downs and on the beach. He'd kissed her. He'd introduced her to the people he loved most in the world, and they'd liked her. The sun had been shining, and life had felt so full of promise.

Today, it was raining. And that was oh, so appropriate.

Jacob was at the house when he arrived.

'You can buy nettle seeds,' he said. 'They take fourteen days to germinate.'

'I can't wait that long,' Hugo said.

'So your ma told me. And there are no nettles in *this* garden.'

Hugo dug his nails into his palm to contain his impatience. 'So where do I get them?'

'I've got friends at the allotments who can't stay on top of their weeds. If you want to come and take them, you're welcome.'

'We prepared seed trays for them this morning,' Serena said. 'So you'll need to put the back seat down for them.'

'Thanks, Ma.'

Hugo spent the day down at the allotments just outside the village, in the rain, weeding patches under Jacob's watchful eye and transferring small nettle plants into the seed trays. Jacob donated his second-best garden fork, spade and trowel and gave him precise instructions on how to make a flowerbed and transfer the nettles. 'I still think you're crazy, mind. Any normal person would do that with flowers. Bedding plants.'

'Trust me, she'd prefer these to bedding plants,' Hugo said.

Sunday was also pouring with rain. Hugo really didn't enjoy digging up a large corner of his lawn, or planting the tiny nettles. He was cold, wet and grumpy by the time he'd finished. And it really wasn't butterfly weather. And it didn't look quite as good as he'd hoped. In the end, he took a photograph from his bedroom window. At least from there you could see the message.

Maybe he'd miscalculated this. Big time.

Especially as now he had to talk Alice into coming here to see it. What if she said no? Then, he decided, he'd have to cheat massively and tell her it was a group thing—and swear Ruth, Andy, Kit and Jenny to secrecy and ask them to turn up an hour later than her, to give him enough time to talk to her.

A hot bath and two mugs of tea did nothing to improve his mood.

What if this wasn't enough?

What if she didn't believe him?

He was about to text her to suggest meeting up when his doorbell rang. He shoved the phone in his pocket and quelled the hope that it might be Alice. Of course it wouldn't be Alice.

James, a friend from his university days who'd qualified as a surveyor and had promised to survey Rosemary's house for nothing as a donation towards the project, was standing there. 'Sorry, Hugo, I know it's a Sunday, but I thought you'd want to know the results of the survey.'

From the expression on his friend's face, it wasn't good news. 'Come in,' he said. 'Tea, coffee or a beer?'

'Coffee, please. Though you might need gin,' James warned, and proceeded to deliver the bad news.

When James had left, Hugo called Pavani. 'Sorry to be pushy, Pav, and I know it's Sunday, but we've got a problem with the house that means we need money. Have you heard back from any of the potential sponsors?' he asked.

'I'm glad you called—yes, I have,' Pavani said. 'Something came in on Friday, and I've only just had the chance to look at what they said. I'll send the details over now so you can take a look. I can set up a meeting for whenever works for you.'

'Thank you. You're wonderful,' he said.

And then he made the call he'd intended to make, except for very different reasons.

It went straight to voicemail; he sighed inwardly. 'Alice, it's Hugo. I need to talk to you about Rosemary's house. We have good news and bad news, but we definitely need to discuss it. Please call me when you're free.'

Half an hour later, she rang. 'Hi. Sorry I didn't pick up your call earlier. What's happened?'

'Good news or bad, first?'

'Bad,' she said.

'The house has subsidence. James did the survey this morning; he hasn't written it up yet, but he came to tell me what he'd found. It's going to take time—and extra money—to fix.'

'There isn't any spare money,' she said. 'We've already allocated everything I crowdfunded and some of the grants won't come through for months.'

'That's where the good news comes in. Pav said she's found us a sponsor and she's sending the details. Would you mind coming over so we can talk about how we move forward?'

She paused for so long that he thought she was going to say no. 'OK,' she said finally. 'I'll come over now.'

CHAPTER TEN

HUGO'S HOUSE. THE place where the dreams Alice had hardly dared admit to herself had popped, empty as a bubble.

But they needed each other to finalise the butterfly house project. And right now they needed to agree on a plan to move forward with Rosemary's house.

She took the Tube over to Battersea and knocked on his door.

There were dark shadows under his eyes when he opened the door, and she felt guilty; had she done this to him, shoved him back into the shadows where he'd been for the last three years? Then again, she'd been selfish in dragging him into the light when he wasn't really ready.

This was such a mess.

He looked as miserable as she felt. She wanted to put her arms round him and tell him everything was going to be all right; but right now she didn't know if everything would be all right.

'Thanks for coming,' he said.

'You're welcome.' And how horrible it was, being reduced to formality with him. Though this was her own doing. She'd been the one to walk away.

'Coffee?'

It would be rude to refuse; plus it might help distract

her from his nearness. Give her something to do with her hands. 'Thank you.'

Once she was sitting at the table with a mug of coffee, he showed her the file James had given him. 'It's quite bad. The house needs underpinning. Although the house insurance will cover repairing the damage, it won't cover preventing future subsidence.'

She looked at James's figures and winced. 'We don't have that sort of money.'

'Which is where Pav's sponsor comes in. Apparently it's a firm of stockbrokers who want to showcase their green credentials, and they think sponsoring us will help them do that. They get their name on our website and a "sponsored by" board in our reception area, and Pav's suggested holding a special event once a quarter for their clients. I think we should accept.'

'OK. So who are they?'

He opened the file Pav had sent over.

Alice looked at it, and her vision blurred.

Rutherford and Associates, Stockbrokers Managing partner: Barney Rutherford

No.

It couldn't be.

She took a deep breath to calm herself. When she thought about it rationally, Barney wasn't an uncommon first name and Rutherford wasn't an uncommon surname.

All the same...

'Can I just check something?' she asked, picking up her phone.

'Sure.'

She quickly flicked into the firm's website, and clicked on the 'about us' section.

And there he was. Barney Rutherford. Expensive suit,

handmade shirt, silk tie. Probably the same kind of shoes that Hugo wore. A little fatter, a little less hair, but still recognisable as the man who'd hurt her so much all those years ago.

'No,' she said.

Hugo frowned. 'Sorry?'

'No. We're not taking that man's money. We'll have to find another way.'

His frown deepened. 'I don't understand. Do you know him or something?'

'Yes, and he has no moral compass whatsoever. He's not having anything to do with the butterfly house.'

'He's offering us enough to fix the house. Otherwise we might be held up for months and months.'

'I don't care.' Anger she'd suppressed for all these years felt as if it was bursting through her. 'We're not taking his money.'

'OK,' Hugo said carefully. 'But, as I can't see the problem, would you mind telling me why?'

She stared into her coffee. 'He was at Oxford when I was there. I hated my first year. Maybe I picked the wrong college, but I didn't fit in. I was the granddaughter of a coal miner and I had a funny accent. I came from a council estate instead of a country estate. I didn't go to a posh school.' She grimaced and shook her head. 'So I just got on with my work, and showed my face where I had to, but social situations were horrible. There were all these invisible tests I kept failing.

'I told myself it would be better in the second year, but it wasn't. And then Barney came up to me one day in the library. He said he'd noticed me in the quad. He wanted to go out with me. I thought it was probably some sort of joke, so I said no. But he persisted, and eventually I agreed.' She looked up at Hugo. 'And it was amazing. He made me feel as if I was special. All these girls from his background were just queuing up to date him, but he'd chosen *me*. I didn't like the people he mixed with very much, but he kind of protected me from them, and he taught me all the little social things that never occurred to me. He got me to change the way I wore my hair, the way I dressed, so I fitted in.'

It was all horribly clear to Hugo, now. He understood why Alice had been twitchy about meeting his parents, about wearing the right things. Especially as it sounded as if his background was similar to Barney's. She must've been terrified that they'd find her lacking.

'You didn't need to change who you were,' he said softly. 'There's nothing wrong with you at all.'

'I changed,' she said. 'I fitted in. And it was wonderful. I'd never been happier. I adored Barney. I really thought he was the one, and he dropped so many hints that I thought he was going to ask me to marry him at the Commemoration Ball. I got this really special dress. I actually used my overdraft, because I wanted it to be special in case he really did propose—it was something I wanted to remember for ever. It started out as the perfect evening, and even the bitchier girls in his set were nice to me.'

Hugo had a feeling that there was a 'but' coming. A seriously nasty 'but'.

'And then I overhead them talking in the toilets. They didn't know I was there. They were saying how Barney was going to win his bet; he was going to win a lot of money from his pals, that night, because he'd managed to turn the oik into one of them. I couldn't believe it. I honestly thought he loved me—but it turned out that he was mocking me as much as the others did. He was only going out with me for a bet. It was a weird kind of Eliza Doolittle thing. Make the girl from t'pit into a toff.'

She dragged in a breath. 'When I walked out of the toilet and washed my hands, the other girls were still there and

they looked horrified. I could see them mouthing frantically to each other, wondering if I'd overheard. I just ignored them and walked back into the ballroom. Barney
was talking to his friends and he didn't see me come up
behind him. But I heard what they said. It was all "tonight's
the night". Earlier, I would've thought that they knew he
was going to propose to me, but after what I'd just heard
I knew it had a different meaning.'

Hugo was shocked by how unkind Barney and his
friends had been, but he wasn't going to interrupt Alice
now. She needed to get this out of her head, once and for
all.

'I asked Barney to come outside with me—I wasn't
going to have this conversation in front of his mates. Then
I said I'd heard that he was dating me for a bet. He blus-
tered, but I could see the truth in his eyes. I asked him if
tonight was the deadline for his bet. And then he said yes.
I asked how much he was going to win. He wouldn't tell
me, and I said if he had a shred of decency he'd donate that
money to a shelter for the homeless. That I never wanted
to see him again. And then I walked out.' She bit her lip.
'I felt so stupid. So used. I thought he loved me. And all
along I'd just been a joke to him. Free sex, because I was
stupid enough to think he mattered and I gave him my
virginity—and no doubt he boasted about *that* to all his
mates, too.' She shrugged.

'The last week of term was awful. Everyone was laughing at me, at how stupid I'd been to think that someone like
Barney Rutherford would ever be serious about someone
like me. I thought about just leaving Oxford so I didn't
have to face any of them again, but that would've meant
they'd won. So instead I went to see my personal tutor
and asked if I could move college. I said it was awkward
because I'd split up with Barney, and I wanted to concentrate on my studies and not get distracted by anything

else. My tutor was lovely and told me to stay at college, and he helped me find somewhere else to live for the third year. I didn't socialise much in my last year, just focused on my work.' She lifted her chin. 'I graduated top of my year and scooped a couple of awards. But best of all I got my place to do my MA and then my PhD in London. And it was a lot better—people actually liked me for myself, here. It didn't matter where I came from.' She dragged in a breath. 'And that is why I'm not taking *anything* from Barney Rutherford.'

He took her hand. 'First off, that was a really horrible thing to do to you. I don't understand the kind of man who'd behave like that, and you really didn't deserve to be treated like that. Secondly, I think you're amazing because you rose above it all and didn't let them drive you out.'

'But did I?' she asked. 'I seem to be completely use-less at picking Mr Right. Every man I've dated since then—well, except you—has wanted to change me. It always starts off all right, but then he wants me to dress differently or do my hair differently or speak differently, or do something more girly and less scientific, or...' She shook her head. 'I think there's something wrong with me. I can't move on from being the oik who doesn't quite fit in.'

'You're not an oik,' he said.

'No? Barney and his lot were right. Appearances matter.'

'Only on a very superficial level,' he said.

'Come off it, Hugo. Look at your industry. It's about beautiful buildings.'

'But if they're beautiful and don't do their job, they're a failure,' he pointed out.

'Everyone dresses in posh suits.'

'It's a convention,' he said. 'Though, actually, if you're a really brilliant architect, you can wear odd socks and crumpled clothes and everyone will just think you're quirky.'

'Even if you've got the wrong accent and the wrong background?'

'There's no such thing as a wrong accent and a wrong background. It's what you do that matters,' he said. 'What's in your head and what's in your heart.'

Why couldn't she believe him? Why couldn't she move on?

'But even you,' she said. 'You wanted me to be something different.'

He shook his head. 'I've never asked you to change the way you dress. Actually, I happen to *like* the way you dress. You're incredibly cute. Especially with those sassy slogans on your T-shirts.'

'I don't mean that.' She looked away. 'That morning... I was so happy, when I woke in your arms. And then you called me Emma, and I knew it wasn't me you really wanted. You wanted her. And I can't be her. I just can't.'

His intake of breath was audible, and she winced. 'Sorry. I didn't mean that to sound as bad as it did.'

'It sounded bad,' he said, 'and it *is* bad, because it's not fair. Other than Emma, you're the first woman I've slept with in more than a decade. And you know I'm an owl, Alice. You can't even talk to me until I've had two cups of coffee in the morning, because I'm so not a morning person and what comes out of my mouth won't make any sense. Yes, I miss my wife. I loved her so much and we were happy together. But she *died*, Alice. She's not here any more and nobody can bring her back. She wouldn't want me to spend the rest of my life, alone and grieving— though that was exactly what I was doing until I met you. And then you started changing things. You changed the way I see things, showed me that there's still light in the world and I need to stop trudging along in my lonely little rut and reach for the sunlight. You showed me there are butterflies. That I can stop existing with boxes around me, that putting flowers everywhere makes life better.'

He stood up. 'Come with me. There's something I need to show you. And I don't care that it's raining and I don't care if you trudge mud all over my floor—or—' He waved one hand in seeming exasperation, clearly failing to find the right words. 'Oh, just come with me, Alice. Please.'

She followed him out into the garden. And then she saw what she hadn't noticed when she'd walked into his house: that the right-hand far corner of the garden wasn't a neat manicured lawn any more. He'd dug a flower bed.

'It's a flower bed,' she said.

'No. No, it isn't.' He shook his head and took her hand. 'Look closer.'

She walked across the lawn with him, and then she realised.

He'd planted *nettles*.

'You're making a wild corner.'

'It's a nectar guide. An Alice guide,' he said. 'And I got it wrong because you can't see it properly at this angle. You need to see it from my bedroom window—and I don't want to tell you to go upstairs and look at it because I don't want you to get the wrong idea.' He pulled his phone from his pocket, flicked into the photo app and selected a photo. 'Here.'

She stared at it.

The flower bed contained a heart shape. And written in nettles were the words *Hugo Loves Alice*.

'You love me,' she said in wonder.

'Yes. I love you enough to change my garden for you— and do you have any idea how hard it is to find baby nettles?'

'How did you do it?' she asked.

'I spent the whole of yesterday digging various people's allotments and taking out weeds—in the rain, and just so you know I refused to move the thistles on the ground that they're important butterfly food sources—in exchange for baby nettles,' he said. 'I brought them back from Sussex in seed trays donated by my mother. And I spent the whole of today using Jacob's second-best spade, fork and trowel to make a proper bed for them and planting them. In the rain. Because I didn't know how else to tell you how I feel.'

'You love me,' she said again, not quite taking it in.

'Yes. I love the real you. The scientist who sends me nerdy facts and teases me about my shoes and worries about ticks. The woman who has slogans on her T-shirt and mad hair. The woman who sees beauty and teaches other people how to see it, too. You're like those Morphos you showed me at the butterfly house—all quiet and hiding in the background, like they are when their wings are closed. And then you start talking about your subject, and you open up, and you're stunning—just like a Morpho flying. I can't take my eyes off you. And I'm not saying that because I've got any hidden agendas. I love you and I want to be with you. I know I messed it up and I hurt you, and I'm sorry. But I really do love you, Alice.'

'I'm sorry, too,' she said. 'I let my past get in the way. I didn't give you a chance to explain. I thought I knew best—and I don't.'

'I'm glad you realise that,' he said. 'Because I think we've got a future. Just we both need to compromise a bit.'

'Yes.' She looked at him. 'I love you, too, Hugo. Even though you're posh and you're a walking clothes horse, you're... You've shown me things, too. Beautiful structures, the way the light gets in. The way you feel about glass and staircases, that's like the way I feel about butterflies. You get me, and I get you. And I hurt you as much as you hurt me, by being proud and stubborn and too scared to take a chance on you. I'm sorry.'

'We're both going to have to work on communication, in the future,' he said. 'But, for now...' He cupped her face in his hand, dipped his head and kissed her. 'I love you,' he whispered. 'And now I think we'd better go back inside before we're both completely soaked.'

Once he'd closed the glass door behind them, he drew her back into his arms. 'If you don't want to take Barney's money, that's fine. We'll find another sponsor.'

She kissed him. 'Why do I feel there's a "but"?'

'Because there is one,' he said. 'He hurt you. He owes you a massive apology. And we could make something good happen out of something bad.'

'How?'

'Take the money. Except *you'll* be the one to take it and make very sure he knows who you are. And that you've won, because you're the one who's made a real difference to the world—to your students, to the butterflies, and to me.'

Could she?

Should she?

'Think about it,' he said. 'I'm here if you want to bounce ideas. Whatever you decide, that won't change how I feel about you. I love you; my family and my best friend think you're wonderful; and I maybe need to work a little harder until you think I'm good enough to meet your family.'

'You're good enough,' she said. 'I think they'll see you the same way Ruth does. And she thinks you're fabulous, by the way.'

'Good,' he said. 'So we get to start again?'

She shook her head. 'We don't need to start again. You were right the first time. We just need to communicate a bit better in future.'

'So was Jacob right and I should've written that message in proper flowers?'

She laughed. 'No. You were right to say it with nettles. Give my butterflies somewhere to lay their eggs and for their caterpillars to feed. It's the most romantic thing I've ever, ever seen.'

'You,' he said, 'are *weird*.'

She grinned. 'Takes one to know one...'

Two days later, Alice headed to Rutherford and Associates, walking hand in hand with Hugo, wearing her favourite T-shirt and jeans and hiking boots.

'That looks like battle gear,' Hugo said.

'It is,' she said. 'I don't need to dress up or have a posh accent; it's who I am and what I can do that's really important. I'm a butterfly specialist—so I'm going to look like one.'

'You've missed a few words out, Dr Walters,' he said. 'You're also brilliant, brave and generally fantastic.' He kissed her lightly. 'I'm going to loiter in the coffee shop across the road. Call me if you need me—but I don't think you will. You're more than good enough on your own, just as you are.'

Ten years ago, she wouldn't have believed him. Maybe even earlier in the summer she wouldn't have been sure. But now, she knew he was right. She was good enough, just as she was.

She took a deep breath. 'I'll come and find you when I'm done.'

Five minutes later, she was in Barney's office.

'Thank you for coming to talk about the project, Dr Walters.' Then he peered at her. '*Alice?*'

She inclined her head. 'You remember me?'

His face suffused with colour. 'Yes.'

'The oik. Your Yorkshire version of Eliza Doolittle.' She

made her accent that little bit broader. 'But it isn't what you look like or what you sound like that matters, Barney. It's who you are. How you treat other people. How you behave.'

He stared at her.

'It's all right. I'm not going to start a fight. I don't expect you to apologise.' She looked at him. 'I don't need your approval or your apologies, because I already have the respect of people who actually matter.'

'So why are you here?' he asked.

'Because,' she said, 'you offered sponsorship for the butterfly house. And I'm looking at this purely as a business transaction. Yes, I could take the moral high ground and refuse your money—but then we'd have to find another sponsor, and I'd rather spend my time on other things. So I'm here to accept your money. And I wanted to do it in person so you know I'm not intimidated by you or your family or your friends—not the way I was at Oxford.'

He looked at her. 'I wasn't very nice to you.'

'No, you weren't,' she agreed.

'I didn't know you were involved in this project.'

'Does that mean you're withdrawing your offer?'

He gave her a wry smile. 'No. It doesn't. Please, take a seat.'

She did so. 'So why did you offer us the sponsorship?'

'My clients want green investments, so it makes sense for us to sponsor something involving ecology,' he said.

'Why the butterfly house?'

'Because I have a daughter. Daisy's four years old and she loves butterflies,' he said. 'I wanted to do something for her, too, something she could be proud of when she grows up.'

So maybe Barney had changed.

He shifted in his seat. 'When she's older, if anyone treats her the way I treated you at Oxford, I'll want to tear him apart with my bare hands. I know you said you didn't want an apology, but you deserve one.' He took a deep breath. 'I'm sorry, Alice. I'm not who I was back then, either. I hope I've grown up, become a better person.'

She hoped so, too.

'I'll match my company's sponsorship personally. In the circumstances, that's the least I can do.'

She hadn't expected that. 'Thank you. Obviously you've had the information from our PR people, but I think you need to know exactly what we're doing.' And she talked him through the project, everything from Viola's work through to Rosemary's, to the design Hugo had made for the butterfly house and the kind of educational resources they were going to offer. As she talked, her confidence grew. And she wasn't The Oik any more. She was Dr Alice Walters. Professional. Good at what she did.

'That,' Barney said when she'd finished, 'sounds amazing. My clients are going to be thrilled.' He smiled. 'And so is my daughter.'

Alice knew she could walk away now, triumphant. Or she could do something better: she could build a bridge. 'We're re-wilding the garden over the summer as well as building the butterfly house. Bring your daughter to see us, with her mum. She can help to plant something, and then she'll always know that she helped make a difference to that little corner of the garden.'

'I'd like that,' he said. 'Thank you, Alice.'

She stood up, and reached across the desk to shake his hand, knowing that finally she had closure on her past. 'You're welcome. And thank you for sponsoring our project. You're helping to make a difference.'

Then she walked over to the coffee shop to meet Hugo.

'Are you OK?' he asked when she sat down opposite him.

She nodded. 'I faced him. I wasn't sure if I was more angry or worried that he wouldn't take me seriously—but then I realised that you were right. I make a difference. It's not just what I do at work, it's who I am as well.' She smiled. 'And he apologised.'

'Good. That was long overdue.' He leaned over and took her hands. 'And I'm guessing he's going to give us the money Pav asked for and a bit more.'

She looked at him, shocked. 'How did you know?'

'Because you, my love, were going to talk to him about the project. And when you talk about butterflies, you sparkle and you light up the room. You're amazing and you're irresistible.'

Hugo valued her for who she was. Loved her for who she was. And that made her hold her head that little bit higher. Finally, she'd moved on from being the oik Barney's set had laughed at. She was herself. She was *enough*.

'We don't have to accept his money,' Hugo said, when she didn't say anything. 'This is your project. You make the call.'

'It's your project too. And Rosemary's, Viola's and Emma's. It's teamwork.'

'But you,' Hugo said, 'are my priority.'

And how amazing that made her feel. He was putting her first. 'We'll accept it,' she said. 'Because this gorgeous architect I happen to know taught me the value of building things with good foundations. His daughter likes butterflies. I told him to bring her to the house and she can help plant something.'

'Great idea.' He inclined his head. 'Congratulations on nailing the deal.'

'With your support.'

'I didn't do anything.' He shrugged. 'I just sat here, drinking coffee.'

'You were here as my backup if I needed you.' She stole

a kiss. 'You believed in me. More than that, you've taught me that I'm OK with who I am.'

'My brilliant, gorgeous butterfly specialist.' He kissed her back. 'I love you. And I can't wait for the future.'

'My brilliant, gorgeous architect. I love you, too. And we're going to build the butterfly house. Fulfil Rosemary's dream.'

'And,' he said softly, 'our own. You, me and the future.'

'You, me and the future,' she echoed.

EPILOGUE

A year later

'I WONDER WHY Philip Hemingford wants to see us in his office,' Hugo asked Alice as they walked through Chelsea together.

'Last time we had an appointment with him, he practically had to referee a fight,' Alice said. 'When you thought I was a gold-digger.'

'And you thought I was a vain clothes horse.'

She looked pointedly at his shoes. 'Says the man with handmade Italian stuff on his feet.'

He laughed, and kissed her. 'And who was it who found me that suit on our honeymoon, Dr Grey?'

'You looked cute in it,' she said with a grin.

Hand in hand, they walked into the solicitor's office. He was already waiting for them.

'Lovely to see you both,' he said, shaking their hands in turn. 'Thank you for the invitation to the opening of the butterfly house next week. I'm looking forward to it.'

'Pleasure,' Alice said.

'So what can we do for you?' Hugo asked.

'I have a letter from Miss Grey. You've met the conditions for it to be given to you,' he said.

'A letter from Great-Aunt Rosemary? For both of us?' Hugo looked confused.

'Yes.'

'Do you have any idea what's in it?' she asked.

He shook his head. 'None at all. Miss Grey was a bit of a law unto herself.'

'Perhaps we should ask you to read it to us,' Hugo said. 'And we promise not to shout at each other.'

The solicitor gave a small smile. 'I'm glad to hear that.' He opened the letter and scanned it.

'What does she say?' Alice asked impatiently.

My dear Hugo and Alice,

If you're reading this, then I know my dearest wish has come true. I've been trying to get you to meet each other for months, but whenever one of you was at the house with me the other one wasn't.

The only way I could think of to get you to meet was to change my will. I knew you'd have to be at the solicitor's, and I hoped that if you worked together—with you in charge of the garden and the butterflies, Alice, and you in charge of the buildings, Hugo—you'd see the same that I do. That you're perfect for each other.

I know you've both suffered a lot in the past, and I think you'll make each other very happy.

Congratulations on your wedding, and I do hope you'll forgive an old woman for interfering.

With much love to you both,

Rosemary

Hugo and Alice looked at each other.

'Matchmaking from beyond the grave,' Hugo said.

'And she was right. We're perfect for each other,' Alice said. 'If she hadn't changed her will and put in those conditions, we probably wouldn't have met.'

'We wouldn't be married,' he said.

She rested her hand on the almost imperceptible bump of her stomach. 'I have a feeling that this little one's going to be a girl. And I also think her name should be Rosemary Viola Emma Grey.'

'Rosemary Viola Emma Grey,' Hugo echoed, and his eyes were full of love.

* * * * *

A WINNING
SEASON

ROCHELLE ALERS

I am privileged and honored
to have had a special editor who guided
and challenged me with every title in this series.

Thanks, Megan Broderick.
I could not have done it without you.

Prologue

Zoey Allen stared at the framed watercolor on the wall in the conference room at McAvoy & McAvoy, Attorneys-At-Law. It had been six weeks since she'd stood at the graveside of her father and stepmother with her two younger brothers, and the shock of losing them still hadn't worn off.

Life as she'd known it had drastically changed the month before she was scheduled to graduate high school; she'd been summoned to the principal's office where the sheriff informed her that her parents had died of carbon monoxide poisoning from a faulty gas heater. Zoey and her brothers had been spared because they were in school at the time. Her plans to attend nursing school and her future were on hold, once she'd petitioned the court to allow her to become her brothers' legal guardian so they would not go into foster care.

"Zoey, are you listening?" Preston asked.

Her gaze swung from the painting to the lawyer. "I'm sorry. I was thinking about something else." Zoey knew she wasn't being truthful. There were times when she deliberately forced herself to think of anything but her current situation. Shopping for groceries, cooking, putting up loads of laundry and seeing to the needs of Kyle and Harper threatened to overwhelm her, and there were times she'd second-guessed her decision to assume full responsibility of a six- and eight-year-old who night after night cried themselves to sleep because they missed their mother and father. There were nights when she also cried because she'd felt so helpless, but Zoey made certain to always put on a brave face for her brothers. They needed to see her strong and in control.

Preston handed her a folder. "The family court judge has signed off on your guardianship of Kyle and Harper. The title and deed to the house is now in your name, along with the title to the minivan."

Zoey forced a smile. "Thank you for everything."

The law firm had taken care of all of her legal concerns pro bono. Her father had drawn up a will after marrying Charmaine Jenkins. His second wife had become his beneficiary, and if she did not survive his children, then everything of worth would be divided equally between their children upon their maturity.

Preston gave her a long look. "Are you all right?"

"I'm just a little tired. Lately I haven't been sleeping too well, but this too shall pass."

Preston ran a hand over his neatly barbered dirty-blond hair. "I can't imagine what you've been going through, but I'd like to give you some advice. Put your brothers in counseling to deal with losing their parents, and you should also do the same for yourself. There are a lot of women who become mothers at eighteen, but to infants and not six- and eight-year-olds. It's not easy now and it's not going to get any easier the older they become, so try to get them some help."

"I promise I will."

Zoey knew she had to get professional counseling for her brothers *and* for herself if only to help her cope with the tragedy and prove to the social worker that she was more than capable of raising her younger siblings. The woman who'd come to the house sought to convince her to put Harper and Kyle in foster care, but she was adamant when she told the social worker that her father, James Allen, had always wanted his children to grow up together.

Zoey did not remember her biological mother, who'd divorced her father and signed over full custody of her two-year-old daughter and then drove away from Wickham Falls, West Virginia, without a backward glance. For years it had been Zoey and her father, until he came home with a new wife when she was nine. Less than a year later she became a big sister to Kyle and two years later to Harper. Her brothers adored her as much as she adored them, and she'd sworn a vow nothing or no one would separate them.

She thanked Preston and left the office. It was the first time she realized that she would be the sole support emotionally and financially for her family. The court had determined she would be legal guardian for her brothers, and they were eligible for their deceased father's survivor's benefits. Fortunately, the house did not have a mortgage, so Zoey was responsible only for repairs and real estate taxes. The entire town had come together to help her cope with the tragedy that had left the younger Allen children orphans.

The rain that had been steadily falling for three days had tapered off as pinpoints of sunlight appeared through watery clouds. She smiled when seeing a rainbow in the distance, and for Zoey it was a sign that everything was going to be all right.

Chapter One

Ten years later...

Zoey Allen maneuvered into the driveway leading to the house where she'd lived all her life and shut off the engine. It was Friday afternoon, and she was looking forward to the weekend where she did not have to adhere to the whims of the elderly woman who spent all day in the only air-cooled room in her home.

She had been assigned several clients since she'd started with a Mineral Springs agency hiring certified home health aides, but her current one was the most eccentric of any with whom she had worked. It was the end of July and West Virginia was experiencing record-breaking heat with near ninety-degree daytime temperatures that lingered beyond sunset. Mrs. Chambers spent all her time in her bedroom with a small window air-conditioning unit that barely cooled the space.

Her client refused to allow her to turn on a fan or a light during the daylight hours because she claimed her electric bill was much too high. When Zoey complained to the scheduling staffer at the agency, she was informed her placement would be a short one because Mrs. Chambers's children were in the process of moving their mother to a Washington, DC, nursing home several miles from where they lived. Zoey had informed the agency that once that occurred, she was going to take a two-week vacation before accepting a subsequent assignment.

"Hello, neighbor."

Zoey closed the door of her minivan and turned to find Sutton Reed smiling at her. Talk that he had returned to Wickham Falls after his retirement from baseball had spread like a lighted fuse attached to a stick of dynamite, and Zoey was slightly taken aback that he was standing less than ten feet away greeting her as his neighbor.

Seeing him up close made her aware that he was more breathtakingly handsome in person than in his photographs. His tall, powerfully built athletic body and large brown eyes, and balanced features in a complexion with shades ranging from rosewood to alizarin, had made him one of *People* magazine's most beautiful people.

A nervous smile flitted over her parted lips. "Hello."

Sutton came closer, extending his hand. "Sutton. I'll be renting Sharon Williams's house until after the new year."

Zoey took his hand, feeling calluses on the palm. She was in her teens and her parents were still alive when Sutton Reed had become a first-round draft pick for the Atlanta Braves.

"Zoey Allen. And welcome home."

Sharon Williams's house had been vacant for several months, and she'd promised the woman she would keep a close eye on her property and alert the sheriff's office if she witnessed any suspicious activity.

Sutton smiled, exhibiting a mouth filled with straight, white teeth. "Thank you." His smile faded. "How's your family?"

"Kyle enlisted in the corps, and Harper will be starting his junior year in a couple of weeks."

He nodded. "It appears as if you've done a wonderful job raising your brothers."

A wry smiled formed on her lips. "I've tried."

Zoey wanted to tell Sutton that it hadn't been easy, that she'd done the best she could to give her siblings what they needed, rather than merely what they wanted, to keep her family intact. Kyle hadn't given her a problem, while Harper tended to make her life a living hell. Everything she proposed he challenged, and she was at her wit's end when dealing with his ongoing defiance.

"I'll be around if you need help with anything," Sutton said, meeting her eyes.

Zoey nodded and smiled. "Thank you."

She didn't know if he'd made the offer because that's what he thought she wanted to hear, or if he was sincere about helping her out. The residents of the Falls had been more than supportive following her family's tragedy. The pastor and the church board had established a college scholarship fund for the Allen boys, and members of the chamber of commerce had arranged for local merchants to make house and auto repairs free of charge for two years.

"I suppose I'll see you around now that we are neighbors. Even if it's going to be only for a short time," Sutton added.

Zoey wanted to tell Sutton that she wouldn't mind having him as her neighbor as long as he didn't host wild parties so loud that she would have to wear earplugs to get a restful night's sleep. She already had to constantly tell Harper to lower the volume on his music when he opted not to wear his buds, which she believed he did just to annoy her.

"It's nice meeting you, Sutton, and it goes double if I can help you out with anything."

Zoey turned on her heel, walked up the stairs to the porch and unlocked the front door. She hadn't realized how fast her heart had been beating until she felt slightly light-headed. During the short time she'd interacted with Sutton Reed, she had managed not to act like a starstruck fan coming face-to-face with a gorgeous famous athlete.

Sutton Reed had put Wickham Falls on the map when as a rookie first baseman he had become the most talked-about player in the league. And instead of his star dimming, it had continued to get brighter until it was apparent he would be inducted into the Baseball Hall of Fame.

Zoey had caught only glimpses of Sutton whenever he'd return to the Falls, but those visits became less and less frequent as the years went on. Her brothers, like many of the young boys in town, regarded Sutton as their hero and role model, while she barely had time to sit and watch television because there were times when she'd felt completely overwhelmed taking care of the house and working part-time during the hours they were in school.

"I can't believe this mess!"

Zoey groaned when she saw articles of clothing strewn on the floor and chairs in the living room. She'd warned Harper repeatedly to pick up after himself. However, threats seemed to go in one ear and out the other. She did not know whether he deliberately ignored her or whatever she said did not make a difference to him.

Dropping her tote on an armchair, Zoey gathered up the discarded garments and deposited them in the hamper in the laundry room off the kitchen, and then walked up the staircase to the second story and opened the door to Harper's room. What greeted her made her roll her eyes upward. Clothes spilled out of open drawers, dirty socks littered the floor, and a plate with a half-eaten sandwich sat on the floor beside the bed.

Shaking her head in exasperation, she picked up the plate and took it downstairs to the kitchen. There was no way Zoey wanted to begin her weekend cleaning Harper's bedroom. She knew he probably was hanging out with his friend Jabari, and she planned to wait for him to come home to read him the riot act. After a shower and a quick dinner, she would be ready to confront the teenager who seemed intent on not following her instructions.

Zoey sat up and reached for her cell phone when she heard the front door open. It was 12:10 a.m., two hours past Harper's curfew. Once the school year ended, she had allowed him to stay out later and had given him a 10:00 p.m. curfew.

"Where do you think you're going?" It was apparent she'd surprised her brother, who came to a complete stop at the staircase. She'd turned off the lights and lay on the sofa to confront his arrival, or he would've tried to convince her that he had come home hours earlier. She flicked on the table lamp. "Come over here and sit down."

Harper Allen exhaled a groan. "Do I have to? I'm really tired and want to go to bed."

Zoey pointed to the love seat. "Yes, you have to." She waited for the tall, lanky sixteen-year-old to sit, hands sandwiched between his knees. Many people had mistaken Harper and Kyle for twins despite the two-year difference in their ages. Both had inherited their late mother's golden-brown complexion, hazel eyes and black curly hair. It had taken them a while to realize although she was their sister, they did not have the same mother.

"I'm only going to say this once," Zoey said in a low, controlled voice. "This is the last time you will break curfew, because the next time I'm going to court to take out a PINS and have you placed in a foster home or juvenile facility until you age out."

Harper sat straight. "What the hell is a PINS?"

Zoey's expression hardened. "What did I tell you about using that kind of language with me? I am not one of your friends." She had enunciated each word. "A PINS is a 'person in need of supervision' petition. It means that a family court judge will mandate what you can and cannot do. And the fact that you were picked up for public intoxication does little to boost your defense that you've done nothing wrong."

Harper pushed out his lip. "I'm not drinking any-more."

She knew he wasn't being truthful, because even with the space separating them Zoey could smell the beer on his breath. "I'm not a fool, Harper. Do you want me to call Sheriff Collier and have him send one of his deputies over with a Breathalyzer?"

Harper shook his head. "No." He paused, the sec-onds ticking. "All right. I had a couple of beers."

"Where?"

"Not at Triple Jay's house. His father would kill him if he found him drinking."

"And you thought I would go along with your underage drinking?"

He shook his head. "No."

"Where were you drinking?" Zoey repeated.

"It was in Mineral Springs."

"You left the Falls to get drunk in the Springs?"

"I have a friend who lives in the Springs and his older brother bought the beer for us."

"I want you to listen to what I'm going to stay because I don't intend to repeat it. This will be the last time you'll go to Mineral Springs to drink anything. Not even water. And it is also the last time you will come into his house after ten. Once school begins, I want you home after your last class. The exception will be extracurricular activities. You are to keep your room clean, and I don't want you eating in there again. We don't need a vermin infestation. And there are going to be some new rules around here. You will have to earn your allowance. Beginning tomorrow, every Saturday you will get up early to mow the lawn and bag the garbage for the Monday pickup."

Harper ran his fingers through a mane of curly hair. "Okay, Zoey, I hear you."

She gritted her teeth. "You hear me, but are you listening, Harper?"

"Yes, I'm listening. I promise no more beer, I have to be in by ten, keep my room clean, and bag the garbage and clean the backyard on Saturdays."

Zoey waved her hand in dismissal. She knew Harper was attempting to placate her. She had never been so embarrassed as when a local deputy discovered him urinating in the parking lot behind a row of stores in the business district. Rather than arrest him, Seth Collier called her to pick him up, with a stern warning that his next offense could possibly result in an arrest.

She watched Harper as he slowly made his way up the staircase, hoping and praying he would keep his promise. She did not like issuing threats, yet she was willing to do it if it meant preventing her brother from ruining his life. Harper had taken his mother's death particularly hard.

Zoey suspected something was causing Harper to act out, and whenever she asked him if he wanted to talk to her, he gave her the pat answer that he was okay. He may have thought he was okay, while continuing with his rebellious behavior. It had been years since her youngest brother was in counseling, and she thought perhaps now it was time to talk to Harper as to whether he needed someone other than her to confide in.

Going from a family of five to three had been not only shocking but also traumatic, and Zoey had had to seek out a counselor help her adjust to becoming a teenage mother to a six- and eight-year-old. At eighteen she was cooking, cleaning, doing laundry, shopping for groceries and helping her siblings with homework in between working a part-time position at Ruthie's, the local family-style buffet restaurant. Other girls her age were dating, holding down full-time jobs or enrolled in college, while she had become legal guardian and surrogate mother to two young boys who'd lost both parents at the same time.

It had taken her more than a year to adjust to caring for someone other than herself and have the Allen family settled into a routine that came as close to normal as it would have been if James and Charmaine were still alive. Pushing off the sofa, she turned off the lamp and made her way to the staircase and to her bedroom.

Zoey changed into a nightgown, adjusted the thermostat on the air conditioner, and got into bed. Although tired, she could not stop thinking about Harper flirting with the possibility of getting arrested. Her fear that he would end up with a criminal record kept her from a restful night's sleep, and it was close to dawn when she finally fell into a deep, dreamless slumber.

Chapter Two

Sutton Reed unloaded a half dozen bags from the cargo area of the SUV with the groceries he needed to stock the refrigerator and pantry in the rental home that was to be his temporary dwelling until next spring when the owner was scheduled to return from Ohio.

He had returned to Wickham Falls in July during Major League Baseball's All-Star break, but for him the break with the sport that had given him the opportunity to live out his dream was finalized months earlier. Sutton had become a free agent at the end of the prior season, and after two stints on the injured list during his fourteen-year career, he'd realized it was time for him to put away his bat and glove and hang up his cleats. Now at thirty-six, he looked forward to life off the baseball diamond and away from the glare of the spotlight.

Sutton knew he had disappointed his agent when he'd declined re-signing with the Atlanta Braves, but his body communicated to him it was time to quit before he seriously reinjured his right knee. Even now, after countless hours of physical therapy, it would stiffen when he least expected.

Yes. He had made the right decision to leave baseball, sell his Atlanta condo and return to his hometown to assist his aunt and uncle in running Powell's Department Store once their daughter opened her craft shop around the corner in Wickham Falls' downtown business district. However, after two weeks, he'd felt manning the sporting goods department was not as stimulating as he had expected it to be and living under the same roof with his relatives felt strange for someone who'd become emancipated within weeks of enrolling in college.

He'd contacted Mrs. Reilly, the local Realtor, who'd informed him there was an available rental, but the owner, Sharon Williams, had given her explicit instructions that anyone who leased her house had to submit a two-month security deposit to cover potential damages and undergo an extensive background check, because she did not want to return from Ohio to discover her home not as she'd left it. Sutton did not have to wait long for the local biweekly's office manager to give her approval, and it had taken only days to finalize the paperwork and for him to move into the comfortably furnished three-bedroom house.

Things had changed since Sutton left the Falls to attend college. However, they hadn't changed so much that he did not recognize the town in which he'd grown up. There were a few new shops along the four square blocks of the business district in a town that still did not claim a fast-food restaurant or big-box store. Residents were very vocal about preserving their small-town ambience with mom-and-pop shops stocking everything the community wanted and needed for daily existence. Their motto was: Live Local. Buy Local.

Sutton had returned to his hometown since leaving to attend college, but as his baseball career escalated and after his mother decided she wanted to move to Atlanta to be closer to him, his visits became less frequent, and he'd had to rely on his cousin Georgina Powell to keep him abreast of the happenings in the Falls.

It took him less than fifteen minutes to put away the canned goods and perishables. The fully furnished, meticulously clean house with an updated kitchen, full and half baths, living/dining/family rooms, attached garage and three second-story bedrooms was perfect for his current lifestyle. The backyard was spacious, and when he unlocked the shed, he'd found a gas grill, lawnmower, smoker and gardening tools.

Divorced and with a graduate degree in history and an illustrious sports career behind him, Sutton had decided to wait a year before making decisions about his future. He had to choose whether to teach, become an athletic coach or go into business to establish a sports camp for underserved youth. Multiple seven-figure contracts, a number of endorsements and conservative investments would allow him to live comfortably for years to come.

Sutton had just finished brewing coffee when he heard a familiar ringtone on his cell phone. Tapping the screen, he answered the call, and then activated the speaker feature. "Good morning, Mom."

"You don't sound as if I woke you up."

"I've been up for a while," he told Michelle Reed. "The company transporting my car from Georgia is expected to be here by nine." He'd stored the car along with his condo's furnishings until he found permanent housing but did not want to leave the vehicle for the next six months without driving it. While in Atlanta, he tended to take the Aston Martin out of the garage every few weeks to keep it running smoothly.

"Do you have some place to garage it?"

He knew his mother had asked because he'd made it a practice not to park the upscale sports car on the street or in the private parking lot behind the row of warehouses that had been converted into condos. "Yes. Sharon Williams's house has a garage, and I'm going to leave it in there until I'm ready to take it out."

"I really didn't call you to chat long, but to tell you I've decided to close up my house for the next six months. After that I must decide whether I want to keep or sell it. I should know one way or the other sometime early next year. I've already called Evelyn to let her know I'm willing to stay with her and Bruce. I also told her that I don't mind helping out in the store."

"When did you decide this?" he asked. The last time he'd spoken to his mother she'd said nothing about temporarily relocating to the town where her family had lived for generations.

And her coming back to work in Powell's Department Store with her sister Evelyn and brother-in-law Bruce Powell also surprised Sutton. He recalled his mother refusing a position of maintaining the books at the retail store because with a degree in business management she preferred working in an office. Michelle began her career as clerk with the Johnson County Public Schools system, eventually advancing to budget manager until she resigned to relocate to Atlanta to live closer to him.

Sutton added a splash of cream to his cup of coffee, and took a sip as he listened to his mother drone on about becoming disenchanted with living in Atlanta, while he wanted to remind her that it wasn't the city but the women in her social circle. Michelle was the pied piper for those always looking for a handout. It had been that way with his father and continued with those she considered her friends. He'd cautioned her over and over that they were users and hangers-on; unfortunately, it had taken years before she'd come to that conclusion on her own.

"You're closing the house for six months, but what do you intend to do after that?" Sutton asked his mother. Six months meant Michelle would be in the Falls through the new year.

"I'll cross that bridge when I come to it. And if I stay here, then I'll buy a one-bedroom condo. I know you got tired of hearing me complain about trying to get rid of those two-faced heifers who acted as if I was running a bed-and-breakfast. I should've taken your advice and chosen a house in a gated community where they'd have to be announced to gain access."

Sutton had promised his mother he would gift her with a house once she'd decided to leave Wickham Falls and move to Atlanta. Michelle had secured the services of a Realtor to show her a few homes and she finally selected a three-bedroom high ranch in a sub-urb subdivision. He smiled. His mother was moving back to live with her sister and brother-in-law. And it also meant they didn't need him to work in the store. The Powells had established a tradition that only those connected to the family were allowed to manage the centuries-old business establishment.

"Now that you're going to be working at Powell's, I suppose this means I'm fired."

"I know you were willing to step up and help Bruce once Georgina opened her own shop, and I also know you didn't go to college and get a gradu-ate degree to become a salesclerk. I told your uncle that I will fill in wherever I'm needed."

His mother was right. He didn't mind helping out his aunt and uncle, but it wasn't something he'd wanted to do for an extended period. Sutton had enrolled in college on a full academic and athletic scholarship. Following his graduation, he'd signed on with the Braves' minor league baseball team as a first baseman. After his tenth year in the big leagues, he'd gone online to earn a graduate degree in American history with the intent to teach once his baseball career ended.

He was more than aware that an athlete's career had an expiration date, and he'd carefully planned for when that day would become a reality. Now that his mother planned to return to Wickham Falls, Sutton knew it was time for him to update his résumé. The new school year was scheduled to begin in two weeks, and he was willing to work as a substitute until he found a permanent position as a history teacher.

"I'm going to ring off because I still need to pack up some of my clothes and ship them to the Falls. I'll call you again before I leave here for good."

"No problem, Mom. And please drive carefully."

Michelle made a sucking sound with her tongue and teeth. "You know I don't speed."

"I know that, but just be aware of the other crazies on the road."

"I will. Love you, son."

"I love you, too, Mom."

Sutton ended the call, picked up the coffee mug, left the kitchen and walked out of the house to wait on the porch for the car carrier. He'd just sat on a cushioned chaise when he saw movement out of the side of his eye. He turned to find Zoey sitting on a porch swing reading. He smiled. She looked nothing like

the young woman he'd met the day before. A revealing tank top and shorts had replaced the loose-fitting
pink smock and matching pants, and he couldn't pull
his gaze away from the smooth brown skin on her
bared arms and long legs. When he'd stood next to
her, introducing himself, Sutton realized she was
taller than the average woman, and the chemically
straightened hair she had secured in a knot on the
top of her head was now styled in a messy bun on
the nape of her long, graceful neck.

Stretching out his legs, he crossed his sandaled
feet at the ankles. He would've greeted his neighbor if she hadn't appeared so engrossed in her book.
Unlike at the home that he'd shared with his ex-wife
or the condo where he'd resided after his divorce, he
hadn't had much contact with his neighbors. But Sharon Williams's house and the Allens' were separated
by a driveway wide enough for only a single vehicle.

Although his interaction with Zoey hadn't lasted
more than two minutes, it was enough for Sutton
to recall her small, round face, wide-set dark eyes
that appeared if she'd been suddenly startled, short,
pert nose and a lush mouth that had held his rapt
attention. He realized he'd been staring, but there
was something about Zoey Allen that had enthralled
and intrigued him. She appeared totally unfazed by
his so-called celebrity persona, unlike a few women
who'd fawned over him because that was what they
believed he wanted. And there was an air of maturity
about her that probably had come from the respon-

sibility of having to raise her younger siblings when she was still a teenager.

He had dated a number of beautiful women, and eventually married one, yet after a while he realized their looks were only window dressing and that he had wanted more. And the *more* was compatibility. It had taken Sutton a long time to grow emotionally and realize that although he had to strive to become what others wanted him to be, he had to be honest enough with himself to do what made him feel secure. He had become a media darling on and off the field, and there were times when he'd felt like a marionette with someone else pulling the strings. And it wasn't as if he was ungrateful that baseball had afforded him a lifestyle he never would've had if he'd chosen a different career. But now it felt good not to have to perform for the public and that he could be himself in his hometown.

Sutton took a sidelong glance at Zoey's delicate profile as she appeared completely absorbed in the book on her lap, unable to pull his gaze away from her long legs and narrow feet. When his mother had called to inform him of the accidental deaths of the Allen parents and that the town was setting up a college scholarship fund for the two minor boys, he hadn't hesitated and had anonymously sent a generous donation. His mother was more familiar with Zoey's family because she'd attended school with James Allen. His contact with Zoey's family was limited because they'd lived in another part of town from where he'd grown up, and he estimated that he was at least eight years her senior.

When he'd complimented her for raising her brothers, her reply had been *"I've tried."* Well, it appeared as if she had done a good job because he knew it couldn't have been easy for a teenage girl to assume the responsibility of raising her younger brothers.

"Good morning."

Sutton had just taken another sip of coffee when he heard Zoey's greeting. Shifting slightly on the chaise, he smiled at her. "Good morning to you, too. I would've said something sooner, but you were totally engrossed in your book."

Zoey closed the book. "I don't get much time to read, so when I do, I try to take advantage of it."

She'd wanted to sleep in late because she didn't have to go to work, but her internal clock refused to cooperate. Monday through Friday she got up at six, made up her bed, showered and dressed before going downstairs to prepare lunch for herself. She always made certain there were leftovers for Harper to microwave before getting into the fifteen-year-old Chrysler Pacifica minivan that had logged so many miles she'd made it a point not to look at the odometer.

"I won't bother you so you can get back to your book."

Zoey set the book on glass-topped rattan table. "You're not bothering me. I just finished it. I'm going to wait a few days before I begin another one."

"Is reading a hobby for you?" Sutton asked.

She nodded. "Between working and taking care

of Harper, reading or bingeing on my favorite television shows are my only guilty pleasures."

"That sounds very safe."

"That's because I can't afford to take risks until my brother finishes school and hopefully goes off to college."

Sutton lifted his coffee mug. "Do you drink coffee?"

She smiled. "Yes."

"Have you had any this morning?"

Zoey shook her head. "Not yet."

He pushed to his feet. "I made enough for several cups. Miss Williams doesn't have a single-brew coffeemaker, so I had to resort to the alternative carafe style."

"Miss Sharon is somewhat old-fashioned when it comes to certain things," she said in defense of her longtime neighbor. Never-married Sharon Williams had become her guardian angel whenever she needed someone to look after her brothers while she made a last-minute run to the local supermarket before it closed. And if it was too late, then she had to drive to the all-night big-box store off the interstate. "And yes, I would like a cup."

"How do you take your coffee?"

"Light and sweet."

Sutton winked at her. "Light and sweet sounds very parochial when I'm so used to hearing caramel Frappuccino with soymilk, caramel drizzle and whipped cream."

Throwing back her head, Zoey laughed. "It sounds as if you've had your share of Starbucks coffees."

Sutton's laughter joined hers. "I did until I brought an espresso machine to brew my own coffee concoctions."

"Lucky you. I have a single-serve coffeemaker that fits perfectly with my lifestyle." She didn't entertain people in her home, and if she did want gourmet coffee, then she would use the dwindling supply of Jamaican Blue Mountain in her refrigerator. However, fancy coffees weren't high on her list of things she needed to make her day.

"I'll be right back with your light and sweet."

Zoey stared at Sutton's back as he turned and went into his house. The black T-shirt hugged his muscular upper body like a second skin, and the relaxed white jeans fit his waist and hips as if they'd been made expressly for his magnificent physique. When she'd gotten up earlier that morning, she went online to google Sutton's name and she discovered things about her neighbor that left her mouth gaping in shock. The young man who'd been raised by a single mother had made it big, yet with fame and fortune had remained humble. He'd also joined an organization with other professional athletes that mentored at-risk youth, children growing up in single-parent households and families experiencing the loss of a family member while in combat. He had also set up his own charity: the Reed Foundation Road to Success.

She'd also examined the photos of Sutton and his ex-wife, wondering what had gone wrong in their eight-year marriage. Zoey had to admit that the tall, stunningly beautiful supermodel known as Angell was his perfect physical counterpart. Their marriage ended without a hint of scandal and when questioned why they were divorcing, Sutton and Angell refused to discuss it with the press, leaving people to wonder if their marriage was a sham as a cover for other proclivities. She'd found herself staring at some of his publicity photos. The one with him sitting on a chair wearing only a pair of jeans while staring directly into the camera was so sensual that it reminded Zoey of how long it had been since she'd had any sexual interaction with a man. The last and only man she'd ever slept with was her high school boyfriend.

The door to the neighboring house opened and Sutton emerged carrying two mugs. He came over and joined her on the porch swing. "A light and sweet for the pretty lady."

Zoey felt pinpoints of heat in her face when he'd referred to her as *pretty*. It was a term she'd occasionally overheard by some men she'd encountered. She wasn't vain about her looks, but she managed to ignore the overtures whenever men attempted to come on to her because she knew nothing would come of it. And for the few who'd asked her why she was so standoffish, her comeback was as a single woman with two kids, she didn't have time to date. She hadn't dated since high school, and once Harper left home her focus would be on nursing school.

But Sutton calling her *pretty* was different. He wasn't a stranger but her next-door neighbor. And interacting with him verified his being a celebrity heartthrob was not a fluke. He was the total package. Looks, brawn and brains. Even his voice, low, beautifully modulated with a hint of a drawl, was hypnotic.

Sutton gave Zoey her mug, noticing her hand had trembled slightly when their fingers touched. "Are you all right?"

"I'm good," she said.

He wanted to believe Zoey was all right but the rigidness in her body said otherwise. He stood and moved to a nearby chair. "I'm sorry if I invaded your personal space."

She lowered her eyes, staring into the contents of her mug. "It's okay."

Sutton drank his coffee, staring at Zoey over the rim. He was perceptive enough to know she had been completely at ease with him the day before, but this morning her body language said otherwise, and he wondered what he'd said or done to make her uneasy.

Suddenly it occurred to Sutton that he may have made a faux pas when he had referred to Zoey as *pretty lady*, especially when he did not know whether she was involved with someone. "I'm sorry, Zoey."

She halted putting the mug to her mouth. "For what?"

"For making you uncomfortable because I called you *pretty lady*. Hell, I don't even know if you're involved with someone."

Zoey swallowed a mouthful of coffee. The corners of her eyes crinkled when she smiled. "I really have to give it to you, Sutton Reed."

A slight frown marred his natural good looks. "What are you talking about?"

"You did not make me uncomfortable, and if you wanted to know if I'm involved with someone, then all you had to do was ask."

A hint of a smile replaced his frown. "Are you?"

The seconds ticked as she met his eyes. "No. And I can't afford to because of a promise I made to Kyle and Harper when they were little boys. I told them it would be just the three of us until they were old enough to take care of themselves."

Sutton set his mug on a side table. "I can understand you making that promise when they were boys, but I doubt if Harper would hold it against you if you decided to start dating."

"Right now, Harper has no say in how I live my life."

"Is he giving you a problem?"

Zoey went completely still. "Why would you ask me that?"

"I was sitting out on the porch when he came home last night. Someone had dropped him off and I noticed he was a little unsteady on his feet."

If Sutton saw Harper coming home obviously under the influence, then Zoey wondered how many of her other neighbors had also witnessed it. Zoey did not want or need people gossiping about the Allen boy drinking or possibly drugging. She had managed to raise Kyle to adulthood without an incident, but life was testing her because Harper had decided he wasn't going to make it that easy for her.

"I don't know you and you don't know me, Sutton, and there's no way I'm going to dump on you about my problems."

Sutton angled his head, giving her a long stare. "You've lived in the Falls all your life and you should know that folks here always look out for one another. Those who have more than they need always share with those who don't have enough. And it's not always about money."

Zoey knew he was right. The people in the town had been more than generous when tragedy struck her family. Even now some folks still asked if she needed anything. She nodded. "You're right. I give thanks every day that I live here and not somewhere else, because without the help of Preston McAvoy, the chamber of commerce and the worshippers at the church, I wouldn't be sitting here talking to you."

The local law firm had handled her legal problems; local contractors had volunteered their services to make certain the house was free of violations; a company selling and installing gas heaters set up an installment plan for her to pay off the cost of the unit over three years.

"So once Harper graduates you plan to stay here?" Sutton asked.

Zoey smiled. "Where would I go?"

He shrugged broad shoulders under his tee. "I don't know. Maybe you'd prefer someplace that has a little more excitement."

She took another sip of the delicious brew. Sutton had made the coffee exactly how she liked it. "The

Falls has enough excitement for the four thousand-plus folks who live here. Someone had submitted a proposal to the town council to open a club and it was unanimously voted down. What we don't need is a club with people getting drunk and acting like fools. The town council in Mineral Springs has closed two clubs in the past four years because of fights and rowdiness."

"The Springs has almost twice our population, so there's bound to be a few more incidents than we have here."

"Speaking of excitement, why did you decide to move back here after spending half your life in Hotlanta?" Zoey had asked the question that had plagued her since hearing word that Sutton Reed was moving back to Wickham Falls.

Sutton closed his eyes for several seconds. "I never really got used to living in a big city. The crowds and noise didn't upset me whenever I was at the stadium, but once the game was over all I wanted was someplace quiet where I could decompress."

"Whenever you were interviewed you seemed so confident, so in control of yourself."

"That was all an act, Zoey. I'd learned early on to switch it on for the cameras and microphones. There was one Sutton for the sports reporters and another Sutton when he was home behind closed doors."

"There is something I don't understand."

He gave her a long, penetrating stare. "What don't you understand?"

Zoey met his eyes. "If you profess to be a private person, why then did you marry a high-profile supermodel?"

Sutton was preempted from answering her question as a truck drove up and parked in front of his house. He stood. "You'll have to excuse me, but I have to take care of a delivery."

She hadn't meant to ask him a question that was obviously personal, but his revelation that he did not like the spotlight appeared completely incongruous juxtaposed to the photos of him and his glamorous ex-wife. The beautiful *Sports Illustrated* model was regularly photographed on and off the catwalk and had countless Twitter followers. Angell adored the camera and it in turn loved her, and she'd used it to her advantage to increase her visibility and popularity.

The screen door opened, and Harper joined Zoey on the porch. She smiled. If she hadn't told him to get up early to clean up the backyard, she knew he wouldn't have gotten out of bed until late morning or early afternoon. Whenever he didn't have school, he stayed up half the night watching the sports channels and playing video games and then crawled into bed just before dawn. She did not have a problem with her brother's waking and sleeping habits because whenever he had classes, he'd set the alarm on his cell phone to get up on time to meet the school bus.

"Holy shit! That's him."

"What did I tell you about cursing, Harper?" Zoey snapped angrily. It was as if her brother deliberately used foul language in her presence because he knew

it annoyed her. It wasn't as if she'd never used an
expletive, but she had made it a habit not to curse,
especially in her home. She was aware that Harper
believed using four-letter words made him feel more
like an adult, and initially she had deliberately ignored it, but lately everything he said was laced with
obscenities.

"Lighten up, Zoey. All kids my age curse."

Setting down the mug, she stood up, struggling
to control her temper. "You're not all kids, but my
brother. And I'm not going to tolerate bad language
in my home, Harper Allen." There must have been
something in her voice, body language or Zoey's
using his full name that changed Harper's expression from cocky to remorseful.

"Okay. I will watch my language."

She glared at him. "You do that."

Harper walked to the railing. "Is that Sutton
Reed?"

Zoey stood beside her brother. "Yes. He just
moved in next door."

Harper's hazel eyes grew bigger. "You're kidding
me! He's living in Miss Sharon's house?"

She heard the awe in Harper's voice. "Yes."

"Have you met him?"

"Yes, Harper, I met him."

Harper grasped her upper arm, his fingers tightened, unaware of his strength. "Can you introduce
me to him?"

Reaching up, Zoey managed to extricate his hand.
Sutton stood on the sidewalk, arms crossed over his

chest. The driver had opened the rear of the truck and lowered a ramp. "He appears to be busy now."

"But can you have me meet him when he's not busy?"

She glanced up at Harper. He'd grown several inches in the past year and now towered over her. There was no doubt he was experiencing hero worship. "Okay."

Harper dropped a kiss on her hair. "Thanks, sis. I'm going to clean up the yard now."

"Once you're finished, you can join me for breakfast with the works." It was only on weekends that Zoey had time to make Harper's favorite breakfast foods: grits, eggs, bacon, sausage or ham, biscuits and home fries.

"You're the best."

Zoey winked at him. "I try." She was the best to Harper only when she wasn't telling him what he should and should not to.

She watched Harper as he sprinted down the porch steps and disappeared around to the back of the house. She hadn't lied to him. She did try to give him what he needed to avoid the problems that had befallen some of the town's teenage boys who were dabbling in drugs and alcohol and, increasingly, fathering babies with different girls.

Zoey turned and went back into the house, recalling the time she'd spent most of her waking hours praying and second-guessing herself about whether she had done the right thing to petition the court to assume full responsibility for her brothers when she'd had to be a mother, father *and* sister. Thankfully it had gotten easier, and the day she witnessed Kyle walk across the stage to receive his high school diploma she felt as if her heart would burst with pride.

Meanwhile, Harper was an above-average student who'd talked about going to college. However, he wasn't certain what he wanted to study, unlike herself, who'd always wanted to go into nursing. Zoey reassured him that he had a lot of time to decide what he wanted to be when he grew up.

With ten years behind them, the next two were certain to go quickly.

Chapter Three

"Well, Mom, you've been back a week now and how are you adjusting to living in the Falls again?" Sutton asked his mother. It was just like old times when Sutton and his mother joined her sister Evelyn, brother-in-law and their son and daughter for Sunday dinners. That was before the unexpected death of the Powells' thirteen-year-old son from meningitis, just a few months after Sutton had first taken the field as a Major League Baseball player. Kevin's passing had sent Evelyn into a downward emotional spiral from which, after more than a decade, she'd only recently begun to recover.

Michelle smiled at him over the rim of her water glass, and he noticed a few new lines added to the network around a pair of clear brown eyes with glints of gold in a complexion reminiscent of polished mahogany. At sixty-one, she still had the ability to turn men's heads, and it had been no different with his father. Sutton had an ambivalent relationship with his biological father, who was unable to care about anyone but himself.

"It's been good," Michelle said.

Evelyn Powell swallowed a mouthful of garlicky green beans. "That's because my sister doesn't have to put up with her fake friends who would drop by because they claim they just happened to be in the neighborhood."

Picking up the napkin beside his plate, Bruce Powell dabbed his mouth. Light from the dining room chandelier shimmered on his shaved pate. The bright red hair from his youth had thinned over the years until the owner of Wickham Falls' oldest family-owned and most profitable business decided to eliminate the graying fringe.

"I thought you came back because you missed us," he teased, dark blue eyes brimming with amusement.

Michelle smiled at her brother-in-law. "That, too." She sobered and her expression grew serious. "If you really want to know the truth, I miss living in a small town where folks know and look out for one another. When I first moved into the subdivision, none of those so-called bougie people said a mumbling word to me until they discovered I was Sutton Reed's mother. Then I lost count of the number of invitations to their luncheon and dinner parties."

Bruce extended his wineglass to Michelle and then Sutton. "Well, I'm glad to have you both back."

"It would have been nice if Georgina could've joined us tonight," Evelyn said. "But when I called her to say we were having Sunday dinner like we used to, she said she's working on a project and wanted to finish it before her next quilting class."

Sutton shared a knowing glance with Bruce when the sisters launched into a discussion as to how their mother had attempted to teach them to knit, crochet and quilt, but they did not have the patience to sit and count stitches or learn to read an intricate pattern, and she finally gave up hope that her daughters would continue the tradition of creating heirloom handicrafts that would be passed down through generations of Reed women. His fondest memories of Grandmother Dorothea, or Granny Dot, were her homemade cakes. Every Sunday she would bake a different cake, and after a while he wasn't able to decide his favorite among lemon pound, carrot, red velvet, hummingbird, coconut or strawberry shortcakes.

He stared at the two women. Michelle at sixty-one was two years older than Evelyn but looked younger. But he had to admit his aunt looked better than when he last saw her. At that time there was a permanent frown between Evelyn's eyes and deep lines had bracketed her mouth, and her once thick jet-black hair had thinned to sparse, graying wisps. However, there was never any sibling rivalry between the sisters, because Michelle never envied Evelyn, who'd managed to marry one of the Falls' most eligible bachelors, while her relationship had been with a man who'd used and left her when she told him she was pregnant with his baby. Michelle had accepted her plight while always maintaining a positive attitude.

Sutton grew up not knowing the man who'd fathered him until after he'd become a first-round draft pick for the Braves. And when they'd come face-to-face in the lobby of an Atlanta hotel, it was as if he had been staring at an older version of himself. Sutton stopped the older man from saying anything when he'd put his hand up and walked past him because he did not want to hear any excuse as to why Gerard Clinton had deserted his mother when she'd needed him at the most vulnerable time in her life. Several reporters had witnessed the nonverbal interchange and the footage was replayed over and over on various sports channels. Years later when the topic of his biological father would occasionally come up during interviews, Sutton's response would be the ubiquitous *no comment* until his publicist issued a statement that the subject of his client's personal family was not up for discussion.

"A Stitch at a Time is the perfect name for my niece's shop," Michelle announced proudly.

Sutton's thoughts shifted from his deadbeat father to his cousin. He'd attended Georgina's grand opening and was awed by her artistic talent evident in the knitted and crocheted garments she displayed along with some of the Reed family's hand-stitched heirloom quilts. She'd done a brisk business signing up people for lessons and others purchasing yarn and accessories to begin new projects. He was proud of Georgi, who at thirty-two had moved out of the house where she'd lived all her life to become an independent adult. Her decision to leave Powell's Department Store, where she'd assisted the father managing it, had prompted him to step up and fill the void.

He had to agree with his mother. Completing any article in the shop required using a stitch. "It is ingenious."

"Sutton, now that your mother is working at the store, what are your future plans?" Evelyn questioned.

"He has lots of options," Michelle said, preempting Sutton's response. "He has degrees in education and history. Which means he can always get a teaching position at a high school or even a college."

Evelyn glared at her older sister. "Can you please let the man speak for himself?"

Sutton saw his mother lower her eyes with Evelyn's sharp retort. There were times when his aunt's tongue was as pointed as a samurai sword, and this was one of them. "My mother is right. I do have a lot of options, which also extend to becoming an athletic coach. Even though the new school year will begin in another week, I'm going to update my résumé and send it to several school districts."

"I know it has been a while, but I still may have a few contacts over at the local school district," Michelle volunteered.

"That's okay and thanks for the offer, Mom. I'd rather do this on my own."

"Sutton is a lot more fortunate than I was at his age," Bruce stated solemnly. "I didn't get the opportunity to go to college because my father and grandfather expected me to come on board and work full-time at the store within days of graduating high school."

"If you'd gone to college, what would you have studied?" Michelle asked her brother-in-law.

A wistful smile parted Bruce's lips. "Veterinary medicine. I was in the second grade and my best friend had a dog who'd had a litter of puppies. I'd go to his house every day to watch their mama feed them until they grew bigger and were old enough to be adopted. When I asked my mother if I could have a puppy, she told me she was allergic to dogs and cats, and that dashed my hopes of becoming a vet."

Sutton wanted to tell his uncle that although it had been a long-held practice that he work in the family business, he could've broken with tradition and pursued his dream to attend veterinary college because he did have a brother and sister who could have stepped in to allow Bruce to live out his dream. The archaic mandate had been repeated in another generation with Georgina. Her dream of becoming an illustrator vanished with her younger brother's passing. However, she'd finally challenged her family to control her own destiny. Sutton had offered to help her because he was transitioning from a professional athlete to a private citizen, and he'd also made his position known to Bruce beforehand that his tenure at the department store would not be permanent.

He never resented having a single mother because she'd raised him believing nothing was beyond his reach if he was willing to work hard to achieve his goal. The salary she'd earned working for the Johnson County school district paid the rent for a small two-bedroom house and put food on the table and clothes on his back. And when he was old enough, he went to work for his uncle at the department store during school breaks. Michelle took him to the local bank and had him open a savings account to deposit his first paycheck, and given her experience as the school district's business manager, she'd taught him how to budget his earnings.

Dinner concluded with Sutton kissing his mother and aunt and thanking his uncle for his hospitality, and he drove the short distance to his house. He parked the sports car in the driveway and went into the house. He toyed with the idea of updating his résumé, then decided it was time to stop procrastinating and do it.

He exchanged his shirt and slacks for a T-shirt and shorts before retrieving a folder with transcripts and copies of recommendations from various instructors and professors. Sutton had just retrieved his laptop when he heard the ear-piercing sound of the Aston Martin's alarm. Taking long strides, he walked to the front door and saw Zoey's brother attempting to open the driver's side door.

He was on the boy before Harper had realized that he wasn't alone. "What do you think you're doing?"

"I… I wasn't trying to steal your car."

Sutton tightened his grip on back of the boy's shirt when he turned to run away. "Where do you think you're going?"

"Home."

"Wrong answer, Harper. I'm going to talk to your sister before I call the sheriff, and have you arrested for breaking into my vehicle."

"Please don't do that."

Sutton ignored the quaver in the teen's voice. "And why not?" he asked, forcibly steering Harper toward his house. He hadn't formally met Zoey's brother, but whenever he sat out on the porch at night, he'd observed him getting out of the same car several nights during the past week. He was coming home earlier than he had when Sutton first saw him with an unsteady gait. His hand went from Harper's shirt to the nape of his neck as he steered him up the porch steps and rang the doorbell.

Zoey raced down the staircase when the doorbell chimed throughout the house. It appeared as if someone hadn't taken their finger off the bell. She flung open the door to find Sutton gripping her brother's neck as he struggled to free himself.

"Let him go!" Her hands fisted. "Now or I'll call the sheriff, and have you arrested for assaulting a minor. And if you've hurt my brother, I'll sue the hell out of you!"

"And what if I tell the sheriff that your dear brother tried to steal my car?"

Nothing moved but her eyes as she stared at Sutton, and then Harper. She hadn't seen her neighbor in more than a week since they'd shared coffee on her porch. "My brother is not a thief!"

Sutton loosened his grip on Harper's nape. "Maybe you'll believe it if your brother will explain what he was doing trying to break into my vehicle."

The tears filling Harper's eyes overflowed. "I... I just wanted..."

Zoey felt as if her head was going to explode. She'd gotten her brother to come home before ten, but now he was attempting to break into someone's car. "You just wanted *what*?" she asked between clenched teeth.

Sniffling, Harper bit his lip. "I just wanted to look inside."

She covered her mouth with her hand to stop the acerbic words from spilling out. She was at her wit's end as to what to do with Harper. Then, she slowly lowered her hand. "Look inside or take it for a joyride?" He'd recently gotten his driver's license and had asked nonstop to let him drive her minivan. It was her only vehicle and she did not trust him with her mode of transportation.

Harper pulled back his shoulders as if girding himself for what was to come. "Both."

Sutton grunted under his breath. "At least you didn't lie about that."

Zoey stood off to the side. "Please come in, Sutton. We need to talk before you make your phone call."

"Zoey!" Harper cried, wiping his nose on the back of his hand.

She rounded on him. "Don't you dare open your mouth to say another word until I talk to Sutton. It's apparent you really want to ruin your life. I suppose being picked up for public intoxication and indecency wasn't enough, so now you have to resort to car theft."

Sutton went completely still. He had no idea Zoey had had to deal with a teenage boy who could possibly be charged as a juvenile offender or, depending upon the discretion of the prosecutor, as an adult. At thirty-six he was old enough to have had a sixteen-year-old son and wondered what he would do if faced with a similar situation.

He pointed to a chair. "Sit down, Harper. Now!" he ordered when the boy hesitated. Sutton waited for Zoey to sit on a love seat before dropping down beside her. There was enough illumination from floor and table lamps to see that her hands were shaking. He didn't know if it was from fear or anger. Reaching for her hand, he threaded their fingers together to stop their trembling.

"I don't know if you're aware of it, but Miss Williams installed a security system that is linked to the sheriff's office to monitor activity if anyone attempted to break in. And that means you were on camera when you tried to open the door to my car."

Harper's eyes appeared abnormally large as he stared at him. "Are you going to have me arrested?"

"That all depends on you, Harper."

"Why me?"

"Do you want to get handcuffed and fingerprinted and become a statistic in the criminal justice system like so many young boys who look like you?"

Harper sandwiched his hands between his knees. "No, sir."

"Then why do you keep messing up?" Zoey asked.

"I don't know."

"You don't know, and I don't know," she said. "I want you to sit on the porch while I talk to Mr. Reed."

Sutton waited for Harper to leave and then gave Zoey's hand a gentle squeeze. "Does your brother have a curfew? Because I've noticed he's come in rather late for someone his age."

"Yes, he does. He has a ten o'clock curfew and every Saturday morning he has to mow the back-yard and bundle the garbage for the Monday morning pickup."

"What about when school is in session?"

"I've told him he has to come home directly after class, and no hanging out with his friends."

"What about sports, Zoey?"

"What about them?"

"Does he play on a school team?"

"No. However, he is an above-average student."

"Academics are not enough. He needs a channel to let out some of his pent-up energy and other frustrations boys his age may be experiencing."

Zoey eased her hand from his loose grip. "Are you talking about sex, Sutton?"

He was slightly taken aback that she was so direct, but then Sutton had to remember she'd shepherded her brothers from boyhood through puberty. "That could be part of it. I've been where Harper is now. Remember he doesn't have a father and that, too, can impact his behavior. I grew up not knowing who my father was until I was an adult, and whenever I saw other boys hanging out with their dads it hit me hard, and I swore if I ever had a son I would strive to have a relationship with him even if I didn't with his mother."

"Are you saying you wouldn't mind being a baby daddy?"

Sutton's jaw hardened. It was apparent Zoey misunderstood him. "No. That's not what I'm saying. I intend to be married whenever I have children." He did not want a repeat of what his mother had had to go through. "However, if my marriage ends in divorce it doesn't mean that I'll divorce my children. Enough about me. Now about Harper."

"What about him, Sutton?"

"I assume it hasn't been easy for you to raise two boys on your own given your age. And you should know I don't want Harper arrested because he doesn't need to be added to the ever-increasing numbers of young black men who are incarcerated."

Zoey closed her eyes for several seconds. "I told Harper that if he got in trouble again, I was going to court to apply for a PINS."

"Don't do that, Zoey. What you don't want is for your brother to become a statistic in the juvenile legal system."

Her hands fisted. "What other option do I have? I can't lock him in the house when I leave for work, and there's still more than a week before the new school year begins. With him in school, at least I'll know where he is and that he has adult supervision between the hours of eight and three."

"What time is your shift at the hospital?"

"I don't work at a hospital. I'm registered with a Mineral Springs home health care agency. I begin work at eight and I'm off at four. I don't accept overnight or weekend assignments because Harper still needs supervision."

Sutton had mentored countless kids as a professional athlete, and he knew this was one time he had to step up to help Zoey with her brother. There was something about Harper that reminded him of himself at sixteen. Sutton had harbored a lot of resentment when he saw the fathers of his teammates who'd come to their high school baseball games to cheer on and support their sons. He didn't know what issues Harper was dealing with and hoped they weren't so deep-rooted that the boy would require professional counseling.

"What if I try to help you with your brother?"

Zoey stared at Sutton as if he'd suddenly taken leave of his senses. She recalled his *I'll be around if you need help with anything*, but she didn't think his *anything* extended to her personal problems. "How?"

"I need to know a little about Harper before I can formulate a plan to hopefully steer him in the right direction."

She paused. "What do you want to know?" The only person she'd ever divulged anything about her family to was a counselor who legally and professionally could not reveal any of their discussions.

"Do you give Harper an allowance?" Sutton asked.

"Yes. I give him twenty dollars a week."

"Other than mowing the grass and taking care of the garbage, does he have any other chores?"

Zoey shook her head. "No."

"Is he into sports?" Sutton asked, as he continued questioning her.

"Yes, but only to watch them on television."

"Does he have a driver's license?"

A slight frown appeared between Zoey's eyes. "Yes, but what does that have to do with Harper?" She hadn't realized she was holding her breath when Sutton outlined his proposal. What he'd planned was so simple that it was almost foolproof.

"Do I have your permission to show him a little tough love and hopefully stop him from going down the wrong road that will probably end with a criminal record?"

Zoey prayed Sutton would do what she had been unable to do for her brother because Harper was in awe of the baseball phenom, and although he'd begun coming in before his curfew expired and getting up early on weekends to mow the backyard and bag the garbage, that still hadn't stopped him from attempting to break into her neighbor's car.

"Yes, you do." She stood. "I'm going to go and get him."

She found Harper on the porch swing, eyes closed and his head resting on the cushioned back. "You can come in now."

Harper's body language spoke volumes as he followed her. He was frightened. In that instant Zoey felt like doing something she hadn't done in years—cry. Her heart turned over when she saw Harper's shoulders slump in defeat, and she curbed the urge to hug him. She had to remember he wasn't a frightened little boy who couldn't sleep during thunderstorms and she had to sit in bed with him until he finally fell asleep. He also wasn't the little boy who insisted on placing flowers on the graves of his parents on the anniversary of their deaths for years until he said it was stupid because they couldn't smell them. Kyle was her quiet, obedient, willing-to-please brother, while it was apparent Harper was acting out in an attempt to mask what she believed were adolescent insecurities.

"Do you want me to stay?" Zoey asked Sutton when Harper retook the chair he'd vacated.

Sutton met her eyes, and then stared at Harper. "Yes, please."

She claimed another chair, leaving Sutton on the love seat. He had outlined what he wanted to ask Harper, and although she'd agreed they were appropriate, she did not want to witness what she thought would become a heart-to-heart talk between the two.

Sutton gave Harper a long glance. "I was talking to your sister and told her I wouldn't call the sheriff's office if you agree to do whatever I propose. Think of it as a plea bargain. Do you understand what I'm saying, Harper?"

Harper shook his head like a bobblehead doll before staring down at the floor. "Yes, sir."

"What I am going to propose will be in effect for the next three months," Sutton told Harper. "Do you think you will be able to do something for three months without giving up?"

Harper's head popped up and he gave Sutton a direct stare. "Do I have a choice?" There was a trace of bravado in his query.

Sutton's expression hardened, and he gave Harper a death stare and she wanted to warn her brother that this wasn't the time to challenge a man whose car he'd attempted to break into and possibly take on a joyride, which translated to car theft.

"Yes, Harper, you have a choice," she spat out angrily. "Now get rid of the attitude." Her reprimand appeared to have an effect because Harper's face and body crumbled like a deflated balloon.

"I'm sorry about that," he whispered. "I'm ready to listen, Mr. Reed."

Sutton leaned forward. "How old are you, Harper?"

"Sixteen."

"You're sixteen and engaging in underage drinking."

Harper lowered his eyes. "I'm not drinking now. And it was only beer."

"Where did you get the beer?"

"I have a friend in Mineral Springs, and I give his older brother money to buy beer for us." He paused. "I can't get it here because everyone knows me."

"Does your friend's brother have a name?" Sutton questioned.

The natural color drained from Harper's face, leaving it a sallow yellowish-brown. "Why do you want to know?"

Sutton flashed a wry smile. "Perhaps the law over in the Springs should know that an adult is buying beer for underage kids."

"You don't have to say anything, Mr. Reed, because I'm not drinking anymore."

"Do you smoke?"

"Smoke what?"

"Cigarettes or weed, Harper."

"Not really."

Zoey let out a groan. Now she knew why Sutton wanted her to stay during his questioning. It was obvious he could get Harper to reveal things to him when he could possibly lie to her. Not only was her brother drinking but he was also smoking weed. She gave him an allowance so he would have some money in his pocket, not give it to an adult to buy alcohol for a teenager. How had she failed so miserably with

Harper when she'd given him the same rules as she had with Kyle?

Crossing his arms over his chest and stretching out long legs, Sutton slumped lower on the love seat. "What do you mean *not really*?"

"I smoked once, and my heart was beating so fast that I thought it was going to explode. It was the first and last time I smoked weed."

"That's because it was probably laced with PCP or something else that could've possibly killed you," Sutton explained. "What about pills, meth, coke?"

"No!"

"That's good because you're going to need to be in good shape if you have to get up at dawn to work out with me."

"Work out how?"

"I run, Harper. We will begin with a slow jog until you build up enough stamina to put in a couple of miles. I'm sure you'll be able to do it because Zoey told me you passed your last physical with flying colors."

"I don't like running."

"And I don't like you breaking into my car," Sutton retorted. "I suggest you get plenty of sleep because I expect to see you standing outside my house at five o'clock every morning—rain or shine."

"I don't have workout clothes," Harper mumbled under his breath.

"Oh, that's not a problem," Sutton drawled, grinning. "I'll pick you up tomorrow morning at ten and we'll go to Powell's. I'll buy you whatever you'll need to jog with me every morning for the next three months."

"I can't believe you want me to jog on the days I have to go to school."

"Believe it, Harper, because your sister has given me her approval. I suggest you get plenty of sleep because you're going to need to stay alert if you are going to compete with me."

Harper rose and walked out of the living room and stomped up the staircase to the second story. Zoey also stood. "I suppose you didn't give him much of a choice. My brother would prefer hanging out and staying up late playing video games and then wasting away the afternoon watching television."

Sutton approached her, smiling. "He'll get over it. Once he begins running, he'll change his attitude. There's something about it that gives you a high you can't get from any drug."

Zoey tilted her chin, returning his smile. "How can I thank you for getting him to open up about things he probably would've lied to me about. I knew he was drinking because I could smell the beer on his breath, but I had no idea he'd smoked weed."

Sutton rested his hands on her shoulders. "You're lucky he had a bad reaction to it. Just between you and me, once he shows me he's changed, I'm going to eventually let him drive the Aston Martin."

"You can't!" She did not want to believe Sutton was going to let a teenager drive his six-figure sports car.

He smiled. "Yes, I can. We'll take it out on the back roads where he can get used to the engine. And don't worry. I'll make certain to bring him back safe and sound."

Her eyelids fluttered. "You promise?"

He dropped his hands. "Yes, I promise."

Zoey studied his handsome face as if committing it to memory. Not only did he look good, but he also smelled wonderful. Despite the seriousness of her situation, it had been much too long since she'd found herself attracted to a man because there had been no room in her busy life to even fantasize about one. But this man lived next door and there was no way she could avoid him, because his connection with her brother for the next three months was what Harper needed at this time in his life: a positive male role model.

"Good night and thank you again, Sutton."

A beat passed. "Good night, Zoey."

She waited for him to leave and then closed and locked the door behind him. Breathing out an audible sigh, she turned off the floor lamp and lowered the settings on the ones on the tables and went upstairs. The door to Harper's bedroom was open. He was sitting on the side of the bed, his head in his hands. Zoey hoped he was thinking about how close he'd come to ruining his life if Sutton had called the sheriff to report him for breaking into his car.

She walked down the hallway to her bedroom and closed the door. Before the doorbell rang, she'd planned to read until it was time for her to retire for bed, but the interruption wouldn't permit her to concentrate. Reaching for the remote, Zoey tuned the television to the Hallmark Channel. Even though she'd viewed the romantic movie before, it was what she needed to relax because she'd had enough excitement for one day.

She managed to watch the entire movie without falling asleep, and when it ended, she went into the en suite bath to wash her face and brush her teeth. After slipping into a nightgown, she checked her cell phone to make certain she hadn't set the alarm because she would not have a client for the next two weeks. Mrs. Chambers's son and daughter-in-law had driven down midweek to take her to a skilled residential nursing facility in Washington, DC.

Zoey had made it a practice to take vacation at the same time every year to shop for school supplies and go through her brothers' closets to inventory what they could still wear and what to donate to the local church's outreach.

After adjusting the pillows cradling her shoulders, Zoey turned off the lamp on the bedside table and closed her eyes. She lay in the darkened room, her mind filled with the image of Sutton's grip on her brother's neck, unaware why he'd sought to use physical force to bring him home. Her initial outrage had turned to embarrassment and shame once he revealed Harper's attempt to break into his car. And she wondered if Harper realized he'd dodged a bullet because if he'd been caught breaking into anyone else's vehicle he would not be sleeping in his own bed but on a cot in a jail cell.

The events of the day were forgotten when Zoey

finally succumbed to the comforting embrace of Morpheus, where when she awoke it was always with an optimism that she was getting closer to her ultimate goal of attending nursing school.

Chapter Four

Sutton waited for Harper to fasten his seat belt before shifting into gear and backing the Jeep Wrangler out of the driveway. When he'd walked out of the house at exactly ten, he'd found the teenager waiting for him. It was a positive sign that the young man was serious about adhering to the terms of their agreement.

"I like your Jeep, Mr. Reed."

Sutton gave him a sidelong glance. "Thank you." He paused. "Do you like cars?"

Shifting slightly on his seat, Harper smiled. "Yes. Once I got my license, I asked Zoey if I could drive her van when she's not using it."

"What did she say?"

"No, because she needs it to get to work, and if I got into an accident, she would be assed-out."

Sutton's eyebrows lifted slightly. "Did she actually say assed-out?"

"Not really. My sister doesn't like it when I curse, but that's because she's old-school about a lot of things. She's not even thirty but she acts like an old fart."

Struggling to tamp down his rising temper, Sutton stared out the windshield. "If your sister, whom you refer to as an old fart, hadn't gone along with our deal, then you would've been handcuffed and shackled while riding in the back of a police van on your way to the court this morning. I'm certain a judge would probably believe putting you in jail is what you'll need to get rid of your feigned badass attitude. And, I don't want you cussing around me." He gave him a quick glance. "I'm running this show, not you, so it's either my way or the highway straight to the county jail. What's it going to be, Harper? I can't hear you," he goaded, when he encountered silence.

"It's your way, Mr. Reed."

Sutton forced a smile. He did not want to bully the boy but knew instinctively that Harper Allen was going to be challenging. One year he'd made a commitment to an organization to mentor at-risk youth and he'd been assigned to mentor several boys living in a Georgia group home. Most were in awe of his celebrity status but there was one training to become an amateur boxer who wouldn't stop harassing him until Sutton put on a pair of boxing gloves and got into the ring with him.

He'd managed to sidestep his opponent's first punch before, with a sweeping motion with his foot, he took him off balance, and he went down within seconds. Not only was he bigger and stronger and had incredible eye-hand control, but Sutton had no intention of hitting the boy but rather embarrassing him. It worked, and in the six weeks that ensued he'd formed a bond with all five boys that continued even after they'd aged out. They continued to keep in touch with him on Facebook and Twitter, updating him on what was going on in their lives. Two had graduated school and enrolled in college; the wannabe boxer who'd had an illustrious amateur career had turned pro; one had enrolled in the military while the remaining one fell through the cracks and was in prison serving a life sentence without the possibility of parole for first-degree murder.

Despite four of the five beating the odds to become productive citizens, it was the last one who grieved Sutton, and although he did not blame himself for the young man's choosing to become a criminal, he was troubled by the fact that there was no hope of him ever venturing beyond the walls of a maximum security prison.

"Now that we've gotten that out of the way, I believe we're going to get along," he said to Harper. "Are you thinking about joining a sports team when you go back to school?"

"No, sir."

"Why not?"

"I like basketball and football, but my sister would never let me play football because she doesn't want me to get concussions. She's studying to become a nurse, so she knows a lot about the human body."

Sutton had to agree with Zoey. If he'd had a son, he would be reluctant to allow him to play football with the increasing numbers of professional players being diagnosed with brain injuries. He then recalled Zoey telling him she was a home health aide. "Is she in nursing school?"

"Not yet. She says she wants to wait until I graduate. She's waiting to become a nurse and she's waiting to get a boyfriend."

Sutton's eyebrows lifted slightly with Harper's reference to his sister not dating anyone, and he did not want to ask the boy if she was dating someone now. "How tall are you and how much do you weigh?" he questioned instead.

"Six one and one seventy," Harper replied.

"You would be perfect for basketball as a small forward."

"I shoot hoops with my friend Jabari. Even though he's taller than me, I'm able to beat him when it comes to three-pointers."

Sutton heard the pride in Harper's voice. "Where do you shoot hoops?"

"We go over to the high school. A couple of years ago they added an outdoor basketball court."

"Times have really changed because when we

wanted to play basketball it was always in the school gym."

"Mr. Reed, why did you decide on baseball instead of football? Because you're a real big dude."

Laughter rumbled in Sutton's chest with Harper's reference to his size. At six four, two hundred and thirty-five pounds, he'd had the speed and bulk to become a linebacker, but since retiring from baseball he'd shed twenty pounds and worked hard not to regain it. There was space in his condo where he'd set up an in-home gym and worked out every other day. The exercise equipment, along with the condo's furnishings, was in a storage unit until he found permanent housing.

"I tried out and made the football team but after sitting on the bench for a year I decided to switch to baseball. It was the best decision I'd ever made, because I really love the game and, thankfully, I've never had a concussion."

"It's not only the head, Mr. Reed. When I see football players sitting in ice baths after a game, I tell myself that's not for me," Harper said, frowning.

"Word," Sutton drawled.

Harper laughed, asking, "Did you ever take an ice bath?"

"The closest I get to something that cold is putting an ice pack on my knee." Slowing and signaling, Sutton turned down the road leading to the downtown business district. "We're going to stop in the shoe store first before heading over to Powell's."

* * *

Zoey had just turned off the vacuum cleaner and stored it in one of the closets off the entryway when she heard her brother's and Sutton's voices. The weather had cooled enough for her to turn off the air conditioners and open windows to let in fresh air.

When she'd gotten up earlier that morning, her intent was to give the house a thorough top-to-bottom cleaning to get that task out of the way so she could enjoy her two-week vacation. Other than working in her garden and catching up on reading, the only other thing on her to-do list was going on Powell's website and ordering school clothes for Harper.

She refused to think of how mundane her existence had become because she had only two years before she could begin to live on her own terms. Harper had made the high school's honor roll and talked about attending college. She hadn't had to withdraw any money from the scholarship fund established by the Wickham Falls residents following her parents' death, and with accruing interest there was enough of a balance to cover four years of tuition for public and some private colleges.

Opening the front door, she walked out onto the porch to find Harper exiting the Jeep holding several shopping bags stamped with Powell's logo.

She rested her hands at her waist. "What on earth did you buy?"

"Stuff," Harper said, grinning like a Cheshire cat.

"Yeah, stuff," Sutton repeated like a coconspirator.

Harper mounted the stairs, Sutton following, and

leaned in close to Zoey. "Mr. Reed brought me the latest Jordans and a pair of Adidas running shoes."

Her jaw dropped and she wanted to go off on her brother but decided to wait to talk to Sutton. Harper had been asking for the Jordans, but she did not have several hundred dollars to spend on a single pair of sneakers that he would either wear out or outgrow in the next six months. And not when she had to buy clothes because many of those he'd worn no longer fit.

"We'll talk about this later." Harper must have registered the censure in her voice when he turned to stare at her.

"I didn't ask Mr. Reed to buy them for me."

"He's right. I offered to buy them," Sutton confirmed.

Zoey gave him a level stare. "*We* need to talk." She did not want Harper to take advantage of her neighbor's goodwill, while she also did not want Sutton to give her brother whatever he asked for. She'd discovered after a few incidents that Harper could turn on and off the charm and he was also quite adept at becoming very manipulative to get his way. Cupping her elbow, Sutton led her to the love seat, waiting for her to sit before he took a facing chair.

Sutton held up a hand. "Before you go off on me, I want you to know that Harper didn't ask me to buy the Jordans. I'd noticed him staring at them while the salesclerk was looking for his running shoes, and I've seen that same expression on the face of countless young boys who want something they couldn't have because their parents need the money to pay the rent or mortgage, or put food on the table. There are times when I asked myself when did a pair of sneakers become handmade designer shoes with price tags comparable to Crockett & Jones?"

"You are preaching to the choir, Sutton."

A hint of a smile tilted the corners of his mouth. "I'm glad you agree." He cleared his throat. "Now, back to your brother. I told him I'd buy the Jordans, but he had to do something to earn them."

Zoey exhaled an audible breath. "What?"

"We worked out a system of barter. Whenever he mows your lawn, he'll also mow mine."

"Was that your suggestion or Harper's?" she asked.

Sutton leaned forward. "It was his. Under another set of circumstances, I would've bought him the shoes with no strings attached."

"Do you make it a habit of buying kids expensive sneakers?"

"I did at one time. I joined an organization nine years ago with other professional athletes that focused on mentoring kids, and even though I'm retired from the game it's difficult for me to step away from that role. Every Christmas we would give the kids one item on their wish lists. Most times it was cell phones and sneakers. They'd get their wish and gift cards so they could buy things for their families. Your brother is a good kid, Zoey, straddling the line between boy- and manhood, and all he needs is someone who's been there, done that to help him with the transition."

Zoey gave him an incredulous look. "Are you saying you also got into trouble?"

"No, because my mother was the queen of tough love. She said she wasn't going to use one copper penny of her hard-earned money to bail me out of jail if I'd had a sudden lapse in judgment and did something stupid that would get me arrested."

"Did you believe her when she said that?" Zoey questioned.

Sutton flashed a wide grin. "Every single word. Michelle Reed was not one to issue idle threats." Suddenly he sobered. "My mother worked hard and sacrificed a lot as a mother raising a boy on her own. And I don't have to tell you that because you've had to raise not one but two boys as a single woman. But the difference is Mom had graduated college and was older than you when she had me."

She nodded. "I have to admit at eighteen I was overwhelmed once I realized I had to become a surrogate mother and breadwinner for my brothers." Zoey did not tell Sutton that she'd been numbed for days up to and including the funeral. It was only when the social worker came to the house to talk about placing her brothers in foster care that she felt a surge of protectiveness that she hadn't believed she possessed. She'd sworn an oath that no one would ever separate her from her brothers. A smile parted her lips. "But when I look back, I'd do it all over again because Dad always said he wanted his children to be raised together because when his mother died his father split his siblings up between different relatives. One brother went to live with an aunt in Texas, another to an uncle in Colorado, and his sisters moved to Michigan to live with his older cousins. And because he was the eldest, Dad stayed with my grandfather. I suppose that's why when my parents divorced Dad convinced my mother to let him have sole custody of me."

A slight frown appeared between Sutton's eyes. "Why sole custody when they could've agreed to joint?"

"Dad said he would've agreed if she hadn't planned to leave the state. His fear was she would take me somewhere and he would never see me again. And if they'd shared custody, he couldn't accuse her of kidnapping."

"Where was she planning to move to?"

"I don't know. Dad wouldn't tell me. James Allen was a man of very few words. He'd get up every day, go to work and then come home expecting to find the house clean and dinner on the table."

"How old were you when your parents divorced?" Sutton had asked yet another question.

"Two, and before you ask, I don't remember anything about my mother. My dad got rid of all pictures of them together once they broke up, but I managed to find a photograph of her in an old high school yearbook and I cried myself to sleep for days because seeing it was like looking in the mirror. Dad paid one of our neighbors to look after me whenever he went to work until he married again. I'll never forget the day when he walked in with a woman to tell me she was my new mother. Charmaine Jenkins was twenty and four months pregnant with my father's baby." Zoey nearly laughed aloud when she saw Sutton's shocked expression once she'd revealed Charmaine was barely out of her teens.

"Did you get along well with your stepmother?"

Zoey smiled. "Yes. She was like an older sister because she was only eleven years older than me. Charmaine was an incredible cook and taught me many of the dishes she'd learned from her grandmother. She also showed me how to style my hair and apply makeup. And whenever I needed a dress for a school dance, she always volunteered to go with me and pick out something she said was certain to make the other girls jealous."

Sutton's smile matched hers. "So, she wasn't the stereotypical wicked stepmother."

"Not in the least." Zoey sobered. "It may sound odd, but I miss her more than my father. This is not to say I didn't love him, but he wasn't the easiest man to get close to because he wasn't prone to displays of affection. There were times when he appeared uncomfortable if Charmaine hugged or kissed him in front of us."

Sutton studied the woman sitting across from him, thinking about all she'd had to go through in less than thirty years of living. Her father had attempted to erase all evidence of the woman who'd given birth to her. Why, he wondered, would a man do that? Especially to a girl who needed a connection with her mother. He wondered if Zoey realized how strong she was—emotionally. She'd survived losing three of her loved ones, counting her mother, and yet she held on to raise her brothers to adulthood.

Sutton wasn't familiar with Zoey's truck driver father because like some small towns and cities, Wickham Falls was divided into neighborhoods based on social class: college-educated professionals, civil servants, blue-collar workers, the working poor and those living at or below the poverty line. His family fell into the second category after his mother graduated college and found a position with the school district. It was only at school and during sporting events that all residents were equal.

He'd found himself drawn to Zoey because of her undying loyalty to Harper, who he suspected did not appreciate it. Sutton had suggested the plea deal more for Zoey than for Harper because he was aware of the sacrifices she'd made and pressing charges would only serve to compound the anguish she'd experienced over the years.

"I hope you're not going to get on Harper about the Jordans."

"I promise I won't say a word." She mimed zipping her lips.

"Thank…" His words trailed off when the sound of a car's horn rent the air. Shifting on his chair, Sutton saw that the vehicle had stopped, and a teenage girl hung out the passenger-side window waving.

"Hi, Sutton!"

Nodding, he returned the wave.

"Aren't you going to say anything to your fan girls?" Zoey teased.

He turned and glared at her. "Very funny."

"I knew when you moved in next door that there would be more than the usual traffic on the block with folks attempting to get a glimpse of you."

"I had enough of that when I worked at Powell's."

"Worked?" Zoey asked.

"Yes. My mother came up from Georgia, so she's filling in for me." Sutton pushed to his feet. "I'm going to let you get back to whatever you were doing. Now that it's cooler, I plan to grill outside later today. You and Harper are more than welcome to join me."

A beat passed. "I'd like that. Is there something you'd like me to bring?"

Sutton hadn't realized he'd been holding his breath as he awaited her reply, because somehow he'd expected her to decline his invitation when she'd hesitated. "No, thank you. I happen to have everything."

"What about a salad and dessert?"

Sutton studied large dark eyes that never wavered whenever they met his. *Strong. Confident.* Those were the two words that came to mind when they interacted with each other. "Bring whatever you want."

Her eyebrows lifted slightly. "Are you allergic to anything? Chocolate? Nuts? Gluten?"

"No. I eat any and everything that isn't raw or moves on the plate."

Zoey smiled. "What about gelatin?"

Sutton laughed. "That doesn't include gelatin."

"What time do you want us to come?"

"Any time after four. By the way, do you eat red meat?" he asked.

"Yes, Sutton, I do eat red meat."

"I had to ask because I want to make sure I have something that you're able to eat."

Zoey stood and rested a hand on his forearm. "I eat meat, vegetables and fish."

Sutton gave the hand on his arm a gentle squeeze. "That's good to know. Oh, I forgot to ask you if you'd be opposed to me setting up a portable basketball hoop in your backyard."

"Why?"

"Because Harper may try out for the basketball team and I'd like to help him perfect some of his moves."

"Why not baseball, Sutton? After all, you were and still are one of the best in the game."

"Your brother admitted he's afraid of a ninety-mile-an-hour ball coming at him, and you don't want him to play football, so that leaves basketball."

"You're really going to coach him?"

Sutton almost laughed when she eyed him with a critical squint. "Yes. Why are you looking at me like that? You don't believe I can get Harper on the team, do you?" Zoey averted her eyes. "How about a little wager?"

"Okay, Sutton."

"What are you willing to put up if I prove you wrong?"

She lifted her chin in a defiant gesture. "It can't be money."

"I don't want or need your money. How about a night on the town?"

There was no doubt his suggestion shocked her when she went frozen. Nothing moved. Not even her eyes. "In Wickham Falls?"

Throwing back his head, he laughed loudly. "No, Zoey. Not here."

"Do I get to pick the place if I win?" Zoey asked. There was a thread of confidence in her query.

"Of course. And it will be the same with me." He extended his hand. "Do you want to shake on it?"

She placed her hand on his outstretched palm. "You've got yourself a deal."

"I'll order the hoop and set it up." Sutton released her fingers. "I'll expect you later." He'd gotten Harper to agree to try out for the basketball team, and practicing with him was certain to bring back memories of the days when Sutton had spent hours playing pickup ball with some of his mentees during the off-season.

"Later it is."

He walked off the porch and over to his rental and around the back to the shed to take out the gas grill. He had asked Zoey if she ate meat because he'd married a woman who'd monitored every morsel she put into her mouth because as a swimsuit model she did not want to appear *fat* in her photo shoots. And it was her refusal to have a child because she felt it would impact her career that had shattered their marriage.

Sutton met Angell Bailey at a party during his last year in college and they hit it off immediately. She'd missed so many classes because of photo shoots that she had earned only enough credits to become a sophomore rather than a senior. They'd continued to date during his time in the minor leagues and married two months before he was called up to the majors. And whenever he cooked for her, he had to be cognizant of how much oil he'd added to the salad dressing and not butter her thin-sliced wheat toast. Angell never ate dessert or drank coffee or tea because she claimed they stained her teeth. However, there were occasions when she would imbibe too much, which she'd called empty calories, and then would embark on a two-week detox cleanse.

Sutton did not want to think about Angell or compare any woman to her; however, he'd found it difficult to erase eight years of marriage to someone he'd loved unconditionally. There were times when he would have preferred that she'd cheated on him if only to make their eventual breakup more acceptable. It was only when he'd suggested they adopt a child or children that he realized his wife did not want to become a mother although they had discussed and agreed to starting a family before they'd exchanged vows.

He forgot about Angell as he removed the cover from the grill and checked the gauge on the propane tank. It was almost empty, and that meant he had to drive into town and get another one from the hardware store. Since his return, a lot of people had gotten used to seeing him in the business district, some approaching to thank him for touting that Wickham Falls, West Virginia, was one of best small towns in which to grow up, while others had asked him to pose for pictures taken with their camera phones.

Sutton realized he was somewhat of a novelty because of his former high-profile status and once the newness wore off he would become another local resident added to the list of those who'd left and then returned to start over.

Chapter Five

I could get used to this, Zoey thought as she lay on the webbed chaise in her neighbor's backyard. Sutton and Harper manned the grill as the mouthwatering aroma of the marinade on the skirt steaks wafted in the warm summer air. Both wore baseball caps, shorts, T-shirts and flip-flops.

Her contribution to the cookout was ripened strawberries from her garden for a strawberry shortcake, and a salad made with arugula, grape tomatoes, cucumber, Mediterranean olives, feta and crispy chickpeas. A bottle of sesame ginger dressing had been set aside to add to the salad just before serving.

It had been too long since she'd used her backyard for other than occasionally mowing the grass and planting and weeding her vegetable garden. And whenever she ventured outdoors to relax, it was always on the front porch. Just peering up through the lenses of her sunglasses at the puffy clouds in the sky as she had as a girl when she tried to see if they resembled shapes of animals brought back memories of happier times. The year she'd celebrated her thirteenth birthday, her father, who'd worked as a driver for an international shipping company, announced that he'd quit and bought his own tractor trailer. All of his life James Allen had talked about working for himself. He accepted moving and shipping jobs to save enough money to pay off the loan for the truck in five rather than ten years.

Zoey had felt her father's joy as surely as if it was her own, but Charmaine refused to join in the celebration because she knew it would take her husband away from home for days and sometimes weeks at a time, leaving her with the total responsibility of taking care of a three-year-old who still wasn't completely toilet-trained and a teething, colicky one-year-old.

Her dad's decision had upset the tranquility of the Allen household, and Zoey knew she had to step in and help Charmaine with household chores or babysitting her brothers whenever their mother was plagued with chronic migraines, and by the time she was sixteen she was able to put palatable meals on the table that garnered praise from the entire family. Never could she have imagined that she was auditioning for a role she would have to assume two years later.

She closed her eyes and let her senses take over as the heat from the sun warmed her exposed skin. The incessant chatter of birds in overhead trees made her smile as she wondered what they were saying to one another. The smell of grilling meat wafted to her nose, reminding her of how long it had been since her last meal. When Sutton had mentioned cooking out, she'd decided to forgo lunch in order to save her appetite.

"Shame on you, Sutton Alexander Reed, for not calling me to say you were grilling out."

Zoey opened her eyes and sat straight when she heard a feminine voice. Standing several feet away was Georgina Powell. Mixed-race, she had inherited the best physical traits from her Scotch-Irish father and African American mother. Georgina's opening her own needlecraft shop several weeks ago had come as a shock for everyone in town who had expected her to take control of the department store once her father retired.

It was obvious the two women were startled to see each other when they exchanged a lingering stare. "Hello, Georgi." Zoey was the first one to speak. "Congratulations on your new business."

Georgina ran a hand through the brown curly hair with glints of copper falling around her face. "Thank you, Zoey."

"I'm sorry I missed your grand opening, but I had to work."

"That day was so hectic that I can't remember who came and who didn't. But I still have some mementos that I handed out to everyone who stopped by. The next time you're downtown, just stop in and I'll give you one. By the way, do you knit or crochet?"

Zoey grimaced. "I knit a little." Charmaine had taught her how to knit and purl, but she was able to follow only an easy pattern.

"A little is what I need for a project to help lift the spirits of cancer patients at the county hospital. However, I have to talk to my cousin first to see if he's willing to participate as one of the sponsors, and if he agrees then I'll talk to you about it."

Sutton handed Harper a pair of tongs when he saw his cousin. "Take over, chef. Once the steaks begin to brown around the edges, you can take them off the direct heat and place them on the side of the burners to keep them warm. I'll be right back."

His gaze lingered briefly on the curve of Zoey's slim hips in a pair of fitted white jeans before he averted his eyes because he didn't want her to catch him ogling her. And if he was truly honest with himself, he liked staring at her. Dipping his head, he dropped a kiss on Georgina's curly hair. "Hey, Georgi. Should I assume you two know each other?"

Georgina nodded. "Zoey and I occasionally see each other around town." She slipped her arm through Sutton's. I'm sorry to barge in on you while you have company, but could you call me later tonight because I'd like to discuss something with you."

"Of course. I hope you're going to hang out long enough to eat with us."

"I'd love to, but I can't."

"Are you sure?"

"Yes."

"Did you not chastise me for grilling and not calling you?"

"Yes," Georgina repeated, "because if you had, then I wouldn't have made prior plans to eat with someone."

"Do you care to enlighten me as to who this someone is?"

Georgina stared at something over his shoulder. "I suppose if I don't tell you you'll find out soon enough. I'm seeing Langston Cooper."

"The Langston Cooper who's the editor of *The Sentinel* and was one of the finest pitching prospects the Falls ever had before he decided he preferred journalism to baseball?"

Her grin was dazzling. "One and the same, dear cousin."

"All right, all right, all right," he drawled in his best Matthew McConaughey imitation.

Georgina swatted at him. "Should I assume that you approve of me dating one of your former high school classmates?"

"It doesn't matter whether I approve or disapprove. I'm just glad you found someone who makes you happy."

"He makes me laugh, Sutton."

His expressive eyebrows lifted. "So, you're not serious?"

"No. We are just friends." Sutton tried to imagine his high school friend and classmate dating his cousin and failed. They were complete opposites. Langston was worldly, while Georgina at thirty-two had spent all of her life under her parents' roof in Wickham Falls.

"Good for you, Georgi."

"I'm going to leave now so you can get back to your guests." She turned on her heel and smiled at Zoey. "Don't forget to stop in whenever you have time."

"I won't," she said.

Sutton waited for Georgina to leave before he moved closer to Zoey and reached for her hand. "We just put the steaks on, and the corn is done, so it's almost time to eat." He did not react when her fingers tightened on his.

She smiled up at him. "Perfect timing, because my stomach is making rumbling noises."

He curbed the urge to kiss her mouth to find out if it was as soft as it appeared. "Come sit and I'll bring you what you want."

"Hey, Zoey, this salad is really good," Harper said as he refilled his plate.

Zoey inclined her head. "Thank you."

He usually complained about eating any vegetable, declaring that he preferred meat and carbs; however, she wasn't ready to admit that Sutton's limited interaction with her brother had positively affected him.

"I have to agree with Harper," said Sutton, who also had a second helping. "At first I thought the crunchiness was croutons before I realized they were chickpeas."

"Do you like vegetables, Mr. Reed?" Harper asked.

Sutton smiled. "Of course. How do you think I got this big," he said teasingly. "My mother wouldn't let me leave the table unless I ate my vegetables. One day she made succotash and when I discovered it had okra, I told her I wasn't eating it. It ended in a stalemate when I spent the night in the kitchen sleeping on the floor next to the table."

"What did she say, Mr. Reed?"

"She woke me up and told me to go to bed. I never had to eat okra again, but I wasn't exempt from the other vegetables she put on the table. As I got older, I realized I couldn't exist on meat and potatoes and learned to eat healthy, and that meant food on a plate should always have color—green, yellow, red, orange, brown and black."

Harper scrunched up his nose. "Black! You can't be talking about burnt food."

Zoey, listening intently to Sutton and Harper, shifted so they wouldn't see her smirking. She was still in awe at how Sutton was able to draw her brother out of his shell. With her he tended to be monosyllabic, and if he did talk it was usually curt and condescending. Most times she walked away before it escalated into a shouting match and threats. What Zoey did not want was a repeat of the arguments between her father and stepmother. Charmaine wouldn't greet her husband with a hug and kiss whenever he returned from driving across the country but with a complaint that she was overwhelmed with all she had to do when he was "gallivanting all over the road with who knows who." James wouldn't hold back when he told his wife that he was working like a dog to keep a roof over her head and provide for their children. Charmaine's veiled accusation that James was cheating on her was based on their relationship, which had begun when he delivered packages to an auto supply company where she'd worked as a receptionist.

Zoey would gather her brothers and sit out on the porch to wait for the yelling to stop. She always cautioned them to be very quiet before they went back into the house because Daddy was going to bed because he was very tired from driving for long hours.

"What about black beans?" Sutton asked.

Harper hit his forehead with the heel of his hand. "I forgot about them. Zoey makes good black bean soup."

Sutton winked at Zoey. "Maybe one day she'll make it for *us*."

"I usually make soup during the cooler months." Harper's favorites were chili and black bean.

"I'm right next door, so you'll know where to find me."

"Mr. Reed, have you ever taken steroids?" Harper asked, changing the topic of conversation.

Sutton's expression changed as a frown settled over his features. "Never."

Zoey felt like an interloper as Sutton answered Harper's questions, but there was nothing in his voice or body language that indicated annoyance, which had probably come from his experience mentoring young people. She took a sip of the raspberry iced tea, meeting Sutton's eyes over the rim of the glass. He appeared so relaxed and natural with her brother that she wondered why he hadn't fathered children. Did he or his ex-wife not want to or couldn't have children?

"Zoey, do you mind if I hang out with Triple Jay?"

She blinked as if coming out of a trance. Jabari Johnson Jr., better known as Triple Jay, and Harper shared a number of classes, lived within walking distance of each other and had become best friends. Jabari's father gave up his position as a postal inspector to own and operate the local dry cleaner/Laundromat; the former owners, an elderly couple, had relocated to a vacation community in Mobile, Alabama.

"Okay, but—"

"I know. Don't come home too late," Harper said, cutting off her warning. He stood up. "Mr. Reed, do you want me to help you clean up before I leave?"

Zoey's jaw dropped. Harper would assist her cooking, but never asked whether he could help her whenever they finished a meal.

"Nah, Harper," Sutton said. "I got this, but thanks for asking. What time did we agree to meet tomorrow morning?"

"Five."

"Then five it is."

She waited for her brother to be out of earshot, and

then shifted to give Sutton a long stare. "You must be a magic genie to have turned Harper into someone I don't recognize."

"I told you before that he's a good boy and probably just needs someone he can open up to."

"You don't think it's hero worship?"

Leaning back in his chair, Sutton crossed his arms over his chest. "No, I don't. There are some boys who need a male figure to answer the questions they don't feel comfortable talking to their mothers or other women about."

"It can't be sex because I've had the *talk* with him. I even bought condoms for him because I told him I had no intention of becoming an auntie when I was still raising him."

A hint of a smile played at the corners of Sutton's mouth. "It sounds as if you really didn't hold back."

"I can't afford to bite my tongue with Harper, because he's the type if you give him an inch he will take a yard."

"Are you saying a hard head makes for a soft behind?"

Zoey laughed softly. "Either a soft behind or grounded for life."

Sutton's laughter joined hers. "I prefer a soft behind because a spanking is quick while grounding can be limitless." He stopped laughing and sobered. "I'd like to ask you a personal question, and you don't have to answer it if you don't want to."

A flicker of apprehension swept over Zoey as she

struggled not to exhibit any uneasiness. "What do you want to know?"

Sutton lowered his arms and sat straight. "Do you regret putting your life on hold to raise your brothers?"

"No, never. The only regrets I have are losing my father and Charmaine, and not knowing my mother. Other than that, I have none."

"So, you don't regret not being married or having children of your own?"

"I'm only twenty-eight, and for me that means there's time to become a nurse, fall in love, get married and even consider having children."

"You want children?"

"Why wouldn't I want children, Sutton? After all, I've had more than enough experience raising Harper and Kyle. And what about you, Sutton? Do you regret growing up without your father?"

Sutton knew when he asked Zoey the question he'd opened himself for her to delve into his past. As a public figure, his professional life had become an open book and fodder for gossip; however, he'd managed to keep his private life a secret. Folks in Wickham Falls knew he'd been raised by a single mother, but no one other than his aunt Evelyn and subsequently his ex-wife knew Michelle Reed had been sleeping with a man who'd drained her bank account and then disappeared when she told him she was pregnant with his child.

"No, because he was a fraud. He used my mother

for whatever he could get from her, and when she told him she was pregnant he disappeared. Years later when he'd heard that I'd signed with the Braves he showed up at the hotel where I was staying, and to say I was shocked to see him is an understatement."

"How did you know he was your dad if you'd never met him?"

"It was like looking at myself thirty years into the future. I walked past him as if he did not exist and that was the first and last time I saw him. A few years later when my mother moved to Atlanta she'd hinted that she'd run into him, and I tried to tell her that it was no accident that he was in Georgia. He knew I'd bought her a house and he figured he could sweet-talk her again and get what he wanted before moving on to his next victim.

"When I suspected he was still hanging around Mom, I refused to take her calls until she got rid of him for good. I was at an away game when she left a voice mail message on my phone that she gave Gerard Clinton his final walking papers and she doubted whether she would ever see him again. I didn't ask what she'd done, and she didn't elaborate. My aunt claims she's a lightning rod for the downtrodden. The folks she calls friends are anything but. They just drop by and hang out because they know Mom will order in whatever they want to eat while drinking up every drop of liquor in her house. And I can't understand why my mother keeps a fully stocked bar when she'll rarely take a drink."

"It takes all kinds to make a world," Zoey murmured. "There are those that give and those that take."

"How true," he said in agreement. His mother was a giver and his father a taker.

Late-afternoon shadows heralded the onset of dusk as the intermittent glow from fireflies and hissing and flickering from lighted citronella candles reminded Sutton that the time had passed more quickly than he'd wanted. Being with Zoey had a calming effect on him. He found her open, unpretentious and nonjudgmental. And there was no woe-is-me when it came to stepping up and assuming responsibility for her younger siblings, knowing there were so many things she could've done and missed as a twenty-something woman.

"Are we still on for dessert?" he asked.

Zoey pushed to her feet. "Yes. I'll help you clean up here and then we can go to my place for cake and coffee."

Sutton also stood. "There's not much to put away. After I take the leftovers inside, I'll be over." He waited for Zoey to walk through the gate of the fence separating the two properties before clearing the table. He took the platter with steak and corn inside the house and into the kitchen, covered it with plastic wrap and placed it on a shelf in the refrigerator.

Cooking outdoors with Harper and Zoey was a reminder of what he'd been missing. It's not that he hadn't entertained in Atlanta, but this afternoon was different. For a moment he wondered how different his life would've been if he'd married someone like

Zoey and they'd had children. Backyard cookouts would've become commonplace with her, his family and their close friends and not the hordes Angell needed to ensure she'd be the center of attention.

He drew the shades, turned on several lamps and then went next door to continue what had become a very special day that had begun with taking Harper shopping. The teenage boy admitted to him in confidence that he blamed his father for spending so much time away from home whenever he went out on the road. And it pained him to hear his mother fight with her husband and cry when he left because she feared she would never see him again. Sutton knew it had to be a heavy emotional burden to carry for so many years, but also knew what Harper had confided to him he would not and could not disclose to his sister.

Sutton rang the bell as he peered through the glass of the outer door. Moments later Zoey appeared from the rear. "It's open."

He opened the door and locked it behind him. "Do you always leave the outer door unlocked?"

"No. But I knew you were coming over, so I decided not to lock it. Please come in the kitchen. I was just going to take the shortcake out of the fridge when you rang the bell."

Sutton followed her through the living and dining rooms to an eat-in kitchen that reminded him of photos in magazines geared for country living. Everything about the space felt like a comforting hug, from the round wooden table with seating for six to the breakfast nook with padded bench seats.

Clay pots overflowing with fresh herbs lined a trio of window ledges.

If it hadn't been for the updated stainless-steel appliances, Sutton would've believed he'd stepped back in time in the all-white kitchen when he spied a wood-burning stove in a far corner that appeared incongruent to the modern furnishings.

"Do you still use that stove?"

"Yes. But only in the winter because it heats up the kitchen and most of the first story. When the older appliances began breaking down and I had to replace them, I couldn't bring myself to get rid of it."

"It adds a lot of character to the kitchen."

"I agree. Initially I wanted to buy a vintage Vulcan stove with eight burners, three ovens and a warming drawer, but it was too expensive, and I would've had to remove some of the cabinets and countertops to make it fit."

"Maybe in the next house you'll be able to get what you want."

Frowning, Zoey shook her head. "I doubt there will be a next house for me, unless I get married and have kids. But that's not going to be for a while. This place will belong to Harper once I graduate nursing school."

Sutton felt a momentary rush of panic. He'd come back to Wickham Falls to find someone with whom he could be friends and possibly in a relationship with in the future, while she was talking about moving away. "Do you plan to leave the Falls?"

"Probably. It would be ideal if I could get a position with the county hospital where I could either rent or buy a condo in Beckley."

"Isn't Harper planning to go to college?"

Zoey turned on the single-serve coffeemaker. "Yes. But he says he wants to commute as opposed to living on campus. Unlike Kyle, he has no intention of leaving Wickham Falls."

"He's going to live here alone while you go to nursing school." Sutton's question was a statement.

Resting a hip against the countertop, Zoey gave him a long, penetrating stare. "No. I plan on getting a bachelor's degree in nursing, which means Harper and I will be in college at the same time."

He bit back a smile. It meant she was going to be around for at least the next six years. "It looks like you've got everything planned out well in advance." Zoey knew exactly what she wanted and intended to do while his future was still up in the air. He'd updated and sent out résumés, and now he would have to wait to see whether he would get a response. And if and when he did, then the next step would be contacting his former colleges for them to forward official transcripts.

"I have to plan, otherwise my life would be a complete mess." She removed two cups and saucers and dessert plates from an overhead cabinet.

He watched her walk over to the refrigerator and remove a pedestal plate with a cake decorated with cream and large fresh strawberries. "That looks delicious. Did you buy the cake from Sasha's Sweet Shoppe?"

Zoey set the plate on the table in the breakfast nook. "No. I made it myself."

"You're kidding."

"No, I'm not. The strawberries are from my garden. I planted several flats last year, but I never got to eat them because critters were feasting on the tomatoes, strawberries, cucumbers and peppers. This spring I bought a portable wire enclosure from the hardware store and it did the trick."

"How long have you been gardening?"

"This is only my second year." She returned to the fridge and took out a container of cream. "Please sit and I'll bring you your coffee. There's sugar on the table if you need it."

Sutton sat, watching her move around the kitchen, using no wasted motion as she placed forks, spoons, napkins and a cake knife on the smooth knotty pine table. The homemade treat reminded him of Sunday dinners with Granny Dot's cakes. His childhood had been easy, uncomplicated with no thought as to the next day except to go to school and play. As he matured, he had come to accept that if his mother had married Gerard Clinton he would've learned to despise his father. And he did not hate the amoral man who preyed on vulnerable women to get what he wanted before disappearing to find his next mark. Sutton was merely indifferent.

The aroma of brewing coffee filled the kitchen and Sutton sprang up to take the cup and saucer from Zoey. The back of his right hand brushed her breast, and she jumped slightly and would've spilled the hot brew if his reflexes had been slower when his fingers circled her wrist.

The seconds ticked as Zoey stared up at him like a deer caught in the headlights. The innocent motion had triggered an awareness Sutton knew he wasn't ready to act on, while he did not want to do anything that would ruin the easygoing camaraderie that seemed to unfold so naturally between them.

"I think it's better if you sit and I brew the next cup," he said in her ear.

"Okay."

Chapter Six

Zoey collapsed on the bench seat like a rag doll. Putting some distance between her and Sutton allowed her to breathe normally. The instant his hand brushed across her breast, it was as if dormant desire detonated and reminded her that she was woman who'd denied her own physical needs for more than a decade. Her breasts felt heavy and she hunched her shoulders to conceal an outline of extended nipples under the white bra and thin tank top.

She knew without a doubt she would be able to get along with Sutton as a friend and neighbor, but nothing beyond that. She had to be careful, very careful, not to succumb to his blatant sensuality that she was aware of but struggled to ignore whenever they shared the same space.

Zoey felt more in control of her body and emotions when Sutton set his coffee on the table and sat opposite her. Light from an overhead pendant illuminated the salt-and-pepper stubble on his recently shaved head. Reaching for the sugar bowl, she spooned two teaspoons into her cup, followed by a liberal splash of cream.

Zoey picked up the knife, cut a slice of cake, placed it on a dish and handed it to Sutton. "As my guest you get the first slice."

Sutton took the dish, smiling. "It looks too pretty to eat. That's what I used to say to my grandmother whenever she served dessert after Sunday dinner. Her comeback was, 'Boy, stop jawing and eat the dadgum cake before I take it from you.'"

Laughing, Zoey cut a piece for herself. "Did she make the quintessential pound or coconut layer cake?"

"Those and many others. Granny Dot was known as the cake lady. I waited all week just to see which one she would make. Each one would become my favorite until the next. After a while I gave up altogether and decided all were equally delicious."

"Did your grandmother ever enter her cakes in the Fourth of July bakeoff competition?" The celebration had been the highlight of Zoey's childhood when Wickham Falls and neighboring towns turned out for the annual three-day festivities. Ripples of excitement were tangible with the arrival of food trucks and carnival rides, and the raising of tents, and it was the only time she and her brothers were allowed to stay out well beyond their bedtime.

"No. Granny said she didn't need someone to judge her cakes, because she knew they were the best."

"Talk about confidence."

"That was something Granny never lacked. She'd warn me and my cousins that she would skin us alive if we did anything that would dishonor our ancestors. She'd mentioned the ancestors so often that I went looking for them. That's when I got a history lesson from Granny about a time in our history when black people were enslaved for hundreds of years yet endured unspeakable acts so we could be free. She told me that my third great-grandmother was a conductor on the Underground Railroad that pieced quilts with designs that were hidden messages that served to guide runaways north to freedom. Her stories fired my imagination, and even before I enrolled in college, I knew I wanted to become a history major."

"Baseball and history, Sutton?"

"It couldn't get any better because I was able to indulge in both my passions."

Zoey picked up a forkful of cake and took a bite, watching Sutton do the same. He had fulfilled his passion to play baseball and earn degrees in history, while she was still waiting to embrace hers. And his talking about his grandmother was a painful reminder that she hadn't had the privilege of having known her grandparents.

Sutton finished his slice, set his fork beside the

dish and touched a napkin to his mouth. "You've got the magic, Zoey."

"Magic?" Her voice rose in surprise.

"Yes. Where did you learn to bake like this?"

Her smile was dazzling. "Charmaine taught me to cook. Her folks owned a restaurant in Morgantown, and by the time she was old enough to look over the prep table, she'd joined the rest of the family in the restaurant's kitchen. When she was older she was entrusted with making pies and cakes."

"She taught you well because you're a definite cake lady."

"Are you saying I'm as good as Granny Dot?"

"Yes. So, own it."

Zoey put her palms together and bowed her head with Sutton's compliment. "Thank you, kind sir."

"There's no need to thank me. I'm certain if Sasha Manning had to judge a blind taste test with other strawberry shortcakes, she would select yours as the winner."

Sasha Manning, like so many others who'd grown up in the Falls and left, had come back to open Sasha's Sweet Shoppe. "I'm like your grandmother, Sutton. I'm not competitive."

Sutton stared at the coffee in the delicate cup. "You're not competitive, while I've spent more than half my life competing. It began with tryouts in high school and continued through college, then the minor and the major leagues. And I had to bring my A game to prove I wasn't a fluke once I signed my first multimillion-dollar contract. Fans are fickle because they boo you when you're in a slump and hail you as a conquering hero whenever you hit a walk-off home run."

"Why do they call it a walk-off?"

Sutton smiled and attractive lines fanned out around his eyes. "The home team always has the field advantage of batting last whenever they're losing or the score is tied. The bases can be empty or there can be men on base, and if the next batter hits a home run or gets a hit to score the runner, the opposing pitcher walks off the mound. Therefore, the term *walk-off.*"

"Which do you find more exciting? A walk-off or a grand slam?"

"So, you do follow baseball?"

Zoey managed to look insulted. "I never said I didn't follow the game. The minute Harper comes home he turns on the television to the sports channel. The few times I watched with him I did see you hit some moon shots."

"It was all in a night's work."

"There's no need to be self-effacing, Beast."

Sutton rolled his eyes upward. It had taken a while for him to accept the soubriquet when a popular sportscaster tagged him with the nickname after he hit home runs in four consecutive games.

"You didn't like being called Beast?" Zoey questioned.

"Not really."

"You were never comfortable being a celebrity."

"Is that a question or an observation?"

Resting her elbow on the table, Zoey cupped her chin on the heel of her hand. "An observation, Sutton. I've seen you during interviews, and everything you said appeared measured, as if you'd been following a script. Hanging out with you now I see someone that is the opposite of the high-profile baseball phenom."

Sutton was amazed at Zoey's perceptiveness. It was as if he'd been two people in one body. There was the Beast for the fans and sportscasters and Sutton Alexander Reed for his family and close friends. Angell also capitalized on his fame once they were referred to as Beauty and the Beast.

He ran a hand over his face. "You're right, Zoey, about having to create an alter ego for the public. I had to smile when I didn't want to and be gracious to rabid fans from opposing teams who would occasionally throw things or spit at me. Becoming a mentor allowed me to be myself. I identified with those kids because most of them came from single-parent homes. I'd lecture them about setting realistic goals for themselves, because eight out of ten wanted to become rappers or play in the NBA. They'd look at me as if I'd taken leave of my senses when I reminded them of the number of rappers that end up in cemeteries, and those who didn't were able to transition into other careers. Their eyes got big when I reminded them of the successful acting careers of LL Cool J, Ice-T, Ice Cube, Queen Latifah, Ludacris, Will Smith, and the list goes on and on. And if they were looking for a career in the NBA, then they had to stay in school, because scouts did not troll parks or playgrounds but high schools and colleges looking for the next Michael Jordan or LeBron James. Occasionally I'd invite drug counselors and life coaches to chair workshops about the risks of substance abuse and how to cope with problems that accompanied the result of becoming a baby daddy."

Zoey lowered her hand. "You were more than a mentor. There's no doubt they saw you as a father figure or even an older brother."

Sutton wanted to remind Zoey that he wasn't actually a father figure, but a sports hero and he had no way of knowing whether he had a biological brother. He drained his cup. "It's getting late, so it's best I head home."

"I'm going to cut several slices of cake you can take home with you."

"Miss Allen, are you trying to sabotage me?"

"What are you talking about?"

"I've managed to lose twenty pounds by eliminating sugar from my diet, but I have little or no willpower when it comes to homemade cake."

"You run, so one slice a day shouldn't wreck your diet."

Sutton stood up and came around the table and eased Zoey off the bench seat. He cradled her face in his hands. "To avoid temptation, I will come over every day for a single slice of your incredibly delicious strawberry shortcake." Lowering his head, he kissed the bridge of her nose. "I'll see you tomorrow, cake lady." He heard someone clear their throat and he turned to find Harper standing at the entrance to the kitchen, eyes as big as silver dollars.

"Mr. Reed, I... I told Jabari that you were going to coach me so I can try out for the basketball team and...and he said... He asked if he can join us."

Sutton knew Harper was caught off guard when seeing him kiss his sister, but it wasn't the time to reassure the kid that he did not plan to take advantage of her. "You can tell Jabari that I'll look forward to his joining us."

Harper stared at the floor. "I'll call and tell him." He turned on his heel and left.

"Sutton."

"Zoey." He smiled when they spoke at the same time. "I suppose Harper and I will have a man-to-man talk tomorrow."

Zoey rested a hand on his shoulder. "I don't want you to bring it up if he doesn't."

"Okay. If that's what you want."

"It is what I want, Sutton."

"Good night again."

"I'll walk you to the door."

Zoey locked the outer and inner door and when she turned she saw Harper standing in the middle of the living room. "Are you in for the night?"

He took a step. "Yes. Is something going on between you and Mr. Reed?"

Her impassive expression did not change. "No. Mr. Reed and I are friends. Why?"

"Just asking."

"Is that it?"

"Yup. I'm going to bed now. I have to get up early to run."

Zoey hadn't lied to her brother. She and Sutton were friends, and while she had to fight the feelings that made her want more than friendship, she knew nothing would become of it.

It had been ten long years since she'd shared her body not with a man but a boy who was just as inexperienced as she'd been. She'd kept waiting to experience the orgasms other girls bragged about, but they never came. Her boyfriend, who'd hinted he wanted to give her an engagement ring, had no way of knowing that she was relieved when he broke up with her because she could not have imagined being married to a man who failed to bring her to climax.

However, it was different with Sutton. Everything about him turned her on, while she'd perfected an air of indifference to the man who made her fantasize about making love with him. And based on her current emotional well-being, she could not afford to act on her fantasy. She'd planned out her life for the next two years, and there was no room for romance when it was her sole responsibility to shepherd Harper through high school and into college and nursing school for herself.

Sutton pulled into the driveway, shut off the engine and waited for Harper to exit the Jeep. "Are you getting out or do you want me to drive back to the track so we can jog some more?" It had been three days since the boy saw him kissing his sister and while he'd gone along with Zoey's suggestion not to bring up the incident with Harper, it apparently had affected him because the teenager was practically monosyllabic.

"Mr. Reed, can we talk?"

Sutton shifted slightly, resting his right arm over the back of the passenger-side headrest. "Of course. What do you want to talk about?"

Harper stared out the side window. "You and my sister."

A beat passed. "What about me and your sister?"

"Are you getting with her?"

Removing his arm, Sutton ran a hand over his face. He'd barely kissed Zoey, and it was on her nose, and now Harper was referring to his possibly sleeping with her. "No, Harper, I'm not getting with your sister. When you walked in on us I was kissing Zoey on her nose and not her mouth." Harper turned to stare at him, a flush suffusing his golden-brown complexion, and Sutton successfully hid a grin once he realized he'd embarrassed the teenager.

"I didn't know."

Sutton gave Harper a reassuring pat on his shoulder. "It's okay. And you didn't have to wait three days to talk to me about something that's been bothering you."

Harper lowered his eyes. "Okay. But I need to know something else."

"What is it?"

"Do you like Zoey?"

A hint of a smile tilted the corners of Sutton's mouth as he stared out the Jeep's windshield. It was obvious Harper was more than curious about him and his sister. "Like her how?"

Harper exhaled a breath. "Like her enough to take her out."

Sutton wanted to tell him that it was a no-brainer. Despite having a wager with Zoey that he would take her out if Harper made the basketball team, there was no guarantee it would happen. Everything about Zoey appealed to him and he looked forward to the opportunity whenever they were able to spend time together.

"Yes, I would like to take her out."

"Mr. Reed, I want you to promise me you're not going to mess over my sister. When Kyle left to join the marines, he told me that I was now the man of the house and that I had to look out for Zoey."

Sutton smiled, and wanted to remind Harper it was the other way around. Zoey was responsible for him, but he didn't want to bruise the boy's ego while applauding that he'd thought of himself as her protector. "I'm going to tell you something—man-to-man. I don't mess over women and that means I'll never deliberately hurt your sister. And that is something you should never do with girls."

"Don't get me wrong, Mr. Reed," Harper countered quickly. "I've seen boys at school do things to girls that just ain't right."

"I'm glad you recognize when it's not right."

Harper pressed a fist to his mouth. "I know that

I sometimes give Zoey a hard time, but I do know how far to push her."

"Why do you feel the need to push her?"

"I hate it when she treats me like a little kid."

"You may not be little, Harper, but you are a kid in the legal sense. You're still in school and there's no way you'll be able to get a decent job that will pay you enough to live the way you do now even if you lived on your own. And what if you need a vehicle to get to work? Where is that extra money coming from if you are only making minimum wage? My advice is not to talk back and to follow house rules."

"Is that what you did, Mr. Reed?"

"Oh yeah. There was just me and Mom and it wasn't easy for her to raise a son on her own, and once I got to high school I promised myself I wouldn't do anything to make life harder for her. And that meant not breaking curfew and asking permission to use her car."

Harper frowned. "Were you some kind of freak?"

"No. I was respectful, Harper," Sutton countered. "If you don't respect yourself, then no one will respect you. I've mentored a lot of boys that are around your age who don't respect themselves."

"Where did they live?"

"Some were in juvenile detention centers and others in group homes. Once they felt comfortable enough with me to talk about themselves, I realized they'd believed what was in the streets was better than what they'd had at home. This is not to say some of them didn't come from homes where abuse was evident."

"Did you like being a mentor?"

Sutton mulled over Harper's question because he didn't want to lie to him. "Yes and no. Yes, because there were occasions when I was able to get through to a young man and convince him to turn his life around, but then there were others that were impossible to reach."

"What happened to them, Mr. Reed?"

"It was either prison or an early grave."

"Damn!" Harper drawled under his breath.

Harper's *damn* was mild compared with what he'd said whenever he'd heard the news that one of his mentees had been murdered or charged with a felony. It had taken several years for him to realize he couldn't save every kid, and that's when he was able to accept his success on the ball field did not carry over to his role as a mentor.

A text message appeared on the phone attached to the dashboard. "The basketball hoop is schedule to be delivered tomorrow afternoon."

Harper's hazel eyes were shimmering with excitement. "Can I call Jabari and tell him to come over tomorrow?"

"Not yet," Sutton cautioned. "I want to see your skills before we invite someone else to join us."

"No problem, Mr. Reed." Harper opened his door. "I'll see you later."

Sutton watched Harper walk in the direction of his house. The first day of his alternating walking and jogging around the track at the high school, Harper was barely able to clock two miles, and Sutton reassured him that after a while he would build up enough stamina to increase the distance. And he reminded him if he wanted to make the basketball team, then not only would he have to run the length of the court while dribbling, but also accurately shoot while in motion to make the basket.

He exited the Jeep and went into the rental, removed the pedometer strapped to his upper arm and headed for the bathroom. The hoop was scheduled to arrive the next day, which meant he had to buy a pump and several basketballs.

Zoey left a sticky note on the kitchen countertop telling Harper she would be out of the house for a while before carrying the last of four boxes filled with clothes Harper and Kyle no longer wore or fit to the minivan to transport them to the local church. Harper was at least two inches taller than his older brother, and still growing, which meant he couldn't wear Kyle's hand-me-downs. She'd washed, dried and placed them in labeled boxes with their contents for the church's outreach program. Volunteers had advertised they needed gently used tees, jeans, sweaters, jackets, coats and hoodies that would be distributed to needy families before the onset of the new school year.

Her plan included dropping off the boxes, stopping by A Stitch at a Time to talk to Georgina about her knitting project, and then going to Powell's to pick up her online order. She'd managed to get Harper to sit with her as they researched the department store's website to select what he wanted to wear. In the past she would take her brothers to the store and spend what had felt like hours going through racks of shirts, pants and jackets and then sitting outside the fitting rooms while they tried them on.

Powell's, like many brick-and-mortar stores, had a website for consumers to order online for shipping or a local pickup. Harper had selected jeans, hoodies and short- and long-sleeved tees. The store also had a special section dedicated to the local school's sports paraphernalia.

It had only been days, but Zoey had noticed a marked change in Harper's personality since he'd begun running with Sutton. He came home in time to eat dinner with her and didn't ask to go out again. She didn't have to remind him to pick up his clothes or not eat in his bedroom, and she knew his interacting with Sutton was responsible for the overt change in her brother's behavior. Harper had to have realized he'd been given a pass once Sutton let him off for attempting to steal his vehicle and sought to make amends by adhering to the conditions Sutton had imposed.

She thought of Sutton's moving in next door as a blessing and a curse. A blessing because of his impact with the changes in her brother and a curse because of the increase in activity along their street. And most of the motorists were women hoping to catch a glimpse of Sutton going into or leaving his house. A few of the bolder ones sat in their vehicles with their engines idling until someone called the sheriff's department to complain about suspicious people lurking on their block. A deputy did follow up on the complaint and cautioned those who did not live on Marshall Street not to loiter there.

Zoey would watch Sutton's reaction to women screaming they want to marry him, but at no time did he appear affected by the attention. He would smile and wave, and if approached by a child he would autograph a shirt or scrap of paper. He had been touted as one of baseball's nice guys and it was apparent he hadn't changed even after he'd retired from the game.

She started up the minivan, backed out of the driveway and groaned inwardly when she heard a rattling coming from under the hood. She made a mental note to call Austen & Sons Auto for an appointment to check out the vehicle while she was still on vacation.

Zoey had made it a practice to save a portion of her salary to add to her nursing school tuition and what she called her rainy day fund, and it appeared as if she would have to dip into it to make repairs on the minivan or use it as a down payment for a low-mileage used car. Over the years she'd become astute in budgeting her income.

She'd used the death benefits from her father's and Charmaine's life insurance to pay off the mortgage on the house, and subsequently sold her father's tractor trailer and deposited the money into the account for her nursing school tuition. She no longer received survivor's benefits for Kyle, and once Harper turned eighteen his benefits would also end.

However, thanks to the generosity of the residents of Wickham Falls and some from Mineral Springs, Harper would not have to apply for financial aid to attend college. Kyle's decision to forfeit his half of the college fund because he would use the military's education benefit afforded Harper more options when it came to choosing an institution of higher learning. Zoey was slightly surprised once her youngest brother announced that he did not want to attend an out-of-state school, but commute to and from classes. She had come to believe the older Harper became the more he reminded her of Charmaine. Not only had he inherited his late mother's complexion, curly hair and eye color, but he was also a homebody. When he wasn't hanging out with Jabari, he could always be found at home. The exception had been when he'd gone to Mineral Springs to drink beer, and she hoped that was behind him.

She made it to the church and rang the bell to the outreach office. One of the workers answered the door and unloaded the boxes from the van's cargo area, thanking her profusely for the donation. Her next stop was the needlecraft shop before she went to Powell's to pick up her online purchase.

Chapter Seven

A bell chimed as Zoey opened the door to A Stitch at a Time and she stopped short to stare at an entire wall of yarn and threads of every conceivable color ranging from snow white to jet-black stored in plexiglass compartments. She smiled when she saw a table with knitted and crocheted monkeys, rabbits, chicks and ducks. There was also a display with babies' and older children's hats, sweaters, blankets and booties in soft pastels. Two women, sitting on matching armchairs, barely glanced up from their knitting when she walked in. There were three more chatting quietly as they sat around a glass-topped table.

Georgina, who'd been helping a woman piecing a quilt, held up a finger, signaling she needed a moment, giving Zoey time to further examine the space with cushioned chairs, love seats, area rugs and framed prints that invited one to come and sit for hours. When asked if she knitted, Zoey had been truthful when she'd admitted just a little. However, her curiosity was piqued when Georgina mentioned cancer patients.

She moved closer to examine several quilts on stands with Please Do Not Touch placards on a table fronting what appeared to be antiques. Some of the threads were missing and the colors on many of the squares had faded.

"Those were made by my great-great-great-grandmothers, some dating back to before the Civil War."

Zoey turned and smiled at Georgina. She was dressed in black and white: black smock with white lettering of the shop's name across the back, white jeans and black-and-white vintage saddle shoes. She had secured her curly hair in a ponytail.

"They should be hanging in a museum."

"I'm seriously thinking about it," Georgina replied. "They were packed away in airtight containers for years and I just took them out to put them on display for those who quilt or want to learn the art of hand quilting. A few of them need repairing, which I plan to get to sometime later in the year." She paused. "I've been running off at the mouth when I need to let you know why I'd asked if you can knit."

"As I said before, only a little. I know how to knit and purl."

"That's all you need to know. Have you heard

about the new wing that's being built at the county hospital that's dedicated for cancer patients?"

"Yes." Zoey was aware of the fundraiser to build the wing so cancer patients could remain close to home while receiving care.

"There's going to be a ribbon-cutting ceremony early next year and I asked Sutton whether he would represent Wickham Falls when we donate chemo caps and scarves for the patients. And meanwhile, I'm asking all my customers that knit or crochet if they would also get involved. I'd like to sign up as many people that I can and hopefully donate dozens of caps and scarves. The patterns are for beginners, so realistically you should be able to finish at least one set. I'm selling all of the yarn at fifty percent off the adult kits, and eighty percent off for children. I know you work, so I don't expect you to complete more than one kit."

Zoey felt a surge of excitement at the prospect of making something essential for patients undergoing chemotherapy. "Sign me up." Georgina flashed a smile. It had taken her a while to get used to not seeing the gap between Georgina's teeth.

"Do you know how to cast on?"

"No," Zoey answered. Charmaine used to cast on for her.

"I'll show you. After you cast on and join the stitches, you're going to be knitting in the round, which means you'll only have to use the knit stitch for the cap. You'll knit one row, purl one row for the scarves. We will only use acrylic yarn for the adults and baby yarn for the children."

Zoey could not realistically predict how many caps and scarves she would make in four months, but instead of reading she would knit. "I can't promise how many kits I can finish before the ribbon-cutting, but I'll do my best," she said, saying her thoughts aloud.

"Thank you so much, Zoey."

"How many have signed on?"

"Right now, fourteen have committed. Once the teachers return from the summer recess I'm going to hit them up, too."

"I have a few more days of vacation left before I go back to work, so when do you want me to come in and begin?" She'd called the agency to find out if they were ready to assign her another client and the scheduler said she would call a day in advance if a case came up. And that meant her two-week vacation would be extended. She'd accrued enough hours to take two weeks off, but anything beyond that would be without pay.

"I'm booked up with lessons for the rest of the week. I close Sundays and Mondays, but if you want to come in either of those two days I'll make myself available for you."

"I'm good for Monday morning."

Georgina smiled again. "I was hoping you would say that. What time do you want to come in?"

"The earlier the better." She was an early riser and tended to get her chores out of the way so she could have the rest of the day to do whatever she wanted.

"Nine."

"Perfect. I'm going to give you one of my business cards and I'll jot down the number to my cell. You can send me a message when you get here. I always keep the blinds drawn when I'm closed." She removed a card from the pocket of her smock and scrawled a number on the back.

"Okay. Georgi?"

"Yes?"

"You're doing a good thing."

Georgina's eyelids fluttered at the same time she bit down on her lip. "I knew I had to do something to give back because when I opened the doors to A Stitch at a Time I had no idea if folks would support me."

Zoey realized Sutton's cousin was becoming emotional. "Isn't that what we do in Wickham Falls? We look out and support one another." She thought about how everyone had come together to make certain she and her brothers would be taken care of so that the family would be able to stay together.

"You're right about that, Zoey."

"I'll be here Monday morning."

She left the shop and walked down Sheridan Street and around the corner. It was late morning and Main Street was crowded with shoppers and browsers. Families were filing into Ruthie's, the family-style all-you-can-eat buffet restaurant, for lunch.

Zoey became one of those window-shopping as she peered into the shoe store that was doing a brisk business days before the start of school. Someone bumped her and she glanced up and recognized the boy she'd slept with in high school. He was with his wife and a toddler son, and he lowered his eyes when she stared at him. They rarely ran into each other, and when they did they acknowledged the other with a nod. After they broke up, he dated a girl from Mineral Springs and married her.

She walked down the block to Powell's, and into the department store and over to the area for customer service/merchandise pickup. Reaching into her handbag, she took out her receipt and handed it to the young man behind the counter.

"I got an email that my order is ready for pickup."

He studied her receipt. "I'll check in the back for you, Miss Allen."

"What are you doing here?" asked a familiar voice.

Glancing over her shoulder, she saw Sutton smiling down at her. He was dressed entirely in black: long-sleeve tee, jeans, baseball cap and low-heeled boots. Whenever he smiled, her pulse would race a little faster, and with her limited experience with the opposite sex she hoped he did not compare her with some of the worldly, sophisticated women he'd met and known, because she could not pretend to be other than what she was: a small-town girl.

"Are you working or shopping?" He'd come to her house two days ago and they'd shared the last of the cake with coffee while sitting on her porch. She'd teased him relentlessly whenever a car came down the street, slowing noticeably in front of his rental with the hope of catching a glimpse of him.

"Shopping. Why are you here?"

"I'm picking up some things I ordered online."

"The hoop was delivered a couple of days ago, so I'm here picking up a pump that was on back order and a few balls."

"Do you really believe Harper will be able to make the team?"

"I won't know, Zoey, until I see him play. He claims he can beat his friend Jabari with three-pointers. The kid may turn out to be the next coming of Steph Curry."

"We will see, Sutton."

He lifted his eyebrows as he gave her a skeptical look. "You doubt his skills?"

"No, because I've never seen him play. He and Jabari go over to the high school several days a week to shoot hoops, but if he makes the team I definitely will attend his games. After all, I have to support my brother."

Sutton smiled. "As long as you don't become one of those family members that act up so badly that they're banned from future games."

Zoey made a sucking sound with her tongue and teeth. "There's no way I would embarrass Harper like that." She'd seen footage of parents leaving the stands and confronting referees because they felt their child has been slighted.

"We will see, Zoey," Sutton said, repeating what she'd said.

"Miss Allen, are you going to need help carrying this to your vehicle?"

Zoey glanced at the large box on the counter. "How heavy is it?"

"It has some weight to it."

Sutton reached around her and scooped the box off the counter. "It's okay, Danny. I'll take it out to her vehicle."

"I'm parked on Sheridan," Zoey told Sutton as she followed him out of the store.

He hoisted the box onto one shoulder. "You never would've been able to carry this that far."

She gave him a sidelong glance. Zoey wanted to tell Sutton that she was a lot stronger than she looked. "That's sexist, Sutton."

"Not only is this box heavy, but it's also bulky."

"FYI, I wouldn't have carried it around the corner, but driven my car around to the front of the store."

"Well, you don't have to do that because I'm playing delivery boy for you."

"And I thank you," she countered, not wanting to appear ungrateful for his assistance. She opened the rear of the minivan and stood aside as Sutton stored the carton in the cargo area behind the rear seats. The tinted rear and back windows concealed the vehicle's contents.

"Where are you off to now?" Sutton asked.

"Home."

"Have you had lunch?"

"No."

"Neither have I. Would you mind eating lunch with me?"

"My place or yours?"

"Neither," he said. "I was thinking more along the lines of a picnic lunch. I can call the Wolf Den for a take-out order and then we can go over to The Clearing to eat."

Going to what locals called The Clearing was like going back in time for Zoey. A forested area overlooking the falls that had given the town its name had been cleared of trees, the trunks fashioned into picnic tables and benches, as a campsite for family gatherings. There were grills for outdoor cooking and designated receptacles for discarded food and charcoal.

It was where kids from the high school hung out during the summer months, after classes and on weekends, and because the town did not have a fast-food restaurant, they'd ordered food from the Wolf Den for their impromptu picnics. The owners of the restaurant/sports bar had a special half-price menu for students with accompanying ID. The Clearing was also closely and regularly monitored by the sheriff's office to make certain there was no evidence of underage drinking and drug use.

A smile parted her lips. "I can't remember the last time I'd hung out at The Clearing."

Sutton's smile matched hers as he reached for her hand. "It's been even longer for me. We'll leave your vehicle here and take mine. Let me know what you want from the Den before I call in our order."

"Everything they make is delicious, so order whatever you like." She stared at him when he took out his phone and tapped an app. "I can't believe you've downloaded the Den on your cell."

He winked at her. "Anything to save time." He tapped the screen again. "Done. I paid so it will be ready by the time we get there."

Zoey noticed furtive stares as she walked with Sutton and realized it was only a matter of time before word spread that Sutton Reed was seen holding hands with Zoey Allen. Not only was he a returning hometown hero, but she hadn't been seen with a man since graduating high school.

Let them talk, she thought. It was the same thing her father said when he returned from a road trip with a new wife who was not only not much older than his daughter but also obviously pregnant. Zoey did not understand the whispers and sly glances whenever she and Charmaine went downtown to shop until Charmaine told her that some people needed to gossip about something to make themselves appear knowledgeable. And then warned her about repeating things she'd overheard because once the words came off her tongue she could not retrieve them.

Although she missed her father, she missed her stepmother more because Charmaine was there with her and her brothers every day. Zoey had looked forward to coming home after school to sit in the kitchen to do homework while Charmaine prepared dinner. What she enjoyed most were the stories about her stepmom's coal-mining ancestors who had taken a leading role in union organizing and were active in strikes that battled scabs and hired private guards the owners brought in to intimidate the workers. And once Charmaine trusted her to use the stove and oven without burning down the house, her cooking lessons began, and by the time she was sixteen she was able to perfect meals for breakfast, lunch and dinner.

It had taken Zoey a long time, even years, to convince herself that her father was gone and not coming back because she'd gotten so used to his being away from home for work, and then coming back days and sometimes weeks later. The day she celebrated her twenty-first birthday she'd locked herself in her room for hours crying inconsolably, until Kyle and Harper knocked on the door and pleaded for her to come out. While experiencing her crying jag, it was as if she could see the events in her young life like frames of film, and they were littered with losses. She'd lost her mother, father and stepmother, and she prayed she would live long enough to raise her brothers to adulthood.

Zoe finally emerged, face puffy, eyes swollen, and lied that she hadn't been feeling well. She managed to laugh when they offered to make toast and tea because they were aware of what she would eat whenever she was threatening a cold. She thanked them for their concern, and told them because it was a milestone birthday she was taking them to Ruthie's to celebrate. Her brothers liked going to the restaurant because they could choose whatever they wanted to eat. Zoey always cautioned them not to eat too much or they would be too full and unable to eat dessert. The dessert selections were kids' favorites with pies, tarts, cakes and soft-serve custard.

Her blue funk continued for more than a week,

and she'd contemplating going back into therapy but feared the therapist would document that she was not emotionally stable enough to take care of her siblings. And for Zoey that was not an option, and she swore an oath that she would do whatever was humanly possible to keep her family together.

Sutton helped her up into the Jeep and waited for her to secure the seat belt before rounding the vehicle and slipping behind the wheel. She stared straight ahead rather than glance at his distinctive profile. After photo shoots where his face and body had appeared on the covers of so many magazines and countless interviews, she wondered if he did miss some of the attention.

"What did you order?"

"Stuff."

Zoey turned to look at Sutton. He was smiling. "What kind of stuff?"

"Chicken, brisket, ribs and a number of side dishes."

"No okra?" she teased.

"You got jokes?"

Her expression mirrored innocence. "No. I've heard that the Den offered fried okra, which isn't prepared the same as the okra in succotash."

"Fried or boiled, I just don't like it."

"What else don't you like, so I can keep that in mind if or when I ever invite you over for Sunday dinner?"

Stopping at the four-way intersection, Sutton

waited for traffic to clear to cross the road. "You're going to cook for me?"

"Not for you personally, Sutton. I'm old-fashioned when it comes to having Sunday dinner, because it is a family tradition I try to keep."

"So, now I'm family?"

"Not quite."

"What do you mean by *'not quite'*? Either I am or I'm not."

"You're my friend and a neighbor, and I've always invited neighbors over in the past. Before she moved to Ohio, Miss Sharon would join us a couple of times a month."

Sutton decided not to get into a back-and-forth with Zoey. Just the fact that she'd invited him to her home to eat something other than dessert should have ended the discussion, but he wanted to know if her inviting him for what she considered a family tradition had any bearing on how she felt about him.

And it was true that they were friends and neighbors, yet he wanted more. Sutton wanted to be able to call and invite her out to dinner or to a movie. In other words, he wanted to date her. He'd had one serious relationship following his divorce and in hindsight he should've ended it before it had begun. He did not blame the woman as much as he did himself because he'd realized too late that his reason for seeing her was loneliness. From the time he'd tried out and made the high school baseball team, he was a part of a group, a crew that depended on one another for success. His squad mentality continued throughout college and his baseball career. However, the exception was his marriage. Once he walked through the door of his house, all he wanted and needed was his wife. He was able to mentally shut out the roar of the crowd and his trash-talking teammates. What he hadn't wanted to come home to was strangers milling inside and outside the home he considered his sanctuary and have them greet him as if he was just another one of Angell's guests.

The woman he'd dated for more than a year was similar in appearance and temperament to his exwife. When he'd introduced her, some people had asked if she was a model. That's when the lightbulb went off. He had a stereotype when it came to a woman: most were tall and slender model types. And Zoey Allen was no exception, because he'd found Zoey to be a natural beauty without the coiffed hair, makeup and designer clothes. If he thought her attractive, then no doubt other men also did.

She's waiting to become a nurse and she's waiting to get a boyfriend. Mr. Reed, I want you to promise me you're not going to mess over my sister.

Harper's words were branded into his brain like a permanent tattoo. Was the teenager sending him signals that he wanted him with Zoey? Or perhaps he was reading more into their conversation because he did want an easygoing and uncomplicated relationship with her.

Not only did he like Zoey, but he also admired her quiet strength and family loyalty. He didn't know how many high school seniors were willing to assume the responsibility of rearing their younger siblings when they were looking and planning their own futures that did not include becoming a guardian or surrogate parent. She had delayed pursuing a career and relationships because her family had become a priority.

He had reached a point in his life when he wanted children, while Zoey talked about delaying marriage and starting a family because after Harper graduated college she needed to experience a time in her life when she wanted to be responsible only for herself.

And for Sutton, it was family he coveted most. It was the reason he relocated his mother from Wickham Falls to Atlanta, bought a house and vehicle for her and deposited money in an account to ensure a comfortable lifestyle. Family was also the reason why he'd returned to his hometown when Georgina informed him that she was leaving Powell's to open her own business and asked if he would step up and fill the void in management. Her request had come at the right time; he'd put his condo on the market and had planned to leave Atlanta with the possibility of relocating to Washington, DC, because he'd fallen in love with the capital city.

"What time is Sunday dinner?" he asked Zoey after a comfortable silence.

"Three."

"What if I return the favor the following Sunday?"

Zoey shifted on her seat and gave him a direct stare. "That sounds like a plan."

"Take my cell and program your number. If for some reason our plans change, then I'll text you."

Grabbing his cell phone attached to the holder on the dashboard, she entered her name and number in his contacts. She then removed her phone from her bucket bag. "What's your number?" He gave her his number and she returned the phone to her bag.

Sutton smiled, believing he'd won a small victory. He didn't know why, but he thought Zoey would reject his offer. Other than grilling steak and corn and inviting Zoey and Harper to join him, it had been a while since he'd cooked for someone other than himself. And one of the best things to have come from his marriage was his mother-in-law's cooking lessons. When he and Angell went house hunting, she insisted they purchase a home with a mother-in-law suite because she wanted her mother to live with them. He had no qualms having his wife's mother sharing their roof because he really liked the soft-spoken widow who had grown close to her only daughter after losing her husband to complications of diabetes.

During his team's home stands, Sutton spent most of his free time in the kitchen with Elizabeth Tompkins, who patiently taught him to duplicate recipes passed down through generations of women in her family. Elizabeth did not bother to hide her frustrations when Angell would permit herself only a tablespoon portion of everything her mother had put on the table. It was obvious his wife had an eating disorder, which she vehemently denied whenever he insisted she seek counseling. The ritual at home was he and Elizabeth cooked and ate, while Angell starved herself in order to stay thin.

"Do you want a traditional Southern Sunday dinner with fried chicken or baked ham with all the fixings or something a little different?"

"How different, Sutton?"

"A pork crown roast stuffed with apple sausage stuffing, braised red cabbage and a sweet potato casserole."

"You're a gourmet cook!"

Sutton shook his head. "Not hardly. My ex-mother-in-law is a caterer and she taught me whatever I know about preparing different dishes."

"Lucky you."

The two words lacked emotion and Sutton wondered if talking about his ex-wife's mother had Zoey believing that he wasn't ready to let go of his past. A pregnant silence followed as he headed in the direction of the Wolf Den and maneuvered into an empty parking space. "Wait here, and I'll be right back."

Chapter Eight

Zoey stared through the windshield and waited for Sutton to return. His voice was filled with pride when he'd talked about his mother-in-law, and she wondered if he still was in contact with the woman or his ex-wife. She enjoyed the time she spent with Sutton, and while attempting to read more into their association, she didn't want to interact with a man who couldn't stop talking about his ex-girlfriends or wives.

After she broke up with her high school boyfriend, a few men had attempted to come on to her, but she'd quickly rejected them with the excuse that she didn't have time for a relationship because of her brothers. All accepted her rejection with the exception of one who tried to convince her that he wasn't put off because she was responsible for raising her siblings. Not only was he nearly twenty years her senior, but he was also a widower with three teenage girls and could not stop talking about his deceased wife. It was obvious he was looking for a stepmother for his girls, and there was no way she was willing to compete with a dead woman. Barely out of her teens herself, Zoey knew she also wasn't equipped to deal with five children and remain sane. It had taken some effort, but she was finally able to convince him to stop dropping by her house on the threat of serving him with a restraining order.

Now, when it came to Sutton she felt as if she was on an emotional roller coaster. She liked him but the fear of becoming too involved caused her to put up barriers to keep him at a distance. There were times when she was ashamed of her less-than-friendly tone and the need to challenge him because she had to remind herself that Sutton was going to be her temporary neighbor. After the new year he would move away, and she would be left with memories of a man who only had to stare at her to remind her of what she'd been missing and denying for more than a decade: a woman who hadn't had sex in a very long time. And Sutton Reed was definitely not a fumbling, inexperienced boy but a mature man who had not only dated women but also married one. Sutton returned and Zoey shifted on her seat to see him place two large shopping bags on the rear seats.

"What on earth did you buy?" she asked, as he got in beside her.

Sutton winked at her. "Stuff."

Zoey couldn't stop the smile spreading over her features. "You and your stuff."

He wiggled his eyebrows. "You'll see."

Ten minutes later she sat on the blanket Sutton kept in his vehicle for emergencies along with a first aid kit, staring at containers of brisket, barbecue chicken, ribs and sides of potato, macaroni, three-bean salads and chilled bottles of water, along with paper plates, napkins, cups and plastic knives, forks and spoons. He'd spread the blanket out under the sweeping branches of a large maple tree.

"I like this."

He handed her a plate. "I'm glad you approve."

"You don't need my approval, Sutton."

He went still, meeting her eyes. "Yes, I do, Zoey. It means a lot to me."

A slight frown furrowed her smooth forehead. "Why?"

"Don't you know?"

She blinked. He'd answered her question with one of his own. "No, I don't."

"Let's eat first, then I'll tell you."

Zoey surveyed The Clearing. Some of the picnic tables were filled with teenagers enjoying their last bit of daytime freedom before the start of classes and others were occupied with families taking advantage of the warm summer afternoon. A group of mothers watched as their young children played tag, their high-pitched screams competing with the incessant chatter of birds flitting from branch to branch and tree to tree. The aroma of grilling meat and the distinctive smell of burnt marshmallows lingered in the air. She recalled bringing Harper and Kyle to The Clearing to make s'mores, and then she would take them to the waterfall that gave the town its name. They never ceased to be in awe of the rush of water falling over the rocks to the rapids below and then flowing into a lake brimming with fish that was a fisherman's nirvana.

Several teenage girls lay on blankets in direct sunlight to deepen their already tanned bodies, while a number of couples sought the cover of trees to escape the harmful rays of the brilliant August sun.

Zoey opened a bottle of water and took a long swallow, and then filled her plate with bite-size pieces of meat, and then followed with salads. Sutton unscrewed the top to his water bottle and touched his to hers.

"Bon appétit," he said, grinning.

"Buen provecho," she countered in Spanish, shifting her position and crossing her legs in an easy pose, then balancing her plate on her knees. Zoey took a bite of brisket and rolled her eyes upward. It was so tender it literally melted on her tongue. "Oh, my gosh. This is so good!"

"How often do you go to the Den?"

"I go there, but only to order takeout. It's a sports bar and not a place I'd wanted to expose my brothers to because they serve alcohol. How about yourself?"

Sutton chewed and swallowed a mouthful of macaroni salad. "When I was in high school some of the kids would stop by after winning a home game and the Gibsons would sit us in the rear of the restaurant while the coaches and parents sat up front closer to the bar. And the few times I came home while still in college I would occasionally stop in, but never to drink."

"You don't drink?"

"Only occasionally. Once I was assigned as the team's first baseman, Coach Evans took me aside and told me something that I've never forgotten. He predicted that if I worked hard and stayed out of trouble I would be able to play in the big leagues. Then he confided that college recruiters were asking about me, and they'd hired a private detective to surveil me and whenever I was randomly drug tested they wanted to see the results. The college did not want to give me a free education for me to mess up. It's the same with professional sports, Zoey. Some dudes are signed to multimillion-dollar contracts only to literally piss it away when they get drunk or high and bust up a joint or assault someone. But, the owners of these teams just don't get it. It is too much money for kids who never had much or are barely out of their teens to handle. They splurge on cars, jewelry, women, buy homes for their family members and try to give the boys they grew up with everything they ask for." He held up a hand. "And before you ask me about the Aston Martin, I didn't buy it. I did a commercial for the manufacturer and rather than accept monetary payment, I asked for the car."

A beat passed. "How did you react to what Coach Evans told you?" Zoey asked.

"I was shocked and frightened, because I hadn't thought I had the skills to play in the majors. I loved playing baseball, but I was also partial to history. My goal was to graduate college and teach, yet knew I couldn't play pro ball and teach at the same time. Teams begin spring training in February and the regular season runs from late March or early April through late September or early October. And if your team makes the postseason, then early November."

"How many games are in a regular season?"

"One hundred sixty-two."

"I suppose that would conflict with you teaching classes."

"You think?" Sutton drawled, smiling. He sobered. "So, my plan A became my plan B."

Zoey imagined she detected a hint of resignation in Sutton's voice. Had he regretted deferring teaching in lieu of a baseball career that had afforded him fame and fortune? "Now that you've retired from baseball, do you plan to execute your plan B?"

Sutton nodded. "Yes. At eighteen I'd believed I'd had my future planned out for myself, but fast-forward eighteen years later and I think of myself as blessed because I'm able to control my own destiny."

"You talked about doubting whether you had the skills to become a professional baseball player, yet you'll probably be inducted into the Baseball Hall of Fame."

"If I am it's because I worked hard, Zoey. I got to

the ballpark early to practice hitting in the batting cage. And I had someone shag balls to me so I could improve my footwork when playing my position. If I made it look easy, trust me, babe, it wasn't. My body has taken more hits than a piñata, and the scars on my right knee look like a road map."

"I suppose you would've been more banged up if you'd played football."

"Talk about a blessing in disguise. I'd made the school's football squad but sat on the bench for a year. That's when I decided to try baseball."

Zoey unfolded her legs, stretched them out and stared at the toes of her tennis shoes. "I have forbidden Harper to play football because of the possibility of sustaining a head injury."

"If I had a son I, too, wouldn't want him to play football."

"What about other sports?"

A beat passed, before Sutton said, "The only exception is boxing and for the same reason as football. I believe in kids playing sports because it fosters confidence and discipline, while teaching them they are no longer an individual but a part of a team. And when the team wins, everyone is a winner."

Zoey thought about Harper trying out for the Wolf Pack basketball team. If he didn't make the cut, would he give up altogether or try again? Unlike Kyle, who hadn't given up when he didn't make the baseball team the first two times. However, the third was a charm when he was selected as a backup catcher.

"Harper's attitude has changed since he's begun running with you, and for that I'm eternally grateful."

"I told you before that your brother is a good kid. It takes him a while to open up, but now we're simpatico."

"Oh, so it's like that now. You two are *that* tight?" Zoey crossed her middle and forefinger.

Throwing back his head, Sutton laughed loudly. "Real tight," he confirmed.

He stared at the woman that unknowingly had also changed him. Interacting with Zoey had a calming effect on him. He'd given himself a year in which to kick back and decompress from the years he'd spent under the glare of the spotlight. There was hardly a time when he walked through an airport terminal that someone hadn't pointed or called out his name. He'd returned to Wickham Falls at the request of his cousin to help at Powell's, and resigned himself to the fact that passing the year in his hometown would fit in easily with his plans for his future.

That was then and this was now. That was before he'd moved into Sharon Williams's house and met his pretty neighbor. And that was before his mother decided she was coming back to Wickham Falls to live with her sister and brother-in-law for the next six months.

His moving to DC to live and teach was no longer on Sutton's wish list because he could live and teach in and around his hometown. He knew he would have to vacate his temporary living quarters before the owner returned and that he could either purchase one of the new homes in the development going up on what had been the Wolfe/Remington land, or he could buy a couple of vacant acres and build a house to his own specifications.

"I don't know about you, but I need to walk off some of this food before I fall asleep right here," Zoey said, breaking into his musings.

"Why don't you take a nap, while I put everything away? We can go for a walk once it cools down a bit." The heat wave had returned, this time hotter than before.

Zoey slipped off her tennis shoes to reveal well-groomed feet. Her toenails were painted a brilliant blood red. She went to her knees. "Let me help you."

Sutton gently pushed her hand away. "Just relax. I've got this." He waited for Zoey to lie on her back, and then he covered the containers and placed them in shopping bags. They hadn't eaten all he'd ordered, but without an ice chest in which to store them they had to be thrown away because of the heat. He walked a short distance and discarded the bags in a nearby receptacle, and then returned to where Zoey reclined on her side.

She patted a spot next to her. "There's room for you."

He sat, took off his boots and lay down facing her. They were so close he could feel the warmth of her breath on his cheek. Sutton studied her feminine features, marveling at their delicateness. She met his eyes for an instant before lowering her gaze.

The length of her lashes rested on the ridge of high cheekbones.

He vaguely remembered her father because he'd occasionally come into Powell's to shop when he'd worked weekends or during the summer school recess. James Allen rarely spoke to anyone but would occasionally stop and chat with Sutton's mother because both had been in the same graduating class.

Sutton still couldn't wrap his head around Zoey's decision to raise her younger brothers when as a teenage girl she was only two months away from graduating high school. He wondered if she had assumed that responsibility because her father stated he wanted his children to grow up together, as it hadn't been possible with him and his siblings, or if history was repeating itself when James Allen became a divorced single father with a toddler daughter.

"I'm as full as a tick," Zoey whispered.

"You didn't appear to eat that much."

She opened her eyes. "I ate enough. I usually have a salad midday so I can save my appetite for dinner."

"What do you usually have for breakfast?"

"Cereal, fruit and coffee. When I don't have fruit, then I'll substitute juice."

"What about dinner?" he asked.

"Harper and I have what we call meatless Mondays. I will make a pasta dish with garlic and oil or with lots of veggies. Then there's taco Tuesdays, wings Wednesdays. I've learned to oven fry my wings, which is healthier than frying. And we always have a salad every night."

"What about the rest of the week?"

"It's turkey Thursdays—salad, sliders, sandwiches and/or meat loaf. We have fish on Fridays, and because Harper really favors Mexican and Italian food, we'll alternate making fajitas and nachos with spaghetti and meatballs or lasagna. Sunday is for chicken. It can be roasted, baked, fried, stewed, stir-fried, broiled or grilled. I always cook enough for dinner so there are leftovers for lunch."

"Can you give me a hint what you're making this Sunday?"

"I hope you don't have a nut allergy because it's chicken in a sweet-and-sour sauce with ginger and almonds."

Sutton leaned closer and pressed a kiss on the bridge of Zoey's nose. "That sounds scrumptious. I know I'm really going to enjoy sharing Sunday dinners with you."

Zoey stared up at him from under lowered lids. "You don't think we'll get sick of seeing each other?"

His expression changed, becoming a mask of stone. "Why would you say that?"

"Every Sunday, Sutton?"

"Why not?"

"What about your family? Don't you have Sunday dinner with them?"

Zoey's mentioning his family reminded Sutton that since his mother's return, she and her sister had resumed the family tradition of eating together after attending church services. "What if we share every other Sunday?" His question elicited a smile from her.

"Now, that sounds like a plan. I'll host the second Sunday in the month, and you can do the fourth," she said, confidently.

"If that's the case, then let me host dinner this Sunday, and you can do it two weeks later."

"Are you sure, Sutton?"

"Very sure."

Sutton resisted the urge to kiss her again, this time on the mouth. The first time he saw Zoey up close, it was her mouth that drew his rapt attention. Women had their plastic surgeons on speed dial to achieve the lips Zoey claimed naturally. Everything about her was natural, feminine. He smiled when she shifted slightly, the movement bringing them even closer, and he rested his arm over her waist.

"Have you selected your nursing school?"

"Yes. WVUIT."

"My mother graduated from West Virginia University Institute of Technology with a business degree."

"Didn't she at one time work at the school's business office?"

"Yes. She really liked it, but once I put down roots in Atlanta, she talked about moving closer to me. I don't know if you're aware of it, but she's back for at least six months."

"I can understand her following you. She raised you as a single mother, so your bond is very strong."

"Like you and your brothers?"

Zoey looped an arm around Sutton's neck. "Yup. We're like the Three Musketeers. One for all and all for one. Kyle emails or sends me messages every week. I didn't tell him I was having problems with Harper because it would upset him, because he's been thinking about signing up to train to become a SEAL."

"You're right about not telling him because he needs to be physically *and* mentally at the top of his game."

Sutton closed his eyes, enjoying the soft crush of Zoey's body against his and the subtle scent of flowers on her body and hair. He managed to ease his hips away from her in an effort for her not to become aware of his growing erection. And in that instant he wondered how much experience she'd had with men to lie that close and not realize he had been turned on by the warmth and soft curves of her body. Gritting his teeth, he forced himself to think of any and everything but the woman lying innocently and trustingly beside him.

"How would you like not having to wait two years to go to nursing school?" he asked. Sutton didn't know where the thought had come from, but he had to say something to take his mind off wanting to make love with Zoey. She dropped her arm and eased back at the same time he swallowed an inaudible breath of relief.

"What are you talking about?" she asked.

"I have a foundation that will pay your tuition if you want to enroll now."

* * *

Zoey sat up and stared down at Sutton as if he had been speaking a foreign language. She'd known of him for years but had actually interacted with him every day since only a little more than a week ago, and meanwhile he was offering to pay for her college.

"It's not about money, Sutton."

He also sat up. "If it's not money, then what's stopping you, Zoey?"

"Harper. I have to be here for him. And you saw for yourself that he needs close supervision. It's one of the reasons why I haven't applied to an online college because I can't work, take care of Harper and fulfill the requirements for my coursework. There wouldn't be enough hours in the day to do all I'd have to do."

Pulling up his legs, Sutton wrapped his arms around his knees. "Tell me why you don't need money and we'll talk about Harper."

She told Sutton about the scholarship fund that was set up for her brothers following their parents' passing. "Kyle decided to enlist in the corps and plans to use his military educational benefit, which left more than enough money for Harper to complete his college education. I invested my share of my father's death benefit and saved the money from the sale of his tractor trailer for my college education, and I try to save at least ten percent from each paycheck to add to it. I had to learn quickly how to manage my resources to make ends meet, because once my brothers turn eighteen they'll lose my dad's social security survivor benefits."

"Okay. It appears as if you've taken care of your financial needs. Now about Harper."

"What about him?" she asked.

"I want to become his mentor. You will have to let me know what you expect from him and I'll execute it. And that means making certain he gets to school on time, does his homework and chores, and hopefully will stay out of trouble."

"Why Harper, Sutton?"

He narrowed his eyes at her. "I've mentored countless fatherless boys in Atlanta and not one in my hometown. What's the expression? Charity begins at home and then spreads abroad. Initially I resented the media referring to me as a role model because I'm of the belief that fathers need to be role models for their kids, but when they're not in their lives, then others have to step up and assume that responsibility.

"I was luckier than those boys because my mother gave me what I needed to believe in myself. I'd talk to boys about not becoming a father unless they're ready to be a daddy. And when they asked what the difference is, I had to explain that any man could father a child, but being a daddy meant being there and supporting their children. Most appeared bored until I admitted as a high school senior I went home, shut myself in my bedroom and cried inconsolably because I'd hit my first home run and my father wasn't there to celebrate with me. My confession was like a punch in the gut once they realized a two-hundred-pound-plus baseball phenom had just admitted to crying because he didn't have his father in his life."

"It must have taken a lot for you to admit that."

"It did," Sutton confessed, "but it was necessary if I was going to relate to them one-on-one and not like a larger-than-life so-called media marketing superhero. These kids saw me as a father figure, but that's something I don't want with Harper."

"But what if he does, Sutton? You can't monitor his emotions like turning on and off a faucet. Harper has a problem making and keeping friends because he's afraid of losing them. He and Jabari have been hanging out together since the beginning of summer, so I'm not certain how long that will last. He lost his father and mother, and it wasn't until Kyle left that he began acting out and breaking curfew. I can't agree to let you mentor him beyond your three-month agreement because once Miss Sharon returns, you will leave the Falls and he's going to be devastated."

"Who said anything about me leaving Wickham Falls?"

Zoey's jaw dropped. "I... I thought I heard talk that you were going to be here for a year and—"

"When I was first interviewed by a reporter for *The Sentinel*, I'd mentioned that I was going to take a year off to plan my next move," Sutton explained, cutting Zoey off. "But everything changed once my mother came back."

"You're not leaving?" Her voice was barely a whisper.

Sutton shook his head, smiling. "No. I'm staying. I've sent my résumé out to various school districts for a teaching position, and I also plan to buy or build a house here in the Falls before Sharon Williams returns."

Zoey felt as if she'd been gut-punched with this new revelation. Sutton Reed wasn't leaving Wickham Falls, and he had volunteered to mentor her brother for at least the next two years. And the time would also allow her to get to know her temporary neighbor better.

"I feel a lot better knowing that you're going to be around for a while."

"A while is going to be a very long time. I left Wickham Falls at eighteen, lived in Atlanta for fourteen years, played ball in every city that has a professional baseball team in this country and Canada, also some winter ball in Puerto Rico, Mexico and the Dominican Republic. Once my mother relocated to Atlanta, I rarely came back to the Falls. It's only now that I've been back for more than a few days at a time that I realized this is where I'm able to feel comfortable enough to be myself. I don't have to worry about cameras or microphones and being asked questions I don't want to or refuse to answer. And if I must use whatever celebrity status I have left, then let it be to help kids stay on the right track."

A smile trembled over Zoey's lips before they parted. Knowing Sutton wasn't moving away filled her with an indescribable joy that left her feeling slightly light-headed and struggling to draw a normal breath. The man whom she'd found herself fantasizing about had further deepened his ties with her family now that he'd offered to mentor Harper. She had no clue if Sutton had feelings for her that went beyond friendship, but that did not matter.

"I'm glad you decided to stay."

His eyebrows lifted. "Are you glad for Harper?"

She gave him a direct stare. "Harper isn't the only one in the equation." Zoey went completely still when Sutton moved closer, their chests rising and falling in unison. She felt a vaguely sensual light flow between them as the seconds ticked.

Sutton cradled her face in his hands. "Who else is in the equation, Zoey?" he whispered in her ear.

She closed her eyes and pressed her forehead to Sutton's. His question appeared to release the restraints she'd placed on her body to keep men out of her life and out of her bed as she pressed her breasts to his chest. "Me."

"And who else?"

Her eyelashes fluttered against his cheek. "You."

The single word was barely off her tongue when Sutton covered her mouth with his. It wasn't as much a kiss as it was a caress. It ended and she buried her face against the column of his strong neck.

Easing back, Sutton met her eyes. "Yes. You, me and Harper."

"All for one and one for all?"

He smiled. "That's us."

It was with a great deal of reluctance that she pulled away, shattering the sensual spell of the man holding her captive. "I think it's time we head back."

Sutton rose to stand. Reaching down, he cupped her elbow and helped her to her feet, waiting until she slipped her feet into her tennis shoes.

They'd spent less than two hours together, but it could've been two minutes. Time had passed much too quickly, but she would be left with the memory of a man who had unknowingly changed her to where she wanted more than friendship.

The return drive to the business district was accomplished in complete silence. Sutton left Zoey where she'd parked her vehicle on Sheridan Street. "I'll bring the box back to your house after I make a quick stop." At the last possible moment when she turned to get into her car, he dipped his head and brushed a kiss over her mouth.

"Drive safely," he said, smiling.

"I will, and thank you for lunch."

Sutton winked at her. "You're most welcome. Do you mind if we do it again?"

"I'd love to do it again." The instant the four-letter word slipped off her tongue, she chided herself for using it. But it was too late and there was no way to retract it.

She got into the van, secured her seat belt, started the engine and backed out of the space. She glanced up at the rearview mirror as she drove down the street, stopping at the railroad crossing. Sutton hadn't moved.

The day had been one of surprises: Sutton had asked her to share lunch with him, they'd agreed to alternate preparing Sunday dinner, he'd volunteered to mentor Harper, *and* the most shocking thing was that he'd planned to stay in Wickham Falls.

Zoey hummed "O Happy Day," and after a while she belted out full-throated the lyrics of one of her favorite songs. She continued to sing when she unlocked the front door and walked inside the house to find Harper sprawled on the sofa in the living room watching music videos.

He waved at her without taking his eyes off the screen.

"Sutton's going to drop off a box with your school clothes."

"Okay."

"Have you had lunch?" she asked him.

"Yeah. I had the rest of the shrimp salad and coleslaw. Can I go to Triple Jay's after dinner?"

"Why don't you have him come here instead of you always hanging out at his house?"

Zoey didn't want him to wear out his welcome.

"We don't have a game room."

She wanted to tell her brother that she had no intention of setting up a game room in the house when in two years most of his free-time focus would no longer be video games but college courses. "Yes, you can go but don't stay too late."

"I won't."

Zoey knew his hanging out with his friend would soon come to an end with the resumption of classes. Every August was a milestone. Now it would be eight years down, two to go, and that meant she was closer to her dream of enrolling in nursing school.

Chapter Nine

"How do they look now, Mr. Reed?"

Sutton peered into the pot with the sautéed onions and slivers of apples. They had turned a pale translucent color. "They're good. Now you can put in the cabbage."

Harper had asked if he could assist in preparing Sunday dinner and Sutton was amazed by his infectious enthusiasm. He'd discovered Zoey's brother was not only eager to learn but was willing to work hard at whatever task he'd taken on.

Sutton had set up the basketball hoop in the neighboring backyard, and the first time Harper put the ball through the net he knew the kid had what it took to make the high school's basketball team. Although he had to perfect his footwork, his ability to make free throws and three-pointers was remarkable.

They'd been running every morning for almost two weeks, and he was able to connect with Harper as a mentee in a way that hadn't been possible with the other boys because of their direct contact. They saw each other every day and he knew it was the reason for the increasing bond between them. Harper would occasionally drop hints about him and Zoey, but Sutton was able to successfully shift the conversation away from him and the boy's sister.

The details surrounding his running into Zoey and sharing a picnic lunch with her at The Clearing had lingered with him for days. However, he'd realized his faux pas when asking if he could underwrite the cost of her nursing school tuition, and knew it was wrong for him assume she would have to apply for financial loans to support her higher education.

He'd also discovered at twenty-eight she was a lot more mature than women he'd met who were ten to fifteen years older, and he attributed that to her taking on the herculean responsibility of raising a six- and eight-year-old when still a teenager.

Her natural beauty notwithstanding, it was her strength, focus, self-confidence and determination that drew him to her. He'd also found her upbeat and positive, traits he had come to admire in a woman with whom he wanted to interact. Sutton totally believed in the adage that if life gives you lemons, then make lemonade, while his mantra was if you fall or fail, then get up and do it over as many times as it will take until you succeed.

Sutton watched Harper as he dropped handfuls of shredded cabbage into the pot, stirring it with a wooden spoon until the leaves were slightly wilted. Harper admitted he enjoyed cooking and would on occasion help prep ingredients for Zoey whenever they made meals together.

"This smells so good," Harper said, smiling.

Leaning against the countertop, Sutton crossed his arms over his chest. "Not only should food smell and taste delicious, but it should also look good."

Harper gave him a quick glance. "Mr. Reed, I think I know what I want to study when I go to college."

"What is that?" Sutton asked.

"Culinary arts. I want to become a chef."

Sutton had no idea that when he'd called him "chef" the afternoon they'd grilled out in his backyard that the moniker was predestined. "You really like cooking that much?"

"Yup. A lot of boys I know want to be rappers or entrepreneurs when they don't know what they want to sell. I don't remember that much about my mom, except the stories she used to tell me about growing up in a trailer next to her family's restaurant. She said everyone ordered their fried chicken and barbecue ribs."

"Is the restaurant still in business?"

"Nope. It burned down. Mom drove me and Kyle to see it. The trailer where she lived was also gone."

Sutton studied the tall, slender boy who'd brushed his hair off his face and styled it in a ponytail. "So, it looks as if you inherited your family's gene for cooking," he teased.

"I guess," Harper agreed. "I went online to re-search cooking schools and the closest ones are in DC, Maryland or northern Virginia."

"That's close enough for you to drive whenever you want to come home."

Harper covered the pot with a lid and took if off the heat. "Were you afraid to leave the Falls when you first went to college?"

"No, because I went to visit the campus for an incoming freshman orientation before the start of classes. The four years I spent at the University of Florida were some of the best and most memorable in my life."

"Do you think Zoey will be all right if I leave the Falls to go to college in another state?"

"Trust me, Harper. Your sister will be okay."

"Can I ask you something, Mr. Reed?"

Sutton sensed a change in the boy's demeanor along with his expression. Something was bother-ing him. "Of course."

"I know you said you're going to live here, but once I leave can you promise me that you'll look out for Zoey?"

Suddenly, Sutton saw Harper in a whole new light. It was apparent that he took his role as man of the house very seriously, while Sutton saw an adolescent on the cusp of manhood. Harper did not know that he would look out for Zoey even if he hadn't asked him. There was so much he liked and admired about Harper's sister, and living next door to each other for the next eight to nine months, and their plan to share Sunday dinner twice each month, while mentoring her brother, was certain to cement their friendship.

"Yes, Harper. I promise to look out for your sister." He gave Harper a fist bump, sealing their deal. The doorbell chimed and Sutton glanced at the clock on the microwave. It was exactly three. "Check on the sweet potatoes while I get the door."

Zoey smiled up at Sutton when he opened the door. It was the first time she'd seen him wearing a dress shirt and tailored slacks, which she doubted had come off a rack because they'd expertly fit his tall, muscular physique. The gray in his black hair was more visible now that it was no longer stubble. She extended a covered container with a dozen miniature cheesecakes.

"Just a little something for dessert."

Sutton dipped his head and kissed her cheek. "They truly are little."

"I know that you're watching your waistline, so I decided to make miniatures that are very close to being guilt-free."

Sutton's eyes lingered on her face before shifting lower to her feet. "By the way, you look very nice."

Zoey no longer felt flustered or uneasy whenever Sutton stared at her because she was more than ready if he wanted a relationship with her. She wasn't so naive that she did not know when a man was either interested or attracted to her—and Sutton was no different. Initially she thought he'd volunteered to mentor Harper as a foil to get closer to her until she recalled his involvement in serving youth during his professional baseball career. However, it was his longing looks, gentle touch and caressing kisses that had awakened her celibate body.

"Thank you."

She'd washed and blown out her chemically relaxed hair and used a curling iron to achieve a profusion of curls framing her face and falling to her shoulders. A light cover of makeup and white silk blouse, ice-blue linen slacks and matching ballet slipper shoes completed her casual chic outfit.

"Please come in and rest yourself. My sous chef is putting the finishing touches on dinner."

Zoey followed him into the house that was as familiar as her own. Miss Sharon was one of two neighbors she could depend on to come through whenever she needed a babysitter. "Has Harper taken over your kitchen?"

"Not yet," Sutton said, smiling. "He's a natural when it comes to following instructions."

"He's like his mother. Charmaine loved to cook."

Sutton rested his free hand at the small of her back. "It looks as if the both of you had a very talented teacher."

Zoey glanced at the dining room table with place settings for three. She walked into the kitchen and was met with a plethora of aromas that tantalized her olfactory nerves. Her eyes focused on a pork roast with apple sausage stuffing on a large platter. Harper, wearing oven mitts, took a casserole dish out of the oven and set it on a trivet.

Her heart swelled with pride when she stared at her brother moving around the kitchen with the confidence he'd acquired when helping her prepare dishes. Harper was a masculine version of his mother; their personalities were similar as well as their likes and dislikes. Unlike Kyle, who would come home from school and go to his bedroom to do homework, Harper would sit at the kitchen table and watch her cook. And once he was old enough to look over the stove, he would ask if he could help her. At no time could she refuse his enthusiasm because she remembered when she would ask her stepmother to teach her how to make a particular dish.

Harper glanced up, smiling. "Hey, Zoey." He pointed to the pork roast. "Look at what Mr. Reed made."

She returned his smile. Seeing the ponytail made her aware of why he'd asked for one of her elastic hair ties. "It looks beautiful and smells scrumptious." The pork, roasted a golden brown, was topped with a stuffing reminiscent of what she would prepare for a Thanksgiving turkey.

Sutton removed a pitcher of chilled lemonade from the refrigerator. "I baked extra stuffing to go with the leftover chops."

Zoey estimated there were more than a dozen ribs

on the large roast. "You will be eating leftovers for days."

"Wrong, Zoey," Sutton countered. "All of us will be eating leftover pork chops. When I told the butcher at the Village Market that I wanted a crown roast of pork for three people with enough for leftovers, he probably thought I was feeding a basketball team."

"I don't mind eating pork every day," Harper announced proudly. "Ribs and pulled pork are my favorites."

"I'm more a chicken man," Sutton admitted, staring at Zoey. "Legs in particular."

She gave him a *what are you trying to say* look as she recalled the morning when she'd sat on the porch in a tank top and pair of shorts, reading. Zoey had noticed Sutton staring at her legs.

"You like legs and I like breasts," Harper added.

"Can I help with anything?" Zoey volunteered. Judging from the exchange of glances between her brother and his mentor, she'd assumed they were referring to body and not chicken parts.

Sutton handed her the pitcher. "You can put this on the table while I bring over the roast."

Ten minutes later, Zoey sat at the table with Harper and Sutton, holding hands while she said grace. What followed was a feast of fork-tender stuffing made with cubed bread, Italian sausage, chopped onion celery, tart Granny Smith apples and fresh herbs she was able to identify as sage, thyme and parsley. The sweet potato casserole topped with ground pecans and sweet-and-sour red cabbage were the perfect complement for the meat and stuffing. To say Sutton was a good cook was an understatement. He was exceptional, and it was apparent his mother-in-law had taught him well.

"Is your mother a good cook?" she asked him.

"Yes. Granny Dot made certain her daughters learned to cook. However, she had less success with teaching them to knit, crochet or quilt. That's when Georgi became her student."

"She learned well, because the handmade garments exhibited in her shop are beautiful."

"You've been to A Stitch at a Time?"

"Yes. Georgina asked me to stop by and I've committed to knitting a cap and scarf for cancer patients whenever they complete the new wing at the county hospital."

"My cousin can be quite persuasive when she wants to be. I told her I would represent the Falls during the ribbon-cutting ceremony."

Zoey smiled at Sutton. "There's nothing wrong with using your celebrity status if it's for a good cause."

"Mr. Reed, can you be one of the speakers at my graduation?" Harper asked.

Sutton set down his knife and fork, and then touched his napkin to the corners of his mouth. "That would depend on the school's administration."

"But you graduated from Wickham Falls High School," Harper insisted.

"I still would have to get authorization from the school board."

"Maybe I'll run for a seat on the student council and we can petition the principal to have Mr. Reed become our commencement speaker."

Zoey shared a look with Sutton; in the past Harper didn't want to become involved in any student government activities, despite her suggestion he join one or two of the school-based clubs because it would look good on his college applications. Good grades weren't enough when college officials also weighed community service and extracurricular activities.

Sutton rested an elbow on the table. "If you're able to convince them, then I definitely will become your commencement speaker."

Harper stared down at his plate. "Zoey has been bugging me to get more involved in school activities because that's what colleges are looking for."

Sutton winked at Zoey. "She's right. I joined the French club, was a student council member and played on the baseball team. I also did community service at the animal shelter in Mineral Springs."

"What did you do there?"

"I was assigned to cleaning cages and walking dogs for exercise. I didn't grow up with a pet, but after caring for dogs and cats that would eventually be put down if they weren't adopted, I'd become a pet lover."

"Have you ever had a pet?" Zoey asked Sutton.

"Not yet. I didn't want one while I played ball because I didn't want to leave it whenever I had away games. And my condo had a no-pet rule."

"We did not grow up with an animal because my father was allergic to pet dander," Zoey said before Sutton could ask her about whether she'd had a dog or cat. "I like cats because they're quiet and independent, but if I had to choose it would be a dog."

"Zoey, would you be willing to come with me to the shelter to choose a dog once I'm settled into my permanent home?"

She smiled. "Of course."

"Which one do you want, Mr. Reed. A rottweiler or pit bull?"

Frowning, Sutton shook head. "Those are breeds I wouldn't consider adopting, because I'm partial to terriers."

Harper appeared shocked. "You want one of those little dogs you can put in a purse?"

"Why not?" His expression was impassive. "What's wrong with carrying a dog in a bag?"

"But…but a big dude like you with a tiny dog."

"So, are you saying big dudes need big dogs and little dudes little dogs? And when the time comes whenever I invite my fur baby into his forever home, he will have hair and not fur, because I don't want him shedding everywhere, and he will be small enough so as not to jump up on my bed or furniture when I'm not there."

Zoey hid a smile when her brother dropped his eyes. It was obvious Harper had come down with a case of foot-in-mouth. And it was apparent Sutton was a neat freak. She dabbed her mouth with her napkin. "If I eat any more I won't have room for dessert."

Harper placed his napkin next to his plate. "I'm going to save my dessert for later. Zoey, is it all right after I help Mr. Reed clean up if I go to The Clearing with some of the kids from school? It will be the last time before classes start on Tuesday."

"How are you getting there?"

"Jabari said he's going to ask his father if he can use his car."

Pushing back his chair, Sutton rose to his feet. "You can use the Wrangler. Just make certain you have your license on you, and I shouldn't have to warn you about speeding, smoking and drinking in my vehicle or doing other things I won't mention at this time."

Zoey half rose. "Sutton?"

He held up his hand. "It's okay, Zoey. I'm certain Harper will bring my vehicle back spotless and without a scratch."

Harper's shock was evident when he stared like a deer caught in the blinding glare of a driver's headlights. "Really, Mr. Reed?"

Sutton nodded. "Come with me and I'll give you the fob."

Zoey swallowed a groan when they walked out of the dining room. It was apparent Sutton trusted her brother enough to let him drive his vehicle with a group of teenagers. She slumped back down to her chair and waited for Sutton to return. She didn't have long to wait.

"Do you know what you've done?" she asked him.

Sutton came over to sit next to her. He rested an arm over her shoulders. "I know exactly what I've done. It's a test, Zoey. He already knows how I feel about smoking and drinking, but the real test is not telling when I expect him to come back." Leaning closer, he pressed a kiss on her temple. "You have to learn to trust him, and he needs to know that you do. And more importantly, you have to be willing to let go. I don't have to remind you that in a couple of years he'll turn eighteen, and he will have a high school diploma, be eligible to vote and enlist in the military without parental consent."

Zoey turned her head and gave Sutton a long stare. "You're spoiling him, Sutton. First a pair of Jordans and now your Jeep."

"They are material things that can be replaced. Let me remind you that Harper never asked me for the sneakers or to let him drive the Jeep."

"Maybe he learned his lesson when he tried to break into your sports car," she mumbled under her breath.

"Lighten up, sweetheart."

"Do you call all women you know *sweetheart*?"

"Just the ones I like."

A smile had replaced her strained expression. "Should I assume I'm one of those you like?"

"Of course."

"How much?"

"This much," Sutton said, nanoseconds before his

mouth covered hers in a kiss that sucked the oxygen from her lungs.

This kiss was so different from others they'd exchanged that Zoey felt as if the heat in her veins had reached the boiling point. She was on fire from the top of her head to the soles of her feet, as an uncontrollable tremor settled between her thighs.

"Sutton. Sutton!" she repeated. She was close to losing control and begging him to make love to her.

Sutton ended the kiss when he felt Zoey shaking as if she'd suddenly taken chill. He knew he'd aroused her, but also knew there was nothing he was going to do about it. Not now.

"Was that enough convincing?" Her shoulders shook at the same time she bit her lip, and then he realized she was laughing. "Was it, sweetheart?"

"Yes-s-s."

"Bummer," he whispered. "I thought maybe you'd need a little more convincing."

Zoey sobered. "That's enough—for now. You cooked, so I don't mind helping clean up."

Sutton dropped a kiss on her hair. She'd shattered the sensual moment with the mention of clearing away dinner. "You don't have to do that."

"Yes, I do. I believe in shared duties."

"If that's what you want." Sutton rose to stand, pulled out Zoey's chair and helped her to her feet.

"I'll rinse, and you can stack the dishwasher."

"Anything for the pretty lady."

Going on tiptoes, she kissed his cheek. "Thanks."

Sutton did not know why she was thanking him when he should've been thanking her and Harper. They'd permitted him to playact that they were a family cooking together and trading stories over dinner. That was something he'd missed when married to Angell. His mother-in-law cooked and his wife sat at the table, stoned-faced, picking at her food because he'd refused to have his home filled with strange people drinking, smoking and sleeping off their high in some of the eight bedrooms in the six-thousand-square-foot mansion. Whenever he came home he wanted peace and quiet, away from crowds, while Angell did not want to give up her fake friends and adoring entourage, and in the end Sutton gave her the only thing she wanted for a divorce settlement: the house.

Reaching for her hand, Sutton led Zoey into the kitchen and filled the sink with hot water and dish detergent before turning on the radio on the countertop. The melodious harmonies of Boyz II Men singing "I'll Make Love to You" filled the space.

After wiping his hands on a terry cloth towel, he curved an arm around Zoey's waist. "May I please have this dance?"

She squinted her eyes as she held up her hand. Staring at the palm, she said, "I have to check to see whether I have space on my dance card. Oh, you're lucky because my suitor is dancing with another woman."

Throwing back his head, Sutton laughed. "I think

you've been reading too many of those romance novels."

Zoey scrunched up her nose. "Don't knock them if you haven't read them."

Her arms went around his waist when he eased her to stand between his feet. "Do you think if I read one I would come to know what women like?"

She tilted her head to look up at him. "Want and need, Sutton. The two things are very different."

He tightened the embrace, bringing her breasts against his chest. "Perhaps you can tell me the difference without having to read one of those books. Hypothetically, what would you want and need from me if I was your lover or husband?"

Zoey blinked once. "Me?"

"Yeah, you. I'm your lover and I want you to become my wife. What would I have to do to convince you to marry me?"

Chapter Ten

Zoey lowered her eyes. She wasn't prepared to pretend they were lovers on the verge of exchanging vows. "But we're not lovers, Sutton."

"I did say hypothetically."

"Which one do you want first? Lover or husband?"

"Lover."

She let out a breath. "I want him to be sensitive to what I like and don't like in bed."

"I wouldn't know that until we make love the first time."

"If I tell you to stop, then I'd expect you to stop."

"That goes without saying," Sutton countered.

"*Stop* is different from *no*, Sutton." He smiled and attractive lines fanned out around his large eyes. "What are you grinning about?"

"What if it's so good that you want me to stop because you're afraid of losing control?"

"I've never lost control."

His smile faded. "Never?"

"No." And there was no way she was going to admit to him that she'd never climaxed.

"Have we finished talking about our lovemaking?"

"I believe in monogamy. If you cheat on me, then it's over between us. I don't believe in second chances."

"I've never been able to sleep with more than one woman at the same time, because it can get messy."

"Not if they both have the same name."

"Now you're being naughty, Zoey."

"I read a novel where the man sought out women with the same or similar names to sleep with so he wouldn't get confused."

Sutton shook his head. "That requires too much research. Have we exhausted the rules for us being lovers?"

"Yes."

"What would you need from me if I were your husband?"

Zoey paused as she contemplated what she'd need from her husband to make her feel fulfilled as his wife. "He must love me unconditionally. I'll need to know and believe that he will support and protect me and our children. That he will put family first, and everything else second. I will tell and show my husband that I love him, and make certain he knows that I will be with him in the good and the bad times. I don't want us to go to bed angry with each other even if we have a disagreement."

"That sounds easy enough."

"If it was easy, Sutton, there wouldn't be so many divorces."

"Some couples use divorce as a way to escape or run away from their problems rather than face them."

Pushing against his chest, Zoey managed to extricate herself, walk over to the sink and stare down at the soapy water. "Is that what happened in your marriage?" She jumped slightly when Sutton rested his hands on her shoulders.

"No. I stayed in a marriage longer than I should have because I wanted it to work."

Zoey turned to face him. "What went wrong?"

"We were complete opposites, but I didn't know that until after we were married. And I'm not going to badmouth Angell because there are things about her I still love."

"Are you in love with her, Sutton?" She'd asked because if he was then they would never cross the line from friends to lovers. She had no intention of becoming that involved with a man who hadn't gotten over his ex.

"No, Zoey, I'm not in love with her. What you see is what you get with Angell—beautiful, outgoing and she can never get enough of the spotlight."

Zoey listened intently as Sutton told how his wife ignored his pleas that he did not want to come home and find his house filled with hordes of people. Many he didn't know. He'd given her his schedule as to when he would be home and traveling for away games, but she claimed she couldn't keep up with it. She would leave town for photo shoots, occasionally flying out of the country, and when she returned it was jet lag that left her out of sorts and unable to keep up with his schedule.

"We'd talked about starting a family before we were married, and Angell asked if we could wait because her modeling career was just taking off. We'd agreed to wait five years, and when that came and went, she asked if we could wait another year. I agreed, and six months later she said she wanted out of the marriage. I asked her what she wanted as a divorce settlement and she said the house. I signed over all six thousand square feet set on three acres and walked away from all of it."

"Does she still live there?"

"I don't know, Zoey. Her mother and I will exchange emails a couple of times a year, but there's never a mention of Angell. I wish her well and hope she's happy."

Zoey's eyelids fluttered as she struggled to control her emotions. "There are winner and losers when it comes to divorce."

"Why would you say that?"

"When my father divorced my mother, she lost her baby daughter and I grew up not knowing my mother. So, both of us were losers. And I suppose that's why I hold on to Harper as tightly as I can. He was only six and very close to Charmaine when she died. That's when I knew I had to be strong for him and Kyle. I'm not even thirty and I've lost a mother, father and a stepmother. And it's as if I'm holding my breath when I think of who's next. I didn't want Kyle to join the marines, because I was afraid he would be deployed, but I couldn't tell him that. He would be in awe during the Memorial Day parade when active and former military would march down Main Street in their uniforms. And once he discovered that Aiden Gibson, one of the owners of the Wolf Den, was a former navy SEAL, that was all he needed to decide he wanted a military career."

Sutton wanted to tell Zoey that if she had to go through any more tragedy in her life that he would be there for her. That there was no need for her to go it alone because he was falling in love with her. But that was something he wanted to show her. That he would be with her in the good and bad times, and he prayed there would be an abundance of good.

"When are you going back to work?"

"I don't know because the agency doesn't have an available client for my hours. Why?"

"I'd like to make plans for us to drive up to Charleston and have an early dinner at a fancy restaurant before coming back here."

"*Fancy* as in *formal*?"

"Maybe I used the wrong adjective. Business-casual attire, and that means no tank tops, flip-flops, booty shorts and sleeveless shirts and torn clothing."

Zoey rolled her eyes upward. "I do wear tank tops and flops, but never booty shorts."

"Well, are we on?"

"If you make it for the weekend, then you've got yourself a partner. I don't work weekends or over-nights because of Harper."

"We don't have anything planned for next Sunday, so that means we'll have Saturday night to hang out a little late. And I'll be certain to ask permission from the man of your house if it's all right if I take his sister out. I'll also reassure him that she will be safe with me."

"You're taking that man-of-the-house scenario a bit too far."

"You have to know he's very protective of you."

"And I of him, Sutton. But, don't forget I'm still the adult."

"Yes, ma'am."

Sutton felt as if he'd scaled a high wall once he'd gotten Zoey to agree to go out with him. He still felt as if he had to walk on proverbial eggshells with her because it would take him a while to be able to gauge her moods. She'd gone through a lot and Sutton wanted to make her life as angst-free as possible.

He must love me unconditionally. I'll need to know and believe that he will support and protect me and our children. She had no idea how easy that would be for him. When he declared his love for her, it would be without question. Support and protection went to-gether with Zoey and the children he hoped would eventually be in their future.

He made quick work of clearing the dining room table and packing away leftovers for Zoey and

Harper. The pork, stuffing, cabbage and sweet potato casserole would last them for several days. Zoey
handed him dishes, glasses and silverware and he
stacked them in the dishwasher.

Sutton gave her a sidelong glance as she used a
brush to scrub the roasting pan. "Are we going to
have coffee with the cake?"

"Yes. Would you mind if we brew coffee at my
place? I have a blend that will complement dessert."

"Of course not. Should I bring the cheesecakes?"

"No. I have some."

"Do you realize you gave me a dozen little cakes?"

"Of course," Zoey said smugly. "There's little or
no sugar in them."

"You've listened to me talk about my ex's eating
habits, but I can assure you that I'm not that nitpicky
with food except where it concerns dessert. Sweets
are my Achilles' heel."

"Have you considered smaller portions?" she
asked.

"I will if you make miniature desserts."

Zoey winked at him. "Your wish is my command.
I will make itty-bitty muffins, cakes and tarts."

"Thank you, sweetheart."

Sutton realized it was the second time he'd called
her by the endearment when he wanted to refer to her
as *my love.* Although they'd grown up in the same
town, it was as if they'd lived thousands of miles
apart.

He was already playing pro ball when the news
reached him that James and Charmaine Allen had

died from carbon monoxide poisoning, leaving their three children orphans. Georgina told him how the town had come together to fundraise for the surviving Allen siblings, and he hadn't hesitated to anonymously send a generous donation.

Fast-forward ten years and the teenage girl who'd challenged the system and won so that she could keep her brothers out of foster care was standing in his kitchen washing dishes. Her selflessness and maternal instincts afforded her the wherewithal to raise both her brothers to manhood, while deferring her own dream to become a nurse. In that instant Sutton swore a vow that he would do all he could to help her to achieve her career goal.

Zoey watched Sutton as he took a sip of coffee. They'd elected to have dessert on her porch. "What do you think?"

Sutton peered at her over the rim of his cup. "It's delicious. What is it?"

"Jamaican Blue Mountain. It is purportedly one the best and most expensive coffees in the world."

He took another sip. "I could drink this all day every day. Where did you buy this?"

"I didn't buy it. I had a client whose son was a coffee broker and he would occasionally send me gifts of coffee. He would grind the beans just before shipping to ensure their freshness with a recommendation to store the grounds in a glass jar in the fridge."

"Does he still send you coffee?"

"No. After his mother passed away, he moved to

Kenya to oversee a coffee plantation there. My supply is dwindling, and I probably have enough for another three or four cups."

Sutton inclined his head. "Thank you for sharing it with me. I've drunk so many bad cups of coffee in my life that I'm shocked when I get one that I can really enjoy."

"When did you start drinking coffee?" Zoey asked.

"It was in college when I spent all-nighters studying for an exam or trying to finish a paper."

"Did you party a lot?"

A smile ruffled his mouth. "Yes and no."

Zoey narrowed her eyes at the man seated opposite her. "It's either yes or no, Sutton."

"Yes, after the team won a game, and no when we didn't."

She popped the last piece of cheesecake topped with a strawberry into her mouth. Zoey did not want to envy Sutton's college experience, which would be so different from hers. He'd left home to attend college at eighteen, while she would be thirty and much older than the average incoming student.

"Now that you're retired, have you thought about writing a book about your life in the big leagues?"

Sutton sank lower on the rocker and stared down at the liquid in his cup. "If I do decide to write a book, it would be a definitive history of the Negro Leagues."

Zoey listened intently as he told her about the formation of the first black professional baseball team, the Cuban Giants, in 1885. She was amazed with the wealth of knowledge and his ability to recall names and dates of every team and their players. It was then she realized he was able to combine his love of baseball with history.

"When are you going to start writing?"

"Once I'm settled where I can set up a home office."

Zoey set her cup on a side table. "Have you looked at the model homes going up on the Wolfe/Remington land? I haven't seen them, but folks claim they're beautiful."

"No," Sutton admitted, "but Georgi told me about them. Right now, she's renting a guesthouse on the property, and she's seriously thinking about buying one of the new homes once construction is completed."

"What's the projected date for completion?"

Zoey was familiar with the property owned by the descendants of the most infamous family in Johnson County, because she remembered her father spitting on the ground whenever he'd mentioned the Wolfe name. James Allen would launch into a tirade about the mine owners who treated their pets better than their workers. His father had been one of the miners who'd been injured during a cave-in, and rather than install government-mandated safety regulations, the Wolfes absolved themselves of all injuries and loss of life when they closed all their mines in the county, leaving thousands unemployed and uncompensated. It was only later that Zoey realized her father had poisoned her mind against the Wolfes and the people who owned the property were not responsible for the actions of their ancestors.

"Early next year."

Zoey moved off her chair and placed both coffee cups and dessert plates on a tray. "Don't run away. I'm going to take these inside the house."

Sutton stood and took the tray from her. "I'll take it in."

She held the door and let him precede her. Zoey knew she would remember the events of this day for a very long time. She'd been honest and forthcoming when Sutton asked what she wanted and needed from him if he were her lover or husband. And despite her limited experience with men, she did not have any preconceived notions about a fairy-tale romance. Yes, she read and liked romance novels with some plots that defied the imagination, yet it was that all-consuming happily-ever-after that she found most satisfying. The authors didn't add an addendum or epilogue five or ten years into the couple's marriage, which Zoey suspected was not without angst or conflicts, but because of the couple's dedication, she knew their love for each other would endure.

When he'd posed the questions, she felt as if she was interviewing for a position in his life and future. She'd found it flattering because she was very attracted to Sutton, but then she was also realistic that if she did sleep with him it did not necessarily translate into her becoming his wife.

"Just put the cups and dishes in the sink," Zoey instructed Sutton. "I'll wash them later."

The hand-painted china pieces were a wedding gift from her father to Charmaine, who would bring them out on special occasions and holidays, and wishing to keep the memories of their mother alive for Kyle and Harper, she would take the china out of the cabinet and set a festive table for their birthdays, Christmas and Thanksgiving.

She'd thought of the day as special because Sutton was the first person who made her question what she wanted from a man. She didn't have a girlfriend in whom to confide, and all her clients were elderly and/ or sickly and needed and wanted her more than she did them. Zoey kept them entertained by reading to them, and her other duties included light housekeeping, assisting them with bathing and making certain they ate their meals.

After the passing of her first client, with whom she had become very attached, Zoey grieved her death as if she'd been a family member. It was the first and last time she'd become that emotionally absorbed in a client.

Sutton turned, angled his head and stared at her as if deep in thought. "I'd like you to think of a few restaurants where you'd want to eat when we go up to Charleston, and I'll select a few and hopefully we'll be able to agree on one."

Zoey's last and happy memory of going to Charleston was with Charmaine, who'd insisted on shopping for a dress at a high-end boutique because her step-daughter wasn't going to prom with something that came off a department store rack.

"I'll let you know midweek." She had to go online and research restaurants in the capital city, but more important, she had to find something appropriate to wear for her date.

Sutton took a step, lowered his head and brushed a light kiss on her parted lips. "Thanks for everything."

"And thank you for a wonderful afternoon."

He kissed her again, this time on the forehead. "It's only the beginning of many more to come."

Zoey watched as he turned on his heel and walked out of the kitchen, leaving her staring at where he'd been. She'd discovered Sutton to be generous and easygoing, yet she wasn't ready to go all in with him. She knew that he liked her the way a man liked a woman, but she kept asking, why her? Her life for the past ten years had been an open book. All he had to do was ask around and anyone in Wickham Falls would tell him that no one had ever seen her with a man, that she worked as a home health aide in Mineral Springs and that she doted on her brothers.

What she didn't want was for Sutton to think of her as a charity case. She knew she'd shocked him when she'd rejected his offer to underwrite the cost of her nursing school tuition. There had been a time when she'd accepted money from the residents and businesses in her hometown, but that was in the past. Zoey had pulled herself up by her bootstraps and with astute planning, she had managed to become self-sufficient. She didn't live extravagantly, and the only big-ticket item on her agenda was getting a new vehicle.

Zoey hand-washed the cups, saucers and dessert plates, leaving them on a rack to dry before she went upstairs to change into a pair of shorts and tank top. Global warming was apparent. Wickham Falls was in a valley surrounded by forests and lakes and was experiencing temperatures that broke decades-old records and had most people complaining about the heat.

Zoey opened her eyes when she heard an approaching car to find Harper pulling into Sutton's driveway. Picking up her cell phone, she glanced at the time. It was a little after eight, and she'd spent the past two hours dozing on the porch. Sitting straight, she raised her arms above her head to relieve the stiffness in her shoulders.

"How was it driving the Jeep?" she asked as he came up the stairs.

Harper grinned like a Cheshire cat. "Nice. Mr. Reed said I could keep his spare fob in case I needed it again."

"When do you think you're going to need to drive his car again?"

The teenager lifted his shoulders. "I don't know. But I'll hold on to it just in case."

Zoey didn't want to come down too hard on him, because the Jeep was Sutton's property and responsibility and if he wanted to entrust it to a sixteen-year-old, then she had no say in the matter.

"I hope you appreciate his generosity," she said instead.

"I do. I'm going to shower and turn in."

"I'll be in once the bugs start biting." Leaving the love seat, she folded her body down to the rocker and pulled her knees to her chest. If Sutton trusted Harper with his late-model SUV, then she had to learn to trust her brother enough to make the right decisions for his own well-being.

Chapter Eleven

Zoey sent Georgina a text message and seconds later the door to A Stitch at a Time opened, and Georgina pulled her inside. "There have been a few folks tapping on the door to see if I'm here because I made the mistake of parking my car outside instead of behind the stores on Main Street."

She smiled at the woman with a profusion of curly hair framing her face. "Do you think they're your regular customers or lookie-loos?"

"They can't be my regulars because they know when I'm closed." She looped her arm through Zoey's. "Come with me and I'll show you the kit I've put together for everyone who has signed up to knit the caps and scarves."

Zoey saw the glass-topped table filled with skeins

of yarns in every conceivable shade of pink, the official color of the fight against cancer. "Did you have all of these shades in your inventory?"

"No. I had to go online and order from different manufacturers. I still have some on order waiting to be shipped. Please sit and select the shade you want. The medium yarn will be for older children and adults and the baby yarn will be for small children."

"I think I'm going to begin with a kit for a small child because it will go faster than if I had to knit for an adult." Zoey pointed to a skein that reminded her of a blush wine. "I like this one."

Georgina smiled. "Good choice. Can you read a pattern?"

"Yes. It's just that I don't know how to cast on." She watched as Georgina checked the dye lots on the skeins to make certain they matched and took out the number she needed for a cap and scarf.

"You'll use a smaller needle for the kids." She selected a set of knitting needles from a supply in a wicker basket. "I always tell my knitters and those that crochet to work up a swatch to make certain the gauge is right for the number of stitches. Some folks knit tight and others loosely."

"I remember my stepmother taking time to wind a skein into a ball before she began knitting."

Georgina pulled her chair closer to Zoey's. "A lot of people still do, but I have a spinner that will do that for you. I'm going to show you how to cast on, then once you knit a swatch, I'll spin up the skeins you'll need to complete your project."

Zoey watched as Georgina tied yarn around the needle, making the first stitch, and then looped lengths of yarn over her thumb and forefinger, and then inserted a needle under her thumb and around the forefinger to cast on the second stitch. She repeated the action until there were ten stitches on the needle. She handed it to Zoey. "Now you try it."

Zoey executed the motion as if she'd tried countless times before. "It's easier than I thought."

Zoey thought of Charmaine, who'd boasted that she came from a long line of women who knitted, crocheted and quilted during their free time. Her stepmother would sit down in front of the television once she'd cleaned up the kitchen and knit while watching her favorite programs. She never bought a sweater for Kyle or Harper because she claimed she could make them for her sons.

"Do you believe needlecrafts are a dying art?" she asked Georgina.

"Not around here. When my father had the crafts section at the store, we sold well. But when he decided to expand sporting goods, I saw my chance to take the inventory and open this place."

"When I came in the other day, I noticed you were busy."

"There are some days when I barely get a chance to take a break with people coming to sign up for lessons and buy yarn. There's been an uptick in an interest in quilting, so I'd be glad to say it's not a dying art."

Zoey spent the better part of an hour in the shop,

working up a gauge before casting on with a set of round needles and completing three rows of a cap for a small child, while Georgina spun the skeins into balls and put them in a large plastic resealable bag along with the patterns. She handed Georgina her credit card for her purchase.

"I'm going to charge you ten percent because now that you're dating my cousin I consider you family."

Zoey froze. What was Georgina talking about? She and Sutton hadn't had their first official date and meanwhile his cousin… Her thoughts broke off and she wondered if he told Georgina they were involved with each other.

"Why would you say that? Sutton and I and neighbors, and we haven't dated, so that doesn't translate into you considering me family."

Georgina made a sucking sound with her tongue and teeth. "Come on now, Zoey. It's all over town that folks saw Sutton kissing you outside the shop."

The rush of heat starting in her chest moved up to her face and Zoey felt as if her head had caught fire. She swallowed a curse. Folks in the Falls didn't need a tabloid newspaper when gossip spread faster than a lighted fuse attached to a stick of dynamite.

"Does he know about the gossip?" she questioned.

"Yup."

"What did he say?"

"'Let them talk.'"

Sutton's reaction was to ignore the gossip. After all, he'd spent half of his adult life in the spotlight, while her being linked to a former superstar athlete would take some getting used to. "It was a friendly kiss."

Georgina looked at her side-eyed. "I happen to know my cousin well enough to know that he isn't prone to public displays of affection, so you may think of it as friendly, but it was anything but for Sutton. Do you two have something going on I should know about?"

"We're just friends."

Georgina's eyebrows lifted. "Me and Langston Cooper were friends before it turned into relationship."

Zoey's jaw dropped and when she tried to speak, no words came out. "You and Langston?" she finally asked. The editor in chief of *The Sentinel* had left Wickham Falls and become an award-winning war correspondent before coming back to take over ownership of the then-failing biweekly. There was no doubt she was truly out of the loop when it came to goings-on in her town.

"I suppose you haven't heard, but yes," Georgina said proudly. "I had a bad relationship some years ago and I told myself I never wanted to get involved again, but Langston proved me wrong. He's the opposite of every man I've known, and I'm not ashamed to say I'm totally in love with him."

"You're like a character in my romance novels."

"I'm a romance novel and fairy-tale heroine, Zoey. And you can be one if you give Sutton half a chance to make you happy."

"I'm not saying he doesn't make me happy but…"

"But what?" Georgina asked when her words trailed off.

Zoey wondered if she could confide in Georgina and not have her go back and tell Sutton. "I need to tell you something, but I don't want it to go beyond this shop." A flush suffused Georgina's face and Zoey realized she'd embarrassed her.

"I don't repeat gossip, Zoey, and believe me when I tell you that I hear a lot of it around here. I only mentioned Sutton to you because he happens to be my cousin."

"I'm sorry. I didn't mean to insult you."

"You didn't," Georgina said quickly. "Come on, girl, give me the deets."

"I've only slept with one boy and that was when I was in high school. But it's so different now. I can't believe it's taken me ten years to feel desire so strong that I fantasize making love with a man."

Georgina's toffee-brown eyes were brimming with tenderness. "What you feel is normal for a woman your age. Some of us go through long periods where we're celibate but by choice."

"Are you speaking from experience?"

"Yes, Zoey. I didn't date any of the boys in high school because they talked openly that I was a good catch because my father owned Powell's and after my brother died they knew I was next in line to inherit everything."

"So, it was all about money."

"Bingo," Georgina drawled. "I dated a few guys, but it ended as quickly as it'd begun because I was still living at home. Then I got involved with a man from Beckley and it reached a point where we talked about marriage and children until our relationship imploded."

"What happened?"

"He asked me to lend him money to cover his gambling debts."

With wide eyes, Zoey said, "You're kidding?"

"I wish. His father owned a successful used car business, so I figured he was someone who was solvent. But I was wrong. He was embezzling from the business and his bookie was pressuring him to repay his debts. That's when I walked away and never looked back. I swore never again until Langston and I were seated at the same table during a fundraiser earlier this spring. He's intelligent, mature, erudite, and he doesn't need my money."

"He sounds like the total package."

Georgina nodded, grinning. "Believe me, he is."

"Money isn't an issue with me and Sutton because I don't want his and I have enough to take care of me and my brother."

"What happened to make you split up with your boyfriend?"

"After my parents died and I became the legal guardian for my brothers, he claimed he was too young to take on the responsibility of raising two school-age kids. I ran into him the other day and he was with his wife and son."

"Did you speak to him?"

"No. We see each other in passing but we never

speak. He said enough ten years ago when he broke up with me when I needed him most. I didn't hold it against him when he said he wasn't ready for kids at eighteen, but when he said he didn't want to raise someone else's kids that's when I knew it was over between us."

"What a loser," Georgina said under her breath. "There are a few men in the Falls who marry women with children and vice versa. There are so many blended families in town that you wouldn't be able to count them on both hands and feet."

"I'm glad we didn't marry because I doubt whether we would've stay together. I don't need a fair-weather partner who will bolt when the relationship turns stormy."

"That would never happen with Sutton, Zoey. I've never been one to play matchmaker, but you won't find a nicer guy than Sutton. And I'm not saying that because he's my cousin. You can't imagine how many women have asked me to hook them up with him when word got out that he was divorced. I told them he would not appreciate me setting him up with someone, but that didn't stop them from asking me over and over. And once they found out that he'd moved back to the Falls, they acted like what my grandmother would call brazen hussies. They came to Powell's in droves and swarmed around him like locusts."

This disclosure piqued Zoey's interest. "What did he do?"

"Sutton is the same one you see whenever he's interviewed. He was polite and charming. He'd signed autographs for anyone that wanted one, and whenever a woman lingered too long he'd excuse himself telling her he had to wait on other customers. After a while, once they realized he wasn't receptive to their flirting they stopped coming in. He may be the Beast on the baseball diamond, but he's soft as a marshmallow off the field. His generosity is phenomenal, and he has donated and raised millions for his scholarship foundation dedicated to the at-risk kids he mentors."

Zoey wasn't ready to admit to Georgina that Sutton had volunteered to mentor her brother. "I've discovered firsthand how generous he can be."

"Yes, my cousin is one of the good guys, but for the life of me I'll never understand why he married that gold-digging wannabe supermodel."

"Wasn't she a successful supermodel?"

"Yeah, right. It all depends on who you talk to. Angell was in a *Sports Illustrated* swimsuit group shot, and if you listen to her brag about it, you'd think she was on the cover. She had what I consider a rather uneventful modeling career. She had been selected to participate in several Fashion Weeks around the world, but that was when she was in college. After the divorce, Sutton's star rose and hers fell because as Beauty and the Beast they'd become a brand. Agencies wouldn't book her without her husband, and that really ticked her off. But she had to know that a lot of models age out in their late twenties or thirties."

"Most of them except my favorite, Naomi Campbell," Zoey added. "The woman still owns the runway. I had…" Her words trailed off when her cell chimed a programmed ringtone. "Excuse me, but I have to take this call." She retrieved her phone from her bag and tapped a key. "Hello."

"Good morning, Zoey."

She recognized the voice of the agency's scheduler. "Good morning, Kelly. Do you have an assignment for me?"

"Yes, but it's temporary. Alison Harrison has a family emergency and she will be out for the rest of the week. I'd like to know if you're willing to cover her shift."

"Of course. What are her hours?"

"Seven to two. Her client is Caroline Raab. She's a retired sixty-two-year-old widowed schoolteacher who is recovering from a stroke that has left her with some memory loss. Alison says she's really sweet."

Zoey wanted to do the happy dance. Sweet she could really do after working with Mrs. Chambers. "Does she live alone?"

"No. Her college-student grandson lives with her."

"Text me her address."

"I'm sending it now. And, thank you, Zoey."

"Thank you."

Zoey ended the call and tapped the message app. Mrs. Raab lived in Beckley. She still did not have a permanent assignment, but she didn't mind working as a fill-in temp. She dropped the phone into her bag and walked over to the counter where Georgina had set the shopping bag stamped with the shop's logo.

"I have the rest of the day to get a jump on my

project because I have to go back to work tomorrow. And thank you for the family discount."

Georgina combed her fingers through her hair, holding it off her forehead. "Don't make a liar out of me, Zoey."

A slight frown appeared between Zoey's eyes. "What are you talking about?"

"You're real and I see why Sutton likes you."

"Thank you, but I think you're getting ahead of yourself, Georgina."

"I don't think so, Zoey Allen. Even my aunt Michelle heard the rumors about her son kissing the Allen girl and she says she wants to meet you. So, don't be surprised if Sutton asks you to come to Sunday dinner to meet the family."

Zoey couldn't believe what she was hearing. How could a chaste kiss blow up into something that had Georgina's family believing she and Sutton were ready to walk down the aisle together? Well, nothing was further from the truth.

Did she like him?

Yes.

Did she want to sleep with him?

Of course.

But was she ready to marry him or any other man?

No.

Zoey had carefully mapped out her life from the instant she accepted responsibility for her younger siblings, and marriage was not a part of that equation until she became a nurse, and that was still six years away. There were two years before Harper graduated high school and four years for her to earn a BSN and then pass the nursing boards. At thirty-six she would be open to falling in love, becoming a wife and mother.

She forced a smile she did not feel. "I'm really not ready to meet Sutton's mother." She and Sutton were friends and their friendship had not reached the level where she needed and wanted to be introduced to Sutton's mother. "I'll stop in again when I finish my project."

Reaching out, Georgina hugged her. "Thanks again for joining the campaign."

Zoey felt Sutton's cousin's warmth and enthusiasm when she returned the hug. "Anytime."

She left the shop, stored her knitting purchase in the cargo area of the minivan and decided rather than return home she would drive to the boutique in Charleston where Charmaine had selected her dress for prom. Sutton had promised to take her to an upscale restaurant and Zoey wanted a new outfit to celebrate their first official date.

Her conversation with Georgina provided her a glimpse into a segment of Sutton's marriage he hadn't revealed. But, then she remembered him saying there were things about his ex-wife he still loved. And he wondered if it was her beauty. Georgina had downplayed her cousin's ex-wife's modeling career, but photos of the woman did not lie. She was extremely photogenic and beautiful.

She turned on the radio, tuning it to a station with old-school jams, and sang along with familiar tunes from a decade ago. It was as if she'd turned back the clock when songs that had been popular when she was in high school filled the interior of the van. Those were the happy times when her only concern was maintaining her grades so she could get into college.

It had taken her a while to accept the curve life had thrown at her and made her aware she was no longer a teenage girl planning her schedules around the Fall Festival and homecoming, but a young woman who had come to acknowledge that she was stronger than she could've ever imagined.

Zoey slipped a note under the door to Harper's bedroom, wishing him luck on his first day as a junior. She had to leave the house an hour earlier because she had to drive to Beckley to clock in by seven. She heard Harper leave the house at five to run with Sutton and return a few minutes ago. The sound of running water coming from behind the bathroom door indicated he was in the shower.

She left the house and waved to Sutton, who sat on the top step of his porch drinking from a mug of coffee. He was still wearing his jogging clothes. "Good morning."

He raised the mug. "Good morning, working girl."

"Have a good day."

Sutton nodded. "Back at you."

Zoey slipped behind the wheel of the minivan, started it up and backed out the driveway. She'd made an appointment for Saturday to bring the van to Austen & Sons Auto for a tune-up. After going over her accounts, she figured out she could afford to finance a certified midsize used car with a substantial deposit to lower the monthly payments.

Traffic was heavier than normal with the start of school, and Zoey groaned when the app on her phone indicated a fender bender near the next exit. She sat idling for nearly ten minutes before cars began moving. Following the GPS, she reached her destination fifteen minutes before she was scheduled to start.

Mrs. Raab lived in a modest unattached one-story ranch house with a two-car garage. She parked her van on the street and walked up to the front door. It opened before she rang the bell and she met the light blue eyes of a young man with a scowl distorting his handsome features. He was totally grunge with ripped jeans, a flannel shirt tied at his waist and a leather choker.

"You're late!"

Reaching into her tote, Zoey removed her ID badge and showed it to him. "No, I'm not. In fact, I'm early because I was told my hours are seven to two."

"The other girl always came at six thirty."

Zoey struggled to control her rising temper. "I'm not the other *girl*. Now, will you please step aside so I can introduce myself to your grandmother?"

Taking a backward step, he opened the door and she walked in. "My grandmother is in her library."

Zoey walked through the parlor, living and dining rooms to an area that was set up as a reading room. A frail-looking white-haired woman sat in a cush-

ioned rocker listening to classical music coming from
a radio on a bookcase packed tightly with books.

"Has she had breakfast?"

"No. It's your job to feed her."

"William! What did I tell you about being rude?"
The words were garbled, as if her tongue was too
large for her mouth.

He dropped his eyes. "I'm sorry, Grandma. I'm
leaving now. I'll be back after my last class."

Caroline Raab held out her thin arms. "Come and
give your grandma a kiss before you go."

Zoey noticed the young man's hesitation before he
hugged and kissed his grandmother and suspected
he really did not want to deal with the woman under
whose roof he resided. The exquisite furnishings in
the house had been carefully selected to turn the
home into a designer showplace.

After the scheduler had texted her Mrs. Raab's address, she had sent her an email with her client's di-
etary restrictions and exercise regimen. She was able
to bathe, dress and eat by herself, while her grandson
was responsible for taking her to her rehab appoint-
ments three evenings a week to meet with a speech
therapist.

She hunkered down in front of the woman. "Good
morning, Mrs. Raab. My name is Zoey and I will be
filling in for Alison until she returns."

Caroline rested a hand on Zoey's head. "You are
very pretty."

Zoey covered the woman's hand with hers. "Thank
you so much. What would you like for breakfast?"

"Oatmeal with fruit."

She stood straight. "Do you want to eat here or in the kitchen?"

"I like it here with my books."

"Would you like me to read to you after you finish breakfast?"

Caroline attempted to smile, and it was the first time Zoey noticed that the left side of her face was paralyzed. "Yes."

The stroke had affected her ability to speak clearly and given her some memory loss and partial paralysis. Zoey hoped with ongoing rehabilitation she would be able to correct her speech and regain some feeling in her face.

Mrs. Raab was the complete opposite of her former client and although it was a temporary assignment Zoey knew she would enjoy it.

Chapter Twelve

It was Friday, her last day with Caroline Raab as her client, and Zoey wished she could become the woman's permanent home health aide. She enjoyed reading and listening to music with the retired music teacher. Her late husband had been a navy test pilot who'd lost his life when a jet exploded and crashed in the Mojave Desert. She haltingly told Zoey her daughter, an only child, had struggled with addiction as a college student and finally overdosed four years after giving birth to her only child. Caroline adopted the boy and with the hope that she would afford him a stable lifestyle he hadn't had with his mother.

Zoey felt, as an overindulgent grandmother, she had raised a spoiled, ungrateful, entitled young man who merely tolerated the woman. Billy, as he'd asked her to call him, didn't have Friday classes and whenever she glanced up, he would appear like a specter that never failed to raise the hair on the back of her neck. She was in the kitchen preparing a pasta salad for her client when William crept in. Stick-straight jet-black hair stood up on his head like little spikes. "Is there something you want?"

"No. I just decided to watch you."

"I'm not on display, so I suggest you go watch something else."

"You really have a smart-ass mouth."

Zoey clamped her teeth tightly to keep from saying something she wouldn't be able to retract. She had only two more hours and then her shift would be over, and she wouldn't have to see his smug face again.

"What's the matter, Miss Zoey? I should take you with me when I take my grandmother for speech therapy."

She'd had enough. "Take a walk, little boy." She must have gotten through to him when he turned on his heel and stomped out the kitchen. She had tried in vain to ignore his stalking and occasional taunts, but she had had enough. And the only reason she hadn't gone off on him was because the assignment was temporary, but it would have been ideal if not for the client's grandson.

Zoey set the plate with the macaroni salad on a tray in front of Caroline and watched as she fed herself. She'd begun including carbs along the protein in the woman's diet in an attempt for her to keep up her strength.

"This is so good," Caroline said.

"I'm glad you like it."

She waited for her to finish her meal. "I'll bring you some water." Zoey had gotten her to increase her intake of water to keep her kidneys functioning well.

"Thank you, Zoey."

Twenty minutes later, she sat across from her client knitting as they listened to the radio tuned to a classical music station. It was Caroline's favorite time of the day when after lunch she would lie on the recliner and listen to music while Zoey knitted. When she'd questioned Billy if his grandmother still played the concert grand piano in a corner of the living room, he'd revealed she stopped playing years ago after they'd buried his grandfather.

The clock on a table chimed the hour and Zoey put away her knitting and gathered her tote. "Mrs. Raab, I'm leaving now."

The light blue eyes she'd passed along to her grandson stared vacantly into space. "Have a good afternoon." It was the same thing she said every day.

"You, too, Mrs. Raab."

Zoey left the house and stopped short when she saw that two of her tires had been flattened, and she didn't have to have an IQ of a genius to know who was responsible. She wasn't going to confront Billy. To do so would give him the satisfaction that he'd bested her. She took out her cell phone and tapped the number for Austen's Auto to tow the van back to Wickham Falls. A recorded voice asked that she leave a message.

Zoey called Sutton next and sighed in relief when he answered after the second ring. "What's up, sweetheart?"

"I need a ride back to the Falls. Right now, I'm staring at two flat tires and when I called Austen's I got their answering service. Can you please pick me up?"

"Of course. Give me the address where you are. After I hang up, I want you to call Austen's again. If you can't reach them, then I'll contact another garage and have them tow you back here."

"Thank you, Sutton."

"Come on now, Zoey. There's no need to thank me. You have to know how I feel about you."

She smiled despite the dire situation. "Yes, I know. You like me."

"Wrong, babe. What I feel goes a lot deeper than liking."

Zoey closed her eyes as she tried to slow down her runaway heartbeat. She knew instinctively what he was going to say because it would echo her own feelings. She was falling in love with Sutton Reed despite her resolve not to allow herself to become that involved with him because it would disrupt or derail everything she'd planned for her future. And she knew if he did mention that other four-letter word, it would change everything.

"And what's that?" she whispered. The sound of

a car's engine came through the earpiece and it was obvious Sutton was in his car.

"I'll show you later. I'm going to hang up so you can call Austen's back."

The line went dead and Zoey tapped the auto body shop's number. It rang once before a gravelly voice identified the name of the business. She related her problem and the man said the tow driver was out on a run and he would call to let him know where to retrieve her vehicle.

"Do you need a ride back to the Falls?"

"No. Someone is coming to get me."

"Leave the keys under the driver's-side mat and lock the door."

"How will you unlock it?"

"Miss, we have tools that allow us to get into most cars. And yours is not one of these new ones that make it almost impossible to break into."

Zoey wanted to tell him he didn't have to remind her how old her minivan was. She opened the door, sat behind the wheel and stared out the windshield. If Billy had cut the tires on her new car, Zoey knew she would've gone ballistic. Pressing her head against her headrest, she closed her eyes and waited for Sutton or the tow truck driver—whichever one arrived first.

Sutton maneuvered up along the curb behind Zoey's van. She got out at the same time he exited his vehicle. She appeared more fragile in the loose-fitting smock and uniform pants, and his heart turned over when he saw lines of tension bracketing her mouth. Sutton held out his arms and he wasn't disappointed as she moved into his embrace.

"I got here as soon as I could."

"Thank you."

He buried his face in her hair. Zoey was thanking him when he should've been the one thanking her for providing him a second chance to fall in love with someone who allowed him a modicum of normalcy for the first time in a very long time. Sutton peered over Zoey's shoulder at the minivan. "How did you get two flats at the same time?"

"You don't want to know."

"Yes, I do want to know," he retorted. Sutton dropped his arms and walked to Zoey's vehicle and ran his fingers over what was obviously a slash in the rubber. "Someone cut your tires. Do you have an idea who did this?" Zoey stared at the middle of his chest rather than meet his eyes. "You know, don't you?"

She blinked once. "I have a suspicion, but I can't prove it."

"Who, Zoey?"

"I think it was my client's grandson."

Sutton didn't want to believe what he was hearing when Zoey revealed her client's grandson's hostility toward her. It was obvious the kid was jerk. "Where is he?"

Zoey caught his arm. "Don't, Sutton."

He flung off her hand. "Don't what, Zoey? Don't give the cretin a throat punch? Or maybe I should break his fingers so he'll think twice about slashing someone else's tires?"

"Please, Sutton. There's no need for violence. This is my last day here and I'll never see him again."

Sutton stared at Zoey, seeing her fear and feeling her vulnerability. He cradled her face in his hands. "Sweetheart, what happened to the woman who said he must love me unconditionally? And I'll need to know and believe that he will support and protect me. I'm here with you because you need me to protect you. I'm just going to talk to the man, and not give him the ass-kicking he deserves."

Her fingers curled around his wrists. "You promise?"

Smiling, Sutton brushed a kiss over her lips. "Yes, babe, I promise."

Zoey watched Sutton walk to the front door and ring the bell. She hadn't realized she was holding her breath when the door opened, and Sutton motioned for Billy to step outside. She wasn't close enough to hear their conversation, but she could see the younger man's expression change from shock to uncertainty as Sutton leaned in and said something in his ear.

She chewed her lip as Billy went back into the house and returned minutes later, handing Sutton an envelope. The two men shook hands and Billy went back into the house and closed the door.

Zoey stared at Sutton as he approached. He wore a pale blue tailored shirt, navy-and-white-striped silk tie, gray linen slacks and brown oxfords, and she wondered where he'd been when he took her call.

Sutton handed her the envelope. "There's enough

in there for you to buy four new tires and cover the tow."

"You shook him down for money?"

"Is that what you think?"

"What else is it, Sutton?"

"I made the creep pay for what he did to you. Would you have preferred that I bitch slap him?"

"No! I don't like violence."

"And I don't like some dude who can't understand when no means no. He admitted it made him mad when you ignored him, because, let me see if I can remember his direct quote. 'I always get any bitch I want because I can pay for whatever they want.' The spoiled little snot is spending his inheritance even before his grandmother passes away."

Sutton was right about Billy being spoiled. He drove a top-of-the-line BMW and always flashed a fistful of dollars, which he probably assumed would impress her. "I suppose I ruined his record of getting what he wants, so he decided to punish me by slashing my tires."

"Guys like your Billy are more common than you realize. They drive luxury cars and flash wads of money and women flock to them like bees to honey."

Zoey recalled Georgina referring to Sutton's ex-wife as a gold-digging wannabe model and wondered if she'd used Sutton's success to elevate her own. "Thank you for being my knight in shining armor."

Throwing back his head, Sutton laughed. "My armor is a little rusty, but I don't want you to forget that I'll always be here for you."

Her eyelids fluttered when she heard the passion in his voice. "Do you love me, Sutton Reed?"

Sutton took a step. "Yes, Zoey Allen. I love you unconditionally."

She gave him a direct stare. "Why?"

"I'm surprised you have to ask me why. You embody everything I want and need. Let's start with family. There is nothing more precious to me than family. They're constant in good and bad times. I grew up with a single mother that sacrificed a lot to give me what I needed to become who I am today and there isn't anything I wouldn't do for her. And when I look at what you've sacrificed for your brothers, I see the same strength in you that I see in my mother. Your beauty notwithstanding, you're smart, sensible and feisty."

Zoey smiled. "You think I'm feisty?" He nodded. "I'm actually rather passive."

"You were anything but passive when I brought Harper to your door after I found him vandalizing my car. You were more like a lioness protecting her cub. All fangs and claws."

"That's because you had my brother in a headlock. And no one, I mean no one, will hurt my brothers without me coming for them."

"It wasn't a headlock, sweetheart. I was holding him by the back of his shirt."

"Same difference because he couldn't get away."

"Now, back to why I've fallen in love with you."

"Oh, there's more?" Zoey teased.

"Yup. Sharing Sunday dinner with you and Harper

is a reminder of what I'd been missing for more years than I can count. Mom and I didn't have much, but the highlight of my week was Sunday dinner. We'd attend early church services, and then she would come home and cook so the house was filled with incredibly mouthwatering aromas. My mother was very proud, and she refused to take a handout from my aunt Evelyn, who'd married Bruce Powell, who at the time was one of the wealthiest men in Wickham Falls."

Zoey blinked as if coming out of a trance. "You're in love with me because I remind you of your mother?"

"No, babe. You have the same qualities I admire in my mother. You're proud, Zoey. Almost to a fault. You refused to let me pay for your nursing school tuition. And you were upset when I bought the Jordans for Harper and let him drive the Jeep. When it comes to Harper because there are times when I relate to him as an older brother and other times when I see him as my son. Meeting and hanging out with you and Harper has allowed me a modicum of normalcy for the first time in a very long time.

"Playing pro ball opened up a whole new world that took some getting used to. I was paid an obscene amount of money to hit a ball with a wooden bat, and I was so traumatized that I put a copy of my first multimillion-dollar contract in a drawer and it was three weeks before I was able to take it out and count the number of zeros. I didn't want to be like some young men who'd grown up not having much and that overcompensated by going on spending sprees. One career-ending injury and everything they had disappeared like a puff of smoke."

"You were lucky, Sutton."

"I'm not judging them, Zoey, but I wanted something to show for the years of working with trainers and coaches to keep me at the top of my game. There were days when I played healthy and others when I played hurt. And I was realistic enough to know when the curtain would come down and I would have to take my final bow. What I didn't know when Georgi asked me to come back to Wickham Falls was that I would rent a house next to a most amazing woman that makes me fantasize about sharing a future with her."

Zoey slowly shook her head. "Sutton, don't."

"Don't what, Zoey? Don't love you? Don't take care of and protect you and Harper?"

"Aren't we moving too fast?"

"*We*, babe?"

She realized she'd said *we* rather than *you*. However, Zoey knew she had to stop denying what was so obvious. She had fallen in love with her neighbor. Sutton was so confident, something in his manner so soothing, that whenever they occupied the same space her whole being seemed to be filled with a waiting that needed to be assuaged. And that waiting was sexual fulfillment. Sutton was no boy about to embark on his first sexual encounter, but a mature man who'd dated women and had been married to a woman. He wanted a wife and a family, and if she married him, then he would get two for the price of one.

Zoey moved closer and wound her arms around Sutton's waist. "What if we take it nice and slow because I'm not going anywhere, and neither are you."

Sutton kissed her forehead. "Deal. I want to tell you that my mother has invited you and Harper to come to dinner this Sunday with the rest of the family. She claims she wants to meet the young woman everyone's talking about that was locking lips with her son in public."

"Did you tell her that you kissed me and not the other way around?"

"I did, but she still would like to meet you."

"Sutton, I'm not really ready to meet your mother. There are some issues we need to discuss and resolve before I meet her."

"Like what?"

Zoey eased back. "Why are you wearing a shirt and tie?"

Sutton laced their fingers together and led her over to the Jeep, opened the passenger-side door, helped her up and then rounded the vehicle and got in next to her. "We can wait here and talk in here until the tow truck driver gets here. When you called me, I was just leaving an interview."

"Where and who interviewed you?"

"Johnson County Public Schools. I got a call from an assistant superintendent that they need a permanent substitute history teacher at the high school."

Her eyes grew wide. "They hired you?"

"I'll know in a week. I have to email the bursars at my colleges to request they send official transcripts."

"I can't believe it. It's like you've come full circle. Teaching at the same high school where you'd graduated."

"Weird, isn't it?"

"No, Sutton. It's wonderful."

He felt Zoey's enthusiasm as surely as if it was his own. The call had caught him completely by surprise; it had been only two weeks since he'd sent out his résumé, and he assumed it would take months before he'd hear back, because most schools were fully staffed before the start of the school year. A teacher in the history department requested and was approved for an extended family leave to care for her husband, who'd sustained serious injuries when he'd fallen mountain climbing.

"I felt as if I was in a machine that took me back in time when I saw kids running down the halls to get to their classroom before the late bell rang, and at that instant I'd become one of them. I had a chemistry teacher that was a stickler for lateness, and he didn't want to hear that you'd come from PE and had to change before making it to his class on time. He was so rigid that I told myself when I become a teacher I would never threaten or intimidate my students."

Leaning to her left, Zoey kissed his jaw. "You're going to be a wonderful teacher."

Sutton hoped he would. It had taken years for him to earn a graduate degree taking online courses. During off-seasons when he didn't play winter ball, he could be found in front of a computer listening to lectures, taking exams and completing papers. He'd spent a couple of years researching the growth, expansion and destruction of every all-black town in the United States following the end of the Civil War for what would become his thesis.

Everything he'd always wanted was coming together, while his life had come full circle. He had secured a teaching position and fallen in love with a woman in his hometown. Zoey was asking for time and he would give her all that she needed to love him as much as he'd come to love her.

"You look nice, sis."

Zoey spun around on the toes of a pair of strappy black satin stilettos, the skirt of the dress flaring out around her bare legs. She had gone online to search for restaurants in the Charleston area and came up with three choices. Sutton had also come up with three choices, with two matching hers, and they finally decided on an Italian restaurant six miles outside the capital city.

"Thank you, Harper."

"Do you guys have a curfew?"

She narrowed her eyes at her brother as he flopped down on a chair in the living room. "Very funny."

"I'll try to wait up for you."

Zoey ruffled his hair. "Don't even try it."

"Would you mind if I stayed over at Triple Jay's?

We've been talking about putting together a gaming club at the school."

Zoey saw an expression of expectation on Harper's face. It was apparent his friendship with Jabari had survived the summer, and that meant he was maturing socially. He could get and keep friends. Whenever Jabari came over to shoot hoops, he'd asked if Harper could spend the night at his house, and so far she hadn't given her consent. But she knew if Harper was going to have a sleepover with anyone, then it would be with the Johnsons. Jabari's father's edict of no smoking, drinking or having kids over when the adults weren't there was strictly adhered to.

"Okay."

The sound of the doorbell echoed throughout the house and Harper jumped up, racing to the door. "I'll get it."

Zoey, reaching for a black silk shawl and evening bag, followed him. Sutton said he would pick her up at six. It would take them an hour to drive to Charleston, and he had made their reservation for seven thirty.

"Yo, man!" Harper shouted. "You're taking the Aston Martin!"

Zoey bit her lip to keep from laughing when she saw an expression of shock freeze Sutton's features. She had decided their first official date called for special attention to her appearance. She had an appointment with Bessie Daniels, the proprietress of Perfect Tresses salon, for her hair, hands and feet. The stylist had worked her magic by touching up the new growth in her hair and applying an avocado conditioner that left her hair soft and shiny. After sitting under the dryer for the better part of an hour for her roller sets to dry, she'd nearly fallen asleep. A mani-pedi was next before Bessie blew out the curls and pinned her shoulder-length hair up in an elaborate twist off the nape of her neck.

Zoey hadn't forgotten the makeup lesson Charmaine had taught her to accentuate her best features when she applied a smoky eye shadow, concealer and two coats of mascara and feathered her naturally arched eyebrows that were dark enough for her to forgo using a pencil. She'd tried several shades of lipstick before choosing an orangey-red that set off the orange undertones in her dark brown complexion.

When she'd visited the boutique, Zoey hadn't had to try on several garments once she spied a royal blue silk off-the-shoulder dress with an attached black slip. The dress was nipped and banded at the waist and the skirt flared out around her hips and ended at her knees. A pair of four-inch stilettos put her five-nine frame over the six-foot mark. It felt good not to crane her neck to look up at Sutton.

Her gaze slowly moved from his neatly barbered hair and clean-shaven face down to his tailored royal blue suit, white shirt and platinum tie, and black slip-ons.

"Wow!" The single word slipped unbidden from Sutton as he stared at Zoey's transformation. She was truly beautiful.

Zoey pressed her mouth close to his ear. "You did say no flops or booty shorts," she whispered.

He cupped her elbow. "I've seen you in shorts and you're a lot sexier in a dress."

Sutton hadn't thought Zoey could improve on perfection, but she had. Even without makeup, her skin glowed with the appearance of good health, and her slender, curvy body never failed to send his libido into overdrive when he would inadvertently touch her breast or hip.

They were going out to enjoy a leisurely meal in a restaurant touted for its intimate ambience, extensive wine list and delicious authentic Northern Italian cuisine. If they were friends with benefits, he would've reserved a hotel suite and ordered room service, but he was more than ready to let her take the lead in their relationship; it would be up to Zoey to make the first overture as to when she wanted him to make love to her.

Sutton opened the door to the two-door, dark gray coupe and seated Zoey, and then rounded the sports car, got in and fastened his seat belt. He and Zoey shared a smile as he shifted into gear. The powerful car accelerated quickly, and he eased off the gas pedal. He didn't want to get stopped for speeding. The car was capable of going from zero to sixty miles per hour in three point five seconds.

"Are you all right?" he asked Zoey as she stared out the windshield.

"Yes, but I can't give you permission to let Harper

drive this car. It's much too powerful for an inexperienced driver."

"You're right. If I take him out in it I'll do the driving."

"Thank you."

Sutton didn't tell Zoey that he would agree to anything she wanted within reason if only to keep her happy. He was beginning to love her just that much.

Chapter Thirteen

"How's your chicken Milanese?"

Zoey's head popped up and she smiled at Sutton across the small round table in the restaurant reminiscent of an Italian grotto. The only illumination came from strategically placed sconces and flickering candles on each table. Diffused lighting, prerecorded soft jazz and the sexy man seated close enough for her to feel his warmth and inhale the sensual fragrance of his cologne had created a spell from which she did not want to escape.

"It's delicious." She'd ordered the crispy chicken cutlet topped with a lemony arugula salad and shaved parmesan cheese, while Sutton had requested chicken pasta with a creamy white wine parmesan sauce. "How's your chicken?"

"Perfect."

She hadn't known when he made the reservation Sutton had asked to be seated in an alcove where they couldn't be seen by patrons coming into the eating establishment. When Zoey had asked about their seating, he'd explained he did not want to risk being recognized and have someone intrude on his time with her. His explanation was a reminder that she was dating someone who was still regarded as a celebrity. Gossip about his kissing her had spread through Wickham Falls like a wildfire, and when she'd walked into Perfect Tresses she felt like a specimen under a slide when eyes followed her every move. Thankfully no one questioned her about her relationship with Sutton, leaving them to draw their conclusions as to their association.

It was apparent Sutton had learned how to deal with being a celeb while all of it was new to Zoey, and she wondered if she would ever feel completely comfortable being linked to him. She'd viewed enough televised entertainment programs to know that once a person became a public figure it was almost impossible to disappear unless they became a recluse. And even after decades there was always someone who would recognize them. A server, standing a short distance away, approached their table and refilled their wineglasses. The man's eyes lingered briefly on Sutton's face before he walked away.

Zoey smiled at her dining partner. "Does it make you uncomfortable when folks recognize you?"

"No, because I've gotten used to it."

"Have you ever refused to sign an autograph?"

Sutton paused and angled his head. "Not that I can remember. This is not to say everyone I meet wants an autograph." Picking up his wineglass, he took a sip. "Does it upset you to be seen with me?"

"No, Sutton. Why would you ask me that when I'm here with you?"

"I'm just checking because if you are uncomfortable I will do whatever I can to keep you out of the spotlight."

"I appreciate your concern, but I'm certain I can handle it, because the most attention I'll get will be in Wickham Falls until everyone gets used to seeing us together. You weren't here when my parents died, and people were constantly asking if I was all right or needed anything. At first I was overwhelmed with the attention because my focus was to make certain my brothers would remain with me and not go into the foster care system. And it wasn't until I met with a therapist that I was able to sort out what was important and what wasn't, and that's when I had to acknowledge that I never would've been able to get to where I am today if it hadn't been for the residents in *our* hometown. Folks gossip and occasionally point fingers, but that happens in most small towns, and the Falls is no exception. However, you can always count on our residents to step up and take care of their own when necessary."

Sutton looked at Zoey as if really seeing her for the first time. He'd asked her about being seen with him because he did not want her well-ordered life to be scrutinized and/or dissected. She'd lived all her life in Wickham Falls, and unlike some of the kids who'd graduated high school and moved away, she'd stayed because she'd become responsible for her younger siblings. She'd had to grow up quickly, while at eighteen his focus was leaving the Falls to attend college and living life by his own set of rules. Knowing he was on a scholarship, he had to maintain his grades, but it was the college social scene that made him aware of the limitations imposed on young people back in his hometown. There were no fast-food restaurants or strip malls for them to hang out at after classes or weekends. The owners at the Wolf Den wouldn't serve alcohol to anyone under the age of twenty-three, and although neighboring Mineral Springs was larger, more populated and did have fast-food joints and a strip mall, kids from his town rarely ventured there because of the history of the high school football rivalry.

It was apparent Zoey liked living in Wickham Falls, but she did mention if she secured a nursing position with the county hospital that she would consider renting or buying a condo in Beckley, while his intent was to buy property in the Falls. But that was years away and a lot could happen between them in six years, while she had reminded him that she wasn't going anywhere, and neither was he.

"I know for certain that is one of the reasons I decided to come back," he said after a pregnant silence.

"You claim you came back to help out at Powell's, but had you planned to stay?" Zoey asked.

Suddenly Sutton felt as if she had put him on the spot, but he didn't want to lie to her. "No."

Her eyebrows lifted. "No?"

"I'm being truthful, Zoey. When I sold my condo in Atlanta, I'd planned to move to Washington, DC, and teach there. Then I got the call from Georgi asking me to come back and fill in for her. I told her I would give myself a year and then leave."

"What made you change your mind?"

"It was a couple of things. My mother decided to close her house for six months and move back to the Falls, so that freed up my obligation to work at Powell's. Meanwhile, she's uncertain whether she's going to sell it." He paused, his gaze making love to Zoey's incredibly beautiful face. "Then I met my sexy neighbor, and that was all she wrote."

Zoey lowered her eyes. "Don't forget I'm your temporary neighbor."

He shrugged his shoulders under his suit jacket. "True, but things have a way of changing when we least expect it."

"Like you teaching at our old high school."

"Yes."

"Do you know your start date?"

Sutton took another sip of wine and then set the glass beside his plate. "No. I got an email from the school that they received my grad school transcript, but they're still waiting for the one from the University of Florida. How about you? Has your agency assigned you a new client?"

"No. The scheduler will always call the day before to give me the background on the client."

Propping an elbow on the table, he cupped his chin in the heel of his hand. "Do you think we can plan to do something together until we're both working?"

Zoey smiled tentatively. "What do you have in mind?"

Sutton wiggled his eyebrows. "I'll leave that up to you. What do you want to do or where do you want to go?"

"Have you been to the National Museum of African American History and Culture at the Smithsonian?"

He nodded. "Yes. A couple of times, but I wouldn't mind going back again if you want to see it."

"I do," Zoey admitted, "but I'd like to save that for a weekend rather than a day trip."

Sutton successfully hid a grin. Zoey talking about a weekend trip meant an overnight stay, but he didn't want to get ahead of himself when contemplating their sleeping together. "Labor Day is coming up in a couple of weeks, and the following three-day weekend will be Veterans Day."

"I prefer Veterans Day."

Sutton was hoping she would've said Labor Day, but three months wasn't unreasonable because to him Zoey was worth the wait. "I have time before I'm appointed as a sub, so maybe we can take in a few day trips before you're assigned another client."

"How do you feel about roughing it?" Zoey asked, smiling.

"I'm game if you are," he countered.

"I'd like to go hiking and whitewater rafting at New River Gorge."

Just when Sutton believed he'd come to figure who Zoey Allen was, she continued to surprise him like when she opened the door earlier that evening. Her dramatic makeup, sophisticated hairdo, the dress that was perfect for her figure and sexy heels had rendered him temporarily mute, and he chided himself for thinking she did not have the wherewithal to become that fashionably astute. It was obvious he'd gotten much too used to the glamorous wives of his teammates.

Since his divorce and retirement from baseball, Sutton had discovered things he'd once coveted now held no appeal. He'd been a small-town country boy who'd caught the attention of one of the most attractive coeds at the University of Florida, dated and subsequently married her. However, it had taken years before he realized he was turning into someone he did not recognize.

The lightbulb finally went off once he decided to go back to college for a master's in history because he knew his tenure as an athlete had an expiration date. Injuries followed by surgeries and rehab turned on the yellow light for him to slow up and prepare to stop and assess his future.

And he'd come full circle once he returned to Wickham Falls because it was where he most felt at home and himself. He still recognized the names and faces of longtime residents who did not treat him as a hero, but as someone they'd watched grow up, leave and then come back like a few others.

"When do you want to leave?" he asked Zoey.

"Early Saturday morning. If we do a day trip, then I will need the next one to recover. Unlike you and Harper, I'm *not* that physically active."

"I'll pick you up at seven and we can stop for breakfast before heading to New River Gorge."

Reaching across the table, Zoey squeezed his hand. "Thank you."

He didn't know why she was thanking him when it should've been the reverse. Sutton was looking forward to visiting the museum, hiking and white-water rafting with Zoey with the anticipation of a small child waiting for Christmas morning to open his gifts. They were outings that could become pleasant memories for him whenever he'd recall his journeys with a woman who had unknowingly affected him as no other had. With Zoey he felt free to say what he felt, and that was liberating after spending the past fourteen years as a professional ballplayer performing for the public on and off the field.

Lowering his head, Sutton reversed their hands and pressed a kiss on her knuckles. "You're welcome." He gave her fingers a gentle squeeze before releasing them. "Do you want coffee and dessert?"

"I'm going to pass on dessert and coffee."

Sutton raised a hand to get the waiter's attention for the check, but before the man could approach the table, a young woman rushed over and handed him a pen and cocktail napkin. "Will you please autograph this? You're my son's favorite baseball player and when I tell him that I got your autograph he's going to be over the moon."

Sutton flashed a warm smile. It was obvious sitting in a secluded corner of the restaurant hadn't shielded him from recognition. "What's your son's name?"

"Tyler Marshall."

Sutton wrote the boy's name on the napkin, and then scrawled his signature and returned the square of paper to the woman. "I hope he'll like it."

Her cheeks were flushed with high color. "He's going to treasure it. Now can I get a picture of you, so he'll believe me when I said I met the real Sutton Reed?" she asked as she removed a cell phone from her jacket pocket.

Sutton groaned inwardly. "Okay." Did she expect him to say no now that she'd intruded on his time with his date? His admirer took two photos in rapid succession, one with him and another with him and Zoey when she shifted to get them in the frame.

She bowed as if he were royalty. "Thank you so much, Mr. Reed. I have to put these on Facebook."

Sutton stared at Zoey when she looked at him from under lowered lids, and he wondered what she was thinking. Was she annoyed by the interruption? Or did she resent being photographed with him without giving consent?

"I'm sorry about that, Zoey."

She shook her head. "Don't apologize, Sutton. You're a celebrity, so it stands to reason people will want your autograph and your picture."

"I'm apologizing because I specially asked for this table so we wouldn't have to be disturbed."

"I'm a realist, Sutton. I knew when I agreed to go out with you that I would have to share you with the public because you can't turn your fame off and on like a light switch. If you didn't want the fame and recognition, then your plan B should've been your plan A, but it's too late to rewrite your history, so I suggest you embrace it and accept it for what it is. You're a hero, icon, superstar and mentor and whatever other labels you've been given over the years."

Admiration shimmered in his eyes. "Do you know that you're an incredibly wise young woman?"

"No, I'm not. I'm just someone that had to grow up faster and assume a lot more responsibility than many high school seniors. This is not to say there aren't eighteen-year-old mothers, but most of them don't have six- and eight-year-olds. Even though Charmaine was a stay-at-home mom, she insisted on teaching me how to run my own household because women in her family married and had kids right out of high school. I know I insulted her when I told her I wanted a career and not to end up as a slave for a man whose intent was to keep me pregnant."

"How old were you when you said this to her?"

"Thirteen, because I knew at that age I wanted to be a nurse. Charmaine and I didn't speak to each other for several days until I apologized and then asked her to teach me to cook. During the week after coming home from school, I'd sit in the kitchen doing homework and watching her cook. On weekends she taught me how to make a bed, use the washer and dryer and give the house a thorough cleaning. I can never thank her enough because when social workers made unannounced visits before I was granted legal guardianship for Kyle and Harper, they'd inspect the house and check out the fridge and the laundry room to document signs of neglect, but never found any. The house was always neat and clean. The fridge was stocked with food, and the hampers weren't overflowing with dirty clothes. One confided to me that the process would go faster if I was married, but that hadn't been an option for me."

"Were you dating someone?"

"No, because he bailed on me the moment I told him I was going to raise my brothers. He claimed he was too young to take on that responsibility and wanted to wait until he was older before becoming a father. He married the year we turned twenty-five and he now has a toddler son."

Sutton wanted to tell Zoey that her ex-boyfriend had done her a favor if she couldn't depend on him when she needed him. "Good riddance!"

Zoey lowered her eyes as a mysterious smile flittered over her mouth. "I said things to him that cannot be repeated in polite company. I know it shocked him that I knew those curses because he'd never heard me use profanity, and I had no intention of apologizing because I meant every word."

Now Sutton understood why Zoey wanted someone who would support and protect her and her children. Her siblings weren't her children, yet she had stepped into the role as a mother figure. The support she was talking about wasn't financial, but emotional.

Zoey quickened her pace to keep up with Sutton's longer legs as they walked out of the restaurant and headed across the street to the valet-monitored parking lot. Sutton had made plans for them to visit a local jazz club featuring up-and-coming bands. Without warning, the sky lit up with electrified energy that turned night into day as a sweltering humidity hung in the air like a heated leaded blanket. A rumble of thunder appeared to shake the ground under their feet.

She glanced at Sutton, who appeared to sniff the air like a large cat. "The sky looks scary."

"I think we better head back home before the skies open up."

Zoey wasn't going to argue with him. The extreme heat and lack of rain had even the skeptics mumbling about global warming. Wickham Falls rarely experienced tornados because it was in a valley, but any amount of rain above two inches meant flooding, and the falls turned into a torrent of rushing water that swelled streams to small rivers.

The valet brought Sutton's car around and, once seated, Zoey breathed out a sigh of relief when he started up the engine and adjusted the air-conditioning, the cool air whispering over her moist face.

"I really can't remember when it's been this hot."

Sutton, who'd removed his suit jacket and hung it on a hanger near the rear seats, gave her a quick glance before shifting into gear. "It feels like Florida during the summer months."

"Which city was your favorite when you played away games?"

Another flash of lightning followed by an explosion of thunder nearly drowned out his words, and Zoey had to strain her ears to hear his response. "I'd have to say New York and Miami. I always tried to see a different Broadway play whenever we were in New York."

"What about Miami?"

"It's the food, babe. Miami has some of the best Spanish restaurants on the face of the planet."

"It's like that?" she teased.

"Yes. Once you have mofongo with pork, beef or shrimp, an empanada, black beans and rice or a Cuban sandwich, you'll be hooked for life."

"I suppose one of these days I'll have to take a trip to Miami to see what you're talking about."

Sutton slowed and came to a stop at a red light. "Do you have any more vacation time coming to you?"

Zoey didn't have to be clairvoyant to know what he was going to propose. "Not until next year. I accrue one vacation day each month. Why?"

"What do you say to a road trip to Miami during the Christmas break? Harper can invite his friend Jabari to come along to keep him company."

She quickly did the math and concluded she would accrue another five days of vacation by December. Her vacations were always spent at home, catching up on projects she'd neglected, but going to Miami would be a welcome change from her predictable staycation.

"I say yes."

Sutton grinned like a Cheshire cat. "What about New York in the summer?"

Zoey punched his shoulder, encountering rock-hard muscle under the shirt. "Slow down, sport. Let's take care of Miami before we go to New York." Fat drops of rain splattered the windshield and Sutton activated the wipers, turning them to the fastest speed.

"Do you want to go to Coney Island and discover why Nathan's hot dog is the best in the world?"

"I have a lot of things on my must-see and to-do lists, but all in good time." Sutton needed to know that as a teacher he had a school calendar with designated dates for teacher-student-parent conferences, and holidays, while she'd insisted on a Monday-through-Friday schedule that did not include evening or overnight cases.

She knew a relationship with him would mean she didn't have to wait years to cross off the items on her to-do and must-see lists. Sutton had moved into her longtime neighbor's house and into her life with the force of a tornado touching down and sweeping up everything in its path. And as much as she tried to ignore him, her body threatened to betray her, and Zoey knew she had to stop fighting the inevitable.

She stared out the side window, unable to make out the passing landscape. The rain was falling sideways, obliterating everything outside the vehicle. A soft gasp escaped her when she felt Sutton's hand on her thigh, the warmth burning her skin through the delicate fabric of her dress. It moved higher and her knees parted of their own volition. She was on fire, the area between her legs thrumming a desire that needed to be assuaged.

"Are you all right, sweetheart?"

Zoey's heart was beating so fast as her heated blood threatened to incinerate her. "No, I'm not all right," she whispered truthfully. Sutton had lit a fire and her whole being seemed to be filled with a wanting for something she desired and needed to experience as a woman.

She closed her eyes and swallowed a moan when she felt a rush of moisture bathe the area between her legs and she pressed her knees together to still their trembling.

His hand stilled. "What's the matter?"

She opened her eyes and briefly met his in the glow coming off the dashboard. "You can't touch me and expect me not to beg you to make love to me."

Sutton removed his hand. "You don't have to beg, Zoey. All you have to do is ask," he said after a pregnant pause.

Zoey closed her eyes again and expelled a breath. It had been a month since Sutton had introduced himself to her as her neighbor, and she had spent countless restless nights fantasizing about the man who made her crave him like an addictive drug. Perhaps if she'd had a relationship or relationships with other men over the past decade, her reaction to Sutton wouldn't have bordered on a need to share her body with his.

However, tonight was different. It would be the first time she would make the initial overture and ask a man to sleep with her. In the past, it had been by mutual agreement between two curious virginal teenagers.

"Will you please make love to me?"

Chapter Fourteen

Will you please make love to me?

Sutton repeated Zoey's entreaty to himself over and over to make certain he wasn't hallucinating. She was unaware that he'd found himself enthralled with her the instant he saw her on her porch wearing a revealing tank top and shorts. He'd felt like a voyeur when unable to pull his gaze away from her delicate features and long legs. In the past, it had taken time for him to get to know a woman before even contemplating sharing her bed, yet that hadn't happened with Zoey Allen.

He was no monk when it came to sleeping with women; however, there hadn't been so many before and after his marriage that he could not remember their names or faces, and he became even more dis-

criminating following his divorce because of his rec-
ognizability. Despite being a public figure, Sutton did
not want to establish the reputation of being linked
to a revolving door of women.

"Yes, sweetheart."

He smiled when she rested her hand atop his, gently squeezing his fingers before removing them from
her thigh. She was still breathing heavily as his respiration kept tempo with hers. He had aroused her
and in turn she had aroused him. Sutton shifted into
another position on the seat to attempt to conceal the
swelling bulge in his groin. He chanced a sidelong
glance at Zoey and found her staring out the side
window, praying she wouldn't look at him because
she would have noticed his hard-on. Tapping a button on the steering wheel, he turned on the satellite
radio, tuning it to a station featuring jazz. Dave Bru-
beck's classic hit, "Take Five," filled the interior of
the car. His college roommate's uncles were professional jazz musicians, and they had turned him on
to the music genre.

"Do you want me to change the station?" Sutton
asked Zoey.

"Please don't."

The drive from Charleston to Wickham Falls
was accomplished with cool jazz competing with
the sounds of the wipers sweeping rain off the windshield and the slip-slap of tire on roadway. He knew
sleeping with Zoey would change both of them. Her
brother had dropped hints about her not dating any-

one, and while she'd admitted having a high school boyfriend, that was a little more than a decade ago.

The rain had accumulated more quickly than it could run off and a few of the local roads had become small rivers, forcing him to turn around and find another route. He encountered several detours where cars and trucks were partially submerged in the rising waters. Meteorologists had hinted of the possibility of precipitation, not severe thunderstorms.

The hour's drive took twice that long when Sutton activated the remote device to the garage door Sharon Williams had left behind for her tenant. "I'm going to back in enough for you to get out without getting too wet. The door to the kitchen is unlocked." He waited until Zoey went inside the house and then backed the sports car into the garage, got out and tapped the button on the wall that lowered the door.

The courage Zoey had summoned up to ask Sutton to make love to her dissipated like a drop of water on a red-hot skillet. She stood in the middle of the kitchen watching like a rabbit, frightened and frozen with no means of escape when cornered by a deadly predator. At that moment she did not wonder if he could please her but whether she could please him. Would he know immediately that she lacked the sexual experience other women her age had achieved?

He came closer, and she could see from the light he'd left on over the stove his gaze going from her eyes to her shoulders and still lower to her breasts that rose and fell heavily with each breath. Zoey wanted him to say something, anything that would shatter the spell that held her in limbo as to whether she should reach out and touch him. Her eyelids fluttered wildly as she forced a nervous smile, and she wasn't disappointed when he returned it.

"I'm not on any contraception." *Damn*, she thought, *where did that come from?* It was the same thing she'd said to her first and only lover.

Sutton's gaze was as soft as a caress as he took the evening bag from her punishing grip. "Don't worry, babe. I have protection."

Sutton's revealing that he had protection jolted Zoey into the realization that she'd asked a man to have sex with her while assuming he had condoms. While she knew how to run a household and budget her finances, she still had a lot to learn about relationships. Sutton's touching her hand sent shivers up her arm. She took a step, bringing them inches apart. Her left hand touched his jaw and then moved down until her arm circled his neck. Leaning in, she pressed her mouth to his, swallowing a moist breath when his lips parted under hers.

Sutton's arms circled her waist, bringing her closer. "You have to let me know what you want," he whispered, his voice lowering until it resembled a growl.

Zoey was mute for several seconds. He was asking her what she wanted as if she had a sexual repertoire.

Gathering Zoey in his arms, Sutton picked her up, walked out of the kitchen and headed for the staircase. Zoey had buried her face against his neck, her breathing quickening. He knew it had been a long time for her, and he wanted their coming together to be special—for her and for him. He hadn't been celibate as long she had been, but it was long enough that he was glad he had waited for her.

Night-lights in several outlets provided illumination along the hallway. He stopped at the bedroom where he slept and walked in. A bedside lamp cast a warm glow in the room. Bending slightly, he placed Zoey down on the bed as if she were a piece of delicate crystal. Her eyes seemed larger when she stared up at him looming over her. He smiled at her while he slipped off the sexy heels. Bringing her bare foot to his mouth, Sutton pressed a kiss on each of her groomed toes. Sitting on the side of the bed, he removed his own shoes and then lay beside her. Lacing his fingers through hers, he shifted on his side to face her. Her hand was icy-cold.

"Are you frightened, love?"

Her breathing sounded unusually raspy. "I don't think so."

His nose nuzzled her scented neck. "Relax, babe. I won't do anything you don't want me to."

"It's okay. I trust you."

She trusted him but Sutton wanted more than her trust. He wanted her love. Releasing her hand, he curved an arm around her waist and shifted her body until she lay on his chest, her legs nestled between his. He had tempered his desire for Zoey so she would feel completely comfortable with him.

His right hand slipped down her spine, fingers

splaying over the firm roundness of her hips. He managed to swallow back a moan when she moved sensually against his groin. His left hand moved down and he cradled her bottom, squeezing gently each time she shifted her hips. Sutton searched for her mouth, tongue easing behind her parted lips, and she opened it to receive all he was willing to offer.

First Zoey was cold, then she was hot, as Sutton's tongue moved in and out of her mouth in a rhythm that sent her pulse racing and her senses spinning out of control. This kiss was nothing like the chaste ones they'd exchanged before. Her mouth and tongue were as busy as his when she caught his upper lip between her teeth, pulling it into her mouth before giving the fuller lower one equal attention. Her fingers massaged his scalp, his ears, trembling as she felt the fires of desire settle between her thighs, and bring with it a rush of liquid.

"Sutton!" she breathed out when he reversed their positions and straddled her body. Closing her eyes, she felt rather than saw him undress her. What seemed like long, agonizing minutes were only seconds when he divested her of the dress. He went still, and she opened her eyes to find him staring at her black lace strapless bra and matching thong.

Supporting his greater weight on his forearms, Sutton lowered his chest to her. "Why did you even bother to put on underwear? They're pretty but hardly practical."

Her gentle laugh floated upward. "I'm not one to go commando."

"Yes, you can," he crooned in her ear. His hands went to the front clasp on her bra, and with a quick motion he released it, baring her chest. "Whenever you're with me you can ditch the bra. Your breasts are too beautiful to cover up."

Zoey felt a surge of confidence with his compliment. "What about the panties?"

Hooking his fingers in the narrow bands of elastic, he pushed the tiny triangle of lace off her hips and down her legs. Dangling the thong from a forefinger, he lifted his eyebrows. "You call this panties?" Shaking his head, he tossed it at the foot of the bed. The bra followed, leaving her completely naked to his hungry gaze. He sat her up as he went to his knees. "I undressed you, and now it's your turn, sweetheart."

The heavy lashes that shadowed her cheeks flew up. "You want me to undress you?"

A smile played at the corners of Sutton's mouth. "Yes. I'm not going to make love to you, and you're not going to make love to me. We're going to make love with each other." He removed his tie and unbuttoned his collar. "I've given you a head start." Beckoning to her with his right hand, he whispered, "Come on, love."

Zoey rose on her knees and placed a hand in the middle of his chest. She wanted to scream at him to take her and end her frustration, but decided to play along. It was apparent he wanted their first time together to be a memorable one. The heat from his large body nearly overpowered her as she undid the buttons on his shirt. Even though she wasn't looking at Sutton, she could still feel the heat from his gaze as he watched her every move. Pulling the hem of his shirt from the waistband of his pants, she pushed it off his broad shoulders. Her hands were steady when she finished undressing him, but Sutton did not give her time to admire his magnificent body when his mouth covered hers in an explosive joining that swept away any apprehension that she had made a mistake to ask him to make love to her.

Soft moans filled the room as his kisses left her mouth, moving down her throat, over her breasts, belly. The harsh, uneven rhythm of her breathing changed, becoming gasps when the heat from Sutton's mouth seared her mound.

Passion catapulted the blood through her head, chest and legs, making it impossible for Zoey to think. Sutton offered her a sweet agony that teased relentlessly while refusing to release her from the erotic torment. His name was locked away in the back of her throat.

Zoey felt the first ripple, soft and pulsing, then the second, and a third. She lost count after the fourth orgasm, and there was no way she could stop her screams of fulfillment as divine ecstasy shook her uncontrollably until she lay motionless, spent, as tears flowed down her face. She was oblivious to Sutton opening a bedside table drawer for a condom to protect her from an unplanned pregnancy. Then she felt his erection easing into her.

Reveling in the exquisite pleasure of Zoey's tight flesh stretching and closing around his erection, Sutton breathed in and out through his open mouth. He was so light-headed that he feared he would pass out before he achieved his own gratification in her fragrant softness. Her hands slipped down his back, her fingers tightening on the flesh on his buttocks, and he knew he'd revived her passion. Slowing his rhythm, he slid in and out of her body with a strong, powerful thrusting of his hips. A moan slipped between her lips, lingering against his throat. The sensuality he found in Zoey's body took him beyond himself as he surrendered to the explosive ecstasy that had come from a place where he'd never been. The throbbing in his lower body continued, leaving him as weak as a newborn.

His head cleared, his respiration slowed, and he finally returned from his exhilarating free-fall flight. Tightening his hold on Zoey's body, he reversed their positions and cradled her to his chest. Placing kisses on her hair, he recalled his vow never to fall in love again, yet Zoey Allen had unwittingly made him a liar. Zoey wanted a career, marriage and children, and he knew with her they could have all three.

He breathed a kiss on her scalp. "Thank you."

She chuckled. "I should be the one thanking you. You were wonderful."

His hand made stroking motions up and down her spine. "That's because you're wonderful." He paused. "Did I hurt you?"

"No, Sutton."

"Then why were you crying?"

She raised her head and rested her chin on his breastbone. "Because it was so good."

He wiggled his eyebrows. "It was better than good, Zoey."

She was good.

And they were good together. He knew it would be several more days before they would be able to make love again, and he would take her suggestion he not fast-track their relationship. They had time—almost nine months before Sharon Williams returned to Wickham Falls to reclaim her house. And that was long enough for Sutton to convince Zoey to marry him, live together and secure Harper's future.

Students were standing around in small groups and some were sitting on the tops of their desks when Sutton entered the classroom, closed the door and wrote his name on the board. It had taken three weeks following his initial interview for his appointment as a permanent substitute to be approved. He had passed the time going over the curriculum and logging countless hours researching topics for his lectures, visiting his mother, who'd urged him to bring the Allen girl to Sunday dinner so the family could meet her, and also reconnecting with Langston Cooper, his former baseball teammate who was also dating his cousin.

Sutton still rose early every morning to jog with Harper, who along with his friend Jabari had made the basketball team. As incoming juniors, they would sit on the bench, but the excitement of suiting up, practicing and traveling with the team left them optimistic they would eventually become starters.

Zoey was assigned a new client and schedule, her workday beginning at seven and ending at three in the afternoon, and although she did not say it, he knew by her refusal to discuss her client with him that it hadn't been an easy assignment, making him aware that taking care of the elderly or infirm was demanding and challenging.

Sutton gave her time to wind down once she returned home, and then brought her dinner, which appeared to lift her lethargy. When he'd ask if she was feeling well, her answer was always the same. She hadn't been sleeping well. She was eating less, and this alarmed him, yet again she professed nothing was wrong. The notion that perhaps she was pregnant had nagged at him, but he dismissed it as soon as it entered his mind. There was never a time when they'd shared a bed that he hadn't used a condom.

All thoughts of his relationship vanished the instant the late bell rang. Standing at the front of the room, he watched a dozen students take their seats. He hid a smile when he saw recognition on the faces of some of them. It was apparent they knew who he was.

"I'm Mr. Reed, and I will be filling in for Mrs. Sellers for the next four months. I have the notes from your previous substitute teacher, and he indicated you've covered the first two decades of the twentieth century, and now we're going to concentrate on the events covering post–World War I through the Great Depression." Sutton leaned against a corner of the desk. "Before we cover the major events of 1920 to 1930, I'm going to give you a pop quiz about what you've learned for the prior decade, so I'll know what we have to review."

A boy raised his hand. "Mr. Reed, how did you go from playing baseball to teaching history?"

Sutton crossed his arms over his chest. "Twenty years ago, I sat in the very seat where you're sitting now and had a teacher that made history come alive for me. He had everyone in the class spellbound with his lectures. He was more of a storyteller than a teacher. He allowed us to role-play with him when he got into the mind of a 1920s woman fighting for the right to vote, and Sacco and Vanzetti, who were sentenced to death even though there was no evidence of a crime and after the outcome of the trial people became aware of corruption in the American government and court systems against immigrants. We'll cover Prohibition and Black Tuesday, the Palmer Raids, and political and cultural changes that will impact the country's postwar society."

A girl with a profusion of braided extensions raised her hand. "Mr. Reed, are you going to test us?"

"But of course." His response elicited a smattering of laughter. "If I don't test you, how will I know if you've retained what I've taught? I plan to give you a quiz every Friday. They will vary between ten and twenty questions. I also want you to think about a topic for a paper on one of events during the decade we're discussing. The paper should be ten pages, double-spaced with footnotes and a bibliography." He held up a hand when a number of arms shot up. "And before you ask, it's due before the Christmas break."

Sutton continued to answer a number of questions from his students about the courses he took in college and his days in the minor and major leagues. The bell rang, signaling the end of class, and the boys and girls lingered behind for him to scrawl his autograph in their notebooks.

He knew it would take some time before his students would regard him as a teacher and not a former big-league baseball player. He'd moved back to Wickham Falls to teach in the same school where he'd attended and graduated from, while falling in love with Zoey made life not only good. It was glorious.

Zoey opened one eye, peered at the cell phone on the bedside table and groaned. It was Saturday and, while she'd wanted to sleep in late, it had proved elusive for the last few weeks. She had fallen inexorably in love with Sutton. She loved making love with him, wanted to lie beside him all day and languish in the aftermath of sexual fulfillment. However, her angst began when she had to leave his bed and return to her own bedroom before Harper got up, and it continued until they came together again with an intimacy that never failed to steal the breath from her lungs.

It was apparent the plans she'd made for her future seemed to implode once she slept with her sexy neighbor. It had been more than two months since she'd experienced multiple orgasms with a man, and each time she and Sutton made love she felt it—all over her body from her head to her toes. It just wasn't sex but everything about Sutton as a lover. He was sensitive to what she liked and didn't like, which brought both of them maximum pleasure. Zoey did not want Sutton to be her lover but her husband.

Zoey got out of bed, pushing her feet into a pair of fluffy slippers. Now that she was awake, she realized she couldn't go back to sleep. Her gaze lingered on her knitting project on the chair in her reading corner. She had finished the chemo hat and had begun making the scarf. Knitting had become therapeutic, helping her to relax.

She and Sutton had decided to move up their visit to the National Museum of African American History and Culture at the Smithsonian to the Christmas recess. They would drive to DC, stay overnight and then continue on to Miami for some fun in the sun.

Forty minutes later, she sat on the porch, wearing a sweater to ward off the early fall morning chill, knitting and enjoying her second cup of coffee when she spied Sutton coming out of his house. He waved to her and, smiling, she returned it. Zoey did not have to wait long for him to join her.

Bending at the waist, Sutton brushed a light kiss over her mouth. "Good morning."

"Good morning."

He folded his body down on a chair opposite her, noticing the slight puffiness under her large eyes. "I didn't expect to see you up and out this early."

"My internal clock doesn't know when it's the weekend."

Sutton angled his head and looked at the woman with whom he'd fallen in love. Instinctually he knew something was bothering her, yet he wasn't able to pinpoint it. Nothing had changed between them whenever they'd slept together, or he would've detected it because he was so attuned to her body.

"I know you're not going to like what I'm about to say. But you look like crap, sweetheart."

Her impassive expression did not change. "Oh, you sought to soften the insult with an endearment?"

"Talk to me, Zoey. What the hell is going on with you?"

"Nothing."

"I don't believe you when you talk about being an insomniac."

"I'm not an insomniac. I just wake up in the middle of the night and I can't go back to sleep."

"Why?"

"Because my internal clock knows the time when I get up and leave your house so I can be here before Harper gets up."

"Do you believe Harper doesn't know we're sleeping together?"

"I don't know what he believes, Sutton, because I don't feel I'm obligated to discuss my love life with my brother."

Sutton gritted his teeth in frustration. He did not know why Zoey continued to treat her brother like a little kid. When he'd suggested Harper go jogging with him every morning as retribution for attempting to break into his Aston Martin, Sutton could not anticipate Zoey's brother would open up to him about his sister. Harper admitted he was concerned that she would spend the rest of her life alone, that he'd witnessed her rejecting the advances of men who'd asked her out.

"Have you ever talked to him about what your life would be like once he leaves the nest?"

"No, because that's not going to be for a while," Zoey stated.

"If that's what you think, then I suggest you talk to him about what he wants for his future." Harper had talked about becoming a chef, and that meant he and Zoey would not be attending the same college.

Zoey narrowed her eyes. "What aren't you telling me?"

Rising, Sutton approached Zoey and pressed a kiss to her forehead. "Talk to Harper." That said, he turned on his heel and retraced his steps, leaving her to stare at his retreating back.

Chapter Fifteen

Zoey went back into the house and opened the refrigerator to take out items for breakfast when a barefoot Harper strolled into the kitchen. His curly unbound hair stood out around his head like a black cloud. He wore a white tee with ripped jeans he refused to let her throw away because they were his favorite.

She stared at her brother. His shoulders appeared broader and his forearms more muscular. He'd complained about not putting on muscle, but since he'd begun shooting hoops and lifting weights at Jabari's house, his body had undergone a visible transformation.

"What do you want for breakfast?" she asked him.

"I was just going to ask you that," Harper said.

"You want to cook for me?"

"Yup. If I'm going to become a chef, then I need someone to test my dishes."

Zoey sat on a chair at the table. Whenever she'd asked Harper what he wanted to be when he grew up, his response was he didn't know, or it was a shrug of his shoulders. This was the first time he'd given her a definitive answer.

"Are you really serious about becoming a chef?"

Harper opened the refrigerator. "Yes. Sutton and I talked about it and I decided I would apply to schools in DC, Maryland or northern Virginia."

Zoey bit her lip. She did not know why, but she felt as if she were losing her brother. He'd confided to Sutton what he hadn't to her, and it was apparent his influence had become paramount in the teenager's life. However, her concern was short-lived because Sutton was a positive role model for Harper.

"I'm glad you've decided on a career choice."

Harper took out a carton of eggs and set it on the countertop. "I really like cooking and maybe one of these days I'll open my own restaurant like my mama's people."

A rush of emotion eddied through Zoey and she forced herself not to cry. It was as if Harper had matured overnight, and she knew it was Sutton's influence that had contributed to his becoming a responsible young adult.

"If you decide not to live on campus, then you'll have to look for an apartment either in or around DC."

"I know. But…"

"But what, Harper?"

He turned to give her a direct look. "Are you going to be okay living alone?"

Zoey nearly laughed when she saw concern in his hazel eyes. "Believe me, Harper, when I tell you that I will be okay. And if I get lonely, then I'll get a dog to keep me company."

"You don't need a dog when you could be with Mr. Reed."

Her eyebrows lifted slightly, and she wondered if Harper and Sutton had had conversations about her. "Doesn't Mr. Reed have something to say about that?"

Harper returned to the fridge to take out ingredients for an omelet. "He already told me that you know he's in love with you, and I know that you're spending a lot of time with him at his house. And when I asked him if he wants to marry you, he said yes. But please don't get mad at him because I promised him I wouldn't say anything to you."

Zoey's eyelids fluttered and she averted her head so her brother wouldn't see the tears welling up in her eyes at the same time her chest filled with an indescribable joy wrapping her in a cocoon of newly awakened confidence. She no longer had to slip out of Sutton's bed in the middle of the night because she didn't want to advertise to Harper that she was sleeping with his mentor.

"What's said in this kitchen stays in this kitchen."

Harper smiled. "Thanks, sis. Mr. Reed said I can

use the Jeep today. A group of us are going to hang out at Ruthie's for lunch."

Zoey did not want to ask who the *us* was. She'd learned not to question Harper and trust him to do what was right and not to get into trouble.

Sutton saved the work on his laptop when the doorbell rang and left the kitchen to answer the door. He opened it, grinning when he saw Zoey smiling up at him. Reaching for her hand, he pulled her inside and closed the door. "You definitely are a welcome distraction because I needed to come up for air."

Going on tiptoes, Zoey kissed his jaw. "So, now I'm a distraction?" she teased.

His arm went around her waist, pulling her close. "I did say 'a welcome distraction.' I've been typing lectures for the next few weeks. Come with me in the kitchen."

Zoey held back. "We need to talk."

He heard something in Zoey's voice that gave him pause, and Sutton wondered what had happened since their conversation on her porch earlier that morning. "What about?"

She smiled. "Us."

His tension eased. "What about us?"

"I'm in love with you, Sutton Hamilton Reed."

Throwing back his head, Sutton laughed as if he'd taken leave of his senses. He'd lost count of the number of times he'd admitted to Zoey that he was in love with her, while waiting for her to tell him when she wasn't in the throes of climaxing. He finally sobered to see an expression of anguish flit over her features.

He dipped his head and kissed her soft parted lips. "Thank you, sweetheart."

"We love each other and now what?" she asked.

"We do what couples in love do. We get engaged, married, and then live together."

She gave him a long, penetrating stare. "Is that what you want, Sutton?"

His eyes made love to her face. "It's what I wanted the first time I laid eyes on you."

Her eyelids fluttered. "But... But you didn't know anything about me." There was a tremor in her voice.

"It's not about what I knew but what I saw and heard. When I asked Georgi about you, she told me how you'd fought tooth and nail to keep your brothers with you and out of foster care, and I wondered how many girls your age would've sacrificed what you have for Harper and Kyle. To me you were superwoman. And it helps that you're sexy as all get-out." Sutton nearly laughed aloud when he saw Zoey lower her eyes. It was her modesty he'd found enthralling. It had taken her a while before she'd felt comfortable enough to walk around nude in his presence. "What are we going to do, Zoey?"

She gave him a direct look. "You tell me, Sutton."

"We get dressed and go to a jewelry store and get measured for engagement rings. Then we announce our engagement to our family, and after that we can set a wedding date."

"Is this what you really want?" she asked.

Sutton cradled her face. "Yes. But is it what you want, love?"

Zoey's eyes filled with tears and she blinked them back before they fell. "Yes, Sutton, it is what I want. I love you just that much, but I'd like for us to wait to make the announcement."

He stared at Zoey as if she were a stranger. Why, he thought, was she sending him mixed messages? "Wait until when?"

"Thanksgiving. I've committed to sharing the holiday with your family, so I think it would be the perfect time to make the announcement."

"What about Harper?"

"We certainly cannot tell my brother," Zoey said, smiling. "He just may let it slip to his friends and we won't have to place an announcement in *The Sentinel*. I'll let him know Thanksgiving morning that he's about to become a brother-in-law when his sister marries his mentor and history teacher."

He kissed her again, this time with a tenderness he hadn't known she possessed. He didn't kiss her mouth. Sutton caressed it. He knew for certain that being married to Zoey would be very different from his first marriage. It would have the normalcy he'd craved when he was off the ball field. Their home would be their sanctuary and not an impromptu club or gathering place for those looking for a place to eat and drink in abandon. He would marry Zoey and support her wholeheartedly while she became a nurse. And he would continue to mentor Harper in his quest to become a chef, while promising his future brother-in-law he would be willing to invest in his future business venture.

Zoey, flanked by Harper and Sutton, was seated across the table from Georgina and Langston Cooper in the Powells' formal dining room. Prisms of light from a chandelier reflected off the near-flawless blue-white diamonds in the engagement ring on her left hand.

She and Sutton had visited a renowned jeweler in the capital where it had taken nearly two hours for her to examine a variety of loose diamonds. She finally decided on a cushion-cut center stone in a platinum setting with a double halo of diamonds, before she and Sutton chose matching platinum wedding bands.

When Sutton introduced her to his mother, Zoey had immediately felt Michelle Reed's warmth and acceptance that she was to become her son's future wife, and insisted Zoey call her Mom instead of Ms. Reed. Her first Thanksgiving dinner with the Powells made her feel as if she'd known them for years. Bruce and Evelyn were friendly and unpretentious, and it was obvious they were proud of their nephew's accomplishments. The topics of conversation floating around the table focused on Sutton's appointment as a substitute teacher, Georgina's chemo cap and scarves project for the new cancer wing at the county hospital, Zoey's plan to enroll in nursing school and Harper's revelation that he wanted to become a chef.

Everyone was taken aback once Langston disclosed that he and Sutton were discussing the possibility of forming a Wickham Falls Little League with the support of local businesses. Bruce was excited with the prospect of a team representing the department store and promised to donate baseball equipment for the entire league. Zoey and Georgina exchanged knowing glances as they stood up to help Evelyn and Michelle clear the table as Sutton, Bruce and Langston launched into a discussion about baseball, football and basketball, while Harper was amused by the spirited conversation.

Georgina pulled Zoey into an alcove off the kitchen. "I can't believe you're going to be my cousin when you marry Sutton," she whispered.

Zoey hugged her. "I can't thank you and your family enough for making me and Harper feel so welcomed."

"Have you and Sutton set a date for your wedding?"

Zoey nodded. "We've decided on New Year's Eve."

"But that's five weeks away!"

"I know, but it's going to be small, private and very informal. We've decided to hold the ceremony and reception in a ballroom at the Wickham Falls Bed-and-Breakfast. And because I don't have any close girlfriends, I'd like to ask you to stand in as my maid of honor. Harper has agreed to be Sutton's best man. I emailed my other brother, who's in the marines, to let him know that I'm getting married, and hopefully he'll be able to get an approved leave."

Georgina smiled. "Of course I'll be your maid of

honor. And I'm honored that you asked." Reaching for Zoey's left hand, she stared at the engagement ring. "Your ring is truly gorgeous." She had enunciated each word.

"Thank you." When examining the loose stones, Zoey had rejected those weighing more two carats. With the center stone and double halo, the ring's total carat weight was three point eight. Any larger and she would have considered it ostentatious.

Georgina leaned close. "My aunt Michelle really likes you and if she didn't then you would've known it immediately. Once Sutton divorced his first wife and he was once again an eligible bachelor, she would complain constantly about women asking her to hook up their daughters, nieces, cousins and even granddaughters with him. My aunt believed they all were after his money."

"I don't want or need Sutton's money," Zoey countered. There was a slight edge in her retort. She didn't have a seven- or six-figure bank balance. Her annual income allowed her to be lower middle class, and if she was able to pay her property taxes, put food on the table, buy the essentials and save a little for the proverbial rainy day, she wasn't looking for man to take care of her. Sutton hadn't mentioned her signing a prenup agreement, and she assumed he did not think of her as someone willing to marry him because of money.

What they did discuss was their living arrangements. Once married he would move into her house and continue to pay the rent on Sharon Williams's house to fulfill the terms in the lease agreement. He had also suggested she not wait two years to begin her college education. If he was able to secure a permanent teaching position at the high school, his hours would coincide with Harper's.

"Good for you. My aunt admires you."

"Why?"

"Because she sees some of herself in you. Aunt Michelle raised Sutton as a single mother after his father sweet-talked her out of the money she'd received from my grandfather's death benefit and then took off when she told him she was pregnant. She worked, sacrificed for herself to give Sutton what he needed, while refusing to accept any financial support from my parents. You've done the same with your brothers."

"Don't forget I did have financial support when the town got together to fundraise to make repairs and pay the taxes on my home and set up scholarship funds for Kyle and Harper."

"I don't know if he told you, but the year before he signed his multimillion-dollar contract when he heard about you losing your parents, he wired a large sum of money to the pastor of the church for your brothers' scholarship fund." Georgina's eyes widened as her jaw dropped when Zoey stared, unblinking. "You didn't know?"

"No, Georgi. Sutton never told me. I was aware of a generous anonymous donation but was never told who the donor was."

Georgina grabbed her arm. "Please don't tell him

that I let the cat out of the bag, or he'll bring holy hell down on me, and I don't want to get on the wrong side of Sutton once he loses his temper."

"I promise not to say anything."

"I want you to be the first to know other than our parents that Langston and I are planning to marry on Valentine's Day."

"You're kidding?"

"No, I'm not. We've had our misunderstandings, ups and downs and lately a slight detour, but we managed to work through our problems because we truly love each other. I want you to remember that when you and Sutton don't agree on something."

"What are you two whispering about?"

Georgina winked at Zoey. "Nothing, Mom."

Zoey wanted to tell Sutton's aunt it wasn't nothing. Georgina had revealed things about Sutton she doubted he would've ever divulged to her, and she hadn't lied to his cousin. She would keep his secret.

"I think I need a nap," Harper announced as Sutton maneuvered the Jeep into the driveway to his house.

"I believe we'll all need naps after eating much too much food," Zoey said in agreement. A slight frown furrowed her forehead when she caught a glimpse of a strange vehicle parked behind her minivan.

"Were you expecting company?" Sutton asked as he shut off the engine.

"No." Zoey got out before Sutton could come around to help her down. Once she got closer to her home, she noticed the late-model SUV had Alaskan plates. It was apparent someone had mistaken her house for someone else's. She wasn't familiar with anyone from that state.

She mounted the porch steps at the same time a woman rose slowly from the rocker. Porch lamps illuminated her dark brown unlined complexion and salt-and-pepper ponytail.

The woman was tall, but not as tall as Zoey, and slender. They stared at each other, not moving for a full minute. However, there was something about her that was vaguely familiar.

"I know you don't recognize me, Zoey."

"How do you know my name?"

"I know it because I gave it to you when you were born."

Zoey felt her legs go weak and she doubted whether she would've been able to remain standing if Sutton hadn't come up behind her. Now she knew who she was when she recalled seeing the photograph in the yearbook. But she looked nothing like the image of youthful girl smiling for the camera. Lines bracketed her mouth, and there was a network of lines around her eyes. "You are my mother?" The query was low, hoarse, as if she'd just run a long, grueling race and had attempted to catch her breath.

A smile parted her lips. "Yes. I'm your mother. I'm no longer Donna Allen but Donna Parker."

Rage and resentment coursed through Zoey, making it impossible for her to formulate her thoughts. "Get off my property and never come back."

"Baby, don't," Sutton crooned in her ear. "Please hear her out."

She rounded on him. "It's been twenty-six years since she abandoned me, and now she shows up as if it's only been twenty seconds. No, Sutton. I don't want to listen to anything she has to say." She brushed past Donna and didn't see Harper staring at the woman who'd introduced herself as his sister's mother and unlocked the front door.

"I'll be at the B and B until the end of January," Donna said quietly, preempting Zoey from opening the door. "After that I'm driving down to Florida. I bought a one-bedroom Miami condo with views of the ocean."

Zoey opened and closed the door, shutting out the images of three people who'd just witnessed more than two decades of the pain and anger she'd managed to conceal from everyone until her father married Charmaine. Her mother had walked out of her life when she was too young to remember her face, and now this woman had shown up without warning claiming to be her.

She walked into the living room, flopped down in a chair and closed her eyes. The day had begun with her and Sutton announcing their engagement and now ended with a stranger attempting to insinuate herself into her life. No, she thought, shaking her head. It wasn't happening, because she could go back or go to wherever she'd come from without her blessing.

"Sis, is that woman really your mother?"

Zoey opened her eyes and stared at Harper. "She

may have given birth to me, but she was never my mother. She left our dad when I was still a baby."

"Why did she leave you and Dad?"

"I don't know, Harper."

"Don't you want to know?"

Zoey waved her hand in dismissal. She wanted to scream at him to leave her alone and stop asking questions to which she had no answers, but did not want to take her frustrations out on her brother. "Please, Harper. I don't want to talk about it." She sat, staring into nothingness as the seconds turned into minutes once Harper retreated upstairs. The door opened and Sutton walked in.

"We need to talk," Sutton announced.

"Not tonight, Sutton."

"When, Zoey?"

She glared at him. "I don't know. Maybe never."

He took long strides, hunkered down and held her hands. "You can't bury your head in the sand and pretend it's all going to go away. You heard what she said. She'll be in Wickham Falls until early next year, then she's leaving for Florida. We're going to marry in another four weeks, and it would be nice to have her attend as mother of the bride."

"Have you lost your freakin' mind? You want me to play nice to a woman who abandoned her toddler daughter with her ex-husband and then went off to do her own thing? That's not happening, Sutton."

"Maybe she has a valid reason for giving up custody?"

"Spare me the melodrama," she sneered, "because

good mothers fight until their last breath to hold on to their children. And you're a fine one to talk because from what I've heard you don't have a relationship with your father."

"This is not about my father!"

"Really, Sutton? Didn't your father show up when he'd heard you were worth millions?"

"That's different, Zoey."

"Really?" she repeated facetiously. "Thanks to social media the entire world must know that Zoey Allen is dating Sutton Reed, so when my biological mother who has been out of my life for twenty-six years believes her daughter has finally made the big time she decides it's a good time to show up to become reacquainted."

"She may have an entirely different reason for wanting to see you."

"Stop it, Sutton. I don't want to talk about my mother," she said between clenched teeth.

"You're going to have to deal with it before you have your own children."

"Have you dealt with your father abandoning your mother, Sutton?"

"Yes and because of that I wanted nothing to do with him."

"It looks as if we have something in common."

"No, we don't, Zoey. The difference is your mother is willing to talk to you about why she left you with your father."

"When I did ask my father why I didn't have a

mother like other kids, he told me she was in love with another man."

"And you believed him?"

"Why wouldn't I, Sutton?"

"Because maybe he didn't tell you the whole story."

"Are you saying he was lying?"

"I'm not saying that, Zoey. But you need to hear both sides, because your mother just told me why she left she left her husband and child for another man."

Zoey felt as if her head had suddenly caught fire. "You went behind my back to talk to her when you know I want nothing to do with her?"

"I didn't go behind your back, Zoey. You rudely left the woman standing on your porch and—"

"Rude!" she shouted. "You call me rude when she knew where I live and could've sent me a letter warning me that she was coming. What happened to your big talk about supporting me, Sutton?"

"I will when you're right. This time you're wrong."

"Maybe I was wrong to agree to marry you."

Sutton straightened. "Maybe we're both wrong. I believed I'd fallen in love with someone willing to listen and perhaps compromise because it's not all about her. But whatever you decide I want you to remember we can go through it together."

"There is nothing to go through together. I have no intention of listening to anything Donna has to say."

"I guess this is either good-night or goodbye. The choice is yours."

Zoey sat, stunned, as she watched Sutton walk

out of her house and perhaps out of her life. Why couldn't he understand where she was coming from? It was very different from his nonexistent relationship with his father. Her mother had married her father and when facing divorce had relinquished total custody rather than agree to joint custody. She could've lived with her mother and had scheduled visits with James Allen.

She twisted the ring on her left hand around her finger; her mind was in tumult. Things were coming at her so fast Zoey couldn't compartmentalize her thoughts to determine her next action.

Wait, the inner voice cautioned her. *Wait and see how everything plays out.*

Sutton tossed and turned, unable to fall asleep until exhaustion won out. It had been the same for more than a week since Zoey's mother had turned up expectedly to shock everyone. It was obvious Zoey was angry and Harper was completely confused.

Donna had struggled not to cry as her words fell over themselves as she attempted to explain why she'd walked away from her ex-husband and daughter that fateful day more than twenty-five years ago. It's not that he'd believed everything Donna told him, but all he wanted was for Zoey to give the woman a chance to explain why she'd left her with her father rather than take her after the divorce. Although he'd pleaded with Zoey to listen to Donna, he did not want to take sides. He loved Zoey too much and was willing to support her but he did not want to begin their marriage with her unresolved issues from her past. She had gone through enough losing her father and stepmother and having to raise her brothers to get mired down in another familial crisis.

Tossing back the sheet, he left the bed and headed for the bathroom. Harper had fulfilled his three-month plea deal, and although Sutton told him he no longer had to get up and go jogging, the teenager said he enjoyed spending the one-on-one time with him. When he left the house, he found Harper standing next to the Jeep. A heavy fog had settled in the valley, leaving visibility close to zero.

"Are we going to jog in the fog?" Harper asked.

"No. Please come in the house. I need to talk to you."

Harper hesitated. "Do you want to talk about my sister?"

"Yes."

"I'm glad, because you have to do something, Mr. Reed. She doesn't talk or eat, and whenever she comes home she locks herself in her bedroom."

"She's going through a lot, Harper."

"She's not the only one going through a lot. Can I stay with you until things get better?"

Sutton dropped an arm over the boy's shoulders. "That's not possible. Zoey is your legal guardian and—"

Harper threw off his arm. "What good are you? I thought you would help me." Turning on his heel, Harper walked back to his house.

Sutton panicked. It was obvious Zoey's reaction to

meeting her mother had thrown her household into turmoil where there were no winners, only losers. Zoey had mentioned Harper's acting out once his brother left to join the military, and even though his sister was still there, she had withdrawn and left him believing he was alone.

He followed Harper, catching up with him as he was about to open the door. "You're sixteen, not six, so I want you to give Zoey some slack. Yes, she's going through a lot, but you're not helping when you talk about leaving her to live me with. One thing I will not allow is for you to desert her when she needs you most. She's always been there for you, now it's time for you to step up and be there for her. What's it going to be, Harper? Are you in or out?"

Harper lowered his eyes. "I'm in."

Smiling, Sutton patted his cheek. "Good. Now, where's Zoey?"

"She's in her bedroom. She's probably asleep."

"It doesn't matter," Sutton said as he crossed the living room and took the stairs to the second floor two at a time. Long strides ate up the length of the hallway until he stood outside the door to Zoey's bedroom. He turned the knob and found it locked, so he rapped lightly on the door. "Zoey, please open the door."

He did not have to wait long before it opened, and his heart turned over when he saw the evidence of the emotional turmoil she'd gone through in a week.

It was obvious she hadn't been eating because her face was thinner and there were dark circles under her large eyes. Bending, he picked her up, set her on the unmade bed and then lay down next to her. He dropped a kiss on her mussed hair. "I know you're hurting, but so is Harper. He asked if he could come and live with me."

Zoey pulled out of his embrace. "No! He can't!"

Sutton hid a smile. He'd gotten a response from her. "Don't worry, because that's not going to happen. I'll never agree to that because he needs you as much as you need him. And he's not the only one who needs you, babe. I need and miss you." He kissed her forehead. "You've spent the past week wallowing in your own self-pity and you've forgotten you're not the only one affected by Donna's pronouncement that she's your mother. You once told me there were three people in our equation—you, me and Harper. Right now, the boy is hurting because you've shut him out, and the next time he acts out you won't be able to blame anyone but yourself. Now, what's it going to be?"

Zoey felt chastised. Sutton was right. She had been so ensnared in her own cocoon of anguish that she hadn't considered how it would affect her über-sensitive brother. "You're right. I've been selfish."

"I didn't say you were selfish. I accused you of wallowing in self-pity."

She managed a small smile. "Same difference. I think it's time I listen to what Donna Parker, or whatever her name is now, has to say."

Sutton smoothed back her hair. "What about us?"

Zoey stared at his mouth. "What about us?" she repeated.

"Are we going through with our plan to start off the new year as husband and wife, or should I call Viviana Wainwright and tell her to cancel our reception?"

Zoey felt a momentary panic. "I never told you that I wouldn't marry you."

"Well, you could've fooled me, Miss Allen."

She scrambled off the bed. "Excuse me. I need to shower and put on some clothes. Then I'm going to the B and B and hopefully put my past to rest and settle more than twenty years of either lies or misunderstandings."

Chapter Sixteen

Zoey knew Donna was shocked to see her when she saw her standing in the parlor waiting for her. Viviana had called her room and told her she had a visitor. Seeing the woman up close and in daylight made her aware of their resemblance. She'd inherited her complexion, eyes, mouth and hair texture.

"I'm sorry I—"

"Please don't apologize," Donna interrupted. "It was wrong of me just to show up unannounced when I should've sent you a letter, but I was afraid you wouldn't believe I was your mother."

Zoey waited for Donna to sit, before settling in an armchair opposite. "You showed up in person, and I still didn't believe you."

"Do you now, Zoey?"

"Yes, because I can see the resemblance. What I need to know is why you left me with my father."

Zoey listened, stunned when Donna revealed she was twenty when she blew a tire and James Allen stopped to help her fix it. She'd thought him handsome and chivalrous, and when he asked her out she said yes. She'd grown up in Wickham Falls but after she graduated her family moved to a suburb of Beckley.

"Meanwhile I was dating someone I was passionately in love with but once I met James I broke up with him. James and I dated off and on and when I didn't see him I'd go back to my old boyfriend. I knew it was wrong but I couldn't make up my mind who I wanted."

With wide eyes, Zoey asked, "You were sleeping both of them?"

Donna nodded. "Yes. I didn't see James for a couple of months and he finally said we had to stop the merry-go-round and get married. Meanwhile I was unaware that I was pregnant with another man's baby when James asked me to marry him. I accepted his proposal because I did love him."

"But not as much as your first boyfriend."

A sad smile parted Donna's lips. "I knew when I married James that I would never love him the way I did Zachary. My parents gave us money for the down payment on the house in Wickham Falls as a wedding gift. All hell broke loose when the doctor confirmed I was three months along when I married, and James knew it wasn't his."

"What did he say?"

"He said because I was his wife he would claim and raise the baby as his own."

Zoey ran a hand over her face. She could not imagine being married to one man while carrying another man's baby. And suddenly it hit her that James Allen wasn't her father and Kyle and Harper weren't her biological brothers. While the woman sitting in front her had handed her over to a man as if he'd legally adopted her. She wanted to say things to Donna she knew would prevent them from having anything that would remotely resemble an association.

"What happened after that?"

"James moved out of our bedroom. He was with me in the delivery room and I thought we could become a normal family after I brought you home, but nothing changed. James wasn't one for displays of affection, but he did fawn over you."

"Did you actually believe he would become the loving husband when he knew you were sleeping with another man while you were also sleeping with him?"

"I don't know what I was thinking at the time, Zoey. After a while, I couldn't take the alienation and asked for a divorce. James agreed, but he told me I couldn't take you."

Zoey narrowed her eyes. "And just like that, you gave me up."

"I was so confused and mixed up that I couldn't think straight. I'd start crying and couldn't stop. It was later when I realized I'd been experiencing severe postpartum depression. The dark moods continued and after the divorce I saw a psychiatrist and I was diagnosed as bipolar. I take medication to this day. And when I don't take it, I have extreme highs and lows."

"What happened after your divorce? Did you look for your baby's father and tell him you'd had his child?"

"Zachary never knew I had his baby. I did go to see him and when I asked his mother for his address, she told me he'd enlisted in the army and was stationed overseas. I wrote him and told him I was no longer married, and I'd given my ex full custody of my daughter, because emotionally I was unable to take care of you." Tears filled Donna's eyes and flowed down her face. "Leaving you was the most difficult thing I've ever had to do in my life."

Pushing off her chair, Zoey went to her knees in front of her mother and hugged her, sharing in the pain and grief both had experienced since that fateful day when Donna Allen was forced to give up her daughter.

"What happened after the divorce, Mama?" The single word validating their relationship had slipped out unbidden.

"I married Zachary, but we never had more children. I'd come to believe it was nature's way of punishing me for abandoning my beautiful baby. It wasn't until I married Zachary that I felt what it meant to be loved. He became a lifer, while I lost count of the number of times we moved from base to base. He retired three years ago. He died in his sleep from natural causes this past spring. I didn't want to move from Alaska because it was the first time I did not feel like a nomad. All my family had left West Virginia, so when I got a call from my last remaining cousin, I decided to drive down to see her. I had no intention of stopping in Wickham Falls, yet something kept pulling me back here. I stopped to ask a deputy if James Allen still lived in town and that's when he told me James and his wife had died from carbon monoxide poisoning ten years ago, but you and your brothers still lived in the house."

Zoey rose and retook her seat. What Donna had just revealed was a lot for her to process. "What was my biological father like?"

Donna smiled. "He was wonderful. Patient, affectionate and overly generous to a fault. He would give someone the shirt off his back or his last dollar if they needed it. I know if you'd met him you would grow to love him as much as I did." Her smile vanished. "I know James remarried. How was your stepmother?"

"She was a wonderful mother, and I loved her unconditionally. She and Dad gave me two very special brothers, and there isn't day when I don't miss her."

Donna closed her eyes as she rested her head against the back of the chair. "It's comforting to know James could give you a better life than I would've been able to. I would've made you crazy with my mood swings." She opened her eyes. "I noticed you were wearing an engagement ring. Are you still getting married?"

Zoey pondered Donna's question. Even though

she had taken off Sutton's ring they hadn't discussed cancelling their wedding plans. She loved him too much not to want to become his wife. "Yes. We've planned to have a New Year's Eve ceremony in the ballroom here at the B and B."

"I know I have no right to ask to become mother of the bride, but I'll be here as long as you need me. By the way, I like your fiancé."

Zoey smiled. "So do I." He was everything she wanted and needed in a life partner: kind, generous, loyal, supportive and compassionate. "Thank you for the offer, but I have everything under control. I know it's not going to be easy getting to know each other after so many years of separation but I'm willing to extend the olive branch and see where it takes us."

Donna returned her smile as the tense lines on her face relaxed. "Thank you, Zoey."

Zoey drove home, feeling as if a weight had been lifted off her heart. She was a realist and knew her relationship with Donna would always pale in comparison to the one she'd had with Charmaine. But she knew it would take time to forgive her biological mother because when she and Sutton had children Donna Parker would be their grandmother.

She opened the door and walked into the house to find Sutton and Harper in the kitchen. She extended her arms and they came over to hug her.

"All for one and one for all," she whispered, kissing Harper and then Sutton on the cheek.

"Does this mean I'm still going to be best man at your wedding?" Harper asked.

"Yes!" Sutton and Zoey said in unison.

"Hot damn!"

Zoey smiled when Sutton winked at her.

Harper dropped his arms. "I'm going to make a special dinner tonight, so can you two please leave my kitchen while I decide what I want to make."

Sutton reached for Zoey's hand and led her into the living room. "How did it go?"

"Okay."

His eyebrows lifted. "Just okay?"

"Let's say it's a new beginning and leave it at that. I've invited her to our wedding."

Sutton brushed a light kiss over her mouth. "Good. Now we'll both have a mother-in-law."

New Year's Eve

The music changed as the familiar notes to the "Wedding March" echoed throughout the mansion's great room. Zoey smiled when her brother's hand covered hers over the sleeve of his dress uniform jacket as they prepared to process over the red, pink and white rose petals littering the white carpet to where Sutton and Harper stood facing the black-robed judge. Kyle had been approved for a three-day leave to attend her wedding. He'd arrived in Wickham Falls the day before and hours before the start of rehearsals and the dinner to follow.

When she'd told Georgina, her wedding was to be small, private and very informal. It had become anything but when the guest list increased exponentially to include many of Sutton's former teammates and their spouses, mentees, college friends and class-mates, and several teachers from the local high school within days after their engagement announcement went viral.

When Zoey called Viviana Wainwright to update the list of invitees, the innkeeper reassured her that she would handle everything needed to make Zoey's day special and memorable, from revising the menu, lodging accommodations for out-of-town guests and hiring a popular local DJ. Her original plan to hold the wedding and sit-down dinner reception in the ballroom was changed to her and Sutton exchanging vows in the great room and hosting a buffet recep-tion in the ballroom.

Kyle's hazel eyes were a startling contrast to his mahogany-brown complexion, further darkened by the California sun. "Are you ready to become Mrs. Sutton Reed?" he whispered, as the assembly came to their feet.

"Yes."

And Zoey was as she placed one foot in front of the other, coming closer and closer to the man who was to become her husband. She smiled at Harper who looked incredibly handsome and mature in his tuxedo as he stood next to Sutton as his best man.

They'd planned for her to graduate nursing school before starting a family. Sutton had teased her about becoming the perfect mother because of her prior ex-perience raising her brothers.

* * *

All of the awards paled in comparison with marrying the woman with whom Sutton had fallen in love and planned to play the best game of his life for. Sharing his life and future with Zoey would become his winningest season. He turned and looked at his bride for the first time in twenty-four hours, his breath catching in his chest. She was breathtakingly ethereal in a cloud of white from the veil attached to the intricate twist at the back of her head to the satin gown skimming her body.

"Thank you," he said to Kyle as his future brother-in-law placed Zoey's hand in his. He increased the pressure on her small hand when he felt her tremble.

The judge waxed eloquently about the significance of marriage and Sutton and Zoey smiled in relief when they exchanged vows, rings and then a kiss seconds before the stroke of midnight, signaling a new day.

The sound of fireworks echoed throughout the valley as the citizens of Wickham Falls celebrated a new year and resilient residents of the Mountain State, while Sutton felt as if he'd come full circle. He'd left at eighteen only to return eighteen years later. And this time it was to stay.

* * * * *

COMING SOON!

We really hope you enjoyed reading this book.
If you're looking for more romance, be sure to
head to the shops when new books are
available on

Thursday 17th September

To see which titles are coming soon, please visit

millsandboon.co.uk/nextmonth

MILLS & BOON

Coming next month

CHRISTMAS REUNION IN PARIS
Liz Fielding

She straightened from her task, took one last glance around. The man was staring out at Paris, already ablaze with lights for the Christmas season, but she didn't see the view, only the face mirrored in the glass.

Chloe gasped his name.

'James...'

It was no more than a whispered breath, but his gaze flickered from the lights of the city to her own image mirrored alongside him.

For a moment, as they looked into the reflection of each other's eyes, her heart stood still. Would he recognise her? Remember her?

The thought had barely formed before he spun around so fast that, as if he had disturbed the earth's rotation, the room rocked.

She flung out a hand as her world tilted, throwing her off balance but there was only air to grasp until strong fingers clasped hers, his body steadying her world as he stepped into her, supporting her, holding her, saying her name.

Not a ghost, but the living man with whom, a lifetime ago, she had shared an intense, passionate teenage love.

A doomed romance that had brought disaster down on both their heads but, in his arms, she had forgotten reality, naively blanked from her mind the future planned for her by ambitious parents.

For a few short months, lying spooned against his body, feeling the slow, steady thud of his heart beating against her ribs, the softness of his sleeping breath against her neck, anything had seemed possible.

Now, unbelievably, he was here, grown into the promise of the youth whose every kiss, every touch had stolen her senses, his fingers entwined in her own, a hand at her back, holding her safe against the breadth of wide shoulders, their bodies touching close. Looking at her as if he could not believe what he was seeing.

His eyes were still that thrilling swirl of grey and green that, for years, had haunted her dreams. To look at his wide, sensuous mouth was to feel his lips angled against hers, feel the heat of his need echoed in the desire pounding through her veins and for a moment, weakly, she leaned into him.

'Chloe…'

Continue reading
CHRISTMAS REUNION IN PARIS
Liz Fielding

Available next month
www.millsandboon.co.uk

MILLS & BOON

THE HEART OF ROMANCE

A ROMANCE FOR EVERY KIND OF READER

MODERN

Prepare to be swept off your feet by sophisticated, sexy and seductive heroes, in some of the world's most glamourous and romantic locations, where power and passion collide.
8 stories per month.

HISTORICAL

Escape with historical heroes from time gone by. Whether your passion is for wicked Regency Rakes, muscled Vikings or rugge Highlanders, awaken the romance of the past.
6 stories per month.

MEDICAL

Set your pulse racing with dedicated, delectable doctors in the high-pressure world of medicine, where emotions run high an passion, comfort and love are the best medicine.
6 stories per month.

True Love

Celebrate true love with tender stories of heartfelt romance, fr the rush of falling in love to the joy a new baby can bring, and focus on the emotional heart of a relationship.
8 stories per month.

Desire

Indulge in secrets and scandal, intense drama and plenty of siz hot action with powerful and passionate heroes who have it all: wealth, status, good looks…everything but the right woman.
6 stories per month.

HEROES

Experience all the excitement of a gripping thriller, with an int romance at its heart. Resourceful, true-to-life women and stror fearless men face danger and desire - a killer combination!
8 stories per month.

DARE

Sensual love stories featuring smart, sassy heroines you'd want best friend, and compelling intense heroes who are worthy of
4 stories per month.

To see which titles are coming soon, please visit

millsandboon.co.uk/nextmonth

MILLS & BOON
MEDICAL
Pulse-Racing Passion

Set your pulse racing with dedicated, delectable doctors in the high-pressure world of medicine, where emotions run high and passion, comfort and love are the best medicine.